# *Lady Valiant*

## Suzanne Robinson

**BANTAM BOOKS**
New York Toronto London Sydney Auckland

LADY VALIANT
*A Bantam Book / July 1993*

ISBN 0-553-29575-6

*Published simultaneously in the United States and Canada*

*Bantam Books are published by Bantam Books, a division of Bantam Doubleday Dell Publishing Group, Inc. Its trademark, consisting of the words "Bantam Books" and the portrayal of a rooster, is Registered in U.S. Patent and Trademark Office and in other countries. Marca Registrada. Bantam Books, 1540 Broadway, New York, New York 10036.*

PRINTED IN THE UNITED STATES OF AMERICA

OPM  0 9 8 7 6 5 4 3 2 1

87922

Ann O'Doherty is one of those rare people who can make everyday life sparkle with humor and excitement. This book is dedicated to her with my thanks for all the hours of editing.

# Lady Valiant

# 1

*There is no more trusting in women.*

—HOMER

**London,
April 1565**

THEA HUNT'S TARGET WAS a man. She lifted the crossbow, steadied it against her shoulder, aimed, and pulled the trigger. The bolt shot out of the groove and impaled its mark. The archery butt shuddered, and Thea lowered her weapon.

She never aimed at plain targets. She painted the outline of a man on a sheet and attached it to the butt. In her imagination the outline took on the form of a dark-haired Frenchman, slight of build yet arrogant of demeanor, noble yet impoverished of honor.

She preferred the crossbow because of the force of the bolt. She could feel the power behind the release of the quarrel, imagine the bolt piercing Henri's flesh. Each time she shot the weapon, she assuaged the pain, the humiliation of her flight from the French court.

At her side, Hobby put her foot in the stirrup of another crossbow and winched the bow back. "Aaow, my bones.

God's truth, mistress, no other lady's maid has to break her back fiddling with these things."

Thea's lips pressed together as she took aim again. She wasn't ready to give up her favorite pastime. "Take comfort. One more bolt in his heart, no, this time in his face, I think."

"Good," Hobby said. "For it's time to change your gown. The sun sets, and the banquet begins soon."

Thea grimaced at the mention of the banquet. She would have to consort with men. Luckily, she'd thought of an excuse that would save her from the dancing.

She glanced across the lawn and garden to the towers of Bridgestone Abbey. Grandmother would be furious at her refusal to dance, but Thea would rather face the old lady's wrath than put herself within touching distance of a nobleman. She wasn't going to be hurt, not ever again.

Hours later at the banquet, she was still grumbling to herself of how she despised men. To be in a room with over a dozen of them made her want to jump into the nearest tureen and pull the lid shut. She could feel her own fear, as if verminous rats were crawling over her body. Her fear had yellow, curved teeth and a spiked tail, and it never left her when she was surrounded by young men. Thea cast a resentful glance at Grandmother. It was Grandmother's fault that she stood there, watching the merriment.

Grandmother had insisted upon giving a banquet. Luckily, at the moment most of the men she wished to evade were engaged in dancing a pavane. Thea hated dancing almost as much as she hated men. Her chief comfort was that she'd found a new way to avoid it. Standing near Grandmother's chair in the high great chamber, she leaned on a walking stick borrowed from her father.

That morning she had pretended to turn her ankle. She

cast a glance at her grandmother. The old lady was surveying the dancers with the look of a milk-gorged calf. Grandmother loved multitudes of persons, especially the powerful and rich. Grandmother had set her heart upon marrying Thea to one of them. This desire was the reason Thea and Lord Hunt were on this prolonged visit instead of remaining at home in peace. Since she and her father had arrived, Lady Hunt had maneuvered to show her granddaughter to as many wealthy young noblemen as she could trap into coming to Bridgestone. Thea had a near escape when Grandmother's favorite got himself killed not long ago in some brawl. Leslie Richmond had been one of those men who felt God owed him wealth, pleasing entertainments, and women of easy virtue. Thea had been considering using him for a crossbow target when he died.

Suddenly Grandmother turned and caught Thea's eye.

"By the rood, where's your father, girl?" she asked.

Thea surveyed the great chamber from one tapestried wall to the other. As usual, Father had wandered away from the merriment, leaving guests to fend for themselves.

"Shall I fetch him, Grandmother?"

"And be quick. I know you, child, and you're as like to vanish as he is."

"Yes, Grandmother."

Thumping her walking stick with ostentation, Thea limped out of the chamber and into the long gallery. Grandmother was especially fond of the gallery. One whole wall consisted of windows while the other was lined with portraits of Hunt ancestors and the kings and queens they had served. Prominent among them was a full-length portrait of Mary Tudor.

She was congratulating herself on her escape when she ran into the Earl of Lynford on her way downstairs. He reached the landing with Timothy Eyre and Lord

Lawrence Gracechurch as she prepared to descend. Of all her grandmother's friends, she could abide Lynford best. His soft brown eyes never held scorn, not even for Father at his most bemused.

Though not yet five and thirty, Lynford had suffered greatly at the hands of the old king, Henry VIII, and his son Edward VI because of his adherence to the old faith. When he was a boy he'd seen his father beheaded for refusing to acknowledge old King Harry instead of the Pope as head of the church. No doubt the horrors of that day were responsible for the sadness that seldom left the earl's eyes. His suffering had given him a quality of sympathy that even Thea found admirable. Still, she didn't want to talk to him for too long, him being a man, and a comely one.

Curtsying to the three, she clasped the banister. "Good e'en, my lord."

Lynford took her hand, though he knew she disliked being touched. He bent over it but refrained from kissing it. When he straightened, his gaze held both merriment and exasperation, and she realized he was as impatient with the crowds of place-seekers as she was. At least Lynford had the wit to recognize Grandmother's true aim in inviting him. He was, after all, one of the few Catholic noblemen Queen Elizabeth tolerated at court.

"Mistress Hunt," Lynford said. "I hope your injury isn't taking you from us so early."

"No, my lord, I but seek my father."

Timothy Eyre bowed to her. "We haven't seen Lord Hunt." Timothy rarely noticed anyone except those wealthy enough to further his own ambitions to rise among the queen's courtiers.

"No doubt he's cavorting with a draft horse or feeding

eels and marchpane to one of his prize cows," Lord Grace-church said.

Thea stared at Gracechurch without smiling. Father ofttimes acted as if he had the wits of a midge, and his ideas of what was important in the world rarely matched anyone else's, but she disliked anyone making jests about him. Especially someone like Gracechurch, who, during Bloody Mary's reign, had accused innocent yeomen of heresy in order to get their land.

"Gracechurch," said Lynford, "you'd do well to keep your thoughts to yourself, such as they are." Lynford bowed to Thea. "Your pardon, Mistress. I for one shall be desolate at your absence."

It was one of those courtly phrases she'd come to resent when addressed to her, yet when Lynford said it, somehow she knew he was telling her the truth. Looking at him, she took in the downturned mouth, the face devoid of any blemish or lump that would bar his being called hand-some. He held her gaze without trying to draw her into a passionate exchange, and for that discretion and the re-spect that prompted it, she was grateful.

She nodded to Lynford, actually smiled at him, then turned her back on Gracechurch and descended the long series of staircases. The high great chamber was on the third floor, and the trip to the kitchen a long one. Grand-mother had designed Bridgestone Abbey herself. The long, winding stone stairs impressed the eye, but the distance from the kitchen caused food to arrive in the great chamber cold.

Not that Grandmother cared. Grace Hunt had wanted an imposing, modern house, and that was what she'd gotten. Situated on the grounds of a ruined abbey, Bridge-stone was more glass than stone. At sunrise and sunset the house lit with flames of reflected sunlight.

Grandmother's pride had been cast in stone, plaster, marble, and glass at Bridgestone. Her initials topped the eight towers of the house; they and her coat of arms decorated every chimney piece and ceiling, every cushion and tapestry in the place. A rectangular block with two towers on each side, Bridgestone dominated the countryside in which it lay. Grace had chosen a sight midway between Westminster and the Fleet River, north of the Strand. The spires of the minster were just visible from the roof of the house.

To Thea, Bridgestone represented Grandmother's thwarted ambition. Grace had enjoyed high favor with the old queen, Mary Tudor, but now Elizabeth sat on the throne. Elizabeth didn't like Grandmother, who had once been so foolhardy as to call the young woman a bastard, though not to her face. Thea didn't like Grandmother either. She hadn't since the day Grace Hunt shoved her on board a ship and sent her to the French court, a motherless little girl, alone and lost and in need of someone who cared about her.

On the ground floor Thea made her way to the kitchen in search of Father because she knew he wouldn't be there. If she looked for him carefully, she wouldn't find him until it was almost time for their guests to leave.

*While her guests drank* Canary wine and danced the lavolta, Grace Hunt rested in her withdrawing chamber. The Countess of Lynford, the earl's stepmother, was with her. Nearsighted, Grace squinted and beckoned impatiently to the younger woman.

"Come nearer, Catherine, and make sure the door is closed."

Catherine Taine, dowager Countess of Lynford, shoved a chair close to Lady Hunt's. "I've heard from Father Jean-

Paul in Scotland. The rumors bruited about are true. Mary of Scotland is enamored of Lord Darnley."

"God's blood, I can't believe it. Darnley's a fool and a drunkard."

"But he's pretty, and she's never had a man before, Grace, only that sickly boy king."

Grace heard a scraping sound in the wall near her chair and glanced at the countess, who appeared not to have heard it. She wrapped a white, gnarled hand around the arm of her chair and pursed her lips. "Time for you to go."

"I just sat down."

"Go away, Catherine."

"But—"

"Tell me, do you still lie with your stepson? The earl was always such a sweet boy. I found it tragic that you should have snapped him up so young, but he never cried for help. Did you spoil him for other women? Did his wife object when she lived?"

Catherine Taine rose, her body quivering. She sputtered, then turned and quit the withdrawing chamber. When the door slammed shut, Grace chuckled and raised her voice.

"You may come out."

The chamber was paneled in oak. There was a click, and one of the panels swung inward to reveal blackness lit by a candle. The candle was held by a man who had to stoop to pass the threshold. Timonty Eyre placed his candle on a sideboard. In his other hand he held a polished wooden box.

"Come in, come in, man." Grace squinted at Timothy, examining him from his sparse black hair to his jeweled shoes. "Has no one ever told you that the clothes should never outshine the man?"

Timothy blinked at her like a dyspeptic halibut, and

Grace curled her lip at him. He was wearing gold damask, a collar of gold and diamonds, and rings on every finger. Men who looked like halibuts shouldn't dress like kings.

"Well, man, what have you?"

His mouth working noiselessly, Timothy imitated a grounded fish for a few moments longer before speaking.

"The Wyvern sent me with the messages."

Timothy opened the box and held it out to Grace. Inside lay five gold buttons larger than her thumbnail. Grace took one. Its top was raised, and she slid it back to reveal a compartment containing a ciphered message. Closing it, she replaced it in the box. Timothy surrendered it to her, and she rested it in her lap.

"He says he likes not this use of Mistress Hunt to convey the messages," Timothy said. "One bearer has already died, and the messages are lost, for the messenger was killed before he could reveal their whereabouts. I never should have trusted that Leslie Richmond; he's near ruined everything."

"Stop whining. My granddaughter will be a much better courier. She knows naught of my doings or of the Wyvern. I will convince her to go to Scotland to try to prevent the Queen of Scots from marrying that lackwit Darnley. I've already obtained permission for her to travel."

"He says there is no reason the girl would attempt such a thing."

"He doesn't know everything." Grace patted the box in her lap. "The Queen of Scots trusts my granddaughter, for grave and privy reasons. They were children together at the French court, and Thea is beholden to her. Besides, my granddaughter has a feather-soft heart full of useless pity.

She'll go. I'll see to it. Now, begone with you. I'll convince her to go to Scotland."

Timothy vanished back into the darkness. The panel clicked shut. Grace smoothed her hands over the button box and tried to compose herself. Timothy always tried her patience. Son of a nobleman and the daughter of the powerful Italian banking family of Tasso, he was her link with the Wyvern.

No one knew who the Wyvern was. He could be any one of a number of English Catholics disgruntled with the rule of Elizabeth Tudor. She knew he was building a network of alliances among the powerful northern barons in the kingdom, for the North was where Catholic strength was the greatest. He and many like him aimed at replacing the Protestant Elizabeth with the Catholic Mary Stuart, Queen of Scots, and thus restoring the true religion to England.

Grace wanted to restore the true religion as well, for that way lay power. She touched the rosary at her waist and smiled grimly. No doubt the Wyvern had tried to ally himself with her son and failed. Edward cared naught for dabbling in matters of state. Edward buried himself in the north country and molted. One conversation with Edward would have been enough to make the Wyvern send Timothy Eyre to her—a profitable move for both of them.

And now she was about to send her granddaughter to Scotland with ciphered promises of support from English Catholics. The buttons were to be a gift to Mary Stuart, who was expecting word from the Wyvern. Word would go separately to the French priest at Mary's court to expect the gift. The priest would warn the queen. Circuitous. But that was the way of the Wyvern. No doubt he'd survived the years since the old queen's death because of his maze-like dealings, his secrecy. Even Elizabeth's secretary of

state, that balding heretic William Cecil, had no knowledge of the Wyvern's existence. Still, it was better that
Thea serve as messenger. No sense in risking herself to
such a dangerous task.

After all, Thea owed her something. She'd returned
from France useless. It had taken all Grace's talent to
conceal the disaster, and now the girl refused to marry. She
stayed with her father in the country and hid. No back-
bone. Yes, Thea owed her something. And if by some
distant chance the girl were caught, who would suspect an
old woman of intrigue when Thea was known to have once
been in the favor of the Queen of Scots? Most convenient,
most convenient indeed.

London,
May 1565

Several weeks later, another grand house—if it could
have spoken—would have protested the indignity of having a young man crawl out of its third-floor window. He
scuffed his boots on its foliated stone walls and nearly
kicked in a pane of leaded glass. The trespass was soon
over, however, and the offender dropped silently to the
ground and into the darkness of the May night. Slinking
over a high wall, he sped past the house of a duke and
quitted Charterhouse Lane at the edge of the city. A beam
of moonlight caught a stray lock of hair that had escaped
the hood of his cloak and turned it silver. A gloved hand
reached up to thrust the rampant lock into concealment.

Flitting from shadow to shadow, crevice to doorway in
Aldersgate Street, Robin St. John, Lord Derry, floated ever
nearer to his destination, the shop and house of the jeweler
Hugo Unthank near St. Paul's Cathedral. Few ventured

into London's dark streets in the hours before dawn. Those who did were apt to do so for fell purposes. Derry's purpose was more benign, and his reputation for merciless and artistic swordplay kept ordinary murderers out of his path.

When he was still several streets away from Unthank's house, Derry paused after turning a corner into an alley and listened. It had rained earlier. Cobbles and piles of slop bore beaded coats. The overhanging second stories of the buildings on either side of him dripped soiled rain-drops on his cloak. They hit near his ear and seemed to echo there for anyone within leagues to hear.

There it was again, that distinctive sound of leather grinding into cobbles with grit caught between them. The footsteps halted. Derry drew away from the corner, deeper into the blackness of the alley. A dagger appeared in his hand. He waited, breathing evenly, quietly. A dog's lonely howl cut through the dripping sounds. Only last night a rich young gallant had been found dead near Shoreditch, his throat slit.

He flattened himself against the side of the building as he heard rapid footsteps. The head of a man emerged from the corner as if the building were sprouting appendages. The head swiveled in his direction. Derry stopped breathing and gripped his dagger firmly.

The head turned away, then vanished, and the footsteps scurried on, leaving Derry behind. A trace of a smile touched his lips as he sheathed the dagger. He faded down the alley, climbed a gate, and took to the rooftops. If his errand weren't so urgent, he would have detained his uninvited companion and inquired of the identity of his master.

He could afford no such delay, however, for William Cecil awaited him, and one didn't keep the queen's chief secretary of state waiting. Cecil was already annoyed with him for hieing himself off to France with Oriel Richmond in search of Blade Fitzstephen. Was it his fault if the reckless Blade had gotten himself abducted by the Cardinal of Lorraine?

No, but Cecil had been annoyed in any case, for Derry had left his band of mad ruffians in Cecil's charge. Cecil knew not the first thing about governing such rogues as Inigo Culpepper, Oakshot, Anthony Now-Now or Simon Spry. Derry had inherited the collection of thieves from his mentor, Christian de Rivers, and they served as a disreputable league of spies and personal war band. Neither Christian nor Derry had completely curbed their less respectable pursuits. The unsuspecting secretary Cecil had set a clerk to lead them—a mistake.

Derry teetered at the edge of a roof, then sprang across a gap five stories high to land below on a slick and precarious slope. He gripped the tiles, and slid. Cursing, he skidded like a metal bead on glass. He flailed his arms and legs. One foot dropped over the edge of the roof, but before he fell, the other boot caught a broken tile and stuck. Clawing at the tiles, he stopped his descent and rested with his cheek pressed against the damp roof.

Slowly he crawled sideways until he reached a dormer window. He clung to its pitched roof, pushed a shutter open with the toe of his boot, and swung his body into the black opening beyond. Closing the shutter and barring it, he stood in the darkness a moment, wiping perspiration and raindrops from his face and cloak. He needed no candle to find his way to the trapdoor at his feet.

He descended a ladder to the third floor of Unthank's house and hesitated at the bottom. Down the hall he could see a landing and newel post. Faint light spread up from the lower floor. He floated, catlike and secret, down the stairs.

Near the foot of the staircase lay a half-open door. Next to it was another, guarded by a man with prominent knees and pointed elbows, the cutpurse Inigo Culpepper. As Derry appeared, he came to attention and grinned. Derry put a finger to his lips, and the man nodded. Drawing close to the open door, he hesitated. In the room beyond, a man of slight stature and even slighter hair paced before a fire. Suddenly he stopped and glared at the fireplace.

"Derry, cease your coy hovering and enter."

Derry walked in, swept a bow to William Cecil, and grinned. "How now, good master secretary."

"How now to you, you evil young pestilence." Cecil ran a hand through his sparse hair. "I care not if you haven't rested from your French travels. You're to take back your band of thieves. I'll care for them no longer. Christian de Rivers left them in your charge, not mine."

"You didn't send for me on this account," Derry said. He threw his cloak across the back of a chair and collapsed into it. "What has stirred you so that you resemble a bee tormented by a honey bear?"

"Those ciphers taken from the traitor Leslie Richmond. Blade sent them to me. His clerk hasn't been able to translate them, and my men have been no more successful."

Cecil strode to a table, opened a wooden casket, and spilled five gold buttons out of it. So large that they were almost brooches, they were of red gold. Each had an ocatgonal base supporting filigreed gold tops in the form of curling serpents. Each top slid back to reveal a compartment.

It was in these compartments that the ciphers had been discovered. The late Leslie Richmond had owned them, and the late Leslie Richmond had been a traitor. Cecil snatched up the buttons and rammed them back into the casket again while Derry watched with lifted brows. Cecil rarely lost his temper.

"We've not deciphered the messages," Cecil said, "but Unthank has recognized the gold work as that of one Andrew Byrd, goldsmith. I have had converse with Master Byrd."

"Marry, sir, I trust the poor man still lives."

Cecil frowned at Derry and went on. "Master Byrd had a commission to make several sets of these buttons."

"Ah. And from whom?"

"I'm not sure. He dealt only with the Hunt steward, who has vanished."

Derry stood and went to lean on the chimney piece. Contemplating the fire, he spoke quietly. "Lady Grace Hunt is a fragile old woman, the mother of Sir Edward Hunt, who closets himself in the country and rarely comes to the city unless rousted by the queen's special command."

"Nevertheless, the three sets of buttons were delivered to the London house of this woman. And . . ."

"And?"

"And Leslie Richmond paid court to Lady Hunt's granddaughter, Mistress Dorothea Philadelphia Hunt." Cecil poured himself a cup of wine from a flagon on the table and glanced at Derry. "The old lady is in the next room. I had her brought here in a closed coach so that she knew not where she was—a useless attempt to frighten her. I've spoken to her, but the experience is like attempting to converse with tatting. Vagueness of mind seems to run in the family. Both mother and son suffer from it. I sent for you to see if you could prise something understandable from the woman."

Cecil waved a hand at the door opposite the fireplace. Derry's eyes widened as he realized Cecil was serious. "Think you I'm more enamored of bullying old ladies than you?"

"Mayhap not, but you've certainly more charm." Cecil gave Derry's shoulder a shove. "Make haste, for there's a task I would set you, an urgent one."

Derry cracked the door open a bit and peered inside. Beside a glowing brazier in a cushioned armchair sat Lady Hunt. Wispy white hair peeked from beneath a widow's cap. She nodded, her chin dipping to a hollow bosom, and he heard a little snort. She had fallen asleep. The joints of her fingers were swollen and reddened, and he could see purple veins through the slack skin on the backs of her hands.

Sighing, Derry eased inside the room and shut the door loudly. The woman snorted again and mumbled, but kept sleeping. Derry clasped his hands behind his back and strode over to her. He cleared his throat. Her head nodded. He filled his lungs and cleared his throat louder while bending close to the woman. This time Lady Hunt grunted and snorted herself awake.

Starting, Lady Hunt slapped Derry's arm. "Thea, must you be so noisy? Oh." The old lady peered up at Derry. "Why, it's Robin. Robin St. John, Viscount Moorefield's boy. What do you here, child, and where has that clerk Cecil gone to?"

"Lady Hunt, I've come to talk about those buttons you commissioned from the goldsmith Byrd. Do you remember what Cecil asked?"

"You have, have you? I vow I've never seen men so entranced with fripperies before. Of course I remember. I'm old, not daft. Has her majesty made a law against ordering gold buttons? Mayhap she's made a law saying

Catholics can't have gold buttons. It's a fine day when God-fearing followers of the true religion can't button their clothing."

Derry shook his head to clear it of confusion, then knelt before Lady Hunt. "I would save you much trouble. Tell me what you know of the buttons and their contents. Her majesty seeks not to pry into the religious scruples of her subjects so long as they remain loyal subjects. But you must tell me of the buttons, and of Leslie Richmond."

"Oh, Leslie Richmond." Lady Hunt cast a glance at him from the corner of her eye. "So, you've heard he's dead and want to take his place."

Derry held his breath, released it slowly, and spoke. "Aye, I've come to take his place."

"Well, she won't have you."

"She?"

"And she's gone. You're too late. So fond of Leslie Richmond she was, and now he's dead."

He had to restrain himself from raising his voice. Instead, he rested an arm on his bent leg and urged gently. "Who was fond of Leslie Richmond?"

"Thea, you addled boy."

"Thea."

"Dorothea Philadelphia Hunt, my granddaughter. Now will you tell me why everyone wishes to know about buttons? I vow I think Cecil is mad. Why does anyone care about my granddaughter's gold buttons?"

"Where is your granddaughter?"

Lady Hunt sighed. "I told you, she's not here."

"Where? Where is she?"

"Gone north, boy. I told you."

Pressing his lips together and trying to keep his temper in check, Derry tried once more. "Where in the North has she gone?"

Lady Hunt cocked her head to the side. "Why, to Scotland. Thea has gone to Scotland. First my son sneaked away and went home, and now my granddaughter. Packed all her belongings in wagons and took herself off. Said she would visit her father and then go on to the border."

Derry rose and stood back from the old lady's chair, clasping his hands behind him.

"How long ago did she set off, my lady?"

"Oh, a few days. Mayhap a week or two. I forget."

"And she took her buttons with her?" Derry asked lightly.

"God's patience, child. Did I not say she packed? Now, find that Cecil and tell him to take me home. Only a varlet would keep an old woman up so late at night for such a foolish reason."

As Lady Hunt continued to fuss and grumble, Derry turned and quit the chamber. Locking the joining door behind him, he faced Cecil.

"You heard."

"Yes," Cecil said. He set his wine cup on the table and beckoned to Derry. "I knew about the granddaughter, but I had to be sure of Lady Grace. She can't abide me, and I've no stomach for rougher questioning. Now there's no need. Leslie Richmond was plotting with the granddaughter, not the old lady."

"And the granddaughter has gone to Scotland, no doubt with messages to the Queen of Scots from certain discontented Catholic lords in England. God's blood, why can't Mary Stuart be content with one throne instead of hankering to steal that of our good Elizabeth?"

"Because she's inherited the blood of her French mother's family. The de Guises have always lusted after power, and they mean to have it. In France, in Scotland, and in England."

Derry picked up Cecil's wine cup and sipped from it. "And this girl, Thea Hunt, she plots and schemes treasonously with Mary Stuart and her French relatives?"

Cecil bit his lip and looked away from Derry. "I fear the case is far worse. My—friends at court have caught scent of a new rumor." Cecil turned back to Derry and lowered his voice. "Lady Hunt has added to my certainty. Her granddaughter goes to Scotland to reveal our true intent regarding the marriage of Mary Stuart and Henry, Lord Darnley."

Derry slammed his cup down on the table, spilling wine and making Cecil wince.

"Did I not tell you the plan was too complex? Such machinations are dangerous. Sending the fool Darnley to Scotland like a Trojan horse, the plan was too circuitous. No matter how handsome the jackanapes is, the Queen of Scots won't marry him if she once suspects we greatly desire her to do so."

"We've argued the matter before," Cecil said. "Better she marries a drunken fool with no spine than the king of France or the heir to Spain. God's wounds, Derry, if France and Spain agree to put aside their differences, if Scotland becomes their ally, England will bathe in blood."

Derry felt the blood drain from his face. Suddenly he was back in the Tower, a boy of seventeen accused of plotting against the old queen. Bloody Mary they called her now. Old Bishop Bonner had thrown him in a cell. He'd stayed in that black, dripping hole of filth, unfed, until he lost count of time. When they finally opened the door, he couldn't stand. The guards had dragged him to a great chamber filled with iron instruments, and a rack.

"No." Derry stopped himself from saying anything else aloud and tore himself from the memory.

Cecil was looking at him, but he refused to meet the man's gaze.

"You, of all my intelligencers, know the stakes," he said. "Mary Stuart wants our queen's throne. Mary Stuart is Catholic. She'll kill our good queen Bess, and our people will burn again."

"I need no convincing of the import of these matters," Derry snapped. He squeezed his eyes shut, but the images of that torture chamber wouldn't recede.

"Then you know why you must find Thea Hunt. Find her, keep her from Scotland and Mary Stuart. Derry, she grew up at the French court when Mary Stuart lived there. They were familiars. The Queen of Scots listens to no one who disparages Lord Darnley, but she would listen to her childhood companion. Find Thea Hunt. Abduct her. Hold her until the Queen of Scots marries. And while you hold Mistress Hunt, obtain from her the key to this cursed button cipher and the names of our noble traitors. Those messages you found were meant for Englishmen. We must know who they are."

Derry retrieved his cloak from the back of the armchair and pulled it over his shoulders. "You would have me do violence against this woman?"

Cecil pursed his lips, but made no answer.

"She is a papist," Derry said.

"Come, my friend. There are more agreeable ways to winnow secrets from ladies."

Derry shook his head. "I almost puke at the thought of making myself pleasing to a heretic-burning Catholic who meddles in matters of great import. You know how I despise English papists like Thea Hunt. If I remember right, she returned from France when Bloody Mary lay dying and refused to come to court after our dear Queen Elizabeth succeeded. No doubt she refused to soil herself by frequenting the court of someone she considers a bastard. God's blood! I hate the conniving treasonous wench already."

"Then I can trust her to your care with no fear she'll suborn you into releasing her."

Derry pulled the hood of his cloak over his golden hair. "You may." He reached the threshold, heading for the stairs to the upper floors.

"Wait," Cecil said.

Derry didn't stop. "I'll send word when I've caught the bitch."

"You can't go."

Derry turned slowly. "All this intelligencing has unhinged your mind."

"You can't go as Lord Derry. We can't have it bruited about the countryside that the son of a viscount has abducted a baron's daughter. You'd be put to the horn and forced to marry her. And inconvenient questions would be asked since it's known Thea Hunt was going to Scotland. In any case, her majesty told me to keep these doings secret, for she has a great fondness for Mistress Hunt's father. He gave her comfort when she was a prisoner of her sister and accused of treason."

"His lordship is the most fuzzy-minded peer in the realm, Cecil. He has memorized every illness that afflicts the draft horse but seldom remembers what tenants work his lands. I doubt he'll notice his daughter's absence."

"Still, I think it better if this task be undertaken by Robin Savage."

Derry paused, then grinned and swept Cecil a low bow. He spun in a circle and whirled over to the minister. When he stopped, his posture had changed. In place of the straight-backed stance of a knight was the slouch of a frequenter of taverns and ordinaries.

"Jesu preserve you, master. I be glad to be of service, for a price. I highly thank you, master, in most humble wise, for your faith in Robin Savage."

"I marvel at how easily you lose the letter H from your alphabet," Cecil said. "One would think you were born in Houndsditch."

"A churl is a churl, good master, be he born in White-hall or a stew." Derry dropped his lowborn accent and frowned at Cecil. "I shall enjoy bringing this lady traitor to the hands of justice. Thank you, Cecil, for bringing me such pleasure and contentment."

At first Cecil was silent, then he put a hand on Derry's arm. "Take care. I'd forgot your hurts in my zeal to stop this treason. Thea Hunt isn't your dead wife, nor is she Bloody Mary."

Derry had been gazing at some invisible scene over Cecil's shoulder. He nodded absently.

"I will treat her as she merits, as all traitors merit."

"Derry."

He met Cecil's worried gaze. "Fear not. I'll remember your commandments, but you must remember what I have said. This woman is the servant of wickedness. I'll not quibble at preventing her from achieving her ends. Indeed, it will pleasure me greatly to hunt Mistress Hunt."

# 2

*A bold bad man.*

—EDMUND SPENSER

THEA REFUSED TO RIDE in the coach. Heavy, cumbersome, and slow, it jounced her so that she nearly vomited after a few minutes inside it. She preferred riding at the head of her party just behind the outriders in spite of Nan Hobby's objections. Hobby rode in the coach and shouted at her charge whenever she felt Thea was riding too fast.

"Miiiiiistress!"

Thea groaned and turned her mare. There was no use trying to ignore Hobby. She only shouted louder. As the outriders entered the next valley, Thea pulled alongside the coach. The vehicle jolted over a log, causing Hobby to disappear in a flurry of skirts and petticoats.

"Aaaoow," groaned Hobby. "Mistress, my bones, my bones."

"You could ride."

"That horrible mare you gave me can't be trusted."

"Not when you shriek at her and scare her into bolting."

"Aaaaow."

Thea pointed down the track that led into the oak- and hazel-wooded valley. "We'll be following this road. No more spiny hills for a while."

She glanced up at the hills on either side of the valley. Steeply pitched, like tent tops, they posed a hazard to the wagons loaded with chests and furniture and to the coach. Yet she was glad to see them, for their presence meant soon they would reach the border, and Scotland. The journey had been a slow one due to the wagons, the coach, and Hobby. She heard the call of a lapwing in the distance, and spotted a merlin overhead. The countryside seemed deserted except for their small party.

After deciding with Grandmother that she should go to Scotland, she'd insisted on taking as few servants and men-at-arms as necessary. She and Hobby were the only women, and the men-at-arms numbered only seven, including her steward. They broke their journey only once to rest a few days at home with Father. A few days were all she could afford if she were to reach Scotland in time.

The Queen of Scots was to marry that fool Darnley. When Grandmother told her the news, at first she hadn't believed it. Clever, beautiful, and soft-hearted, her majesty deserved better than that selfish drunk. Thea had pondered long upon Grandmother's suggestion that she go to Scotland. Grandmother said Mary Stuart would listen to no criticism of Darnley, but that she might listen to Thea. After all, they had shared quarters and tutors with the French royal children. In the end she'd decided to go in spite of the original idea being Grandmother's.

Thea had been honored with Mary's friendship, for both found themselves foreigners among a clutch of French children. Later, when Thea had need of much more than friendship, Mary had given her aid, had seen to it that Thea was allowed to go home.

Slapping her riding crop on her leg, Thea muttered to herself. "Don't think of it. That time is over. You'll go to Scotland and then return to the country, where you don't have to see any nobleman at all except Father."

Nudging her mare, she resumed her place near the front of the line of horses and wagons. Only a cause of great moment could have forced her to forgo returning to the seclusion she loved. Her long visit to Grandmother had been made reluctantly, and only because the old woman had threatened to come north to fetch her granddaughter if she didn't come to London. Neither Thea nor Lord Hunt wanted Grandmother swooping down, vulturelike, upon their peaceful nest.

In the years since she returned from France, she'd made her own life far away from young noblemen. Some called her a hermit. Some accused her of false pride. None suspected the true reason for her seclusion. Even now the memory tortured her, though it was seven years old.

She had been sixteen when she met Henri, and one of those girls whom elders entrusted with responsibility— steady in her character, honest to the point of awkwardness. The death of her mother had brought adulthood to her early, and she'd found herself looking at the world through the eyes of a woman when her peers were still entranced with dolls.

Her staid and sensible demeanor had earned her no friends at the French court, and certainly no suitors; therefore, Henri's approach had startled her. This young French gallant had been the first man to court her. Here at last was a man who valued her practical nature. He didn't mock her interest in nature or her love of the great Italian artists such as da Vinci. How was she, to whom duplicity was as foreign as a native from the New World, how was she to know to what lengths a bored nobleman would go to amuse himself?

Thea muttered to herself, irritated that her own sense of loyalty to the kindhearted Scots queen had forced her on this journey. She'd just spent many weeks enduring the company of noblemen, and now she was going to a foreign court, where there would be dozens of them, nay, hundreds. God's mercy, hundreds of Henris!

Her steward interrupted her thoughts. "Mistress, it's close to midday. Shall I look for a place to stop?"

She nodded, shoving aside unwelcome memories, and the man trotted ahead. Hunger had crept up on her unnoticed, and she tugged at the collar of her riding gown. Her finger caught the edge of one of the gold buttons that ran down the garment, and she felt a sting. Grimacing, she looked at her forefinger. Blood beaded up in a cut on the side. She sucked the wound and vowed to demand that Hobby remove the buttons. They'd been a gift from Grandmother along with another set for the Queen of Scots, but one of them had a sharp edge that needed filing.

It was a good excuse to replace them with the old, plainer buttons she preferred. These were too ornate for her taste. She always felt she should be wearing brocade or velvet with them, and a riding hat, which she detested. Only this morning Hobby had tried to convince her to wear one of those silly contrivances on her head, jeweled and feathered. Refusing, she'd stuffed her thick black hair into a net that kept the straight locks out of her way.

She examined her finger. It had stopped bleeding. Pulling her gloves from her belt, she drew them on and searched the path ahead for signs of the steward's return. As she looked past the first outrider, something dropped on the man from the overhanging branches like an enormous fruit with appendages. The second outrider dropped under the weight of another missile, and at the same time she heard shouts and grunts from the men behind her.

"Aaaaow! Murder, murder!"

A giant attacked the coach, lumbering over to it and thrusting his arms inside. A scrawny man in a patched cloak toppled into her path as she turned her horse toward the coach. He sprang erect and pointed at her.

"Here, Robin!"

She looked in the direction of the man's gaze and saw a black stallion wheel, his great bulk easily controlled by a golden-haired man who seemed a part of the animal. The stallion and his rider jumped into motion, hooves tearing the earth, the man's long body aligning itself over the horse's neck. Stilled by fright, she watched him control the animal with a strength that seemed to rival that of the stallion.

The brief stillness vanished as she understood that the man who was part stallion was coming for her. Fear lanced through her. She kicked her mare hard and sprang away, racing down the path through the trees. Riding sidesaddle, she had a precarious perch, but she slapped her mare with the crop, knowing that the risk of capture by a highwayman outweighed the risk of a fall. Desperately wishing she'd carried her crossbow on her saddle instead of packing it in a wagon, she bent low over the mare's neck. Her heart pounding with the hoofbeats of her mare, she fled.

The path twisted to the right, and she nearly lost her seat as she rounded the turn. Righting herself, she felt the mare stretch her legs out, and saw that the way had straightened. She leaned over her horse, not daring to look behind and lose her balance. Thus she heard only the thunder of hooves and felt the spray of dirt as the stallion caught up. The animal's black head appeared, and she kicked her mare in desperation.

A gloved hand came into view, then a golden head. An arm snaked out and encircled her waist. Thea sailed out of the saddle and landed in front of the highwayman. Terror gave her strength. She wriggled and pounded the imprisoning arm.

"None of that, beastly papist gentry mort."

Understanding little of this, caring not to at all, Thea wriggled harder and managed to twist so that she could bite the highwayman's arm. She was rewarded with a shout of pain. Twisting again, she bit the hand that snatched her hair and thrust herself out of the saddle as the stallion slowed to a trot.

She landed on her side, rolled, and scrambled to her feet. Ahead she could see her mare walking down the trail in search of grass. Sprinting for the animal, she felt her hair come loose from its net and sail out behind her. Only a few yards, and she might escape on the mare.

Too late she heard the stallion. She glanced over her shoulder to see a scowling face. She gave a little yelp as a long, lean body sailed at her. She turned to leap out of range, but the highwayman landed on her.

She fell. The force of his weight jolted the air from her lungs. The ground jumped at her face. Her head banged against something. There was a moment of sharp pain, and the feeling of smothering before she lost her senses altogether.

Her next thought wasn't quite a thought, for in truth there was room in her mind for little more than feeling. Her head ached. She was queasy, and she couldn't summon the strength to open her eyes. She could feel her face because someone had laid a palm against her cheek. She could feel her hand because someone was holding it.

"Wake you, my prize. I've no winding sheet to wrap you in if you die."

The words were harsh. It was the voice of thievery and rampage, the voice of a masterless man, a highwayman. Her eyes flew open at the thought, and met the sun. No, not the sun, bright light filtered through a mane of long, roughly cut tresses. She shifted her gaze to the man's face and saw his lips curve into a smile of combined satisfaction and derision. She could only lie on the ground and blink at him, waiting.

He leaned toward her, and she shrank away. Glaring at her, he held her so that she couldn't retreat. He came close, and she was about to scream when he touched the neck of her gown. The feel of his gloved hand on her throat took her voice from her. She began to shake. A slight smile appeared upon his lips, then she felt a tightening of her collar and a rip. She found her voice and screamed as he tore the top button from her gown. Flailing at him weakly, she drew breath to scream again, but he clamped a hand over her mouth.

"Do you want me to gag you?"

She stared at him, trapped by his grip and the malice in his dark blue eyes.

"Do you?"

She shook her head.

"Then, keep quiet."

He removed his hand, and she squeezed her eyes shut, expecting him to resume his attack. When nothing happened, she peeped at him from beneath her lashes. He was regarding her with a contemptuous look, but soon transferred his gaze to the button in his palm. He pressed it between his fingers, frowned at it, then shoved it into a pouch at his belt.

"I'll have the rest of them later," he said.

Reaching for her, he stopped when she shrank from him. He hesitated, then grinned at her.

"Sit you up by yourself, then."

Still waiting for him to pounce on her, she moved her arms, but when she tried to shove herself erect, she found them useless. He snorted. Gathering her in his arms, he raised her to a sitting position. She winced at the pain in her head. His hand came up to cradle her cheek, and she moaned.

"If you puke on me, you'll rue it."

Fear gave way to anger. In spite of her pain, she shoved at his chest. To her chagrin, what she thought were mortal blows turned out to be taps.

"Aaaow! Look what you've done to my lady."

"Get you gone, you old cow. She's well and will remain so for now. Stubb, put the maid on a horse and let's fly. No sense waiting here for company any longer."

Thea opened her eyes. The highwayman was issuing orders to his ruffians. From her position she could see the day's growth of beard on his chin and the tense cords of muscle in his neck.

"My—my men."

"Will have a long walk," he snapped.

"Leave us," she whispered, trying to sit up. "You have your booty."

The highwayman moved abruptly to kneel in front of her. Taking her by the shoulders, he pulled her so that they faced each other eye to eye.

"But, Mistress Hunt, you are the booty. All the rest is fortune's addition."

"But—"

He ignored her. Standing quickly, he picked her up. Made dizzy by the sudden change, she allowed her head to drop to his shoulder. She could smell the leather of his jerkin and feel the soft cambric of his shirt. An outlaw who wore cambric shirts.

She was transferred to the arms of another ruffian, a wiry man no taller than she with a crooked nose and a belligerent expression. Her captor mounted the black stallion again and reached down.

"Give her to me."

Lifted in front of the highwayman, she was settled in his lap a great distance from the ground. The stallion danced sideways, and his master put a steadying hand on the animal's neck. The stallion calmed at once.

"Now, Mistress Hunt, shall I tie your hands, or will you behave? I got no patience for foolish gentry morts who don't know better than to try outrunning horses."

Anger got the better of her. "You may be sure the next time I leave I'll take your horse."

"God's blood, woman. You take him, and I'll give you the whipping you've asked for."

His hand touched a whip tied to his saddle, and she believed him. She screamed and began to struggle.

"Cease your nattering, woman."

He fastened his hand over her mouth again. His free arm wrapped around her waist. Squeezing her against his hard body, he stifled her cries. When she gave up her struggles, he released her.

"Any more yowling and I'll gag you."

Grabbing her by the shoulders, he drew her close so that she was forced to look into his eyes. Transfixed by their scornful beauty, she remained silent.

"What say you?" he asked. "Shall I finish what I began and take all your buttons?"

Hardly able to draw breath, she hadn't the strength to move her lips.

"Answer, woman. Will you ride quietly, or fight beneath me on the ground again."

"R-ride."

Chuckling, he turned her around so that her back was to his chest, and called to his men. The outlaw called Stubb rode up leading a horse carrying Hobby, and Thea twisted her head around to see if her maid fared well.

"Look here, Rob Savage," Stubb said, "if you want to scrap with the gentry mort all day, I'm going on. No telling when someone else is going to come along, and I'm not keen on another fight this day."

"Give me a strap, then."

A strap. He was going to beat her. Thea gasped and rammed her elbow into Rob's stomach. She writhed and twisted, trying to escape the first blow from the lash. Rob finally trapped her by fastening his arms about her and holding her arms to her body.

"Quick, Stubb, tie her hands with the strap."

Subsiding, Thea bit her lower lip. Her struggles had been for naught. Rob's arms left her, but he shook her by the shoulders.

"Now, be quiet or I'll tie you to a pack horse."

"Aaaow! Savage, Robin Savage, the highwayman. God preserve us. We're lost, lost. Oh, mistress, it's Robin Savage. He's killed hundreds of innocent souls. He kills babes and ravages their mothers and steals food from children and burns churches and dismembers clergymen and—"

Thea felt her body grow cold and heavy at the same time. She turned and glanced up at the man who held her. He was frowning at the hysterical Hobby. Suddenly he looked down at her. One of his brows rose, and he smiled slowly.

"A body's got to have a calling."

"You—you've done these things?"

"Now, how's a man to remember every little trespass and sin, specially a man as busy as me."

He grinned at her, lifted a hand to his men, and kicked the stallion. Her head was thrown back against his chest. He steadied her with an arm around her waist, but she squirmed away from him. He ignored her efforts and pulled her close as the horse sprang into a gallop. She grasped his arm with her bound hands, trying to pry it loose to no avail. It was as much use for a snail to attempt to move a boulder.

The stallion leapt over a fallen sapling, and she clutched at Savage's arm. Riding a small mare was a far less alarming experience than trying to keep her seat on this black giant. She would have to wait for a chance to escape, but escape she must.

This man was a villain with a price on his head. She remembered hearing of him. He and his band roamed the highways of England, doing murder and thievery at will. Savage would appear, relieve an honest nobleman or merchant of his wealth, and vanish. No sheriff or constable could find him.

As they rode, Thea mastered her fears enough to begin to think. This man wanted more than just riches and rape. If he'd wanted only these things, he could have finished his attack when he'd begun it. And it wasn't as if she were tempting to men, a beauty worth keeping. She'd found that out long ago in France. And this Savage knew her name. The mystery calmed her somewhat. Again she twisted, daring a glance at him.

"Why have you abducted me?"

He stared at her for a moment before returning his gaze to the road ahead. "For the same reason I take any woman. For using."

He slowed the stallion and turned off the road. Plunging into the forest, they left behind the men assigned to bring the coach and wagons. Several thieves went ahead, while Stubb and the rest followed their master. Thea summoned her courage to break the silence once more.

"Why else?"

"What?"

"It can't be the only reason to, to . . ."

"Why not?"

"You know my name. You were looking for me, not for just anyone."

"Is that so?"

"Are you going to hold me for ransom? There are far richer prizes than me."

"Ransom. Now, there's a right marvelous idea. Holding a woman for ransom's a pleasureful occupation."

As he grinned down at her, fear returned. Her body shook. She swallowed and spoke faintly.

"No."

There was a sharp gasp of exasperation from Savage. "Don't you be telling me what I want."

"But you can't."

His gaze ran over her face and hair. The sight appeared to anger him, for he cursed and snarled at her.

"Don't you be telling me what I can do. God's blood, woman, I could throw you down and have you right here."

She caught her lower lip between her teeth, frozen into her own horror by his threats. He turned her away from him, holding her shoulders so that she couldn't face him. Though he used only the strength of his hands, it was enough to control her, which frightened her even more.

"I could do it," he said. "I might if you don't keep quiet. Mayhap being mounted a few times would shut you up."

Thea remained silent, not daring to anger him further. She had no experience of villains. This one had hurt her. He might hurt her worse. She must take him at his word, despite her suspicion that he'd planned to hold her for ransom. She must escape. She must escape with Hobby and find her men.

They rode for several hours through fells and dales, always heading south, deeper into England. She pondered hard upon how to escape as they traveled. Freeing herself from Savage was impossible. He was too strong and wary of her after her first attempt. She might request a stop to relieve herself, but the foul man might insist on watching her. No, she would have to wait until they stopped for the night and hope he didn't tie her down.

Her gorge rose at the thought of what he might do once they stopped. She tried to keep her body from trembling, but failed. Her own helplessness frightened her, and she struggled not to let tears fall. If she didn't escape, she would fight. It seemed to be her way, to keep fighting no matter how useless the struggle.

As dusk fell, they crossed a meadow and climbed a rounded hill. At the top she had a view of the countryside. Before her stretched a great forest, its trees so thick she could see nothing but an ocean of leaves.

Savage led his men down the hillside and into the forest. As they entered, the sun faded into a twilight fostered by the canopy of leaves above them. Savage rode on until the twilight had almost vanished. Halting in a clearing by a noisy stream, he lifted Thea down.

She'd been on the horse so long, and the hours of fear had wearied her so much, her legs buckled under her.

Savage caught her, his hands coming up under her arms, and she stumbled against him. Clutching her, he swore. She looked up at him to find him glaring at her again. She caught her breath, certain he would leap upon her.

His arms tightened about her, but he didn't throw her to the ground. Instead, he stared at her. His grip loosened, and he went still. To her surprise, his glare melted away. Drawing his brows together, he cocked his head to the side as if puzzled. Upon beholding Savage's confusion, Thea's fears lessened. She stared back at him. Moments passed while they gazed at each other, studying, wary, untrusting.

Eyes of gentian blue met hers, and she felt minute jabs of lightning in her arms, then in her legs and torso. With sudden clarity of thought she realized that looking at him had caused this strange, stinging sensation. It was her first long look at him free of terror.

Not in all her years in the fabulous court of France had she seen such a man. Even his shoulders were muscled. They were wide in contrast to his hips, and he was taller than any Frenchman. He topped any of his thievish minions, and yet seemed unaware of the affect of his appearance. If she forgot what he was, she could imagine him in gold and blue damask that matched his coloring, for this man belonged in the raiment of a king. Beholding him was like watching the sun take the form of a man. And until that moment she hadn't realized a man's mere appearance could delight to the point of pain.

Despite his angelic coloring, however, he had the disposition of an adder. Suddenly he scowled at her, as if something had caught him unprepared and thus annoyed him. Wariness and fear rushed to the fore again.

"Golden eyes and jet black hair. Why did you have to

be so—God's blood, woman." He thrust her away from him. "Never you mind. You were right anyway, little papist. I'm after ransom."

Bewildered, she remained where she was while he stalked away from her. He turned swiftly to point at her.

"Don't you think of running. If I have to chase you and wrestle with you again, you'll pay in any way I find amusing." He marched off to shout ill-tempered orders at his men.

Hobby trotted up to her and began untying the leather strap that bound her hands. Thea stared at Robin Savage, frightened once more and eyeing his leather-clad figure. How could she have forgotten his cruelty and appetite simply because he had a lush, well-formed body and eyes that could kindle wet leaves? She watched him disappear into the trees at the edge of the clearing, and at last she was released from the bondage of his presence.

"He's mad," she said.

"Mad, of course he's mad," Hobby said. "He's a thief and a murderer and a ravager."

"How could God create such a man—so, so pleasing to the eye and so evil of spirit?"

"Take no fantasy about that one, mistress. He's a foul villain who'd as soon slit your throat as spit on you."

"I know." Thea bent and whispered to Hobby. "Can you run fast and long? We must fly this night. Who knows what will happen to us once he's done settling his men."

"I can run."

"Good. I'll watch for my chance, and you do as well." She looked around at the men caring for horses and making a fire. Stubb watched them as he unloaded saddle bags. "For now, I must find privacy."

Hobby pointed to a place at the edge of the clearing,

where bushes grew thick. They walked toward it unhindered. Hobby stopped at the edge of the clearing to guard Thea's retreat. Thea plunged into the trees, looking for the thickest bushes. Thrusting a low-hanging branch aside, she rounded an oak tree. A tall form blocked her way. Before she could react, she was thrust against the tree, and a man's body pressed against hers.

Robin Savage held her fast, laughing at her. She cast a frightened glance at him, but he wasn't looking at her. He was absorbed in studying her lips. His anger had faded, and his expression took on a somnolent turbulence. He leaned close and whispered in her ear, sending chills down her spine.

"Running away in spite of my warnings, little papist."

Thea felt a leg shove between her thighs. His chest pressed against her breasts, causing her to pant. He stared into her eyes and murmured.

"Naughty wench. Now I'll have to punish you."

# 3

*I will neither yield to the song of the siren
nor the voice of the hyena, the tears of the
crocodile nor the howling of the wolf.*

—GEORGE CHAPMAN

DERRY HAD STEPPED INTO the clearing to see
Thea Hunt and her maid disappear into the trees
while Stubb hefted the saddle off his horse. Stalking over to his servant, he had waited until Stubb had
placed the saddle on the ground, then given him a nasty
smile.

"Having a nice afternoon?"

"Aye, my lor—Robin. Haven't been out this way in a
long time."

"Too bad you've already lost our prisoners though."

Stubb whirled about, looked back at his master, and
rubbed his hands on his breeches. "They were here but a
moment gone."

Cuffing Stubb on the side of the head, Derry raced for
the trees.

"They headed for that tree with the split trunk. You
find the maid. I'll find the mistress. If you don't catch her,
don't come back."

Derry plunged into the trees again, shoving aside vines and branches. He felt that burning in his chest, the same burning he'd carried with him since that time in the Tower, the same burning he always felt when having to deal with Catholics. Yet he was almost glad Mistress Hunt had run away.

He hadn't looked to enjoy this task of capturing a woman and forcing her to reveal secrets, but he'd changed his mind the moment she'd begun to fight him in spite of her own fears. She had courage. Instead of weeping, as most women would have, she'd attacked. He was beginning to think he'd enjoy her once she'd been schooled properly. Mayhap he would amuse himself with her after she confessed her wrongdoings.

Circling around to the area he last saw Thea Hunt, he saw the flash of a green gown against the grayish-brown of tree trunks. He flattened himself against a thick oak. Her steps came nearer. He stepped in her path, and she ran into him. She cried out when he caught her between his body and the tree trunk.

"Running away in spite of my warnings, little papist."

He pressed against her, and to his surprise found his body rubbing against hers. His gaze flitted over her, then caught the glint of a gold button. He remembered what she was. Staring into her eyes, he murmured: "Naughty wench. Now I'll have to punish you."

Burying his hand in her hair, he lowered his mouth to hers. She tried to turn her head, but he held her still. His lips touched hers, and he thrust his tongue between her lips. He felt her gasp and pulled away to look at her. Her breathing was rapid and shallow, and the color had drained from her face so that her hair seemed darker than ever. He grinned at her and thrust his hips against hers, causing her to catch her breath and hold it.

"Shall I let you choose your punishment?" When she failed to answer, he went on. "No, you're right. I'm better at deviltry."

He held her gaze when he shifted his weight. Holding both her hands behind her back with one hand, he grasped the gold button below the missing one. Ripping it from her gown, he watched her start and shrink away from him. No doubt she'd reconsidered her actions and decided to play the helpless maid.

"You won't need these anymore," he said.

The neck of her gown had fallen open to reveal the swell of a breast above the low neckline of a shift. She wore no other undergarments. Well, after all, she had been raised at the French court.

A hot, slow smile played over his lips. Which of them would admit their desires first? He was determined it would be she. Already she was breathing heavily. He lowered his head and pressed his lips to the place where her breast began to swell. She turned her head aside, closed her eyes, and bit her lip. Noting her determination, he kissed his way up her chest and throat, licked her jawline, and whispered in her ear: "Tell me about the buttons, and I'll give you more of the same, mistress."

Her eyes popped open. Staring at him, she seemed to wake from some trance.

"Mother of God, save me. He's right mad, and belongs in Bedlam."

Ignoring her, he resumed his punishment. He touched another button. This one lay between her breasts, and she squirmed. He grasped it, holding on while enjoying her attempts to escape his touch, then ripped it. In quick succession he tore three others until the whole top of her gown lay open. Her breasts spilled out, barely contained by the shift. Of the thinnest lawn, it revealed her completely.

She was fighting him now, trying to kick and bite him. Laughing, he tossed the buttons aside, opened his jerkin, and thrust himself against her so that her breasts flattened against his chest. She cried out again, but the force of her exclamation was dampened by her inability to draw a deep breath. Derry held her still, enjoying the feel of her breasts heaving against him.

"How now, mistress. Do you surrender? No point in doing battle when you've already lost, eh? Come, tell me about the buttons and your traitorous allies, and I'll give you a tumble you'll tell all your lady friends about."

He captured her lips once more. They remained closed, so he brushed his own against them, murmuring persuasions. She wouldn't stop writhing beneath him. Every movement caused her hips to rub against his groin, and his skin grew hot, as if he were roasting naked on a spit. When she continued to struggle and nearly bit him, he lost patience.

"Still pretending innocence, are we? Then mayhap you need to lose more than a few buttons."

Derry wanted to end the play, for his part was growing burdensome. Holding her wrists again with one hand, he began to pull her skirts up. At his actions she redoubled her struggles, though there was little she could do, pinned as she was against the tree trunk. His hand snaked under her skirts to find her leg. It was clad in a silk stocking. He held her gaze as he ran his hand up her inner thigh. As he neared their juncture, she screamed, and something hit the back of his neck.

"God rot your vile soul."

Derry whirled around in time to block another blow from a log wielded by the maid called Hobby. The log hit his arm. Cursing, he grabbed it as Stubb raced up and launched himself at Hobby.

"Got you, you venomous sea serpent."

The two wrestled with each other as Derry cast the log aside. Rubbing the back of his neck, he turned back to Thea. She was gone. He saw her skirts vanish in the trees ahead, chuckled at her composure in the face of defeat, and began to walk back to camp. If she ran awhile, she would grow tired and surrender more quickly.

He pursued her on horseback for less than half an hour. She had fled deeper into the forest, it was easy to follow her tracks. He jumped the stream she had just crossed, and walked his horse carefully down a path newly made by her passage through high ferns. Suddenly he pulled his horse up and waited. The tracks had stopped. She must have heard him and gone to earth. Women. They knew nothing of the hunt.

Resting his arm on his thigh, he studied the ground. As he was leaning over, a boulder in skirts landed on him from above. Thrown off balance, his feet flew out of the stirrups. Thea Hunt shoved him out of the saddle. He landed on his back with a jolt, banged his head on the forest duff, and lay gasping as she quickly settled into the saddle. Gathering the reins, she kicked the stallion into motion.

"God's blood." Derry scrambled to his feet and charged her.

Her foot shot out and rammed into his chest as she passed him. He stumbled backward, swearing and rubbing his breast. She was getting away.

"Jove!"

He whistled, three sharp bursts, and the horse stopped so suddenly the woman almost lost her seat. Derry whistled again, and Jove turned on his hind legs. Thea pulled the reins, and the stallion abruptly reared high. Derry sprang into a run as she tumbled backward off the horse. He reached her a moment after she landed on her shoulder and crumpled, facedown, unmoving.

Throwing himself down at her side, he reached for her, hesitated, then touched her back, feeling for broken bones up and down the length of her body. There were none. He gathered her in his arms and turned her over. A thick veil of black hair covered her face. He brushed it aside. Unconsciousness had smoothed the fear from her face. Her straight brows were black ink against the pallor of her skin. The pallor was made more noticeable by the blush of her lips.

"Foolish maid," Derry muttered.

He laid her on the ground, lowered his head, and listened for her heartbeat. It was steady. As he lifted his head, she drew in a breath and moved. Sitting beside her, he put an arm across her body and rested his weight on the ground beside her. When she opened her eyes, he was frowning at her. She stared up at him without recognition at first. Then she knew him, and for the first time Derry saw the terror in her face and recognized it. She thrashed at him weakly, and when she realized her helplessness, two lone tears appeared beneath her lashes.

"Here," Derry snapped. "You stop that, silly gentry mort. Stop it, I say."

"At l-least, before you make me—me—I need privacy."

"So you can run away again? No, thank you. There'll be no more running off into the trees."

"But—but I only wanted to relieve myself!"

Derry looked at her burning cheeks and closed wet eyes, and swore. "You were looking for privacy?"

She nodded, still not meeting his gaze. Feeling foolish,

Derry cursed his own rashness. He scooped his captive up in his arms. She cried out as she sailed into the air.

"Don't squawk so. I'm only setting you on your feet so you can find that privacy you were needing."

He stood her in front of him, but she swayed, and he caught her again. Lifting her, he carried her to Jove, where he allowed her to stand while he retrieved a water bottle from his saddle. Holding it to her lips while she drank, he watched the color return to her cheeks. Still, when she finished she wasn't steady on her feet. Without a word he took her arm and marched her slowly into the ferns near the stream they had crossed shortly before.

Planting her in the midst of the tallest ferns, he gave her a threatening look and marched off to stand with his back to her. He heard rustling, then silence.

"If you run off, you'll regret it."

A small voice at his shoulder made him start.

"I can't run anymore."

She walked past him, limping and holding her gown closed. He gazed at her straight back and curved hips, and felt his sex swell.

"Derry," he whispered to himself, "you do belong in Bedlam."

He followed her to Jove. She was waiting for him, her hands clasped tightly together. He was about to put his foot in the stirrup when she spoke.

"If you're going to, I wish you would now and be done."

The reins dropped from his hand. He couldn't have understood her. He glanced at her face. She met his gaze unsmiling, and stood her ground when he traced her half-exposed body with his glance. He was tempted. Would she comply? He studied her set and trembling jaw.

The request had been made out of fear. He'd heard a challenge, but it had not been a challenge. It had been a plea for release from the anticipation of pain. She hadn't asked for mercy, merely an end to suspense. Only once before had he encountered such bravery—in the dank, black cells in the Tower.

Until now he hadn't thought of her as a prisoner like he himself had once been. The comparison sat ill with him, for close on its heels came guilt. If she were the prisoner, then his part resembled too closely that of Bloody Bonner, the mad bishop who—best not think of it.

"You want me to take you now?" he asked to gain time.

"I don't want it, but—"

"I choose the time and the place, woman," Derry said, his voice crackling with ill temper.

Mounting, he pulled her up in front of him. She leaned over the horse's neck and put a hand to her head. Derry turned sideways, disregarding her protests, and pulled her into his arms so that her head rested on his shoulder.

"None of your carping. I can't hold you for ransom if you're dead from weariness and from banging your head on the ground five times a day. You rest and do it quiet. Foolish besom."

At first she lay stiff and still, as if expecting him to ravish her on horseback. A tempting thought, but an impractical one. Instead, he took his cloak from a saddle bag and wrapped it around her. She was asleep before they reached the camp despite her fears. Derry slid down from his horse with her in his arms. It was dark, and fires had been lit. Stubb had tied the maid to a tree, and she glared at them and mumbled through a thick gag.

His bedroll had been prepared. He laid Thea on the one next to it beside a fire. As he lowered her head to the pallet, she opened her eyes.

Once again he beheld terror as she recognized him. He was growing to hate that look. It reminded him of a trapped fox surrounded by hounds. Best get the questioning over with before it became any less palatable. He would begin while she was bemused from sleep and still frightened and no doubt hungry. She hadn't eaten all day.

Motioning to Stubb, who crossed the camp to stand beside Hobby, he helped Mistress Hunt sit up. She clutched the cloak about her shoulders. Her hair tangled about her face, and she watched him without blinking. As he took a place in front of her, his men gathered around. He saw that she gave them a glance and then gathered her legs under her as if to spring at the slightest movement from any of them.

To regain her attention, he drew a dagger from his belt. Of Spanish steel, it had a double edge and the hilt was embossed with gold and etched with a serpent design. Drawing up one knee, he rested an arm on it. He balanced the dagger on its point on the tip of one finger. It flashed in the light of the fire. He had her attention.

Caressing the flat of the blade, he smiled at her. "Now, Mistress Hunt. To the heart of our business."

She glanced at them, then at him, frowning. He sheathed the dagger. From the pouch at his belt he produced one of the buttons he'd torn from her gown.

"What is this?" he asked.

Like a minnow eyeing a bullfrog, she gaped at him. "That," she said slowly, "is a button."

"In truth, but this, Mistress Hunt, is far more."

He snapped his fingers, and Inigo presented a polished wooden casket to him. Opening it, he showed the contents to her. Delving inside, he retrieved another button, much like the first.

"Do you deny these are yours?"

She nodded, still staring at him.

"You're of the habit of carrying someone else's buttons among your possessions, are you?"

"They're a gift."

"Ha!"

She yelped and jumped back from him, but he caught her wrist in one hand, and with the other shoved the button in front of her nose.

"A gift for what pig's offal?"

She was trembling again, but he tightened his grip on her wrist and shook it. "Who?"

"The Queen of Scotland."

He examined her closely, but she had offered the answer without resistance. It annoyed him that she continued to regard him as if he were addled. It was she who was the traitor. He held the button between them and slid the top back to reveal the hollow compartment he'd discovered when Inigo showed him the casket. Lying inside was a tightly rolled scrap of paper. Again he shoved it in front of Mistress Hunt's face.

She stared at it for a long time before looking at him and speaking in tones of wonder. "There's something inside."

"Oh, my," he mimicked, "there's something inside."

He heard a snicker from Inigo, and a guffaw from Simon Spry. Giving her a mocking smile, he closed the button.

"Your villainy has been discovered. Those ciphers were meant for the Queen of Scots. Your own words condemn you, they do. Bloody papist gentry mort. What do the ciphers say?"

She gasped, then pointed at him. "You're no plain highwayman."

Simon Spry burst into renewed guffaws while Anthony Now-Now bellowed. Inigo knelt beside Derry and poked him in the ribs with an elbow.

"No ordinary highwayman. Hear that? God's arse, half the bawds and ladies in London know that."

Derry scowled at Inigo, then returned his gaze to his indignant prisoner. She was glancing about, surveying his men. She met his gaze, and he noticed that her fear had receded in the face of his revelation.

"Who gave you these ciphers, woman?"

He hadn't expected her wide-eyed reaction to his first accusation; now she lowered her gaze suddenly. All candor vanished from her manner. She didn't answer.

"You've been screeching at me all day. Don't stop now."

Still no answer. Then she looked up at him, her golden eyes reflecting the firelight.

"You've named your horse Jove."

At first he thought she'd lost her wits. Then he beheld the intelligence in her gaze, the assessing look in her eyes. This was no zealot full of papist idolatry. This was a clever, logical woman who until now had been too frightened by unaccustomed violence to think clearly. He should never have called the stallion by name.

"How," she continued, "does an ignorant peasant thief know about the chief god of ancient Rome?"

"I heard it somewhere, I did. Now don't you be questioning me. I'm the grand inquisitor here."

It was time to bring back her fear before she asked another discomforting question. He reached for her before she had time to stop him, and flipped open the edges of her cloak.

"I never did get the rest of those buttons."

She tried to draw the ends of the cloak together, but he drew his dagger and laid the flat of the blade against the folds over her breast.

"Put your hands down," he said softly.

Around him his men drew closer. When she complied, he snagged a fold of the cloak and twitched it aside. Her torn gown lay open, revealing the valley between her breasts. She was quivering. He flicked the tip of the blade. It caught in the fragile lawn of her shift. He tugged gently and spoke.

"I told you I'd choose the time."

Pulling with the dagger, he increased the tension on the shift so that her breasts thrust against it. Night shadows concealed them from everyone but him, for he was sitting in front of her. But one cut from the dagger, the slightest movement on her part, and she would be displayed before everyone.

"I give you one last chance," Derry purred to her. "Who gave you the ciphers?"

She was trembling so hard, he could feel it through the dagger. So pale he thought she might faint, she had closed her eyes when he'd touched her shift. He wasn't surprised, however, when in reply to his question she shook her head. Trembling or not, pale or not, she had courage. He would have to break that courage.

Maintaining the tension on her shift, he drew close to her, so close he could see the rose of her nipples.

"So, Mistress Hunt, your punishment and my pleasure begin."

# 4

*Lord, I have sinned, and mine iniquity*
*Deserves this hell; yet Lord deliver me.*

—FULKE GREVILLE, LORD BROOKE

THEA FELT HER SHIFT tighten against her breasts. Though she had her eyes closed, she perceived a sudden darkness as Savage drew close and blocked out the light from the fire. Her body hadn't stopped trembling since he'd begun toying with her.

She heard his voice—quiet, deceptively gentle. "You're a courier of messages between English traitors and the Queen of Scots. I know this. I've been sent to stop you from convincing Mary Stuart not to marry Darnley, and to prise from you your foul secrets. Come now, sweet. You're too gentle a maid, and far too unseasoned to play against me and win."

As he spoke, she struggled to control her terror. She'd landed in the middle of a treasonous plot. Grandmother. Grandmother had been meddling in great matters. She'd always chafed at her son's lack of ambition, constantly harangued him to come to court and strive for place and power. Grandmother had used her without her knowledge.

Those buttons, they'd been a gift from Grandmother. She'd been instructed to present them to the Queen of Scots personally. Treason. If this man found out about Grandmother, she'd be thrown in the Tower, tortured, given a traitor's death mayhap. Dear God, they might suspect Father, sweet, loving, absentminded Father.

She couldn't reveal the truth, not to this man. Savage wasn't a highwayman, at least not only a highwayman. He served someone powerful, most likely a minister of the queen, for he knew too many privy and dangerous things. She couldn't tell the truth and risk Father and Grandmother falling into his hands.

It seemed hours that Savage held her pinioned by the point of his dagger, yet it was only a few moments before he spoke again, and she felt the warmth of his hand brush against her breast. She sucked in her breath as he put his lips near her ear and whispered, "Tell me what I want to know, Thea *bella,* for though I'm skilled, I doubt you'll enjoy my talents when they're practiced upon you. I ask you for the last time. Who gave you the ciphers?"

Before she lost her courage, Thea shook her head. The hand on her breast lifted. She shrank, hunching her shoulders in anticipation of his attack. She felt him move back, but nothing happened. Opening her eyes, she found him sitting opposite her once more. He rested his weight on his heels, twitched her gown closed with the dagger, and contemplated her with a bemused expression.

"Stubborn gentry mort," he said lazily. When she looked at him, he continued. "Being a leader of men, even these men, takes wits, it does. Managing a stubborn woman's worse than ordering this lot. That's why I've given a lot of thought about how to break you."

Glancing over his shoulder, he called out to Stubb.

"Ready," Stubb shouted.

Savage moved to Thea's side and pointed across the camp. At the edge of the clearing she could just make out Hobby still sitting tied to a tree with a gag in her mouth.

"Yes," Savage said. "A leader has to know his men." He put his arms around her shoulders and placed a kiss on her temple. "Or, in this case, his woman." He nodded to Stubb.

Past the fire, half concealed by shadows, the man moved to stand in front of Hobby. Thea strained to see past him, but Savage pulled her against his body, trapping her there. Hobby screamed. Thea cried out and lunged, trying to escape Savage's grip and run to her maid. Another scream sent panic racing through her. Thea clawed at Savage, pounding his chest and trying to bite him. He grabbed her wrists. They struggled on their knees as Hobby screamed for the third time.

Thea shrieked at Savage, but he calmly grasped her wrists in one hand and pinned her against his chest with the other. Once he'd captured her, he lifted her chin, forcing her to look into his eyes. The dark blue of the sky at sunset should have been an entrancing sight. She beheld a flat, emotionless slate blue and unconcern.

"Now I ask my question again," he said. "Who gave you the ciphers?"

She tried to free her chin, but he held her fast, and she was impaled by a gaze of casual cruelty.

"I don't know," she said. Hobby screamed again, and she rushed on. "I got them from a jeweler named Byrd."

"Yes?"

"I didn't know they contained messages. He must have put them there secretly."

"And Leslie Richmond?"

Her thoughts stopped. Leslie Richmond? Leslie Richmond was dead. He'd visited Grandmother frequently—oh, Leslie Richmond, the lazy gallant and denizen of frowzy taverns. Leslie Richmond must have been one of the intriguers, one of the traitors.

She wet her lips and stared into Savage's implacable eyes. "Y—yes, I suppose he could have put the ciphers in the buttons. It was he who recommended the jeweler Byrd. He even went to the shop with me."

There. She'd lied, but it was a lie about a dead man, and she'd kept Grandmother and Father out of it. Did he believe her?

He was studying her, raking her face with his gaze, then he released her chin and tightened his grip on her so that she was pressed hard against his length.

"There's more," he said with his lips close to hers.

"No."

"Then you like hearing your maid scream?"

"No!"

He seemed everywhere, inescapable. She wanted to scream as loudly as Hobby had. She couldn't move, so great was his strength compared to hers. Her muscles quivered with fatigue from her futile attempts to do battle with him. Suddenly she began to shake. Gasping, she looked up at him in confusion as her strength flew from her body. He was glaring at her, then he said something, but she couldn't hear him. Images of him flying at her, landing on top of her, looming over her, flashed into her perception.

"Thea!" His grip loosened, gentled.

She stared up at him, her mouth working. It was as if her blood had begun to flow from her body. Her skin grew heavy. Her eyelids grew leaden. Abruptly Savage shifted his hold on her, lowering her to the pallet once more.

"I can't . . ." Why did her voice sound as if it were floating in the trees overhead?

Savage's face appeared above her. The firelight turned his hair into a glittering shower of flames.

"Rest you," he said. He took her hand and rubbed it between his own. "I can't do battle with a swooning, cowering little chick. No entertainment in that."

She batted at him with her free hand. "God rot your entrails. I didn't swoon."

"Oh, forgive me, mistress. Then you were overcome by my nearness."

"Overcome by your ungodly cruelty. Where is Hobby?"

"Not dead yet." He released his hand. The man called Inigo appeared with a bowl and cup, which Savage took from him.

He snapped at her as he dismissed his man. "I'm always cruel to traitors who seek to betray her majesty and deliver the kingdom into the hands of Protestant-burning papists. Here."

He tugged her arm so that she sat up, then shoved the cup to her lips. She drank deeply, but he snatched the cup away and thrust the bowl into her hands. It was so large, she had to hold it in both hands. He produced a wooden spoon, dipped it into the bowl, and held it to her lips. The spoon knocked against her teeth so that she was forced to open her mouth. She swallowed a mouthful of stew, and in spite of her continuing fears, she found herself ravenous. The stomach, it seemed, could ignore impending torture if it were empty enough.

Savage kept feeding her until she turned her face aside. Taking the bowl from her, he offered the water cup. As she drank, he watched her. She grew fearful again under that assessing stare. Seeking refuge from it, she kept her gaze on the cup. He hadn't spoken, and as he continued to examine her, her apprehension grew.

"Tomorrow we go to Ravensmere," he said quietly. "We'll reach it by late afternoon. I pray you, use the time to consider your predicament, Thea *bella*. You're right to be afeared. I give you until we gain Ravensmere to confess all. I want to know the names of every person involved in these foul designs against her majesty. I want to know what the ciphers say."

She'd lost her voice again. Glancing up at him, she shook her head.

He waited, then stood. Planting his legs apart, he put his fists on his hips. "Trust not to my mercy, Thea *bella*. You've seen the last of it. At Ravensmere I'll have the truth from you, or soon have you begging to tell it to me."

He turned and stalked away then. She watched him walk through the camp with the ease and rhythm of a dancer and the strength of one accustomed to hard riding. When he vanished into the shadows, she let out the breath she'd been holding. Weary though she was, she glanced about the camp in search of some way to escape. That tall, scrawny Inigo was watching her. So was the monstrous Stubb. Hobby appeared to be sleeping or unconscious, and she couldn't tell from this distance how the woman fared.

A tattered and dirty ruffian dropped down at her side. She yelped and scrambled away from him.

"Here! You be still." The man grabbed her arm and slipped a leather noose over her wrist, then tied her hands together. Without another word he left.

She tried to free herself, but the leather only tightened as she attempted to undo the knots with her teeth. As she gnawed at her bonds, a shadow cut out firelight. Savage loomed over her.

"Turning rat, are you?"

She dropped her hands and glared at him. "I want to see my maid."

"No. Now give me your hands. Stupid dell, you've cut off the blood to your paws." He knelt and loosened the straps, then produced another. Dangling it in front of her face, he grinned at her. "Shall we go for a walk?"

At her look of horror, he scowled. "God's arse, woman. This is your last chance for a few privy moments before we sleep."

"Oh."

She tried to get up. He rose and helped her stand. They repeated their actions of that afternoon. He stood guard while she went into the bushes. Managing with her hands bound was difficult, but she succeeded. This time she didn't run. He would only catch her, and he might punish her by hurting Hobby again. She returned to find him slouched against a tree, slapping the leather strap against his leg. He straightened when she appeared and smiled a gloating smile at her.

"At least you learn. Takes a while though."

"I can bide my time." She marched past him, ignoring his chuckle.

Her dignity was ruined when she stumbled over a vine. He leapt forward and caught her before she fell. He righted her but kept hold of her arm.

"You're making this harder than it warrants," he said as they walked. "We needn't be enemies. Come, tell me what I want to know, and I'll release you."

"I've told you."

"No, you haven't." He stopped abruptly and swung her around to face him. "I can be merciful, Mistress Hunt, merciful and friendly. Most friendly."

He stepped close and took her in his arms. Frightened in a new way, Thea shoved at his chest. He laughed and enclosed her in his arms. He startled her by nipping the tip of her nose.

"I never saw such a stubborn gentry mort. Content you, Thea *bella*."

He brushed his lips across her forehead and down her cheek. Torn between fear and a strange shivering titillation, she shook her head. He kept murmuring her name and soft reassurances. Wrapping her in a warm mist of caressing words, he touched her lips with his fingertips, then replaced them with his mouth. Unable to quite believe what was happening, Thea submitted when his lips forced hers open. His tongue slipped inside her mouth, and he sucked. Caught off guard, she fought the memory of the only other man to touch her. He hadn't been like this. Nothing had ever been like this.

His hand rubbed its way down her back to cup her buttocks. He squeezed, and Thea's eyes flew open. God's mercy, she'd lost her wits altogether. Tearing her mouth from his, she thrust herself out of his arms. He chuckled and captured her again, this time holding her arms behind her back and nibbling at her throat. Alarmed and furious with herself, Thea stomped on his booted foot. He cursed and shoved her away.

"Witch!"

"Randy cozening debaucher."

Breathing heavily, Savage stalked up to her. "Tease. Must have learned it from the French. Even we peasants here in England hear about that gold-encrusted bawdy house the French call a royal court."

Unknowing, he'd come too near the truth. Thea clamped her jaw. Fighting ugly memories and her present nightmare, she whirled about and fled. He raced after her, snatched her arm, and planted her in front of him. She faced him and saw that his mood had changed again.

Holding her by her bound wrists, he swept his gaze up and down her body, smiling contemptuously.

"So, there's more secrets in that pretty head than just treasonous ones. Such a good little player of parts. Come, show us what you learned at the French court, love."

He put his hand on her hip, dragged her close, and rubbed himself against her. Furious, Thea clasped her hands together, brought them up quickly, and banged them against his nose. He yelped and grabbed her hands. Cursing, he held her while shaking his head to clear it.

His head shot up, and she tried to back away as she beheld his fury. In her haste she tripped and fell. He let her, and followed, dropping on top of her. Landing between her legs, he grasped her hands and pulled them over her head.

Her gown had fallen open, and her breasts were exposed again. Thea writhed beneath him, and he laughed, which caused her to struggle harder. She made the mistake of trying to buck him off. Her hips drove into his, and she felt his sex nudge against hers. She gasped and fell back. Trying to shrink into the ground, she found herself completely covered by his body.

He began to move on her, flexing his hips and rubbing them against hers. Sticks and pebbles poked into her back and legs. She heard him moan, and knew she was in peril. His head dipped to her neck. He nuzzled her, and the heat of his skin burned her. His voice sounded harsh in the dark forest.

"Forget our quarrel, Thea *bella*. Forget everything for now."

His tongue stroked her neck, and he put a hand on her breast and cupped it. Thea tried to slide from beneath him, but he was too heavy. Soon it would be too late. His mouth sucked the swell of her breast, then kissed a path to her lips.

"Sweet, sweet Thea, don't fight me," he said against her mouth.

She bit him. He cried out and yanked at a handful of her hair. Resting on a forearm, he touched his fingers to his lips. They came away with a drop of blood.

"You filthy little bawd."

Taking advantage of his distraction, she scrambled away from him. On her hands and knees, she faced him, panting.

"You said I had until tomorrow."

"What?"

"You said I had until we reached this Ravensmere before you tried to make me submit again."

He sat up and gave her a scowl of indignation. "I wasn't—"

"You were."

"You let me."

"You forced me."

They glared at each other. After a few moments Savage broke into a pained grin. He seemed governed by mysterious and unpredictable moods, which made him all the more threatening.

"God's arse, woman, you turn a man's privates to boiled turnips."

"It's your own fault," she said. "I did nothing."

"Pig's swill."

Standing, he pulled her to her feet and shoved her in the direction of camp. "It's late. If we're not going to couple, at least we can get some sleep." He swatted her on the bottom.

Thea yelped, whirled, and kicked at him.

"Make haste," he said with a chuckle, "or I'll change my mind and have you whether you will or no."

Thea marched back to camp and kept well ahead of Savage while she did. She tried to go to Hobby, but her captor stepped in front of her. Pointing to her bedroll, he waited until she was on it, then took his place on the one next to hers. She lay between him and the fire. He scooted his own blankets closer to hers. They almost touched.

"You needn't hover over me," she said.

"Yes I do need. Every time I think you're broke, you start to rear and buck again."

He snatched her hands. He tested her bonds, loosened them a bit, and fastened to them the leather strap he'd kept all this time. He tied the other end to his wrist. She sat gawking at him while he arranged his bedding. When he lay down on his back and threw an arm over his eyes, she was dragged across his chest. He grunted and caught her shoulders.

"Why, Mistress Hunt, I thought you were afeared of my very touch."

"Knave, you've tied the lash to the wrong wrist." Thea pushed away from him.

He grinned and transferred the strap to the wrist nearest her. His glance caught hers, and he lingered there. She tensed. He watched her draw into herself and sighed.

"Close your gown."

She looked down to find her torn gown gaping open again. Her breasts were thrust toward him. She snatched the ends of the bodice and tugged them together. They would never stay. As a remedy she pulled a blanket over her, up to her neck, and lay down on her back. Taking care not to tug on the lash that bound her to Savage, she closed her eyes.

Savage's men were still moving about the camp. Some stood guard, others drank and talked while warming themselves at one of the other fires. They left their master and his captive alone. She couldn't see Hobby. What had that man done to her? Vowing to see the maid upon the morrow, Thea tried to compose herself for sleep. She needed rest if she was to escape this unpredictable ruffian.

Beneath her lashes she stole a look at him. He had settled down again once she had stopped moving. His features had relaxed, as if he were already asleep. Once again she was startled by the contrast between his angelic coloring and his nature.

At once charming and ruthless, he kept her in a state of alarm by his mere presence. He took a deep breath as she watched him, and turned his face toward her. It was the face of a wanton, but not a lowborn wanton. This man wasn't a peasant, though he spoke with the cant of a London rogue.

Mayhap he was a disinherited son of some yeoman or landed gentleman. Many roamed the rubbish-strewn streets of south London and frequented the stews and ordinaries of the towns. Whatever his heritage, he had cast it in the dirt to become a spy and a thief. To his chosen profession he applied a frightening talent for cruelty, frightening because it was wielded with studied, deliberate artistry rather than the crude simplicity of the cur.

He moved again, this time resting his free hand on his breast. The long, slender fingers seemed meant for plucking the strings of a lute rather than hefting a sword. The hand was clean and less threatening when it lay limp and placid in sleep. A deceptive vision.

Thea turned on her side and buried her face in her pallet. Her fears battered at her thoughts. She would never sleep if she let them in. Casting her imagination across the miles to home, she went for a walk in the dale near the house. She counted saplings and listened to the call of a meadow pipit. As she drifted into sleep, she held a flower in her hand, its petals a deep, deep blue, a gentian.

# 5

*I came into a place void of all light, which
bellows like the sea in tempest, when it is
combated by warring winds.*

—Dante Alighieri

IN THE CITY OF London there are taverns and ordinaries in the stews of the south bank that waited, jowls open and slavering, for the entrance of the unwary and the ignorant. In these places the air is as foul as the ale, the customers unclean, and the vice refined and nasty. The White Hart Inn possessed none of these qualities. The White Hart Inn would have pleased the fastidious requirements of a Knight Hospitaler.

This night the White Hart hosted one of its more frequent but rather retiring patrons. A personage of means, this patron paid well for service, though he boasted no title and his clothing spoke more of the merchant than of the city gallant.

This patron occupied one of the more luxurious rooms. He never stayed long, never invited familiarity, seldom spoke to the servants. A creature of the evening, he never appeared until after sunset, when the inn yard boasted deep shadows, and the common rooms were lit only by candles.

Tonight the patron received a visitor. Timothy Eyre crept into the inn yard, glancing behind him every few moments. He mounted the stairs to the east gallery, sped along to the third door, knocked twice, paused, and knocked three times. The door opened, and he slipped inside without causing comment from the stable boys below in the yard.

The chamber into which he shambled was lighted with a single candle on a table. A pair of boots was propped on the table, and they were all that the visitor could see of the room's occupant, who leaned back in his chair out of the light.

Timothy danced before the table on skittish feet. "She's dead. Have you heard? She's dead. What did she tell Cecil? We're found out, I know it."

From the darkness came a voice as tranquil as Timothy was agitated.

"Be at ease, you fool. I know she's dead."

Timothy Eyre paused in his Morris dance. He was one of those men whose attempts at reasoning are accompanied by contortions of the facial muscles and much furrowing of brows. The more complex the reasoning, the more tortuous the spasms.

"You killed her!" Timothy squawked.

"Quiet, fool. Do you think I'd trust the task to you? You're as overwrought as a mare in a pen with three studs."

"But Cecil!"

"Knows nothing. And now we will proceed as I intended, *Dei gratia,* my dear Eyre, *Dei gratia.*"

*Derry awoke with his* face buried in long black tresses, unrested, as troubled as when he'd drifted off to sleep only a few hours before. He plucked fine strands of Thea's hair from his face. His body had surrounded hers in sleep like a shell around a snail. Slipping the tie that connected them from his wrist, he removed himself from her warmth without disturbing her. He was already disturbed.

Running a hand through his hair, he stood above her, contemplating her pale face. She had lied to him. He wasn't sure how, but he knew when a woman was lying to him. Running the leather strap through his fingers, he mused on what he'd forced her to tell him the previous night.

She was protecting someone, someone who was trying to destroy England. It could be someone in her family, even a beloved familiar. The button ciphers in Leslie Richmond's possession had been discovered many weeks earlier. They resembled those in Thea's casket. At the top of Richmond's ciphers had been drawn designs, mythical creatures used in armorial bearings.

Cecil's cipher clerk said that the messages had been addressed to persons symbolized by the mythical creatures. Thea's ciphers contained the same symbols—a unicorn, a griffin, a leopardlike creature called an ounce, a merman called a triton, and a two-legged, winged dragon called a wyvern. In Thea's ciphers, the wyvern appeared at the bottom of each piece of paper. Each paper mentioned one of the other symbols. It was Derry's guess that the wyvern was the leader of the English plotters.

Too many messages were flowing between England and Scotland. A wasp was building a nest, cell by cell, in the heart of England. He needed to know the identity of the wyvern, and only Thea could tell him, or provide the key to the cipher. He had been gentle. He could ill afford to be gentle much longer.

The strap twisted in his hands as he reviewed the

various ways he could force the truth from her. He must coerce her into revealing everything she knew, and quickly, within the fortnight. Glancing up, he saw Stubb bending over a pot suspended over a newly kindled fire. He gave his captive a last glance and refrained from touching that soft hair and even softer cheek.

He joined Stubb, who was sniffing porridge as he stirred it. Behind him Hobby snorted in her sleep. Her gag had been removed.

"Well done," Derry said.

Stubb grunted. "She don't like having her hair pulled, the old sow. Kicked me shin, she did."

"Still, it served. She sounded as if you were breaking her arms."

"But the old sow don't know nothing, my lord. I let her see what you were doing to her mistress. Told her you was going to have her and then let the others take turns, and old Hobby squawked like a threepenny hen. She don't know nothing, and thinks her mistress as innocent as the Christ Child."

Derry rubbed his chin. "Very well, then Oakshot and Hadow will take her north to Blade Fitzstephen for safe-keeping. I can't have Mistress Hunt waking to find her maid untouched after all that screaming. It would ruin my fearful reputation with her. Have them leave at once, and quietly, before the lady wakes. I'll send another man to Cecil with the new ciphers."

"Aye, my lord."

Scooping up a chunk of bread from the cloth beside the fire, Derry snarled at his man. "Call me Rob, you fool."

"Oooo. Right distempered we are this morn." Stubb poked at his porridge with a wooden spoon. "All randy and cock-swollen, are we?"

Derry scowled at Stubb, stuffed the bread in his mouth, and tore off a piece.

"I seen you looking at her," Stubb said. "Though why this one's got you walking bandy-legged is a marvel to the rest of us. Mind you, this one's not ugly, but she's no Marvelous Mag, nor half as fulsome as Jenny, who, by the way, will meet us at Ravensmere."

"How would you like to spend the entire stay at Ravensmere cleaning the offal from those three-hundred-year-old latrines?" Derry lowered himself to the ground and continued eating.

Stubb lifted the pot from the hook that suspended it over the fire. "She don't look hard, that one. You could pleasure the truth out of her if you wanted."

"She's too frightened of me."

"Oh, so you tried already." Stubb held his pot while he chuckled. "I could make my fortune telling that story to a few ladies at court. There's three I could name would crow at the thought of a woman refusing you for once."

Tossing a scrap of bread aside, Derry rose. "Stubb, I'm going to spend the whole of this day contriving delicate methods of torture for Mistress Hunt. If you don't close your mouth, I'll try them on you first."

He stalked away with Stubb's guffaws ringing in his ears. The man knew too much. Stubb had been with him since shortly after he'd been released from the Tower and knew the evil spell that came over him when faced with a beautiful woman.

His wife had been beautiful, and he'd loved her with the foolish rapture of an innocent despite his experiences on the continent. Yes, Alice had been beautiful.

They'd been married by their parents as children, then taken home again. Alice had come to him again when she was fourteen. He'd been enamored from the start, for Alice demanded that everyone be so. Proud of her red-gold hair and lush body, she had insisted on going to court, in fine raiment. He'd given her everything.

As long as she was the center of his existence, they had dealt well together. Then one day Tom Wyatt had come to his house with his plots and grudges against the Catholic Queen Mary. Derry had refused to join his friend, and Tom went away to rebel against his queen and fail.

One day soon after, while Derry was away, men came from Bishop Bonner, inquiring of his relationship with Wyatt. Fearing for herself, Alice blamed Derry, accused him of treason to save her own hide. They waited for him, and when he returned home, she stood on the steps of their home and pointed at him, abjuring them to take him away.

He'd been seventeen, and frightened, and determined not to betray his friend. He'd paid for his honor with his blood, and almost with the health of his mind. Of all the pain, all the things they did to him, the worst had been being thrown into a black cell beneath the Tower and sealed up in it. He had been sure they'd left him there to die of starvation, slowly, alone in that lightless void of stone.

Derry paused in his walk across the camp. The worst had been that cell. Glancing at the sleeping Mistress Hunt, his body went cold. Who better to plan torture than one who had been its victim? Already she would have lost her only companion. Bereft of her one solace, surely such a frightened creature couldn't long endure. She would break. He would have her secrets, and then what? The Tower? Mayhap Cecil would find some more congenial prison for her.

Derry turned to look over his shoulder. Hadow and Oakshot were mounted and leading the maid on a horse out of camp. Gagged and tied again, she cast bellicose glances at him as she left. When she was out of sight, he went to Thea and touched her arm. Her lashes rose slowly. At first she seemed not to know him, then she scrambled upright and away from him.

"Peace, woman. I got lots to do and no time for your nattering." He whistled to Inigo, who brought a sack full of clothing. Taking it, he thrust it at Thea. "Here, put these on. Can't have you prancing about like that in front of my men. Well, go on. And mark you, I'll be nearby, and you know what happens if I have to chase you."

Soon he had her dressed and fed and tied to a mount. To his relief, she gave no trouble until they were ready to set out.

"Where is Hobby?"

"Gone."

"Gone!" She began to tug at the leather straps that bound her to the pommel of her saddle. "What have you done?"

"Naught, yet. Here now, you stop your wriggling. You're upsetting the nag."

"What have you done to Hobby?"

"I told you, naught. But if you try my temper, I might change my mind. Now, be quiet."

They rode in silence most of the day. Stubb and Inigo acted as scouts, riding ahead to warn of anyone else in their way. Deeper and deeper into the forest they went, leaving behind all trace of man.

Stopping seldom, they rode steadily until the sun dipped low, and cast long shadows with a sparkling deep gold light. A breeze whispered, barely stirring the heavy branches of the trees high above. And all through the long day he could feel the woman's eyes on him, watching, fearful, suffused with loathing. Yet he still wanted her.

Their way grew rocky, and they began to climb beside

a frothing stream. Gnarled, grasping trees closed about them, and he saw Thea cast apprehensive looks at them. Bent and twisted, they crouched as if ready to leap at passers-by. As the horses picked their way through boulders and fallen branches, their progress slowed.

Emerging from the tree cover at last, Derry pulled Thea's horse to stand next to his and waited for his men to catch up to them. Ahead a path sprang out of nothing, skirted the stream, and led to a dilapidated bridge that arched over the water. Parts of its stonework had fallen into the stream, and rapids lapped at its underbelly. He smiled as he realized Thea was surveying it with uncertainty.

Pointing to the trees that crowded close to the bridge on the opposite bank, he said, "Ravensmere."

Barely visible through the dense greenery were the towers of an abandoned castle. From their vantage point they could see three slender towers, the tallest of which had a conical roof, the tiles of which had been pierced in some long-ago siege so that the rafters were visible. If they'd been closer, they could have seen that another hole in its side revealed a winding stair. Shutterless, narrow windows dotted the surface of the tower. Ravens perched on its summit and screeched an eerie welcome.

Thea cleared her throat. "That? That is Ravensmere?"

"'Course. What'd you think, I was taking you to my palace?"

"But it's so, so . . . Even in daylight it looks forgotten by man and God."

He didn't answer at first, and she looked at him.

"Remember that," he said.

Turning away, he threw the reins of her horse to Simon Spry and rode ahead. Inigo was at the bridge, waiting for him.

"I'm taking her into the castle," he said. "I want no interference, no protestations, nothing."

"But, my lord, you can't—"

Derry stared with raised brows at Inigo, who lowered his gaze to the ground.

"You bloody lords are all alike," Inigo muttered. "You'd skin your mother if it suited your purposes."

"There are few wolves in the forest now, Inigo, but I'll find one and feed you to it if you cross me."

"I'm going."

He made no reply. Returning to Thea and Simon, he took up the reins of her horse again. He ordered the others to stay behind and led Thea slowly to the bridge.

"Why aren't the others coming?" she asked as he guided her over the bridge.

"I don't need them."

"Why?"

He ignored her. On the other side of the bridge, the trees closed in again, concealing from all but the nearest the overgrown path that wound through them. He took the path, but the horses had to step carefully over the increasingly rocky ground. The stream disappeared. Thea kept glancing back as if she longed for the sight of the ruffians she despised. He kept his expression blank, for it wouldn't do for her to see his satisfaction.

They climbed through the forest toward Ravensmere to the serenade of the stream and the raucous calls of the tower inhabitants. Now he could see the remains of the gate house. A spray of fallen stones marked the grave of the portcullis, and in the gap grew frothy saplings. Their leaves fluttered as he gazed at them. Suddenly, on a broken block of gray stone, a black figure appeared as if conjured there.

He halted. Staring at the lithe form draped lazily across

the stone, he motioned to Thea to stay where she was. Riding forward, he guided Jove to stand beside the intruder.

"What do you here?" he said quietly.

Long, black-clad legs uncrossed. Supple leather boots rested on the stone as the young man sat up. His clothing matched the color of his hair and eyes. So dark were they that it seemed as if some magician had ensorcelled a raven into the form of a youth.

Derry repeated his question.

"My love for you sped me hither."

"Your love? God's eyes, brother, if you try to kill all those you love, I'll take your hate. I say again, Morgan, what do you here?"

"I but carry a message from Christian de Rivers. A certain name is whispered about the streets of Edinburgh and London, in stews and palaces alike. A name he likes not, for it stinks of treason—the name is the wyvern."

"I know this name."

"He sends me to tell you of its import. If you gain knowledge of the wyvern from the woman, you are to send word to him. I'll be nearby to offer aid should you need it."

"God's blood, why did he send you?"

"To twist the sword in your heart, sweet brother. To twist the sword in your heart."

Derry opened his mouth, but Morgan slid off his perch, quick as a merlin in flight, and danced over the stones to vanish in the forest beyond. Anguish flaring, Derry hauled Jove around and galloped back to Thea. She gave him a startled, questioning look, but he glowered at her, and she said nothing.

Pulling her mare behind him, he guided her around the fallen stones, beneath battered walls, and into what was once the bailee of Ravensmere. Remnants of stables and mews greeted them. Collapsed walls sprouted young trees and twisted bushes. Their horses' hooves clattered over broken flagstones. The noise shattered the abandoned silence of the castle and disturbed the ravens. Flapping their wings, they clambered into the air and cawed their outrage.

Crossing to the inner ward, they passed the square keep. He stopped and dismounted before the Raven Tower, which was set in the defensive wall behind the keep. He cut Thea's bonds, grasped her by the waist, and lifted her to the ground.

She looked around. "There's no one here."

"The ravens stand guard."

Not giving her a chance to ask more questions, he took her by the wrist and pulled her toward the Raven Tower. He shoved open a door set with rusted iron studs. Dust billowed out at them, and the setting sun cast a single beam of gold into the darkness in front of them. It bounced off the stones of the wall opposite. Ducking his head, he stepped in and dragged Thea after him.

Inside the door a stairwell curved up, winding toward the top of the tower and the ravens. It also pierced the floor and sank into the bedrock. Derry stepped down, turned, and tugged on Thea's arm.

"Where are we going?"

"Down."

"But there's no light."

"I can feel my way."

He fastened his arm about her waist and took her with him. Together they stumbled down the winding stair. He'd forgotten how endless the trip seemed. With each step they left light and life behind. The air grew cool and still. He could feel her body tremble as the last of the sunlight vanished, leaving her alone with him in rock that seemed to close about them.

His steps slowed. He didn't remember the stair being this long, this deep. He was feeling his way along the wall, keeping Thea close so that she wouldn't trip. He could hear her breathing rapidly. She was truly frightened now. If he hadn't been there before, he would be too. Mayhap he was anyway.

His boot hit a flagstone. The bottom, at last. Thrusting a hand out ahead, he felt along the wall until he hit wood. A door. Shoving it open, he guided Thea through. Once inside, he put his back to the door and paced from it eleven steps. With the last step he hit an iron ring. He released Thea, knelt, and grasped the ring. Pulling with his full strength, he slid a trapdoor from its grooves.

"Please, where are we going?"

"You're going down this ladder."

He heard her footsteps rushing away from him. He raced after them, felt her skirts at his legs, and pounced. She screamed as he caught her and dragged her back to the trapdoor. In the blackness he couldn't see her, but he could feel her terror. Before he had time to consider, he shook her hard. She stopped screaming.

"You can climb down, or I'll throw you."

"Don't. I've done nothing."

"You're a traitor. I got no time to dally with papists. This way nobody has to arrest you or put you on trial."

He lifted her and held her over the gap where the ladder rested. Her feet flailed, then hit the first rung of the ladder. Pushing on her shoulders, he forced her down into the pit.

"Don't try to come out. I'll hit you with the door."

All he heard was a sob. Wincing, he wrestled the trapdoor back into place. As it scraped closed, he heard one last sob. He stood up and covered his face with his hands. He could almost smell her scent in the dead air.

Lifting his head, he stared into blackness. "'Into the eternal darkness, into fire and into ice.'" Was that her voice? Could he hear her through the stone? Gasping, he covered his ears with his hands, his shoulders hunching as if he'd been stabbed in the back.

"Forgive me, Thea *bella*, forgive me."

Blind and desperate, he flung himself toward the door. He banged against stone, thrashed about, and found wood. Without care he raced up the stairs. The beam of golden light pierced his eyes, searing them. Shutting them against the pain, he stumbled outside and slammed the door closed.

Leaning against the portal, he gulped in air. At last he opened his eyes. How could the sun still shine? He remembered being bewildered by the sun's existence upon his release from that black cell.

Nearby, a fallen wall grew a head, then another, but Derry didn't move as Inigo and Stubb emerged from hiding. Behind them several more men appeared.

Walking heavily, as if he bore the weight of the tower on his back, he went to Jove. The stallion met him and nuzzled his face. Derry patted the soft muzzle, then leaned against the animal's neck. The sun faded, drawing the golden light with it, and still the men waited for their master.

Derry lifted his head and glanced at Inigo without seeing him. He wiped sweat from his chin and heard himself utter a harsh laugh.

"I am come up from hell, my birthplace, to show the world its fell pleasures and break the wings of a dove."

# 6

*Hades is relentless and unyielding.*

—HOMER

TIME HAD VANISHED. SHE had tried to hold on to it, but with no light, all measure of its progress vanished. Now she struggled to keep hold of her wits, to stave off horror and confusion. No one knew she was here except that madman, who wanted her dead. No one would come to release her. This place had been abandoned for at least a hundred years. Lying at the base of the ladder, Thea pressed her clasped hands to her lips and tried not to cry.

After Savage had left her, she'd clawed and pounded at the trapdoor, but it had been too heavy for her to move. No one answered her shouts. After a while she tried exploring the pit into which he had cast her. Deep and square, at least it was dry. It smelled of dust and rock, and old chains hung from rings in the walls.

There was no way out, for she had examined every bit of the place. Constructed of the same great blocks of stone of which the Raven Tower was made, the walls felt seamless. The only gap lay between two blocks near one corner, and it was barely wide enough to admit her finger. Air flowed in through this gap. She would die of starvation rather than lack of air.

Hours passed. At least she thought they did. Mayhap they were days. Her hunger grew until she began to feel dizzy. Light-headed, she fought off nausea. She pressed her hands to her stomach as the nausea turned to stabbing pains.

When she realized how weak she'd grown, terror took possession of her and she forced herself to climb the ladder again and shove at the stone. Standing on a lower rung, she placed her palms on it and shoved hard. Dizziness took her, and she swayed, lost her footing, and slipped. Crying out, she clawed at the ladder as she fell and her arm caught a rung.

The jolt wrenched her shoulder. She clung to the ladder with her legs dangling. Slowly she regained her footing and clambered down to slump at the ladder's base once again.

As she lay there, panting and half sobbing, she realized how close to delirium she was. She must fasten her thoughts upon something. Savage. Indeed, he must be mad. His moods shifted like light upon turbulent water. He was trying to drive her to madness as well. He would be back once he thought she was subdued. She would show him she was made of better stuff.

Someone had hired him to abduct her. Someone powerful. Someone at court, who had heard rumors of plots, most likely. Only someone with power would know so much about her doings. Mayhap there was a spy at Grandmother's house in London. Whatever the case, she must protect Grandmother. This powerful person might even decide that Father was also a traitor.

She tried rolling her shoulders, for the pain in her left

one had increased. The movement caused stabbing pains to lance through her back to her chest, so she cradled her left arm close to her breast and lay flat. The pains sent glittering sparks shooting against the backs of her eyelids. Biting her lower lip, she told herself not to succumb to Savage's game.

As time passed, the stinging in her shoulder grew worse, but at last she dozed. Strange dreams gave her little rest—dreams of a black stallion chasing her, his hooves pounding, eyes red. She could smell his sweat as he reared over her, stretching high over her fallen body.

She woke screaming. Her chest heaved and ached. Though she was shivering, beads of sweat trickled down her face and neck. Thea sat up with her back against the ladder. Wiping her face on her sleeve, she gave way to tears. The sound of her own weeping, the blackness that robbed her of all comfort, magnified her desolation.

When her tears slowed, she tried to distract herself with memories—a glowing childhood memory of a hot summer day, walking with Father and Mother, chasing beetles and butterflies. Later, she was older and impatient with Father, who would not pay attention, who would rather talk to horses or to flowers than to her.

Grandmother, who longed to move in court circles, who did so when old Queen Mary succeeded. Silver-haired Grandmother, who didn't care for what one wanted or needed, only for what would advance the family. Grandmother, who came one day and demanded that Thea go to France to be groomed at the fabulous court of Henri II and Catherine de Medici. Grandmother, who ignored her tears and left her on the deck of a ship, weeping, with her hand in that of a strange lady governess.

She reached out to Grandmother as the ship glided away from the dock. She floated away from the shore, away from home, and the ship vanished. Suddenly she stood in the midst of a great blackness. Thrashing about blindly, her arms met nothing but emptiness. Then she heard a snort, and a stamp of a hoof against stone, and saw a spark.

In front of her the blackness took form, grew red eyes and a muzzle full of teeth that parted and snapped at her. She screamed as a black stallion raised itself on its hind legs. She darted out of the way as the hooves sailed down at her. As she leapt aside, the red eyes glowed white, then turned a deep gentian blue. Her breath caught in her throat. She threw up her arms and fell, backward, into the darkness.

*Derry leaned on the* broken stone sill of a window at the top of the Raven Tower. The sun was setting again, and he could hear the ravens circling the roof and landing on exposed rafters. All about him he could see nothing but the tops of trees. Frothy, light green clouds of leaves swayed in the wind and lashed at the steadier, darkly verdant oak leaves. Branches scraped the rounded stone walls of the tower.

Below he saw the remnants of a wooden bridge, a part of the wall walk that ended abruptly in a gap just before it reached the tower. Stooping, Derry picked up a chunk of stone that had broken from the wall and tossed it at the bridge. The stone hit the bridge with a snap, then clattered and tapped its way to the ground far below.

"You up here again."

Derry whirled around, his sword half drawn before he recognized Stubb's voice. He turned back to gaze out at the forest. The sun had dropped below the tree line.

"Don't do no good wasting away up here," Stubb said, holding out a plate of food. "We all know you had no choice. Other men would have been harder. She don't know how blessed she is. Here, I brought your supper."

"I don't want it."

"You didn't want it last night or the night before. You got to eat more. Just because she don't got victuals, don't mean you have to go without."

"I eat when I please; now, leave me alone."

He walked away from Stubb, skirting a hole in the flooring, and sat on the edge of a gap in the wall the size of three men. Grit and pebbles loosened beneath his hip and fell in a jumble over the edge of the wall. Stubb walked up to him.

"See here, my lord, it's been three days. You can't—"

He heard himself shouting. "Hold your tongue!" Clamping his hands on the edge of the wall, he kept his face turned away from Stubb. "I know how long it's been. By my soul, I know how long to the minute."

"Then there's no need for this."

Rounding on Stubb, Derry slid off his perch. The man backed away toward the stairs, and Derry kept coming.

"At first she won't have believed I would leave her there to die. She will have tried to get out, mayhap hurt herself trying. Then the waiting begins, and the fear crowds close upon it, then the hunger, and then more fear. After that the pain, the sickness, then the nightmares that grow and grow until you can't tell whether you're in a waking vision or a dream."

Stubb backed up until he nearly fell down the stairs. Righting himself, he put the plate of food on the floor.

"You're riled because of Morgan."

A new voice intruded. "Is he? How congenial."

Both men turned to meet the newcomer whose footsteps had gone unheard on the tower stair. Derry whirled away from them to resume his post at the window.

"Get out, both of you."

Stubb complied with haste, but Morgan sauntered over to Derry, taking care to avoid the rotting floorboards in the middle of the chamber. He drew near and leaned against the wall beside Derry.

"I came upon Inigo and Simon and the others below. They're besotted with worry over you. Their villainous hearts ache at the thought of you grieving and wasting away up here. I told them not to weave fantasies."

"There's no news yet," Derry said without glancing at his brother. "Go away."

"Inigo is worried you'll lose heart for the work and let the lady out too soon. I told him there was no chance." Morgan began removing his gloves, pulling at the fingers one at a time. "After all, you managed to murder the brother who stood between you and inheriting Moorefield. You won't cavil at torturing a woman."

Derry turned his head slowly until he faced the younger man. "I won't fight with you, Morgan."

"I'm much relieved. Though I can see why you wouldn't bestir yourself. I'm the younger by five years, and no threat to your title."

The two stared at each other, Morgan watchful and intent, Derry closed and silent. When Derry failed to reply, Morgan went on.

"How haps it that you're so damnably clever? Did you make a contract with the devil when they had you in the Tower? Is that how you know what evil to work upon a helpless woman to make her betray her friends?"

"Yes."

Morgan paused then, and Derry smiled, for he knew his brother hadn't expected agreement.

"I've visited hell, wallowed in its muck, breathed its stench. Its putrescence has filtered into my very bones, and now I turn it to my own purpose." Derry held out his hand. "Touch me."

Morgan looked at the hand but didn't move, and Derry lowered it to his side.

"Afraid, sweet brother?" He laughed. "I marvel you come so near and risk contamination."

Swinging away, he headed for the stair, but Morgan grabbed his arm and yanked Derry around to face him. "Time grows short. France plots to swallow England and Scotland, and you languish in a tower as rotten as your heart."

Derry jerked his arm free. "You lack variety in your calumny. Your song is of one note, a single, wearisome screech. Begone."

Derry turned swiftly and descended the stairs. At ground level he met Inigo and Simon Spry. He snatched a water bottle from Inigo's hand, a torch from its wall sconce, and continued his plunge down the stairs. At the bottom he stuck the torch in another wall sconce. After setting the bottle to one side, he placed his hands on the ring of the stone door to the pit. He hesitated, knowing he would find a broken girl behind it.

The door shoved aside easily. Again he paused and this time listened. No sound. Clutching the water bottle, he descended into blackness. He left the torch above, for Thea's eyes would be sensitive to light. Thus he could see little beyond the ladder, especially when he reached the bottom rung. As his foot touched the floor, something snagged the end of his leather jerkin and tugged at it.

"Shhh." Thea lay on her side, favoring her shoulder, and reached up to him with a shaking hand. "Shhh, Father. That man is here somewhere, and he wants to hurt us."

He should have expected the terror to have done this to

her. Heart pounding, Derry sank down beside her and took her hand. It trembled, and he could feel the bones.

"Thea, you have to tell me about the ciphers now. You can't remain—"

"Shhh." She stared up at him with eyes widened by darkness and fear. "He mustn't know you're here. I never thought you would find me."

Derry removed the stopper from the water bottle and held it to her lips. She stopped to drink, gulping noisily.

"Not too much at first," he said as he took back the bottle. "Just tell me what I must know."

"You mustn't speak so loudly. He'll hear us, and I'm trying to keep him from finding out about Grandmother."

The water bottle stopped in midair. After a moment he said, "What about your grandmother?"

. Thea shushed him again, then her head wobbled. He enfolded her in his arms so that her head rested on his shoulder. He patted her cheek, hoping he was doing it in a fatherly manner.

"You brought light with you, Father. I'm glad." She darted quick, feverish glances about the pit, hooked a finger in his shirt, and pulled him closer. "Grandmother has been stirring a pot full of troubles. You know how furious she was at losing place when that terrible Bloody Mary died. Somehow she's begun to dabble in matters of great import. And do you know what?"

"What?"

Thea looked about her suspiciously. Her hands worked in his jerkin, twisting the leather. "She tricked me, Father. She . . . I don't feel well."

"How did she trick you?"

"Water."

He held the bottle to her lips again, then urged her to continue.

"She gave me a set of buttons as a present from her to the Queen of Scots. And do you know that they concealed ciphers? She didn't tell me."

Derry went cold. Touching her cheek, he asked, "You knew nothing of the ciphers?"

Thea moved her head from side to side. "Why has she always been like that, Father? Using people instead of loving them. She sent me away to France."

"You knew nothing?" His voice rose, and he shut his mouth.

"Grandmother . . . she weaves secret webs and snares her own in them." Touching her fingers to her lips, Thea closed her eyes. "And she cares not if we're hurt, you and I."

Derry brushed black tendrils from Thea's face. "Before God, woman, listen to me." He stopped, for she was laughing.

"I thought I was going to Scotland to help her majesty, to tell her about Lord Darnley. Grandmother sent me as a courier, an ignorant one, but a courier."

He leaned closer as her voice faded, then lightly patted her cheek. She moaned in response.

"Thea, the key to the ciphers, know you where it might be? Thea?"

He got no answer. Cursing, he picked her up and stood. She had never been heavy, but now holding her was like holding a bag of feathers. He draped her over one shoulder and climbed out of the pit. Above, he tied a kerchief over her eyes against the light, and shouted for Inigo. Inigo clattered downstairs as he picked Thea up again, and with the thief lighting the way, he carried her out of the darkness. Emerging from the Raven Tower into the court, he was greeted by hovering vagabonds.

Crossing the court to a tower opposite the Raven, he climbed the stairs behind Inigo. At the top he entered a room as light and airy as the pit had been dark and close. He placed Thea on a cot. She grimaced as her shoulder hit the mattress. A glance at Inigo sent the thief out of the chamber.

From a stool beside the cot he took a cloth and rinsed it in a basin of water. He dabbed Thea's face, especially her dry lips. Dipping his fingers in the water, he patted them over her brow above the kerchief. He prodded her shoulder gently, but found no bones broken. She must have strained it. As his hands kneaded the flesh, she moved, sighed, then touched the cloth over her eyes.

"Don't," he said, and put his hand over hers. "You are unused to the light."

At the sound of his voice, she jerked her head in his direction, then tried to scramble away from him. She knew him now.

"Oh God, how came I here? What are you doing? Don't—don't touch me."

He clamped both hands on her shoulders and pushed her down onto the cot. "You've no strength. Rest instead of wasting my time."

"What have you done?"

"Got you out of that hole, I did."

"Why? Wait—my father. No, that was a dream." Placing a trembling hand over her lips, she caught her breath on a sob.

"No weeping, do you hear me?"

She sniffed. "Leave me."

"Not until I've fed you."

"I'll tell you nothing. God's mercy, I hate you."

"God's arse, I care not. And I already got what I need from you."

"I don't believe you."

"And I said I cared not."

"May Satan take your soul to hell." Her voice broke, and she turned her head away from him.

Derry eyed the blindfolded and weeping woman. She had faded like a wraith, and he could almost imagine seeing through her. He wanted to touch her, to lend her his strength, but she would fight him. Before he could decide what to do, Inigo returned with hot broth. Derry took the bowl and dismissed Culpepper.

He heard a little sniff. Balancing the bowl in one hand, he dipped its spoon into the broth and guided it to her lips. Her mouth opened, and the liquid vanished. He smiled, relieved that she was well enough to take food. Half the broth was gone when she sighed and turned her head away. He put the bowl and spoon on the floor. She shouldn't eat too much at first anyway. He listened and heard the even breathing of sleep.

He left quietly and barred the door from the outside. As he dropped the bar into place, he shook his head. The old woman. It had been the old woman all along. The old harpy had fed her granddaughter to him rather than risk her own dried-up hide. What a nest of thorns and nettles he'd come upon. Lady Hunt seemed to care not a wit for the danger in which she'd placed Thea. A plague take the old sow. He'd set out for London upon the morrow and catch her. That he would enjoy, for Thea's sake.

He went out into the courtyard once more. His men had gathered around a fire in the center to watch a roasting boar. Stubb held out a chunk of meat on a plate.

"Now will you eat?"

He took the plate and sat down on a broken block of

stone. He scowled at the meat. She hadn't fared well in that pit. She was too thin, and as pale a winter cloud. He set his plate aside. She'd been innocent, in part, as he had been. His crime had been to befriend a man who rebelled against a queen. Hers had been to be the granddaughter of an intriguing old she-wolf.

"Stubb."

"Aye, Robin."

"We leave for the city upon the morrow. Inigo will remain here to watch the lady."

Stubb nodded. A shadow fell across Derry's line of vision, and he turned to see Morgan strolling toward him with his arm around the waist of a woman with red-gold hair and rounded, wide hips. She snaked an arm around his brother's waist and squeezed. Morgan noticed the direction of Derry's gaze and smiled at him.

"Well met, brother. They tell me you've been torment-ing your poor prisoner again." Morgan came to stand before Derry and squeezed his companion by the shoul-ders. "I have found a more delightful pursuit."

Derry reached out and jerked the woman from his brother's grasp. Morgan stumbled, then grabbed for his companion, but Derry pulled her out of his reach.

"Here now!" the woman said, kicking at Derry's shins.

Holding her at arm's length, Derry grinned at her. "Jenny, I warned you to keep your hands from my brother."

"A pox on you, you bleeding whoreson fish piss."

Morgan put his hands on his hips and lifted a brow.

"Marry," he said to Jenny, "I'm glad you were too busy earlier to speak. By my troth, if you'd have opened that foul mouth, I would have shriveled to the size of an earthworm."

Jenny darted forward. Before Derry could drag her

back, she kicked Morgan's shin. Derry snatched a handful of red-gold hair and yanked her back. Jenny howled, tore herself free, and scrambled to the other side of the fire, where she stood, glaring at the brothers. Derry vowed to send her back to London with his next messenger.

Morgan was rubbing his leg and cursing. "Jesu Maria, I think you're jealous. Afraid she'll compare us to your disadvantage?"

"You're leaving with me. Tomorrow. For London."

"I'm not your minion. I'll leave when I wish."

Derry slapped Morgan's arm, knocking it away from his injured leg and throwing the younger man off balance. He hauled his brother upright.

"The center of all this plotting is Lady Grace Hunt, not Thea. It is the old woman who holds the key to the ciphers."

"Ah, another woman to torture. What good fortune."

Clenching his jaw, Derry turned away from Morgan. The sun had gone down, and the last daylight was vanishing. Stubb and Inigo and the others had retreated with their food away from the warring brothers. Derry was headed for the Raven Tower, leaving Morgan by the fire, when a distant whistle brought him up sharply. Another whistle sounded closer, and then a rider appeared. The man rode into the courtyard and dismounted before Derry.

"My lord."

"Tugman, what brings you so far from your master?"

"Urgent news, my lord." Tugman pulled a sealed letter from his doublet and presented it to Derry.

After motioning Tugman away, Derry took the letter to the fire, broke the seal, and read. He stared at the paper for a long time before dropping it into the fire. Across the flames Morgan's dark eyes bore into him. He lifted his gaze to his brother.

"You've gotten your wish. Neither of us will go to London. Grace Hunt has been murdered. Four nights ago. Stabbed in bed, her chamber riffled but not robbed, as though it had been searched."

"Murdered? By whom?" Morgan asked.

"Cecil knows naught for sure, but he had set inquiries about the city, chasing the identity of this creature called the wyvern. He had questioned Lady Hunt about him that very day, and by that night she was dead."

"By my troth, it seems surpassing unhealthy to befriend the wyvern."

"Yes," Derry said, casting a glance up at the tower room where Thea lay. "And now the only person who might know who the wyvern is lies yonder."

Morgan snorted and joined Derry in looking up at the tower. "More merriment for you, then."

Derry glanced at his brother and laughed bitterly.

"Perchance you would like the work?"

"Thank you, no. It is your endearing custom to break women, brother, not mine."

# 7

*When wert thou born, Desire?*
*in pomp and prime of May.*

—EDWARD DE VERE,
EARL OF OXFORD

THE OWL FLEW OVER the city wall, and as it coasted across the fields north of London and to the west of Bishopsgate, mice scurried for cover. The owl failed to dive for any of the plump denizens of the fields. Perhaps it was curious about the five cloaked men who had invaded its territory—the deserted ruins of the church of St. Botolph. Little was left of the church except the Roman arch of its entrance and one side wall with its massive, half-cylindrical arches. The flagstones had disappeared under a cover of turf and grass. Thus the footsteps of the men inside the skeleton of the church were muffled. One of them peered out around the front arch.

"Nothing," he said, and turned to Timothy Eyre. "You said he would come."

Another man hunched his shoulders, then started as the owl landed on top of the side wall and hooted. "God's blood, I vow there are Saxon and Norman ghosts in this place. I tell you, it isn't safe."

A sixth cloaked figure appeared from the shadows at the end of the wall. "The only surety in life is death."

The five men turned quickly, but said nothing until Timothy found his voice.

"I told you he'd come."

One of the others took a step in the direction of the newcomer, who backed up and drew his sword as Timothy put an arm in front of his companion.

"Wyvern, it's time we learned who you are," the companion said.

"Oh? You wish to die this night?" said the Wyvern.

"Wyvern is as good a name as any for him," Timothy said.

"You know who we are," the companion protested. "It's been months. And now Leslie Richmond is dead, and Lady Hunt. We've been betrayed, and that stoat William Cecil is behind it all. I know it."

The Wyvern approached, which caused the men to retreat. Moonlight caught the folds of a black cloak, a hood, and a mask. "Close your mouth, you fool. I killed them."

"You. Then—then our ciphers haven't been captured?"

"You'd be headless in Shoreditch if they had," said the Wyvern. "I came to put you at ease. I've dealt with the traitors in our midst. The rest of you are safe. Your pledges went to Scotland by an unsuspecting messenger."

The Wyvern sheathed his sword and backed into the shadows once more. "I like not this whining and puking at every noise and rumor. It would be well if you all went home and stayed there. Do it quietly, and without haste. Wait for word from me in the customary manner. I'll not send until the Queen of Scots bears a living son."

"But Leslie Richmond wasn't a traitor, and Lady Hunt—"

With snakelike speed the Wyvern was on the man, who gasped as a knife appeared at his throat. The others backed away from them. The Wyvern chuckled while he pricked his victim's throat with the tip of the knife.

"None of you knows the whole of my design. None of you knew Richmond as I did, or Lady Hunt. Would you rather I'd left them to betray you to the queen? Richmond carried messages from me to the rest of you."

"No, no, no, no."

The knife vanished, and the Wyvern merged with darkness once more. "Then go, and keep yourselves quiet and calm, or you'll end up like the others."

With protests of obedience, four of the men scurried away into the night. Timothy remained behind, watching until they were out of sight. Then he turned to study his master.

"Why did you lie to them? You didn't kill Leslie Richmond."

"They fear me more than ever now," said the Wyvern. "And though I know not who the killer was, I'm certain Cecil and his band of intelligencers had their fingers in those doings. It is better that they fear me more than Cecil."

"And Lady Hunt?"

"Was questioned by Cecil himself. I can't have that. But enough of old affairs. You sent a man to follow Mistress Thea. Has he returned?"

"Er, I was going to . . ."

The Wyvern darted at Timothy. A gloved hand wrapped around Eyre's throat. Timothy clutched it and gargled a protest. The hand squeezed, then tossed him aside. Timothy fell back against the church wall, gulping in air.

"Say it straight out, you puling cur."

"She—" Timothy hauled in a deep breath. "She's van-

ished. He was less than half a league behind, close to the
border. He rode into a dale and found her gone, along with
her men, the wagons, the horses, and pack animals. He
found nothing. He said it was as if they'd been spirited
away by some demon."

"By the rood, I'll skewer you and him both and flay you
with a needle. No, say nothing or I'll do the deed at once."
The Wyvern stalked back and forth in front of Timothy
Eyre, who stayed huddled against the wall. "Someone
knows of my designs. Mayhap they learned something
from Richmond, though I thought he died without revealing anything. Mayhap Lady Hunt was the fool
who—no matter."

"We could send men to look for the girl," Timothy
said.

"Not from London. London is too dangerous now."

The Wyvern stopped abruptly by an arched window.
He gazed out at the moonlit field that stretched between
the church and the houses far away along Bishopsgate
Street. Removing his gloves, he placed a hand on the stone
sill. Silver light caught the reflection of a single ruby ring.
Timothy remained where he was, licking his dry lips and
watching his master. At last the Wyvern spoke again.

"I'll send word by ship to my friend in Scotland. He's an
unlikely warrior, and a skillful one."

The Wyvern lapsed into silence once more. The owl
grew impatient with the remaining invaders and
screeched, making Timothy Eyre jump. The Wyvern
glanced at him while he drummed his fingers on the
windowsill. As the owl sprang into the air and flew off
toward London again, the drumming stopped.

"This disappearance is an ill omen, and no accident. We
must needs find out who caused it." The fingers rapped on
the sill again. "We must draw him out. Draw him out and

make him expose himself to us. I should never have listened to Grace Hunt. That girl was too great a risk, and now she and her captor must be removed."

"But how?" Timothy asked.

The Wyvern drew on his gloves while gazing out the window. "First we find them. Then we discover what they know. And then we make sure they never tell it to anyone else. The task is a delicate one, but no more delicate than many I've undertaken. The key, you understand, is to make certain that your prey never knows your true design.

"Misdirection, dear Timothy, misdirection and disguising, but, *nihil nimis,* nothing in excess."

The Wyvern walked past Timothy. "Don't cower so, you fool. If they knew who we were, we'd be in the Tower having our bones broken. Fare you well, Timothy, and do be of good cheer. I intend to find this pestilential meddler, and when I do, he'll wish he'd been found by the devil rather than me."

*Thea prowled the round* chamber at the top of the tower. Her skirts snapped with the violence of her pacing. She was tired of being afraid. She'd been so afraid for so long that it wasn't possible to maintain the exhausting state. In addition, it was the fifth morning since Robin Savage had plucked her from the black pit and stuck her in this new prison, and she was growing to hate it almost as much as the pit.

The room had a new floor and a patched, conical roof. The morning light made the white-plastered walls glow as it sprayed in through an arched window set low enough for her to see the courtyard below. She hadn't seen Savage since he'd left her there. She'd been given plenty of food and some of her clothing. And now she was strong enough to leave behind her desolation, strong enough to despise Savage's cruelty, strong enough to be furious.

Thea rubbed her sore shoulder, which still twinged if she moved it sharply, and contemplated her situation. She knew not what had happened to her maid or to her men. Time was passing, and thus danger was growing. She remembered little of her stay in the pit except for nightmares and pain, and yet that monstrous Savage seemed content to hold her in this tower forever. If she didn't escape, he would kill her. He might already have killed Hobby. What would happen to Father, and who would warn Mary Stuart of her danger?

The bar across the door thumped as someone removed it. Inigo Culpepper appeared with a tray bearing bread, ale, and a bowl of stew. He had attended to her since that first day when she had tried to rip Stubb's hair from his head. Stubb had hurt her maid, and she longed to shove him out her tower window and hear his body land with a thud in the courtyard. Inigo, however, had managed to win from her a promise of safe conduct. Once or twice he'd stayed awhile and watched her eat. He stood on one leg and then the other, wringing his hands and making apologies for himself and the other thieves. She stopped him when he tried to explain Savage's conduct.

"Feeling better today, mistress?"

Thea crossed her arms and scowled at Inigo as he set down the tray on a bench at the foot of her bed.

"What's to be done with me, Inigo?"

"Now, mistress, you know I can't talk about that. I told you, Robin would beat me into curds for so much as smiling at you."

The disquiet that frayed her calm gnawed at her fragile peace and sent Thea darting for the tray. Grabbing a knife stuck in the bread, she swiped at Inigo with it. He squawked and jumped away from her, but she pursued him. He bounded for the door, burst through it, and ran into Robin Savage. Savage thrust him aside, dived at Thea, and caught her wrist. Twisting the knife from her grasp, he tossed it aside and swept her into his arms. She was off her feet before she could protest.

He tossed her onto the bed. Thea scrambled away from him and to the floor as he retrieved the knife and thrust it in his belt.

"And what do you think I'd do to you for killing one of my men?" he asked her.

"Something worthy of your cruel nature, I've no doubt."

Savage scowled at her for a while longer, then his features relaxed, and he sighed. "This is all wrong."

Thea braced herself for another attack. He would turn nasty at any moment. She blinked at him when he walked to the window, leaned on it, and stared at a scarred boot. After a few moments he lifted his gaze to her. It was a brooding, angry look, a baited-bear look.

"Thea *bella,* you and I have been cast at cross-purposes."

"Marry, you're at cross-purposes with the world."

He seemed not to hear her. "My master thought you a traitor."

"Your master is a fool."

"He thought so because your grandmother told him you were."

She heard the note of complaint in his statement. Thea opened her mouth to ridicule the idea, then closed it. For the first time since she'd met this horrible creature, she believed him. He sounded at once irritated and regretful. Before she could speak, he began again.

"Lady Hunt sent the ciphers without telling you. I

found them. They proved you were the blighted traitor I was sent to find. God's arse, what a confusion."

"How do you know this?"

Savage left the window and came to stand on the opposite side of the bed. She kept her gaze on him all the while.

"When I went down to get you, you thought I was your father and told me."

Thea retreated to the wall, shaking her head. "My father has nothing to do with these intrigues and plots, I tell you."

"I know that, silly gentry mort. I come to make peace."

"Then you'll release me?"

"Ha! And let you go trotting off to Scotland and interfere in great matters that concern you not? I'm here to make peace, not stick my head out for you to chop."

"You can't hold me forever."

"Won't have to. Only until it's too late for you to make trouble. A month or so will do."

Savage rounded the bed and approached her. Thea scooted along the wall, and since the chamber was a tower one, they scurried around in a circle until Savage stopped abruptly and cursed at her.

"Here now. I got no time for this."

"You're not going to touch me again. God, I can hardly bear to be in sight of you."

"Will you stop cackling and listen? I'm trying to ask pardon for what I did."

Thea eyed him. "Why?"

"What mean you, why? I was mistaken. I ask pardon. I won't hurt you anymore. God's blood, woman, can't a man err a bit in this life?"

Outrage burned all caution from her. Thea put her hands on her hips and stalked up to Savage. She jabbed a finger into his jerkin. He winced and backed up as she crowded him.

"You nearly killed me. You're foul and base and low and mean and—"

"And you're a traitor and a papist."

Thea stopped jabbing him and threw up her hands. "Will you stop calling me that? I'm no papist."

"What are you, then, a pagan?"

She poked him in the chest again, emphasizing each word with a jab. "I'm a God-fearing, loyal subject of the queen's majesty." She swept her arms about, indicating the chamber. "Do you see a rosary? Did you see any rosaries or a Latin Bible when you plundered my belongings?"

Savage glanced at her, then at the chamber. Hunching his shoulders, he ran a hand through his hair and rubbed the back of his neck. She couldn't hear what he mumbled.

"What?" she asked.

"Didn't see no rosaries nor no Latin." He had been scowling at the floor. Now he glanced up at her and smiled ruefully. "'Nother confusion, I'll wager."

"For a famous outlaw, you go about addled a great deal of the time, sirrah. Now, get out."

Savage stood erect. "I'm still master here. I'll go when I'm of a mind to go. If you're such a good Christian Englishwoman, you have to forgive me for—for . . ."

"Ask God for forgiveness."

Thea turned her back on Savage, but he caught her arm and pulled her back to him. Holding her by the shoulders, he trapped her gaze with his and brought her near.

"I'm asking you, you stubborn gentry mort. What was I supposed to do? Let you plunge us into war? Did you ever see a burning? Did you see the poor sods old Bloody Mary set on fire? Mayhap you don't care."

Thea yanked herself free. "God preserve me. The high-wayman seeks to teach me compassion. You're too late. I learned it in France when I saw priests laugh at burning children."

They glared at each other, each breathing hard and seething with righteousness until Savage suddenly broke into a grin.

"Seems we got no quarrel, at least a lot less of one than I thought."

"It's all your fault," Thea replied. "You should have talked to me instead of pouncing like a wolf on a ewe."

She felt her body relax. It seemed that she had been stiff and wary for a century. Weariness came over her without warning, and she dropped to the bench beside the tray of cooling food. Savage startled her by dropping to one knee beside her.

"Mistress Hunt, even had I not been set to find you, had I come upon you, I would have pounced."

"It's as I said, you're low and base, a thief and mur-derer."

She tried to get up from the bench, but he put his arm across her lap.

"When I saw you, I was angry."

"This is not a surprise," she said while she tried to shove his arm away.

"I was angry because you were a traitor, lady, and one who set fire to me."

Thea stopped trying to escape. Growing still, she waited for him to continue. He leaned closer. She backed away, but she couldn't go far without overbalancing. He was so near, his body almost touched hers.

"Thea *bella*, when you're not afraid of me, you catch fire as well. Look at me. I promised not to hurt you. Can you not see I know these past few days have been a mistake?"

"Get away."

She shoved him again, and he sat back, regarding her sadly.

"You're still afraid. Even a highwayman hates it when a lovely woman looks at him as if he were a rabid weasel."

She had been wary before. The compliment sparked her distrust and incredulity. Only one other man had looked at her with those sleep-heavy eyes that weren't in truth sleepy at all. Only one other man had cozened her with lies about her beauty. God's breath, she'd near lost her wits.

Thea shoved at Savage with both hands. He toppled to the floor. Springing to her feet, she stood over him.

"Lying, deceitful wretch. Cozen me not with your sticky praises. Now that you've no other use for me, you've decided to entertain yourself." Uttering a cry of desperation, Thea kicked him as he rose, sending him rolling on the floor again. "If you intend to do me harm, do it and be gone. Otherwise, leave me in peace in this prison."

"Addled little bawdy basket, what are you screeching about?" Savage rolled to his feet and faced her.

"If you think me witless enough to submit to you after what you've done to me—God give me strength—how haps it that you think me so stupid that I could suddenly forget your cruelty, lie down, and spread myself for your pleasure simply because you've changed your opinion of me?"

Savage stuck his face in front of hers. "I told you what happened."

"You're trying to get me to bed you." Thea dashed to the bench, picked up the bread from the tray, and threw it at Savage. "God, I detest men. Full of satisfaction with themselves and their parts and their prowess. Using women like they use piss pots, then tossing them away when they're through, as if they stank." She could hear her voice rising, but she couldn't stop it. "I hope you all burn in hell, every last randy, callous sod of you."

Savage was glaring at her. His great, dark blue eyes were so entrancing, she picked up the bowl of stew and threw it at them. He ducked, and the bowl hit the wall. Stew splattered over the stone. He darted a look at it, then turned on her.

"It's muddled in the head, you are."

"Get out!"

"I'm going," he said as he made for the door. "Think you I want to listen to any more ranting. You sound like a pox-ridden bawd whose coney has slipped away without paying."

Thea swore, then glanced down at the mug of ale, the only thing left on the tray. Savage saw the direction of her gaze as he opened the door.

"Don't you try it." He darted behind the door as the mug sailed at him. Sticking his head back around the door, he stared at the wet wood. "I warned you."

He lunged for Thea, who darted for the protection of the bench. Reaching it, she picked it up. The tray flew off it as she thrust it at Savage. Savage caught the bench, tossed it aside, and kept coming. He snagged her by the waist as she raced for the bed. He turned her in his arms and let her fight him until she lost strength. When she could only jerk her body back and forth uselessly, he gave a soft chuckle and brushed his lips across her cheek. She cried out, but he traced the line of her jaw with his tongue. Shivering, she cursed him.

"Thea *bella*, someday you'll curse me for not doing this."

She tried to spit at him, but he kissed her. So suddenly was his mouth on hers that she froze. As quickly as it had captured her lips it was gone, and his tongue tickled its way down her neck. Goose bumps formed at her throat, on her arms, her chest. She gasped as he suddenly turned her so that her back was to his chest. He nibbled his way from her ear to her throat while keeping her trapped in his arms. His hands cupped her breasts, and he murmured promises and little sounds of pleasure. The words made her tingle from her ears to her toes.

"Don't be angry," he whispered. "Forget, Thea *bella,* forget. Only feel. Feel my hands, feel them."

"No!"

Thea tore his hands from her breasts and jabbed backward with her elbow. Savage grunted, then dropped his arms. She whipped about and braced herself for another attack. He was standing there, panting and glaring at her.

"I was right," he said. "You're a bleeding tease." Kicking aside the fallen bench, he stalked to the door and flung it open again. "This is the last time you tease me, woman. Remember that. If you fight me, well enough, but stop fighting again, and nothing you do or say will stop me."

"You try it, sirrah, and I'll kick your testicles into your throat."

Her answer was a slammed door. She heard him cursing as he stormed down the winding stairs. Wiping perspiration from her upper lip and forehead, she dabbed a tear with her sleeve. She went to the window and looked down at the courtyard. Savage emerged from the tower, raced across the flagstones, and disappeared through a gap in the ruined curtain wall. As he vanished, Inigo called out to him. Savage hurled a lurid curse at him, and the man broke into a guffaw that echoed from tower to tower.

Thea went to the bed and sat down. She remained

unmoving for a timeless space, then sank to the floor on her knees. Folding her hands, she prayed.

"Dear God, make him leave me alone. Make him vanish, or release me. Don't let him touch me anymore, and most of all, don't let me want him to. I beg you, don't let him touch me again."

# 8

*My soul thirsteth for thee, my flesh longeth
for thee in a dry and thirsty land,
where no water is.*

—PSALMS 63:1

DERRY CLAMBERED OVER A spray of wall debris.
Inigo's merriment echoed in his ears as he hurried
to put some distance between himself and Thea
Hunt. He plunged into a stand of sycamores, then kept
walking until he came to the stream. The banks fell away
to form a wide pool, shaded and glassy, before they narrowed again where the water continued downhill.

An old log spanned one end of the pool. Derry walked
out on it and sat in the middle with his legs dangling. He
heard Stubb calling his name, but he didn't answer. He
was peeling bark from the log and tossing it into the pool
when his man found him.

Stubb came to the edge of the water, stuck his hands in
his belt, and regarded Derry. "What did she say? Does she
know anything?"

"I don't know."

"You were going to ask her about the cipher key and
Lady Hunt's doings."

Derry hurled a piece of bark at Stubb. "A pox on you! Don't tell me what I'm about as well. I swear by the cross, you're just like her. Dealing with her is like doing a May dance in a forest fire. God's blood, I want to turn her over my leg and take a belt to her." Derry turned to straddle the log and glare at Stubb. "She doesn't listen, and she takes offense at honest affection."

Stubb was grinning at him, so Derry fumbled at his belt in search of his dagger. Stubb's grin vanished. He retreated behind a sycamore.

"You were going to befriend her," he chortled. "You were going to make amends. You were—"

"God rot your hide." Derry launched himself off the log and stood glaring at Stubb. "You attend to your own affairs and leave mine to me."

"She don't like me either," Stubb said. "Can't abide me since I touched her silly maid. Near took my ear off when I brought her food once. That's why Inigo serves her. Appears she don't like you any better, but you said we had to find out what else she might know before we take her back to London."

Derry marched past Stub. "I'm going. Job had no greater trial than reasoning with that woman, but I'm going. May God give me patience to endure it."

He heard Stubb grunt as he plunged into the sycamores again.

"She might be more willing if you'd let her out of her cage a bit. Inigo says she likes to wander about the countryside at home. Loves plants and birds and such better than people. He says she knows the names of all the birds hereabouts."

"Marvelous strange. She'll talk to that rag picker's spawn but not to me."

He burst out of the forest as discomforted as when he

went in, and paused at the edge of the trees. He surveyed the ragged curtain wall, the Raven Tower, the lichen-covered stones of the old gate house. As he stared he felt as if he were imprisoned in his own body.

Craving had taken hold of him, pumped boiling lead through his sinews. He couldn't leave it behind. His body wouldn't calm as it always had when he commanded it. He had but to gaze at the tower where she was, to build the appetite into a ravening frenzy over which he had little governance.

Derry turned and ducked back into the shadows of the forest. He was so intent on fleeing, his shoulder bumped a sycamore. He scowled at the tree, then fell against it so that his forehead met the trunk, and he groaned. He hadn't foreseen this perplexity. How could he have guessed? Women were usually so biddable, so pliant, like wet silk. How was he to foresee that bravery allied to recalcitrance, black hair, and a heart-shaped face would make his body roil with passion?

"Derry," he said to himself, "you'll never gain her trust if you try to make love to her every time you get within an arm's length of her. Think of your duty. Time grows short."

Unfortunately, he made the mistake of thinking of how her body felt when he pulled her against him. Closing his eyes, he pounded his fist against the tree trunk. Pain shot through his fist, up his arm, and to his shoulder. Pain, that was the answer. Use one pain to fight another. He punched the tree again and again until the skin split over his knuckles.

"Piss on it." He shook his hand, then sucked at the bleeding wound. "Not a good idea."

He lifted his face to the sun. Light glowed through his closed lids, causing him to see red. He wanted her to be a papist traitor, an enemy, not a misguided innocent. As it was, she provoked his desire and his distrust, for he had wanted a woman like this before, and she had cast him into hell.

Yet he found himself wanting to explain his actions to Thea Hunt, but if he allowed her to become important to him, she would discover his past. He'd made peace with his own conscience in the last few years. No longer did he whip himself for that accident with his brother as if he could have prevented it. Still, he shied from revealing himself to anyone who could use that past against him. Morgan near killed him with every accusing glance. He would take no more.

Sighing, he flexed his bruised hand and headed for Thea's tower once more. He must face her again despite his remorse and his wariness. Giving himself no chance to question his new resolve, he unbarred the door and threw it open. She was standing in the middle of the chamber, eyes wide with alarm. He hated that look, that frightened-mouse gaze.

"I didn't kill her."

She said nothing.

"The maid, I didn't kill her."

"Oh."

"She's not even hurt. Marry, she boxed Hadow's ears and near took Oakshot's nose off."

The fear faded from her eyes, and he felt as if he'd won a tourney.

"Where is she?"

"Safe, with a friend of mine, and your men as well." He held up a hand. "Now don't you be asking me to bring her to Ravensmere. You and me got some talking to do. Come."

She looked at the hand he held out to her. The fear sparked in her eyes again.

"God's breath, woman, I give you my word I'll not so much as kiss your skirt."

"Your word? Marry, sirrah, I trust not your word."

He reached out and snatched her wrist. "Do you want out of this tower or not? You'd think after days in this room you'd be eager for a change, by God's toes."

They engaged in a tug-of-war for her wrist. Finally she cried out in exasperation.

"Very well." She stopped trying to free herself. "I'll come, but you needn't hold on to me."

Derry dropped her wrist, bowed to her, and indicated the door with a sweep of his arm. One battle won. He followed her to the landing but insisted on taking her arm as they went down the stone stairs. Upon gaining the courtyard, he allowed her to inspect it. She kept clear of the thieves who had congregated about a roasting haunch of venison, waved at Inigo, and headed for the Raven Tower.

He followed her, entranced with the way her waterfall of black hair swayed with each step. She stopped at the base of the Raven Tower and bent over some primroses that grew there. She picked one and held it to her cheek.

"I've been looking at these for days," she said.

He joined her, fascinated with the way the pink, almost transparent petals caressed her skin. "I'm told you spend most of your time at your father's manor in the North. He says you wander about the countryside alone. I marvel your father allows it."

"My father does the same."

She met his gaze, hesitated, then dropped her own to the grass at their feet. Her cheeks grew more pink than the primrose.

"In truth, he wouldn't notice if I turned the manor into a bawdy house unless the women trampled on his flower garden or disturbed his prize draft horses. All Father's sense is invested in his roses and his horses."

He heard the note of loneliness, though her comments were made lightly.

"Come," he said.

His voice broke as he spotted a rapidly beating pulse at her neck. After clearing his throat, he turned and led the way out of the castle. Once beyond the curtain wall, she drew ahead of him and went to a tree covered with pink blossoms.

"I watched the buds burst," she said as he came to stand beside her. "It's a crabapple."

"Come, I want to show you something."

He touched her hand, but she drew away from him, so he went ahead into the sycamore stand. She followed at a distance, still carrying the primrose. He led her to the pool. As they approached, she passed him and went to the log he'd perched on a short time before. To his surprise, she lifted her skirts, hopped onto the log, and tiptoed across it to the opposite bank. He sprang after her, cursing his lack of watchfulness. He jumped to the ground, but she hadn't run away. She'd stopped in a patch of sunlight. Strolling over to her, he watched her kneel and touch the purple, caplike blossoms of a plant.

"Hyacinth."

Putting her nose near them, she drew in a deep breath. He drew in his own breath, but not to smell flowers. He eyed the rise and fall of her breasts. He couldn't stop.

"I hear a blackbird," she said. "Is there a meadow nearby?"

"Hmm?"

"Is there a meadow nearby?"

He shook his head, dragged his gaze up to her eyes, and lifted his brows. "What meadow? Oh, leave off this prating of birds and flowers and such."

He stooped, caught her hands, and pulled her to her feet. Tugging on one hand, he led her back across the pool. When they gained the bank, he turned, placed his hands about her waist, and lifted her to a high rock that jutted out into the water. Standing with his legs braced apart, he put his hands behind his back and surveyed her.

"Now you can't dart about sniffing flowers and counting birds' eggs."

"I thought we were to walk."

"We're to talk, Thea *bella*."

"Don't call me that. And how haps it that you know even one word of Italian?"

"My master told it to me." He stopped her with an upheld hand. "Don't you be interrupting me, chattering gentry mort. You must tell me if you know where the key to those button ciphers is. Did Lady Hunt give you anything else? Any other gifts for the Queen of Scots? And then you must tell me of your grandmother's doings in London."

"No, I'll tell you nothing. I know nothing of you except that you're a craven thief and a mean one. I trust you not. Oh, don't snarl at me. Before you begin your threats of black pits and starvation, I'll tell you it's no use to ask me. I know little of Grandmother's doings. I spend most of my time in the country."

He said nothing. Running his gaze over her face, he frowned. Slowly, with deliberation, he said, "Thea, I don't want to put you in that hole again."

Watching her fear grow caused him physical pain. His hands balled into fists as he saw her body shake, but he kept his face blank, his thoughts cool. She swallowed, then whispered so low, he had to lean close to hear her.

"No cipher key, nothing."

"Give me your word."

She didn't answer. He moved so that he stood against the rock. He grabbed her wrists.

"You know what I can do, Thea. Swear."

"I swear," she said while staring at him as if he were a changeling. "I know nothing of the cipher."

He released her, and she tried to move away from him. His hand caught her ankle, and she started, then went still.

"I—I know nothing of Grandmother's doings or her friends. I saw her and them seldom."

"What friends?"

"Let me go."

He continued to stare into her eyes while encircling her ankle with his fingers. "What friends?" Still she hesitated, so he went on. "Come. I can inquire upon the matter without your help. I ask because it's easier than prising the information from servants."

"Lord Lawrence Gracechurch, Sir Anthony Clark, Timothy Eyre, the Earl of Lynford and the dowager countess, the Marquess of Bridewell. There is Grandmother's companion, Ellen Dowgate. If you're curious, she also entertained the queen's favorite, Robert Dudley, and the Duke of Norfolk and the Earl of Westmoreland."

She knocked his hand away from her ankle. "I could go on. Grandmother liked to give banquets and all sorts of entertainments. She was furious with her majesty for not inviting her to court, where the greatest festivities are held."

Derry stepped back and let his glance roam over Thea. She had recovered from the fright he deliberately gave her, and he could tell she was angry with herself for submitting to him.

"God's blood, woman, do you always balk when asked to comply with a simple demand?"

"You threatened me."

Chewing his lip, he studied her while she glared at him. Then he lifted her to the ground.

"You'll write those names down, and I'll give them to my master."

"You write them down."

"Can't spell so good."

"No doubt your head's too thick to contain much learning."

"I can read the rewards posted for my head."

She tried to walk away, but he stepped in front of her and grinned. "You're hot because you had to obey. You hate having to yield to me. It makes you sputter and spark, it does."

She backed away from him, and he came after her.

"You said you wouldn't even kiss my skirt."

"I changed my mind."

She bolted. She dashed past him, jumped onto the log bridge, and raced across it. He was a step behind her as she landed on the other side. He sprang at her, lifted her in the air, and swung her in a circle before setting her down and wrapping her in his arms. He lowered his mouth to hers. A stab of pain shot down his leg as she raked her foot down the inside of it. He cried out, flinging himself away from her.

As he grabbed his leg, she turned and flew toward the forest. He sprang after her, but his hurt leg wobbled. He hopped on the good leg and shouted at her. She glanced over her shoulder and ran into a barrier. Derry watched Morgan snatch her into his arms while she kicked and clawed at him. The two were still fighting when he limped up to them. As he arrived, Morgan succeeded in trapping both her arms, and Thea's struggles subsided. She spat curses at them both. Glaring at Derry, her hair in wild tangles about her face, she kicked at his groin. Derry jumped back, and Morgan laughed.

"Jesu preserve me, dear brother, I never thought such a fair maid would best you."

"Shut your mouth, Morgan, and release her."

Morgan held on to Thea and gave Derry a pleased smile.

"Afraid she might like my bridle better than your whip?"

Thea gawked at Derry. "You have a brother?"

"I agree it's a hard thing to credit," Morgan said. "He does seem to be more like one of those creatures spawned from mud and offal."

"I said be quiet."

Derry grabbed Thea and tore her from Morgan's grasp.

Morgan startled him by latching on to one of her arms. "Shall we have a contest? Which of us will she take? How much will you wager?"

"Bloody Hades!" Thea lunged at Morgan.

Derry grabbed at her but missed, for she hurled herself at Morgan, flying through the air to land on him. She slashed Morgan's face with her nails while she brought her knee up between his legs. She drew blood from his cheek, and he dodged her knee just in time to avoid mortal pain.

Derry grabbed her, but she threw him off again. Snatching handfuls of Morgan's hair, she tried to tear it from his head. He howled, and Derry had to pry her fists open. Using his full strength, he hauled Thea off her feet. He fastened his arms around her so that she couldn't move her arms.

He heard Morgan swearing, and looked up to find him

pressing the back of his hand to a long scratch on his cheek. He glared at Thea.

"Damned bitch. Gone mad over a little wager."

Thea snarled at him. "I'll cut your entrails out and braid them in your hair."

Derry looked down at her, astonished at the violence of her reaction. All at once she turned in his arms, buried her face in his shoulder, and sobbed. Her hands clutched his jerkin. He put his chin on the top of her head, stroked her hair, and shushed her. Lifting his gaze to Morgan, he smiled.

"She's chosen, think you not?"

"I wish you joy of her," Morgan said, "for she's right mad."

Morgan disappeared, but Derry failed to see him go. He felt Thea's body shake and heard her wail.

"God, I despise men. There are too many men around here. I would highly thank the Lord if he would rid the world of all of them, especially him."

Derry rubbed his face against the silk of her hair and murmured to her. "Who, Thea?"

"Him, you, the one who—all men who make wagers."

She lifted her face then, and looked into his eyes. He saw distrust grow in hers. She straightened, standing in the circle of his arms.

"I'm so tired."

He picked her up.

"Not that tired."

"Quiet, foolish gentry mort."

He carried her across the water again and placed her on the flat rock. Once she was seated, he took her hand.

"I have never seen a gentry mort attack a man like that. What's wrong, Thea?"

"He wanted to make a wager about me, as if I were a pair of dice, something to be used."

"It was but a jest."

"I wish I could put a knife in his heart."

"Thea, this fury matches not the cause." He stared at her, but she had lowered her gaze to their joined hands. "Some other cause lies at the bottom of this cauldron of rage. Someone else. Someone else and a wager about you—"

He caught his breath as a suspicion entered his thoughts. He knew how most men regarded women, especially French noblemen. France. The court. A shy little black-haired wren.

"Thea," he whispered. "Tell me about France."

She hadn't lifted her gaze from their hands. She shook her head.

"I am your friend, Thea."

That brought her head up. Her mouth went slack, and she stared at him wordlessly. He felt his cheeks grow red.

"Mayhap it's hard to believe."

She nodded.

"It's true."

She said nothing.

"God's arse, woman, I give you my word."

He gentled his voice when she shied away from him. "Thea *bella*, the world brims full with men of evil nature toward women, but I am not one of them. Though our dealings together have made me cruel, I was forced to it by fear of bloodshed and war, not out of enjoyment."

He waited for her to reply, but she appeared to be absorbed in studying him. He looked down at their hands. He held hers in both of his. They covered hers completely. Removing one of his hands from hers, he kissed her fingertips, then lifted his gaze to hers in a mute appeal. At last she responded.

"Highwayman, I thank you for your kindness, but it matters not. I find it wondrous, you know. Women are supposed to be evil, insatiable, and in need of governance by men."

She slid down from the rock and shook her skirts. "And do you know what I have discovered?"

He shook his head.

"I have discovered that if the evil of men were put on the balance scales of heaven and weighed against the evil of women, men would tip the scales in less than a heartbeat."

She brushed dust from her sleeve, turned, and began to walk slowly toward Ravensmere. Her steps were slow, and her head drooped. Derry followed her, watching her shoulders slump and her pace waver as she lapsed into thoughtfulness.

She hadn't answered his question. He found himself drawn by the mystery, and to his dismay, he sank deeper into the spell of Thea Hunt, into a spell she cast without intent. He tried to shake it loose without success.

Summoning his will, he turned his thoughts to his task. He was no closer to finding the key to the button ciphers, no closer to discovering the allies of Lady Hunt or the identity of the wyvern. He would search the baggage he'd captured along with Thea once more, pry more details from her regarding Grace Hunt's familiars. Then he would return to London to help Cecil search for the unknown traitors.

Ahead, Thea had reached the curtain wall. Beyond it, Morgan was standing in a circle of thieves. He saw her hesitate. Catching up with her, he took her hand and placed it on his arm. Keeping his body between her and Morgan, he began to escort her across the courtyard.

# 9

*All my senses, like beacon's flame,*
*Gave alarum to desire . . .*

—FULKE GREVILLE, LORD BROOKE

AS SAVAGE TOOK HER arm and put himself between her and the laughing group that contained his brother, Thea tried to keep her thoughts from racing in whirlwind circles. Her tormentor had transformed himself into her defender. It was not a transformation she found believable.

Yet she longed to put aside her distrust, for Robin Savage intrigued her almost beyond endurance. She had never met a man like him. Though, in fairness, she had never encountered a highwayman before. And he was more bearable at the moment than his brother. She peered past Savage at Morgan, who was in the midst of a group of laughing thieves. Their gazes met, and he glanced from her to his brother.

"Jesu, my lads," he said, "you should have witnessed the squalling and scraping in the wood just now. When the lady's about, your master's a randy stallion protecting his favorite mare from a poacher."

Savage paused, then faced his brother while keeping Thea behind him. "I warn you. Find something else to quarrel over."

She wasn't staying to endure Morgan's taunts. God's truth, she despised dark-haired men above all others. And this one had hair as dark as a well filled with pitch. Though he had the wide shoulders and long legs of his brother, his dark coloring made him seem more evil. More evil than Savage, a merry thought.

Thea edged away from the two brothers, but Morgan saw her. Darting around Savage, he captured her in his arms. Cries of amusement went up from the thieves as Thea tried to kick and punch her way free.

Savage let out an obscenity that would have mortified her had she not been in a fight when she heard it. He sprang at Morgan, who jumped away from him, taking Thea with him. The air rushed out of her lungs as he hefted her in the air by one arm and rested her on his hip. Her body tilted. Her head dipped, and she cried out as her nose banged his knee. At her cry, Savage leapt at them. As he moved, Thea shook her head to clear it, then bit Morgan's thigh.

Morgan yelped and dropped her. She landed on all fours and scrambled out of the way as Savage flew at his brother. Two large bodies landed near her and rolled over and over. Thieves scurried for safety, and Thea did as well. Inigo Culpepper helped her to her feet, and they raced out of the way as Savage and Morgan tumbled over each other.

Morgan wedged his knee against Savage's chest and shoved. Savage sailed backward, bumped the ground, and sprang up again. Morgan had rolled to his feet and was heading for Thea.

"Morgan!" Savage cried.

The whole castle went silent. Morgan turned slowly and faced his brother.

"If I must choose," Savage said, "I will choose her."

Morgan's lips curled into a sneer. "At last I've found the catalyst. Who would have thought it would be a little bitch hardly worth tupping."

The callous words rained over her. Rage filled her, and Thea hurled herself at Morgan's back. Morgan turned as she reached him. She clawed at his eyes. He grabbed her wrists and twisted one, making her cry out again. As she tried to bite the overpowering hands, she was swept up in Savage's arms and torn from Morgan's grasp. Savage hurled her out of the way. She jounced into Inigo, and they slumped against each other.

As she landed, Savage turned on his brother. Panting, she watched his expression change. All the fury that had sprung into being at Morgan's attack had vanished. Laundered of emotion, his features smoothed so that he resembled a Botticelli angel.

"You hurt her," Savage said quietly. "I must needs teach you how dangerous a thing that is."

Thea shivered at the hushed and untroubled lightness of his tone. While she leaned weakly against Inigo, Savage abruptly and calmly punched his brother's face. Caught off guard, Morgan's head jerked on his neck. Savage punched him again, this time on the other side of his face.

Stunned, Morgan swiped at him, but Savage delivered a series of punches to his stomach. Over and over he hit first Morgan's face and then his gut until the younger man could no longer stand. When Morgan fell to his knees, Savage lifted his head by the hair and backhanded him once, twice, and a third time.

Morgan could no longer hold himself erect. Savage slipped his arms under his brother's shoulders as Morgan fell. Laying him gently on the ground, Savage rose, wiped his mouth on his sleeve, and turned to Thea.

She knew her eyes were as round as planets. He joined her, and they stared at each other. At her wild-eyed glance, Savage shrugged and looked in his brother's direction, then back at her.

"He hurt you."

Still frightened at the violence she'd just seen him do, Thea only nodded. Savage smiled at her. His eyes crinkled at the corners and reflected the light of the lowering sun. He bowed to her and held out his hand. Confusion and amazement danced in her head.

Thea gazed at his hand, all bruised, but held in a courtly gesture. She put her own in it. Savage bent over it and brushed his lips to the back of her fingers, then placed her hand on his arm. With a warning glance that sent his ruffians scattering for the castle wall, he led her across the courtyard and into the tower.

They stepped into the open doorway.

"Can you manage the stairs?" he asked.

Even in the enclosed space of the tower his voice sounded gentle. Thea found herself lulled into a curious state of serenity by his sudden temperance. He helped her to her room. By the time they reached it, she had found her voice. Dropping to the bench, she stared up at him.

"I don't understand," she said.

He merely lifted one brow.

"Why would you defend me when you've done worse to me yourself?"

"I got things to do." Savage headed for the door.

She rushed after him, touched his arm lightly and quickly, as if it were hot. "Why?"

"Don't know." He hooked his thumbs in his belt and glared at his boots.

"I don't believe you."

Savage's head came up. He snarled at her.

"God's arse, you're a cursed torment, you are."

She stared at him in confusion. Then she narrowed her eyes.

"You never intended really to hurt me at all. Did you?"

"Ha!"

Enlightenment burst upon her, and she felt giddy from the change. Her face must have reflected her consternation, for Savage met her gaze, swore, and pulled her into his arms. This time she understood. He would never admit the truth, but he couldn't hide it from her.

His mouth came down on hers, almost in desperation. She felt his tongue slip between her lips, felt the tug of his own lips. He sucked and teased her lips. His tongue tickled her.

To her surprise, she giggled. She felt his lips move as he smiled, and he nipped her lips. The little bites sent chills down her back, and she began to wriggle. He chuckled and nibbled at her nose and cheeks, which made her shriek and tug his hair in defense. She succeeded in pulling his head back. Staring at his merry face, she watched his good humor fade. His mouth settled into a straight line. A hardness came over his features.

"He hurt you, and I felt—by the rood, Thea *bella,* I do believe I can't abide the thought."

His palm came to rest against her cheek. Entranced, she realized he was talking more to himself than to her. His gaze traced her hair, her jawline, then settled on her lips. He bent over her, holding her still with his hands on either side of her face. This time his mouth had forgotten gentleness. His lips covered hers, pressed hard until they opened. His tongue entered her, penetrated and explored without hesitation.

His hands moved to flatten themselves on her back. One stroked its way down and found her buttock. It squeezed, then shoved her into his hips. Thea's chest was heaving. Her hands were shaking, so she buried them in the folds of his jerkin and shirt. The movement brought their bodies closer. His heat penetrated her own gown and set fire to her skin. Their hips rubbed against each other.

Suddenly Thea felt his arms shift. He sucked on her mouth and his hands steadied her as he lowered her to the floor. He settled between her legs. At the feel of his weight, her sense almost returned to her. She shoved at his chest.

Perceiving her reluctance, Savage caught her face again, kissed her forehead and cheeks, then took her mouth again. Visions of another chamber, in another castle far away, crowded close in her mind, only to burn away when he sucked rhythmically on her mouth.

His hands smoothed a path from her throat to her waist and back up again. Without warning, her bodice came loose, and his hand cupped her breast. He put his hot mouth on her nipple. Her legs stiffened, and she gasped as jolts of arousal arced down her torso to the joining of her legs.

Now her body burned and ached. Rivers of feeling boiled beneath her skin. She raked her hands through his hair as his mouth roamed from one breast to the other. Then he lifted his body. His fingers touched her ankle. They skimmed up the inside of her leg to her thigh. An aching knot formed at the apex of her thighs. It nearly exploded when he touched her. His hand lay on her, then began to stroke. She sucked in her breath. Her eyes closed.

She heard him murmur something, but she was possessed. The ache grew with each stroke of his hand, and she had to move or scream. She rubbed against his hand, and he gave a pleased laugh. His fingers twitched. Thea cried out, and he lowered his body to her. His hand vanished, but its place was taken by hard flesh.

By now Thea didn't care as long as she assuaged this terrible ache. His hand came back, caressed her, smoothed her, then urged her legs farther apart. She felt his sex nudge against her, separate her, then penetrate her. Somehow, the penetration only made the ache between her legs grow. She shoved her hips upward, and he slid deep inside her easily, as if she'd been made to take him.

As he seated himself fully, she heard him gasp. Her eyes flew open, and she found him staring down at her in shock. The look was gone immediately, for he moved and groaned. They clutched each other, riding each other, feeding their pleasure. Thea felt him ram deep inside her, over and over until she began to moan in time with his thrust.

Her voice rose higher and higher as sensation burst upon her. She arched upward, nearly bucking him off, then sank down as he thrust deep into her and cried out. He stiffened, his head thrown back. Falling forward, he came to rest on her. They panted together, then fell into a lazy stillness.

Thea felt him inside her. He moved aside, then turned her so that she faced him. He touched her nose with the tip of his finger and smiled at her.

"Thea *bella*."

The words jolted her out of her drowsy complacence. She sat up and looked down at him.

"Oh, no." She drew her knees up and put her forehead on them. "Oh, no, no, no, I've done it again."

He sat up beside her. "What is that?"

"Fallen prey to—" She stopped, hardly daring to breathe.

Savage poked her gently on the arm. She lifted her head and met a look of concern where she expected condemnation.

"Come, Thea, you've kept your secret long enough."

"What secret?"

He smiled at her and shook his head. "Very well. I will tell it instead. Some arse with a pretty face cozened you when you were quite young. Wooed you with fair words and gained your trust."

She buried her face in her arms and nodded. To her chagrin, he untwisted her body and made her look at him.

"I'll not play the part you've given me. Look elsewhere for someone to judge you." He lifted her chin with his fingertips so that she was forced to look into those soft blue eyes. "I know you, Thea *bella*. You're a trusting, sweet little soul, and a wounded one. Tell me what happened."

She shook her head again. "God's mercy, I can't."

He looked down at his torn shirt and the scratches on his neck and chest. "He was a turd in the guise of a man, and a foolish one too. God, a woman who can mark me like this is a treasure beyond ransom."

Thea looked at the scratches, then gave a long, low wail. "What ails me? I'm depraved. I hated you. I did. I would have gladly skewered you with your own eating knife."

"And what of me?" Savage said on a chuckle. "I thought you a papist traitor."

"And you're a highwayman. A highwayman!" Her eyes hurt from filling with tears. She looked away from Savage, for he was too beguiling with his clothes half off and his skin moist with passion. "I have no virtue at all."

"Good," Savage said. "Can't abide virtuous women."

Thea shoved at him. "You fool. My family will—my grandmother! She'll never forgive me."

Savage busied himself with his clothing. "Um, mayhap she will."

"You don't know her."

Standing, Savage helped her up and began straightening her gown. "I got something to tell you."

She cocked her head to the side and gazed up at him. He brushed a long strand of black hair from her face while he chewed his lip.

"I got word from London," he said at last. "Lady Hunt is dead."

When she didn't reply, he cleared his throat and went on. "She was murdered. Stabbed in her own bed after Secretary Cecil questioned her."

Thea went to her cot and sat on the edge. Slowly she felt herself taking in the meaning of his words. Dead. There had been times as a lonely little girl when she'd wished Grandmother dead for sending her off to a foreign land with no one to love her, not even a friend. That had been long ago.

Grandmother hadn't wanted her love, only her obedience. She'd given up trying to make the old woman love her, but still, she had been family. Deep sadness filled her, only to be thrust into the background when she remembered how Grandmother died. When she looked up, she found Savage standing before her, gazing at her anxiously.

"Murdered," she said. She rubbed her finger over the wrinkled skirt of her gown. "Murdered."

She was grateful that he remained quiet, waiting for her to adjust, to think.

"You truly are loyal to her majesty?" she asked.

Derry threw up his hands. "By the rood, woman, if you don't trust me now, what can I do to prove it? Mayhap when a French and Scottish army marches across England you'll believe me."

"You think someone killed Grandmother because Cecil suspected her."

He folded his arms and looked at her quizzically.

"I think you may be right. God's mercy, she cast me into muck, did she not?"

"Then there'll be no more attempts to tattle tales into the Scottish queen's ears."

Thea rose and went to the window. The sun was dropping behind the trees, and shadows stretched long and sinewy. Simon Spry traipsed across the courtyard with an armful of hay. Stubb was turning a haunch of meat on a spit at the fire.

"She befriended me," Thea said.

Savage was at her side. He touched her shoulder lightly.

Thea continued. "I have never been one of those women who charm, the kind who draw people, who—well, at the French court there was no one like me. I preferred works of art, flowers and trees and birds and other creatures, to masking and dancing and simpering at men." She looked up at Savage, felt her face grow hot. "To be honest, if I had been well liked, no doubt my tastes would be different."

"That's all they do, them court ladies? Dancing and such?"

"Many of them."

"All day long? All the time? Sounds wearisome. Rather be a thief, I would. No wonder you didn't belong. You got too much sense."

She looked out of the window so that she wouldn't have to see his face. "But when I was in France I was young, and I would have liked to belong. You see, I never danced or masked, or anything. No one asked me. I used to hide in water closets and withdrawing rooms so that people wouldn't notice that no one wanted to dance with me. When someone came into the withdrawing room, I would leave so that no one would suspect what I was doing. I was ashamed.

"Then, one night when I was about to retreat before the dancing began, a miracle happened. A young man asked permission to dance with me." Thea smiled as she watched Stubb below in the courtyard poking his meat with a knife. "It was as if I were magically transformed. Suddenly I was worthy. I was like other girls."

Thea sighed and glanced at Savage. He was gazing at her with wide, fearful eyes, and she realized he was dreading the rest of her story.

"The tale is so piteous that it angers me. I still castigate myself for being such a lackwitted fool, making myself into a curiosity, an object of scorn. I believed him, you see. I wanted to love him, and I did, even afterward, when days went by and he ignored me. I spent a whole morning searching the palace for him once."

She turned back to the window and rushed on before she lost her courage. "And I found him taking payment on a wager from five of his friends." Stubb's figure blurred, and she blinked away tears. "They hadn't even bothered to wager on his success. Instead, they wagered on how long it would take."

"*Christ,*" Savage said softly. He came to stand beside her, then rested his arm on the wall next to the window and his head on his arm.

Thea resumed her contemplation of the courtyard. "The Queen of Scots befriended me, you see. She found me bawling in an antechamber and made me confess. She arranged for me to come home. That's what I wanted, you see, to come home and never have to go to court again. Never have to be near men."

"We aren't all—"

"Spare me the lesson," she said. "I was young, just

sixteen, and I've had seven years in which to accustom myself to my degraded state. And now look what I've done." She shook her head. "Coupled with a thief."

"You make it sound as if I were a leper."

"Robin Savage, you know what I mean."

He tweaked her nose. "Mean you that a high-and-mighty lady shouldn't bed a common lout such as myself?"

"No matter your birth, you've never been common."

"I thank you."

Thea walked away from him, turned, and surveyed him. "Which brings us full circle. When I set out to warn the Queen of Scots about Lord Darnley, it was in return for her kindness in helping me. She aided me when I wanted to die. I can't let her make the mistake I did. Not when I might prevent it."

"Thea, don't you see? Whatever her personal kindnesses, her ambition threatens the safety and peace of our country."

She scowled at him and hissed impatiently. "Saints' bones, I know that. Now. But my conscience won't allow me to condemn her to a beast of a husband."

"Elizabeth loves England," Savage said. "Queen Mary loves thrones. I'll not release you as long as you persist in meddling in great matters."

"I know that," Thea snapped. "And call me no foul names. You're helping to create a monstrous marriage. That too is a sin."

Savage walked toward her lazily, like a figure in a dream.

"So you're angry with me?"

"Yes." She shrugged off his hands when he came near and put them on her shoulders.

He kissed her neck, and she brushed him away.

He put his lips near her ear. "Mayhap you're also still furious at yourself for lusting after a highwayman."

Rubbing her ear, she sniffed but said nothing.

Savage touched her earlobe with the tip of his tongue, then brushed his lips down her neck, ending in a kiss at the base of her throat.

"We're both ruined," he said as he kissed his way up her neck. "They'll hang me for taking you if they ever find out. Come, Thea *bella*. If I'm to hang, show me more of what I'm to die for."

# 10

*. . . a lover ought to appear to his beloved wise in
every respect and restrained in his conduct,
and he should do nothing disagreeable that might
annoy her.*

—ANDREAS CAPELLANUS

ERRY WOKE WITH HIS face buried in a cloud of
black silk. His eyes flew open, and at first he was
startled by the feel of a soft shoulder nudging his
chest. Then he realized he was curled around Thea. Her
hair was spread over his face. He kissed the top of her head
and eased out of the bed. After drawing on his clothes, he
tiptoed from the chamber. Outside, he thrust his arms
through his jerkin, then turned and lifted the bar into
place across the door.

She would be furious. Again. After a night of lovemak-
ing, they had quarreled in the early morning hours because he refused to release her, and because she refused to
obey him. He should have known she wasn't the kind of
woman who would give him proper deference, even after
he'd made himself her master in bed. A pox on her. A few
more nights such as this first one, and she'd do anything
he wished. Mayhap.

He grinned to himself, then tried to stop himself from

so foolish an action, then forgot and grinned again. He'd made a discovery, and felt like those explorers who first encountered the New World. She loved art. When she had compared being with him to her first sight of a painting by Titian, he'd had difficulty in concealing his understanding. Pretending ignorance, he'd invited her to describe the works of da Vinci, Botticelli, and bronzes by Antico. He'd promised himself that one day he would show her his treasure room.

He never thought to find a woman who shared his passion for art. Most admired it as they would a pretty sunset. Thea seemed to feed upon its beauty as a babe feeds upon mother's milk. And best of all, unlike his father, she couldn't conceive of his own love of art diminishing his virility. Of all the treasures he'd collected, mayhap Thea was the most precious.

After washing quickly and changing in the dusty chamber he used as his own bedroom, Derry went into the courtyard. There Stubb was gathering men for a dawn patrol. His scouts had reported signs of a large party of riders in the area, and Derry had been sending out his men for the last day and a half trying to find them. Perhaps Thea's father was searching for her.

Derry found a water pail and dipped a cup in it. Stubb joined him.

"There you are. Inigo said you'd forgot all about us, but I told him it would take more than a bit of—ehhh!"

Stubb coughed and sputtered on the water Derry threw in his face. Derry scooped up another drink while his man finished choking.

"After what I did to my own brother, one would think you'd have a care for how you spoke of my lady."

"Your lady, is it?" Stubb wiped his face on his sleeve, then glanced around at the chuckling Inigo and Anthony

Now-Now. "A bit sensitive, aren't we? Time was when you wouldn't have minded that us poor hardworking sots couldn't get a peaceful night's sleep for all the howling and bumping and cooing that went on in that tower."

"Stubb!" Derry advanced on his servant, but Stubb scrambled behind the mountain that was Anthony Now-Now.

"Was that why you had us fix the floor in that chamber? Oh, I see. You was testing the floor, giving it a good thump to see if it held."

Lunging around Anthony, Derry grabbed for Stubb. Stubb shot out from behind his protector, who was guffawing as he spread his arms to protect Derry's tormentor. Derry chased Stubb around the morning fire, but the servant whizzed around a pile of hay. Derry rounded the fire only to bound into Inigo, who wrapped his arms around him and swung him in a circle while he chortled. Dizzy, Derry stuck his foot between Inigo's legs. Inigo collapsed, taking Derry with him, and they fell in a tangle in the dust. Elbowing Inigo off his stomach, Derry sat up, then coughed and sneezed as the thief slapped dust from his clothing.

"Stop that, you fool."

Derry kicked at Inigo, who was laughing. Disgruntled, Derry realized his mistake and proceeded to ignore his amused men. Brushing dirt from his own clothing, he looked up to find Morgan staring at him from the doorway of the Raven Tower. His brother's face bore purple and red marks, and he held one arm close to his ribs. He picked himself up and stalked over to Stubb, who was preparing to ride out.

Stubb patted the neck of his horse and lowered his voice. "No need to scold yourself. He's just a little bruised about the face and ribs. No real harm done. 'Course, he hasn't tried to jest with you about Mistress Hunt like I have this morn. She's turning you into a simpleton, she is."

"Enough, you fool of a whoreson," Derry said. "You tend to the task I've set you. Find this party of strangers. If they're drawing near, we'll run them off before they gain Ravensmere. And try to discover who they are. It's not likely to be anyone but her father's men, but we must take care. Now, go before I box your ears."

He watched Stubb leave. He would have preferred to go with the men, but he had to search Thea's belongings again for the key to the button cipher as well as make a list of her grandmother's familiars. Prising more details from Thea would take all his skill at cozening.

Turning back to the fire, his gaze met his brother's again. Morgan was still on the threshold of the Raven Tower, but when their glances locked, he shoved himself forward and walked slowly over to face Derry. Derry stood his ground, praying Morgan wouldn't try to corner him again.

"I'll ask her pardon, so don't belabor me," Morgan said.

"I've said nothing."

Derry knelt by the fire where Simon Spry was stirring porridge. Simon handed his wooden stirring spoon to Derry and hurried away. Derry began spooning porridge into two bowls.

"I'll do it for her sake, damn you, not because I fear you."

Derry fished in a sack for bread. "Marry, dear brother, there's no need to remind me of how little you fear me."

Morgan knocked a loaf of bread from Derry's hand and dropped to his knees beside his brother. "Why? For once, answer my question straightly. Why did you kill him?"

Picking up the bread and dusting it, Derry resisted the

compulsion to try to explain. Morgan never wanted explanations; he wanted a confession. He put the bread on a tray next to the bowls of porridge, then met Morgan's turbulent black gaze.

"Since you're possessed of godlike omniscience, you tell me why I killed my own brother."

"I know why," Morgan said, "but was it of such import that you be Viscount Moorefield? Why couldn't you content yourself with your own inheritance?"

Kneeling in the dirt opposite his younger brother, Derry glanced down at the whitish mess in the pot suspended over the fire. The porridge turned red, thinned, and became blood, and the memory of that day came back to him. Had it been fourteen years? Almost, for he'd been fourteen when it happened.

The trouble started as soon as he'd been old enough to undertake a knight's training. His father, a soldier who had served in Henry VIII's wars, had nearly succumbed to apoplexy upon discovering his second son's penchant for learning, for reading about Greek myths and geometry rather than practicing his swordplay. As different as papists and Protestants, the two fought constantly. Derry still writhed at the memory of the day his father taunted him in the tilt yard in front of the men of his household.

"By God's robe, the way you hold that sword, I swear I spawned a girl."

They had all laughed, including his older brother, John, and he'd wanted to die right there in the tilt yard so he wouldn't have to hear their jeers. That day he vowed to learn the arts of war. He would show his father and everyone who laughed at him for his clerkish ways.

He'd been ten years old, and for the next four he worked. Swordplay, riding, jousting. The hunt, the skirmish, spear throwing. Gaining more scars than boys much older, he slowly acquired the skills his father admired, only to find that all his pain brought him mere tolerance. How could he have known that his father had a small and mean little heart in which he'd made room for John, his firstborn, and no other?

Heartbroken, Derry endured his father's disdain. Then the disdain turned to purposeful goading. *You'll never match your brother at dueling. He's no mincing, lady-faced craven.* Derry blamed John for taking all their father's affection and challenged him to a contest at swordplay. The sixteen-year-old John accepted with amusement. John had learned from their father to scorn his younger brother. They began at midday in the practice yard with the family and household looking on.

Of course John began well. He drove Derry about the practice ring as if he were a stray cow, mocking and taunting as he did so. Rage made Derry careless, and he turned on John. The years of hurt gave impetus to his attack. His vision blurred with sweat, he fell on John, slicing at the older boy as if he were facing a wild boar.

Startled by the ferocity of the attack, John stumbled as he parried. Their swords scraped together, then their bodies slammed into each other. John kicked Derry. Derry doubled over, then sank to his knees with his sword tip buried in the dirt.

Above him he heard a triumphant yell. Desperate to prove himself to his father and to himself, Derry jumped up, and at the last moment pulled his sword free. The tip wobbled, then pointed up just as John hurled himself at Derry. He ran onto Derry's blade.

To this day he wondered if he'd known John had dropped his sword. Had he seen it, or heard it drop? His father nearly killed him, he bellowed like a lost soul, then picked up John's sword and charged at Derry. It had taken five men to hold him back.

For years he'd wondered if he'd meant to kill John all along. That's what his father told Morgan.

"Answer me."

Morgan's demand jolted Derry back to the present. He was still kneeling beside the fire.

"Was it because of Father?" Morgan asked.

Derry put the bowls of porridge on a tray with the bread, stood, and regarded his brother with a slight smile.

"Fie, brother, such innocence. Of course it was for Moorefield. Why else?"

He left Morgan glaring at him and went back to Thea's chamber. She was waiting for him when he entered, surrounded by buckets of wash water. She took the tray from him, gave him a look of displeasure, and turned her back on him. After placing the tray on the bench, she picked up a bowl and began eating. The spoon jabbed into her mouth like a sword. It clacked against the side of the bowl. Derry began to eat his food in silence.

"You locked me in," she said as her spoon clicked against the lip of the bowl. "You left me and locked me in after you made love to me."

He glared at her and dropped his bowl on the tray. "You won't do as you're told. Give up this misguided attempt to rescue the Queen of Scots."

"She was kind to me!"

"She's kind to dogs."

Thea choked on the ale she'd been drinking. "You likened me to a dog."

"Forgive me," Derry snapped. "I should have likened you to a stubborn little ox, a black and white one." He gulped down ale and muttered, "Bleeding gentry mort."

He heard a little snort and glanced at her. She was grinning at him over her mug.

"What you laughing about?" He narrowed his eyes and peered at her suspiciously.

"Whenever you've failed to make me do something, you call me a gentry mort, whatever that is."

"A gentry mort is you, a stubborn, high-mannered, highborn bit of annoyance."

"Who's an annoyance?"

"You, you pestilence. Ever since I laid eyes on you I've had nothing but predicaments and afflictions. God, the nights I spent swollen and—never you mind."

Derry thrust his head out of the window and yelled down to Simon Spry. They waited for the thief. He glared at her. She smiled at him complacently. Simon came in, bringing her portable writing desk. When he was gone, Derry pointed to the desk, which Simon had placed on the cot.

"Remember those names you told me, the familiars of your grandmother? I want you to write them down."

"You write them."

"Don't want to."

"Why not."

"Don't write so good. Now, write those names, or I'll find a strap and use it on your bottom."

She folded her arms over her chest. He lunged at her, caught her before she could run away, and twisted her hands behind her back. When she stopped fighting him, he nibbled her ear and whispered, "I'll do it. You know I will."

"Go to Hades."

He began gathering her skirt in his hands, baring her leg. Running his finger up her thigh, he found her buttock and squeezed.

"Nice plump little target."

"No!"

"Are you going to write those names?"

"Only because you already know them."

He laughed and released her. "So long as we agree."

Thea glowered at him as she straightened her gown. She crossed to the cot, opened a drawer, and brought out quill, ink, and paper. "You're being common and low again, and I know why. You can't write at all. Admit it."

"I can too," he said. Glancing at her from the corner of his eye, he went on. "I know all fifteen letters of the alphabet."

She paused as she dipped her quill in her ink pot. "All fifteen?"

"Didn't I say so? A, B, D, G, H, K, L, O, P, Q, R, S, T, U, V. There. And you thought I was ignorant."

"You forgot some."

"Nah." He pretended to count on his fingers. "I got all fifteen."

"But, Robin, there are more than fifteen."

"Oh? Name some."

"You forgot C and E and I and J, and a lot more." She finished writing a name. "I could teach you."

He strolled over to look at what she was writing and pointed at the name she was forming. "What's that?"

"Lord Gracechurch."

"Gracechurch it is not." He raised his voice in indignation. "It's too long. It doesn't take that long to say it. You're writing something else."

She sighed and shook her head. "Robin, why did you want me to write the list if you don't trust me?"

He picked up the half-finished list, then discarded it with a sniff. "I can read most of it."

Leaving the bed where she'd been writing, Thea wandered to the window and looked outside. "Will you let me go?"

"I told you, no."

"I mean afterward. Are we to bid each other farewell, the highwayman and the lady?"

Derry stopped breathing for a moment. He hadn't thought of anything but his lust and his mission in so long. What was he going to do with her? He couldn't keep her. Eventually she must go home. Yes, that was the answer. Much as he wanted her, his lust would fade. True, it didn't seem likely to fade at the moment, but he hadn't had her long.

"We don't have to think about farewells just yet," he said to gain time.

Hugging herself, she faced him. "I've thought and thought, but I know my father would never allow me to marry a highwayman."

"Marry?" His voice cracked. "God's blood, ladies don't marry highwaymen."

He watched her come to him. She laid her hand on his arm and looked up at him with such openness that his conscience began to drive spikes into his heart.

"Robin," she said quietly.

He touched her lips with his fingertips, then kissed her. He wondered what she would think of Robin St. John, Lord Derry, the man Morgan hated, the man his father hated? Then, without warning her face blurred and changed until it wasn't her face at all, but Alice's. He felt again the chill of his cell in the Tower. Disturbed by the antics of his own mind, he drew away from her, but she didn't appear to notice the way he closed himself up like a crypt. She went back to the window and gazed out at the courtyard. She leaned forward to look at something.

"Robin," she said. "How fond are you of Inigo?"

"Best thief I got."

"Then you wouldn't like it if Simon shot him with a longbow."

"Where!"

Derry sprang to the window. In the courtyard Inigo was parading about in a breastplate stolen from one of Thea's men-at-arms. Simon had strung a longbow and was taking aim. Inigo faced him and patted his armor. He waved his hands and made faces while Simon drew back on the bow.

Filling his lungs, Derry bellowed at Simon. "Simon Spry, you pig's arse, don't you move!"

Leaving a chuckling Thea behind, he rushed out of the tower and up to Simon. "You lackwitted whoreson, give me that bow. Inigo, strap the breastplate to that water barrel."

He waited quietly while Inigo obeyed his orders. The other men in the courtyard gathered behind Derry. Inigo joined them, and Derry knocked an arrow, turning his body sideways to the target. He put his weight behind drawing the bow. When the fingers gripping the arrow drew even with his jaw, he let go. The arrow buzzed, and there was a clang as the metal tip buried itself in the breastplate. Behind him there was silence. He handed the bow to Inigo, whose face was the color of Thea's petticoat.

"Cheap armor," he said as he headed back to the tower.

He glanced up at Thea's window to see her hanging out of it. He met her startled look and grinned at her. Simon Spry ran to the water barrel and tipped it on its side.

"By the cross, Inigo, this would be your blood if I'd shot you."

Howls of laughter issued from the men in the courtyard as Derry entered the tower. Thea was still hanging out her window when he joined her. He went to stand beside her and gaze out at the men gathered around the breastplate and water barrel.

"My thanks, Thea *bella*."

She nodded, but kept staring at the men.

"Haven't you ever seen a man shoot that far?" he asked. "With a longbow you can hit a target two hundred yards off."

"Mmmm." She didn't seem to have heard him.

He tapped her arm. "Thea, the list."

"Oh, I've finished that."

He took the paper from the desk on the bed, folded it, and stuffed it in his jerkin. "Would you like to come with me? I got to look at your belongings again. Make certain I haven't missed the cipher key before I leave."

"You're leaving?"

"Tomorrow morning."

He ushered her downstairs and into the chamber below hers. There his men had stacked all her belongings— bundles, baskets, trunks, and boxes. On top of a trunk lay the wooden box containing the cipher buttons. She picked it up. Holding it in both hands, she rubbed her thumbs across the top of the box. He watched her for a moment, but she said nothing and he began digging in a box of bed linens. He was holding one of the sheets up to the light when she spoke.

"Robin, I'm thirsty."

"There's a bottle of water in the corner, I think."

She retrieved the bottle. Sitting on a chest, she held the bottle in one hand and the button box in the other. He noticed she hadn't taken a drink. She was staring at the box in her hand again.

"What ails you?"

Looking up at him, she brought the box to her breast and hugged it. "I must be certain before I . . . If only I could be assured that . . ." She lapsed into silence while she contemplated the box, then looked up at him. "You didn't have to—to treat me well."

Now he was confused. He shook his head. "What mean you?"

"You still won't confess that all this time you've tried not to do me harm. Saints, you could have whipped me until I had no skin to get the truth from me. Why didn't you?"

"Whipping's crude."

"Why?"

"Then you'd be no good in bed."

"You could have had me and then whipped me."

He searched for a reply, but she continued, still clutching the box as if it were a reliquary.

"No one has ever cared for me like that, not even my father, and you, my enemy, you protected me."

"I got my reasons for keeping you well."

"I know," she said.

She was watching him, studying him, waiting for some admission from him. She wasn't going to get it. She'd gotten too much from him already. Women! Always trying to pry a man open and expose his entrails. He couldn't meet her gaze and reveal his anger, for she wouldn't understand, so he stared at her body instead. No comfort there, for looking at her evoked a spurt of hot arousal in his own damned unruly body.

"I hate most men, you know." She stopped, then cleared her throat. "Robin, I don't hate you."

"Be quiet!" He thrust himself upright. His legs tangled in the sheet he'd discarded. After fighting his way free, he rushed out of the room before she could finish.

He was certain he didn't want to hear what she had to say next.

## 11

*What should I say*
*Since faith is dead*
*And truth away*
*From you is fled?*

—Sir Thomas Wyatt

Thea watched Robin Savage rush out of the chamber. The door slammed, but she didn't hear him bar it. She hurried to the window and saw him race out into the courtyard and across to the Raven Tower. Through a gap in the crumbling wall she watched him charge up the winding steps to the top of the edifice, where he burst into the upper chamber, startling a raven.

He must have gone to the window to look out, for she couldn't see him. She glanced down at the water bottle and the box she still clutched in both hands. Seeing the thief topple the water barrel had jarred her memory. Upon giving the button box to her, Grandmother had warned her to take care of it. She remembered being perplexed at such a warning, for Grandmother had cautioned her not to get the box wet. A marvelous strange thing to say.

Thea set the bottle and the box on top of a chest. She opened the box and emptied it of buttons. Then she ripped a piece from one of the sheets, wet it, and dabbed the top of the box. Nothing. Mayhap she'd been wrong. She turned the box over and wiped the bottom. Again nothing.

She poured more water on the box. All she got was a pool of water that spilled onto her skirts. She mopped it up with part of the sheet, then opened the box. Swirling her cloth over the inside of the lid, she noticed that it turned brown. Stains appeared on the lid. They darkened and took the form of numbers and letters. Thea wiped the lid harder, and soon five lines of letters and numbers became visible. The cipher key.

Gathering the box and the buttons, Thea rushed to her chamber and found her quill and paper. She quickly copied the writing on the lid, then opened one of the buttons. Its compartment was empty. She should have realized Savage wouldn't leave the ciphers lying about where anyone could get them.

She folded the paper and stuffed it in her bodice. The box she set aside on the bench. As she went to the window to see where Robin had gone, she heard the pounding of horses' hooves. Stubb and his party clattered around fallen stones and into the courtyard. Hardly waiting for his horse to stop, Stubb sprang to the ground and ran to Inigo, who pointed at Thea's tower. Robin must have gone to his own chamber while she'd been busy with the cipher key.

Stubb ran toward the tower, and Thea rushed out of her chamber and down the stairs. The light faded quickly as she turned a sharp bend. She kept close to the wall and had to go slowly so as not to miss her step. As she neared the bottom of the stairs, she heard Stubb crash through the outer door and raise his voice.

"My lord!"

Thea stumbled and fell against the wall as she neared the last turn in the stairs.

"Quiet, you arse." Robin's voice was low and near the foot of the staircase.

Stubb lowered his voice. "My lord, there be a large party of men searching the wood, and the way they're sweeping about, they'll find Ravensmere by the morrow."

Staring down into the darkness, Thea felt her heart bang against her breast. It fluttered, then began to beat rapidly. Her ears rang. When they cleared she could hear Robin's voice, only it wasn't Robin's voice, for the nasal quality of the commoner had vanished. Grammar suddenly appeared along with the ability to pronounce H's.

Thea pressed her back against the wall and edged down the steps to hear better. Robin's new voice was quiet, yet clipped and spare.

"Gather the men. We'll lure them away from Ravensmere, then lose them on the moors at nightfall. If they survive, they'll be in no condition to resume their search. You're sure they wore no livery or badges?"

"No, my lord. They've got a young demon leading them though. Rides like he's on hell's scent and drives his men like he's searching for his own soul."

"I like it not, Stubb, for I doubt if Lord Hunt would know such a man, or send him in search of his daughter. Go now, and tell Inigo he's to remain behind to guard Mistress Hunt."

Thea whirled and raced upstairs to the chamber in which Robin had left her. After throwing the torn and wet pieces of cloth out of sight behind a chest, she opened a box containing her ruffs. She was digging in it when he appeared.

"Thea *bella,* I must go, and you must stay in your chamber until I return."

In silence she left, keeping well ahead of him until she entered her prison room again. As she walked in, she saw the button box. Speeding to it, she sat on the bench and spread her skirts over it. Robin came to her, lifted her hand, and kissed it.

"We'll talk when I return, we will. You be a good gentry mort and don't give Inigo no trouble."

She nodded, not trusting herself to give a civil answer. It took all her determination not to shrink away from him when he kissed her. As his lips tugged at hers, she balled her hands into fists and buried them in the folds of her gown.

"You're quiet," he said when he lifted his mouth from her.

"I'm weary—from last night."

She managed to return his smile. Then he was gone. She sat still and listened to the commotion as Savage and most of his men rode out of the castle. When all was quiet, she remained seated and let her tears trickle down her cheeks.

The pain was going to come, and she wished she could stop it, avoid it, lock it away inside her. She felt a howl of anguish well up in her chest. Covering her mouth with both hands, she sank to the floor on her knees. Bending in half, she crouched in the middle of the chamber and sobbed silently. When her cries threatened to burst from her throat, she stuffed her skirt and petticoat into her mouth.

She lost count of time as she sank into an abyss of misery. She'd been cozened into giving herself to a man who was worse than a thief. He had guided her this way and that for his own purposes, and amused himself as he went. Puppetlike, she'd danced jigs and May dances for him.

Thea opened her eyes. She was still crouched on the floor, and she had no notion of how long she'd lain there. Sitting up, she found that her legs were numb. Her hands were sore, and she realized she'd beaten her fists against the floor. She carefully maneuvered herself upright and stumbled to the bed. Sitting on its edge, she stared at her feet.

He was a nobleman. An English nobleman. She'd known he was no mere highwayman, but never had she suspected him of nobility—not with that gutter accent. A nobleman. A master of contrivings and disguises, no doubt. A man who lied as easily as he breathed, as easily as he made love. Now she realized he'd beguiled her for his own purposes, to gain her secrets. He must have been disappointed at how meager and unimportant hers were.

Thea halted and stared at the wall. She should have known better than to trust her own abductor. God, she was witless. She'd made herself ridiculous, the object of jests and mockery—again. Biting her lip, she fought the old feelings of debasement. She was like a pebble, worth kicking for amusement, but not worth keeping.

With tears welling in her eyes, she cringed at the thought that she would have to face Savage again. She couldn't. But there was the cipher key.

Regardless of her own misery, she couldn't ignore the cipher key, and she could on longer deny the danger she'd unwittingly helped create for her beloved country. No personal obligation to the Queen of Scots could outweigh her duty and love for England. She must reveal the existence of the cipher key, but she must escape Robin as well. Leaving the key behind was impossible without entrusting it to him, yet she grew queasy when she imagined encountering her abductor.

There was another choice. She could take the key with her. She would return to London and give it to her father. The queen liked Father. Her majesty would give him an audience, and he would place the key in her hands. And she would never have to see Robin Savage again.

Thea wiped her eyes. The tears kept coming, but she ignored them. She snatched up the button box. Spilling the buttons into her hand, she shoved them under the bed covers. She tested the door but found it barred. At the window she saw Inigo tending the cooking fire and realized it was past midday. He would bring her something to eat soon.

Leaning out the window, she paused to swallow and steady her voice, then called to him. "Inigo, I'm so wearied of this chamber. Don't bring food up to me, take me down to it, I beg of you."

He smiled and waved at her. Thea backed away from the window. She smoothed her hair and wiped her face dry of tears. Turning the button box over her knee, she broke the lid from it. She piled porridge bowls and stale bread over it on the tray Robin had discarded by the bed and was holding it when Inigo came for her.

She refused his offer to take the tray and asked him to precede her out of the tower. They went to the cooking fire, where Inigo busied himself turning a row of rabbits on the spit. She saw only one other man in the castle, Simon Spry. To her relief, he was propped up against a block of fallen stone, snoring and clutching a mug of ale.

"Inigo, your fire is low. I'll fetch more wood."

"Thank you, mistress."

Setting the tray on the ground, she retrieved the lid while Inigo turned the rabbits. Holding it close to her leg so that her gown concealed it, she strolled over to a pile of kindling and logs. She gathered a small armload into the middle of which she stuffed the lid. At the fire she began placing wood on it.

"Oh, I dropped a nice limb back there. Would you fetch it?"

While Inigo retrieved the wood, she shoved the lid into the fire and dropped kindling on top of it. She smiled at him as he handed the wood to her.

"A good fire now, think you not?"

She watched the lid burn while Inigo poked the rabbits. Glancing around the courtyard, she saw that Simon was still dozing heavily. Past the crumbling gate house two horses were tethered. She knelt by her pile of wood and began gathering several heavy logs.

"I've brought too much," she said.

She stood, swallowed hard, and walked past Inigo. His back was to her as she dropped all but one log back on the pile. She tiptoed back to him with the log grasped in both hands. As she went, she saw her shadow race ahead. She hesitated, then extended her arms and crept forward. She raised the log over her head and banged it down on Inigo's head.

There was a crack. Inigo stood still, then his knees buckled. Thea snatched his shirt before he could fall into the fire and gently lowered him to the ground. There was a pouch at his belt. She felt inside. Coins. She was pulling it off the belt when she heard Simon Spry.

"Whuh?"

She jumped at the sound. Grabbing her log, she ran to Simon as he sat up and rubbed his nose. She hit him on the back of the head, and he fell back, his mug of ale still clutched in one hand. The log fell from her hands. She raced for the horses, snatching up a water bottle as she went.

One of the horses was her mare. They'd kept her mare, the bastards. Thea rummaged through tack piled in the shelter of the curtain wall and managed to saddle her mare with shaking hands. She mounted, then untied the second horse, a gelding, and drove it before her into the wood.

Once beneath the trees, she ran the gelding off in a northerly direction. Then she turned south. If Robin chased after her, he would expect her to go north to Scotland and would follow the tracks of the other horse.

She rode hard, taking chances by galloping through thickly wooded country. Several times she crossed meadows, and then came upon a lake. Her mare was winded, so she stopped to rest her and allow her to drink. Sooner or later she would encounter fields and crops, and then villages, but unless she could gain a town or the shelter of a nobleman's house, Savage might find her.

She walked her horse up and down along the bank, knowing the creature must rest, but also knowing she was visible from great distances, for grassy meadows surrounded the lake on all but the south side. There the land rose up to form a long ridge. She'd ridden over it to reach the lake.

Uneasy, she allowed her mare to drink while she climbed the rise. As she neared the top, she heard a horse whinny. She dropped to the ground at once, then lifted her head. Riding toward her at the head of his band of thieves came Robin Savage. She could tell it was he by the way the sun glinted off his hair. She crawled backward, stood, and raced for her mare.

She leapt into the saddle, then burst into a gallop and rounded the lake in a desperate sprint for the cover of the forest. As she rounded the lake, she heard Robin shout her name. Fear made her kick her mare hard, and the animal tore past the water and into the trees.

The brown tree trunks flew by on either side of her, and she pulled hard on the reins. As the horse slowed, she cantered into a stand of oaks and into the midst of a party of mounted men. She yanked on the reins. The mare slowed, wheeled, and turned to face the men, who hadn't moved. They sat on their horses and gawked at her.

Quieting the frightened mare, she watched as a young man in rich velvet and leather with hair as dark as her own separated from the group and rode toward her. Another nobleman. He smiled at her in welcome. One of his men called out to her.

"Mistress Hunt?"

She sighed and called back. "Are you from my father?"

The dark-haired leader chuckled. *"Mais non, demoiselle.* Does it matter?"

A Frenchman. Dear God, a Frenchman. What was a Frenchman doing looking for her? Kicking her horse, she slapped her reins and swerved away from the man as he approached. Riding hard, she cleared the trees only to run into Robin and his men.

She pulled up on the reins again as Savage galloped toward her. Before she could swerve to avoid him, he was on her. While she fought her mare, he came alongside, leaned over, and scooped her from the saddle. She clawed his face just as the Frenchman and his party burst from the trees. Savage knocked her hands aside, then stared at the men bearing down on them. Whistling to his men, he threw her over his saddle on her stomach and drew his sword.

From her position Thea could see only horses' legs. She tried to right herself, but Savage shoved her back down. She felt him bent forward, heard the clash of swords, and the noise of battle surrounded her. The world spun around her. Horses and men screamed, and dirt sprayed in her face. A man's body dropped to the ground below her. Robin's arm came down with it, and his sword.

She watched him withdraw his blade from the body. He

cursed, and his legs heaved under her. His stallion reared, and she felt his body jerk. As Jove tried to climb the air, she slipped. Robin clutched her, and they fell backward together.

He hit the ground, and she hit him. Stunned, she lay still for a moment. As she tried to move, someone lifted her off Savage and laid her on her back. She opened her eyes to a whirling sky. The dark-haired Frenchman bent over her, and she gasped.

"Content you, *demoiselle*. There is no need to fear me."

"R-Robin."

"This one?"

The Frenchman moved aside to reveal Savage. He lay on his back, blood streaming from a cut on his temple. She pushed the man aside and knelt over Robin. With shaking hands she explored the wound. It wasn't deep, but the blood must be stanched. She tore strips from her petticoat while the Frenchman waited in silence. Around them his men were gathering their wounded and stray horses. As she worked she glanced about but saw no other prisoners. Robin's men had escaped, and the thought comforted her. They would be back.

She turned to the Frenchman. "Water?"

Their gazes locked, and he regarded her with solemnity.

"This is the one who abducted you?"

"He's hurt."

"*Attendez, demoiselle.* If you wish to help him, answer me. Is this the one who abducted you?"

"Yes, yes. God's mercy, now will you give me water?"

"*Oui, demoiselle.*"

He motioned to a man waiting in attendance at his side, and a water bottle was produced. Wasting no further attention on the strangers, she cleaned Robin's wound and bound it. When she finished, the Frenchman drew her away from Savage. Handing the water bottle to her, he waited for her to drink. When she finished, he swept her a bow to which she'd grown accustomed at the French court.

"*Bienvenue, demoiselle. À votre service, s'il vous plaît. Je suis Jean-Paul, Sieur de la Rochefort.*"

"Please, I haven't spoken French in years."

"Forgive me," he said. "Demoiselle, her majesty of Scotland sent me to find you. I thank God for his guidance and for your safety."

Wondering whether to believe him, she looked past him to Robin. He lay as she left him, and he was so still, she almost thought him dead.

"We must take him to my home. He needs the care of a physician."

Jean-Paul chuckled softly and shook his head. "*Ma petite demoiselle,* we go not to England, but to Scotland."

"But I want to go home."

Still smiling at her, Jean-Paul took her hand and kissed it. Then he stood back, lifted his right hand, and made the sign of the cross in blessing to her. He murmured Latin words but broke off at the look on her face and smiled.

"*Oui, demoiselle.* You may call me Father Jean-Paul if you wish, and *non,* we will not go farther into the land of the heretics."

Speechless, she listened to him give orders to his men. Before she could regain her composure, she was lifted upon a fresh horse, the reins of which were placed in Jean-Paul's hand. As the sun began to sink toward the horizon, he led her past the lake and over the ridge once more. She glanced behind her to find that Robin had been tied to a horse facedown. His head swayed with the gait of the animal, and his eyes were closed.

They rode hard for three days. For the first two Thea feared for Robin's life. He never woke during that time, except to surface in a delirium in which he muttered unintelligibly. At nightfall on the third day their captors hauled him from the horse he was tied to, while she waited nearby. The first time they'd done so, the men had tossed him on the ground like an old saddle. She'd attacked the nearest offender and given him a bloody lip. Jean-Paul had interfered before the wounded man could do her harm. Afterward the priest saw that his men were more careful.

On this third night they carried him to a blanket under her watchful gaze. She knelt beside him and removed the bandage from his head. Touching his forehead and cheek with her palm, she was relieved to find it cool. He'd run a fever since being wounded. When she removed her hand, he turned his head to the side, sighed, then slowly opened his eyes.

Wincing, he turned his head and looked at her. Suddenly he grabbed her wrist and tried to sit.

"Where—ahh!"

He fell back, and she placed a hand on his chest while he put both hands to his head. His chest heaved, and he breathed rapidly. The edge of a cloak swung into view, brushed his torn sleeve, and he opened his eyes again.

"You're awake. *Bon.* You see, *ma petite.* Did I not tell you he would recover? A thick English skull, that. I shall fetch some broth."

Robin's eyes widened, then closed as he winced again. Thea put a water bottle to his lips, and he drank. When he shoved the bottle away, she ordered him to be still.

"A pox on you. What in Hades possessed you to try to kill my men and trot off? Stupid gentry mort."

He was going to live, and she could hate him again. Pulling her shoulders straight, she said, "I stitched your wound while you were senseless—my lord."

Robin started to speak, then studied her face and fell silent. They examined each other.

"How could you think—"

"Abandon your low accent, my lord. Cozen me no further with bawdy talk and lewd caresses. I may be a fool, but I'm a fool who knows when she'd been made sport of by a vile spy."

"*Oui, mon seigneur,* do set aside the mask. You're not strong enough to play the part."

Jean-Paul had been standing at her back all this time. Thea gave him a tense glance, then met Robin's gaze. To her astonishment, he was looking at her as if she were a pile of offal. He spoke in the quiet, clipped tones of an aristocrat faced with a leaking water closet.

"Bloody Hades, you led us into a trap. For revenge, I trow, like every other woman who finds an old lover inconvenient. God's blood, couldn't you have thought of your queen and England before your own trivial concerns?"

## 12

*Pray for me! and what noise
soever ye hear, come not unto me,
for nothing can rescue me.*

—CHRISTOPHER MARLOWE

ERRY'S HORSE SLOWED, THEN stopped, and he swayed in the saddle. The ground swung back and forth beneath him, and he clamped his teeth together as pain stabbed through his skull. He had alternated between dizzy awareness and a kind of waking senselessness the whole day.

One of his guards grabbed him and hauled him from the saddle. His knees collapsed, but the man caught him. Another guard joined them, and they held him suspended between them. Thus supported, he was able to lift his head and survey his surroundings. The Frenchman had called a halt at the summit of a hill surrounded by moors. Before him lay the ruins of an abbey.

Blank, arched windows rose up three stories. Roofless, the structure was a skeleton through which he could see the darkening sky. Beyond the abbey, almost lapping at its foundations, was a lake, a blue windowpane laid flat on the earth. The Frenchman walked beneath the pointed arch in one wall, and Derry was dragged in after him.

In a patch of dark gold sunlight stood Thea. The Frenchman was talking to her, and she seemed to be pleading with him. Derry's lip curled into a sneer. He'd allowed lust to make him careless, no, witless. The moment he'd begun to trust her, she betrayed him, as Alice had, and to a Frenchman who served the Queen of Scots. Or did he?

Mayhap this Jean-Paul was more than a royal servant. He had to be. A priest who rode like a warrior, it had been Jean-Paul who had struck the blow that felled him. Any priest who used a sword like a fencing master was no ordinary priest. As he studied Jean-Paul, the priest lifted Thea's hand and brushed his lips to the backs of her fingers.

Derry's head pounded. Watching them created an inner whirlwind that swept him back eleven years. He was at his manor, standing between two guards in the doorway. They dragged him down the steps while Bishop Bonner, Bloody Bonner, leaned over his wife's extended hand.

He turned his head away, and his gaze fell on the sun. Framed by a soaring window, it burst into a glowing orange-red. He had trusted a woman again. This time he would most likely die for it. Jean-Paul hadn't kept him alive to bring him to justice. *Holy Father, if I'm spared, I vow never to trust a woman again.*

Even as Derry pondered what would be done with him, Jean-Paul beckoned to his guards. He was dragged to stand before his captor and Thea. Jean-Paul waited for him to steady himself by bracing his legs apart. Then he began walking back and forth in front of Derry. Derry watched him, and was sorry, because the movement cost him his hard-won balance. Jean-Paul's figure blurred, and the ground dipped. He felt hands tighten around his arms.

When his vision cleared, Jean-Paul was peering at him. The priest pointed at the ground, and his guards clamped their hands on his shoulders and shoved. He dropped, boulderlike, to his knees. Jean-Paul knelt in front of him.

"Sit, *Anglais*. If you fall and hit your head again, my questions will be delayed further."

The priest shoved him gently, and Derry dropped to a sitting position. He leaned forward and rested his weight on his palms while waves of pain arced through his head. Fingers lifted his chin, and Jean-Paul examined him, frowning. He jerked his chin free, and gasped at the stiletto jabs that resulted. When he recovered, Thea was at his side.

"Did I not caution you not to move suddenly?" she asked.

"God rot your traitorous little soul."

"I pray you," Jean-Paul said, "refrain from quarreling with him, *demoiselle*. I have business with our *Anglais*."

"Get her out of my sight if you wish to speak with me," Derry said. "'In the extravagance of her evil she has brought shame both on herself and on all women who will come after her.'"

He winced as Thea gave a shrill cry.

"Vile, cozening miscreant, a pox on you. Fifteen letters in the alphabet? You liar. God's bones, I'll wager you even lie with your—"

Thea shut her mouth, whirled, and marched from the abbey. Derry watched her leave, then was jolted from his fury when Jean-Paul moved near him.

"So, *Anglais*, you lie with your body as well as with your tongue. That is what she meant to say, *n'est-ce pas?*"

Jean-Paul clicked his tongue against the roof of his mouth. "For shame. To seduce such an innocent."

"Get on with it," Derry said. "She may not understand what you are, but there's no need to pose and prance for me."

Jean-Paul sat back, bent a knee, and hooked an arm around it. He regarded Derry for a moment with a pensive smile.

"*Bien.* Now that you fare better, we may begin."

"Who sent you?"

Jean-Paul threw back his head and laughed. "*Mon Dieu, Anglais,* you are the prisoner, not I. I will ask questions. You will answer."

"Why waste time?" Derry asked wearily. "You know I won't answer and then you'll try to make me answer. Why not begin with the beatings or whippings or whatever torture you favor. I vow it all seems a bit pointless."

He met Jean-Paul's gaze without flinching. Neither looked away, and he became fascinated with the utter blackness of the priest's eyes. This man's very coloring concealed his thoughts. The black eyes crinkled, and Jean-Paul smiled. He darted forward to hiss in Derry's face.

"*Sacré Dieu, Anglais,* I do believe you'd welcome such crudities. Can it be that you've had a taste of the crucifix?"

Derry was caught by surprise when the priest knocked his arms out from under him and shoved him on his back. Guards held him down while Jean-Paul palmed a dagger. The blade sliced through the ties of his jerkin, then his shirt. As the last sunlight faded, Jean-Paul ripped aside the cambric to reveal his chest and three long, thin scars. A guard shoved him on his stomach, and he heard the priest draw in his breath.

He was released abruptly. Rolling over, he found Jean-Paul looking at him quizzically.

"You surprise me," the priest said. "Most men who've borne such treatment grovel and whimper at the least threat of more." Jean-Paul tapped the hilt of the dagger against his palm. "Unfortunately for you, *Anglais,* I have been schooled in the more subtle arts of questioning by my master, both in France and in Italy."

Derry felt nausea churn in his stomach when the priest unclasped his cloak and shrugged it from his shoulders. He kept his gaze fastened on the man's hands as he drew off his gloves and loosened the ties of his leather doublet. When the fingers delved beneath it and came up with a gold chain, he blinked. From the chain swung a phial of green Venetian glass, its fragile top sealed with silk thread and wax.

At Jean-Paul's command, his men had built a fire within the walls of the abbey. Its flames climbed high now and cast dancing shadows on the soft grass that grew between cracked flagstones. Jean-Paul held the phial by its chain, and the glass caught the light as it swung back and forth. The green was the color he'd seen when the sun shone through new leaves.

"The de Medicis first made this potion over two hundred years ago," Jean-Paul said. "It brings the *cauchemar,* terrible waking dreams. I call it the nightmare potion." He caught the phial, tossed it in the air, and caught it. "It is my judgment that to make you speak will take longer by the whip than by use of the potion. Therefore I will, as you say, waste no more time. Will you tell me your name and who sent you to abduct Mistress Hunt?"

"*Au diable,* priest."

Jean-Paul sighed and broke the seal on the phial. Removing the stopper, he sniffed the contents.

"The smell of lemons and roses. Such a pleasing odor for so vile a mixture."

The priest held out his hand. One of his men produced a cup half filled with water. He poured but two drops into the cup, then swirled the concoction around while motioning to Derry's guards.

Robin tried to fight them off, but they slammed him down on his back. His head nearly burst open, and his arms and legs went numb. He went limp. When he recovered, four men were on him, pressing his arms and legs into the ground. Jean-Paul was leaning over him, blocking out all light. He whipped his head to the side as he felt the cup touch his lips.

The priest chuckled, then pressed the bandage above the wound on his temple. Derry cried out, and liquid poured into his mouth. He choked and spat, but he was too late. Cold water gushed down his throat. He could feel it crawling down to his stomach. He tasted lemons and roses, and his mouth and throat burned.

Sputtering, he swore at the priest as he was released and hauled to a sitting position. Held upright by two guards, he shook his head, then faced Jean-Paul. To his amazement, Thea appeared behind the priest.

"What have you done to him?"

Jean-Paul kept his gaze fastened on Derry. "Helped him take a drink. Henri, I told you to keep her away. Her majesty the Queen of Scots likes not the thought of her friend being disturbed by violence."

Derry listened closely, but their voices seemed to be floating away from him. He went still in an effort to hear what was being said.

"What have you done to him? Look at him, he's shaking, and look at his eyes."

Derry covered his ears. Their voices had grown suddenly loud, and Thea's had climbed an octave while the priest's had sunk to a low boom.

The fire went out. Derry uncovered his ears, for all the voices were gone, everyone was gone, and he was alone in a deep black cell. He heard himself cry out. Whipping about, he searched the cell. He was alone. But they would come soon. Bloody Bonner would come again, all sweaty in priest's robes, all fat and swollen with lust for blood and pain—his pain, and his screams.

As suddenly as darkness had come, the light burst upon him, a pool of light. He was naked and stretched on a rack in a pool of light. The ropes groaned, the machine moved, and Derry screamed. When the tension released, he lay gasping, sobbing, a seventeen-year-old heap of disconnected bones.

*"You killed him."*

The light shrank, fastened on a dark-haired figure. It raised an arm and pointed at him. It spoke with his father's voice.

*"You killed my John, you killed him, you killed him, you killed him."*

He was standing before the figure, bloody sword in one hand, boots and shirt wet with his own perspiration and John's blood. He dropped the sword. Slowly he brought his hand up and looked at it as if it belonged to someone else. It had to, for it was covered in something wet and red.

*"You killed him."*

He shoved his hand behind his back and shook his head. He tried to deny the accusation, but his voice had vanished. Someone had sewn his lips together. He pleaded with the dark-haired man with his eyes. The man drew a sword, lunged, and Derry felt the tip pierce his gut. Slowly, the blade slid into him, incising his entrails.

Derry watched the stately progress of blade, felt the

agony of severed flesh. The sword hilt appeared, rammed into his body. He looked up at the man holding the sword.

"Morgan?"

Morgan's face was suffused with exultation.

Derry felt his own blood draining from his body, and with it his strength, his spirit. "Morgan, why?"

Morgan stepped back and kicked him while still holding the sword. Derry flew backward, off the blade. He hit the ground, and blood splashed up from the hole in his gut. Morgan walked over and stared down at him.

"Morgan, why?"

*"I hate you. You killed him."*

The words echoed, grew louder, expanded until they filled his senses, until he became sound itself. He threw his arms up, covered his head and ears, but still the sound buzzed inside him. It filled his head and grew louder. He screamed. Blood flowed over his chest, and he screamed again. His body arched with the pain, and then, when he thought he would die from the horror, he began to fall. Faster and faster, deeper he fell into a black void, until, at last, it consumed him.

*Derry tried to open* his eyes, but the effort was too much for his little strength. He lay between waking and sleep, uncertain of which he was in. He couldn't move his body, yet he was aware. In vain he struggled to raise a hand, turn his head. Then someone lifted him, and he was cradled against a hard leg.

He felt a slap on his face, and his eyes flew open. A dark-haired man hit him again, and Derry mumbled. Another slap.

"Morgan?"

"Awaken, *Anglais.*"

"I didn't kill him. It was a mischance. He ran on my sword."

Cold water hit his face. Derry gasped, then sputtered and shook his head. An unwise move, for it immediately swelled to the size of a gorged pig and tried to burst. He fell back and was lowered to the ground. A cold cloth slithered over his neck and face, then settled on his brow.

At last he felt as if he inhabited his own body. He opened his eyes to find the priest staring down at him. Beyond him stood Thea, her face reflecting horror, which brought back his own memory. He turned his face away and bit the inside of his cheek to enforce his will over his rampant emotions. He heard the priest chuckle softly.

"How convenient, *Anglais*. The Tower, the rack and whip, Bishop Bonner, and one called Morgan who is dear to you and yet hates you."

"You've learned much—and nothing."

"Not this time, but it's early, and next time, mayhap, I shall be Morgan for you. Would you like that?"

Thea launched herself at Jean-Paul. Yanking on his arm, she forced him to face her.

"You can't give him more of that vile stuff. Look at him. A larger dose would kill him."

"Not just yet," said the priest, and produced the phial.

"Wait," Thea said. "I can tell you who he is. He's Robin Savage, the highwayman."

Jean-Paul stared at her, then gave a chortle. "A highwayman! *Dieu*, Mistress Hunt, you yourself called him my lord."

"One of his disguises. He plays at being a lord to suit his designs, but he's a thief, leader of the band of ruffians who abducted me for ransom."

Making an impatient sound, Jean-Paul beckoned to his men. "Take her away."

"No!"

Derry watched with mild interest as Thea fought the men who came at her. Two of them lifted her and carried her out of the abbey. As she went, she screamed at Jean-Paul. At a look from their master, the guards set Thea on her feet and gagged her. She disappeared outside into the darkness.

Jean-Paul turned to him. Kneeling beside him, the priest offered a cup of water.

"I'm not thirsty."

Placing the cup in Derry's hands, Jean-Paul held it steady and brought it to Derry's lips. "Drink anyway, *Anglais*. You're not well, and it will refresh you."

Derry drank, and was startled by the taste of lemons and roses. Somehow familiar, he grew uneasy as the taste grew stronger. He tried to shove the cup away, but the priest tipped it, and the water emptied into his mouth. He swallowed, then knocked the cup away. When he looked up, the priest was smiling. Derry blinked slowly at him. Between one blink and another, he fell into deep emptiness and slept.

When next he woke, it was still dark. This time he remembered nothing but a low, insistent voice commanding him, lashing him with questions. He had no notion of how long he'd been senseless this time, but since Jean-Paul wore the same clothing, it must be the same night. It felt like a millennium.

He was lying on his back. His head still felt swollen, and his tongue as well. His ears buzzed incessantly. What was worse, his heart beat so quickly he felt like an overheated dog. He tried to sit up and failed. A boot landed near his shoulder. His gaze traveled up the length of it to black hose, then skipped up to the face of the priest.

"Robin St. John, Lord Derry." Jean-Paul smiled viciously at him. "How haps it, *Anglais,* that the favorite of the bastard English queen abducts the unknowing courier of the Wyvern?"

"Bloody Hades."

Jean-Paul laughed and squatted beside him. "*Passionné, mon ami.* Such fire. Indeed, you're amusing."

The priest settled beside him, and Derry gave him an uneasy stare. How much had he revealed? God, he'd babbled like a silly virgin.

"Come, there's little use in clinging to silence. One more dose, and you'll end up a lackwitted, tractable slave. Save yourself the degradation, *Anglais.* No secret is worth the loss of your spirit."

"God rot your entrails, priest."

Jean-Paul rolled his eyes. "*Nom de Dieu,* what tenacity." Suddenly he leaned close to study Derry.

"Get your puling face away from me," Derry snarled.

"Take my hand."

Derry stared at the priest without moving.

Jean-Paul grabbed his hand. Derry swore and tried to pull free. His arm jerked weakly, and the priest dropped his hand. Without warning, Derry felt hands on his face. His eyelids were pulled wide, then released. Fingers pressed against the pulse at his throat.

"I believe another dose might kill you," Jean-Paul said. "*Infortuné,* for your nightmares are most intriguing."

The fingers at his throat lifted. Jean-Paul smiled at him. He snapped his fingers, and guards appeared, escorting Thea between them. Jean-Paul held out his hand. Thea came to stand beside him. He grabbed her arm and hauled her down to his side. Dread turned Derry's entrails to boiling acid.

"Are you certain you don't wish to tell me about the ciphers?" Jean-Paul asked.

"What ciphers?" Derry asked.

Jean-Paul began to stroke Thea's hair. Derry stirred, then went still as he saw her alarm. She edged away from the priest, but he caught her arm. His free hand touched the collar of her gown, then her lips, then fell to her hand. He kissed her palm.

"I was a youth when I was taken into the household of a prince of the church. He believed as the old church did, that one cannot fight sin unless one knows what sin is. He taught me sin. I found it much more interesting and satisfying than virtue. Cardinal's robes and naked woman's flesh."

Rage bubbled through his veins, bringing with it clarity of thought and strength. Cardinal's robes. A cardinal. A French cardinal. There was only one French cardinal powerful enough to send intelligencers into Scotland and England—Mary Stuart's uncle, the Cardinal of Lorraine.

Jean-Paul kept hold of Thea's hand and turned to Derry. "I've bethought me of a new amusement, *Anglais.* Mayhap if you see me taking my ease with the delightful Mistress Hunt, you will remember what you did with the ciphers. After all, the battle between you and her speaks of much desire. No doubt you'll wish to keep the secret of her passion for yourself."

Rising, the priest pulled Thea after him. Derry thrust himself upright, but his guards hauled him down again. Thea dug in her heels. Jean-Paul yanked hard, and she flew into his arms. He lifted her off her feet.

Derry bellowed at the priest and fought his captors as Jean-Paul carried the struggling Thea through the arched doorway of the abbey. Standing beneath the arch, Jean-Paul turned to face him.

"If you wish to silence her screams, it is within your power. Do me a courtesy, *Anglais.* Don't break too soon."

The priest turned and vanished with Thea still trying to claw her way free.

Derry lurched and kicked at his guards. He was knocked back to the ground. Struggling to his knees, he bellowed Thea's name into the darkness.

# 13

*Wreath the cauldron with a crimson fillet of fine wool;*
*That I may cast a fire-spell on the unkind man I*
*love . . .*

—THEOCRITUS

THEA FOUGHT JEAN-PAUL as he dragged her from the abbey. From within the ruin she heard Robin howl her name in fury. Once they rounded the front corner, the priest released her. She stumbled, then pulled herself erect to face him.

"I confess I'm wondrous amazed we've come to this, *ma petite,* but the *Anglais* has a will of mythic strength." Jean-Paul shrugged off his cloak, then paused at her disbelieving expression. "Content you. It will be no worse than when the *Anglais* had you. Better, for I'm no rough English lout."

"You're a priest!"

Jean-Paul sighed and chuckled softly as he removed his belt and sword and dropped them. *"Quelle innocence."* He reached out and ripped the front of her gown. It tore almost to her breasts.

Caught off guard, Thea cried out, pulled free of his hands, and clutched her gown. As she did so, the forgotten paper containing the cipher key slipped between the torn ends. Jean-Paul's hand darted out, and he snatched it before she could stop him. He opened it, signaling for a torch to one of the guards standing at a distance. Perusing it quickly, he dismissed the guard and studied her. His smile remained, but his gaze was speculative. He folded the paper, held it between two fingers, and swung it to and fro.

"So," he murmured. "The Wyvern has a new intelligencer. I admit you deceived me with your innocent demeanor. God's blood, *ma petite,* does her majesty of Scotland know?"

"What mean you?" Thea watched the paper dance in his hand, her fears growing with each swing.

"We work for the same end, you and I—to put Mary Stuart on the throne of England. There's no need for pretense. The Wyvern asked me to find you, after all."

"But you said . . ." Thea's wits began to frazzle as she realized the depth of the plot into which she'd fallen. A highwayman, a priest, two queens, and the unknown Wyvern.

Jean-Paul laid the paper on a fallen stone and turned back to her. "Never mind the details, *ma petite.* I've delayed too long."

"Leave me be." She backed away from him as he approached, but he kept coming.

"Why object to what is necessary and pleasureful? Is it not fortunate that my prisoner has conceived such a desire for you, or was that your design all along?"

As he finished, the priest leapt upon her. Thea dodged to the side, but he anticipated her and moved as she did. She screamed as they both hit the ground, and she heard Robin shout the priest's name. She landed with Jean-Paul beside her. He pinned her arms to the ground, spread her legs with his own, and pressed his body down on hers. She twisted her body sideways, stretched, and bit his hand.

He yelled, but her attention was distracted by several flashes and then an explosion that seemed to come from all around them. Jean-Paul sat up, and she scrambled out from under him. Three guards were rolling on the ground and screaming. Thea looked past one of them to see Stubb drop a hackbutt and powder, draw his sword, and run in the direction of his master. All around them rose the banshee howls of Robin's men as they swooped down on their startled prey.

Jean-Paul grabbed for his discarded belt and sword. She jumped to her feet, but he was too quick for her. Pulling his sword from its sheath, he grabbed her hair. She cried out as he yanked her close. She turned and tried to claw him, and he raised the hilt of his sword as if to hit her with it. His body jerked before he could do her harm, and, with her in his grasp, he swung around to face the man who had pricked him with his blade.

"Robin!" Thea took a swipe at Jean-Paul, but he held her at arm's length, and her reach was too short.

Robin held his sword so that the tip aimed at the priest's heart, but his hand shook. She caught her breath as he swayed, then recovered before Jean-Paul could thrust at him.

"Priest or no, you touched her," he said slowly, "and I will kill you for it."

All around them the priest's men were fleeing in the face of the onslaught of howling ruffians. Skirmishes ebbed and flowed around them.

Jean-Paul surveyed the wreckage of his camp while holding his opponent at bay. "Jesu, *Anglais,* you have cost me much this night."

"And the Cardinal of Lorraine, I hope," said Robin.

The priest lifted his brows, then sighed. "*Infortuné, mon fils.* This quick wit of yours has brought you a death sentence."

He thrust at Robin, but Thea hurled herself with him as he lunged and knocked his blade aside. Cursing, Jean-Paul kept going with the force of their movement, and slung her at Savage. She flew, stonelike, and hit Robin. They fell with her on top. As they hit, she heard him cry out, and his body went limp. She scrambled upright to face Jean-Paul's attack, but he was gone. Most of his men were gone as well.

As she turned back to Robin, a figure in black loomed over her. It was Morgan. Bloody sword in hand, he scowled at her, knelt beside his brother, and felt for wounds. Robin's lashes fluttered. He opened his eyes and stared at Thea. Relief obvious in his gaze, he shifted it to Morgan, and Thea beheld the sudden assault of terror.

Robin thrust himself away from his brother, staggering to his knees. "No, please."

Morgan reached for him, but he shied away.

"Derry, it's me."

"No more."

Robin tried to evade Morgan's grasp, twisted, and struck out, only to wobble and finally sink to the ground. Thea shoved Morgan away and put her hand over Robin's heart.

"What have you done to him?" Morgan snarled. "He fears me."

"I've done nothing. It was that foul priest."

"That was a priest?"

Robin stirred, and Morgan gathered him in his arms. Thea took his hand and patted it, more to comfort herself than him. The gentian eyes opened. He saw Morgan and began to fight. Morgan caught his brother's wrists and swore.

"God's blood, Derry, stop."

When his order was ignored, he slapped his brother lightly across the cheek. Thea poked him in the ribs.

"Don't you hit him."

"He's addled."

"And hurt, and you're making it worse."

"Jesu, woman, how am I to care for him if he fights me?"

"If you hit him again, I'll stick your backside with your own sword."

They stopped at the sound of Robin's voice. "Thea?"

They hovered over him as if he were a newborn babe. Morgan still held his wrists, but Robin was devouring Thea with his gaze.

"He hurt you not?"

She shook her head.

Morgan thrust his brother's wrists from him. "Thankless sot, I rescue you with a grand stratagem, and you're worried about this vicious little adder."

Robin's worried expression vanished. "She betrayed us."

"I did not."

"You happened upon the priest by good fortune?" he asked sweetly.

Thea crossed her arms over her chest. "He was looking for us, you fool. Oh!"

She jumped up and darted for the flat stone on which Jean-Paul had placed the cipher key. It lay there untouched. Returning to the brothers, she deliberately ignored Robin and addressed Morgan.

"Whom do you serve?"

"Why, myself, lady."

Robin let out a deep breath and touched his bandaged head. "It's no use, Morgan. She's found out I'm not Savage, and you just called me Derry."

"Very well," Morgan said, "since you're in our keeping again. We serve her majesty Queen Elizabeth."

Thea studied Robin's face. He met her gaze openly. He blinked at her slowly, a pale figure of indignation. Suddenly a thought came to her.

"Derry?" she said. "Lord Derry?"

Morgan chuckled and glanced at his brother. "Yes, my beloved murderous, sinful brother Derry. The lodestar of the court and curse of my life." He lowered his voice and chanted a street cry. "'Sweep chimney sweep, with a hey derry sweep, from the bottom to the top, sweep derry sweep.'"

Thea felt her face and neck grow hot. Her own humiliation returned to her, and her mouth went dry. The fabled Lord Derry, so beautiful and so graceful that it was bruited about the kingdom that the queen favored him as much as her beloved Dudley. Robin St. John, Lord Derry. Dear Savior, he'd played with her like a top, and she'd spun for him. Swallowing hard, she stuffed her hurt away and thought of her duty. She held out the cipher key to him.

"This is what you've been seeking. And now that you've got it, I want my maid and my men back."

Robin took it from her, frowning. His hand shook as he read it, and he relinquished it to his brother. Morgan glanced at it and whistled.

"The priest gave it to you, and you seek to buy your honor with it," Robin said coldly.

Furious at his distrust, Thea snapped at him. "No, my lord, I found its hiding place and copied it before I escaped. Though you don't wish to believe it, I am a loyal

subject. I was taking the cursed cipher key to my father so
that he could give it to the queen."

She paused, lifted her chin, and forced herself to meet
Derry's contemptuous and disbelieving stare. "I can admit
when I've erred, my lord. I know I must sacrifice my
personal obligations for the good of England, but remember this, sirrah. My mistakes were made in ignorance.
Yours were not. Now, if you please, I would like to ride
from this place before Jean-Paul comes back for us. I've no
wish to couple with a priest, even if you do."

Thea left Derry to Stubb's care and rode beside Morgan
as they picked their way carefully through the night. She
had little choice but to accept Derry's protection, with
that depraved priest lurking in the countryside. She tried
to comfort herself with the thought that she'd be rid of
him once they reached London. She failed. Knowing herself to have been the dupe of the queen's favorite scalded
Thea's temperament. She snapped at everyone except
Derry, whom she ignored.

Morgan had examined his brother and declared him
unfit for a long trip, and therefore they were going home
to Moorefield Garde. Riding north and west, they jour-
neyed through tree-covered hills that surrounded glassy
lakes until they came to the river that fed them. The land
became more rugged as they skirted the river, and they
began to climb until they reached a waterfall at midday.
Bubbling white foam thundered down from cliffs high
above her head and spattered the surrounding trees and
rocks with a coat of sparkling moisture. A perpetual mist
hung in the air.

Derry hadn't stirred all morning. He'd ridden in a half
doze, but at the sound of the waterfall he straightened and
pulled up his horse, thus halting the whole party.

"Not Moorefield Garde," he said.

Though he hadn't raised his voice, Thea heard him and turned her mount. Morgan was arguing with his brother.

"Unless you can enforce your will, we stay at Moorefield Garde," Morgan said.

"God curse your soul, Morgan."

Derry began to turn his horse, but Morgan snatched the reins and refused to free Derry. When Stubb and Inigo followed Morgan's orders rather than Derry's threats, the battle was over. Thea noticed the rigid set of Morgan's jaw—and the fury in Derry's face, fury at his own helplessness, no doubt. They rode for Moorefield Garde.

Not long afterward they entered a wide valley. Though the sun was high, the air snapped and bit with the cold of a north breeze. Riding beside the river, they began to encounter farms and people, many of whom were headed in the same direction on the river road. All at once the valley narrowed, and the river took a sharp turn around an outcrop of gray rock. From this spit of stone rose a tiered castle—Moorefield Garde.

Built on three levels that climbed the cliffs above the river, the castle was guarded by polygonal towers. The top story of each projected outward to form parapets, and massive curtain walls connected each tower. The highest and most distant of all was one that seemed to be made of black marble.

Thea grew apprehensive as she rode over the stone bridge that crossed the moat. Moorefield Garde was a fortress. Surrounded by steep cliffs, it was a place from which she couldn't escape. She glanced at Derry. He seemed to feel as she did, for he rode with his back straight, looking neither right nor left, his lips pressed together in a straight line.

The journey between the outer, middle, and inner wards was a long one, and wondrous strange to Thea.

Servants and men-at-arms alike halted in mid-stride when they beheld Derry. Caps were swept off heads, curtseys made, all in silence. Ahead of them a buzz arose, and she could see a crowd gathering before what must be the great hall.

Finally they dismounted. People milled about in front of the steps. A man with a chain of office chattered at Morgan as he helped Derry dismount. Then the crowd backed away from the brothers as the doors to the hall banged open and a man with silver hair and the walk of a youth stormed up to them. Thea stared at him, for he had Derry's gentian-blue eyes. The father, however, had spoiled his appearance by cultivating the look of a man who had recently sat on the point of his own dagger. In addition, he constantly held his mouth in a pinched distortion that had etched vertical lines above and below it.

Derry had been leaning on Morgan's shoulder. He dropped away from his brother as their father barreled down on them. He inclined his head stiffly.

"Well met, Father."

Viscount Moorefield made no answer. He glanced at Morgan and snarled.

"He lives."

Morgan said nothing.

The viscount turned away. "Get you gone from here."

Derry began to laugh. Thea took note of his face and moved toward him. She was in time to put her shoulder beneath his arm so that he remained on his feet.

Morgan called after his father. "We're staying."

The viscount stopped with his back to them. "Put him in the Black Tower. Three days, then I throw you both from it into the river."

"'God, these old men!'" Derry said. "'How they pray

for death! How heavy they find this life in the slow drag of days!' "

Viscount Moorefield turned and gave his son a stare filled with loathing, then he continued into the hall. Suddenly Derry thrust Thea away from him. Her compassion for him vanished.

"So," she said. "The highwayman knows Euripides." She ground her teeth together. "Fifteen letters in the alphabet indeed."

Derry swung around on her and would have stumbled if Morgan hadn't caught him.

"Traitor," he snapped.

"Liar. When are you going to return Hobby to me, you honorless degenerate?"

Morgan made a small sound of impatience. "Content you, Mistress Hunt."

She threw up her hands. "The vile cozening lout sits in judgment upon me."

"Both of you, silence!" Morgan hustled his brother back onto his horse and mounted his own. "Come, mistress, he'll get no rest if you aren't housed nearby. It's to the Black Tower for us all."

"And this time don't try to leave," Derry said. "The guards will be warned to prevent it."

She mounted and followed the two brothers around the great hall, past stables, orchards, and gardens and out a fortified gate. As she rode she pondered the viscount's odd greeting. The man hated his own son, his heir. What kind of man hated his own son, or, what kind of son evoked the hatred of his father? Contemplating Derry's slumping shoulders, she recalled the malice that chained the brothers together. God's mercy, what evil had created such enmity between the three?

They climbed a steep slope to the summit of the castle

where the river bent to form the bottom of a rounded V. There rose a tower almost two hundred feet high. As she drew close, the darkness of the stone faded somewhat, and Thea realized that age had deepened the gray of the rock from which the tower was built. The structure appeared black only from a distance.

She trailed after Morgan as he helped Derry inside. Stubb aided Morgan as he guided Derry up the winding stair. Servants passed them on their way, carrying food and baggage. All showed an apprehensive deference to Derry. They climbed higher and higher until they reached the top floor. There the tower split into two chambers. Derry vanished into one, and Inigo conducted her to the other.

She hadn't begun to explore the chamber when she heard the brothers' voices raised in argument again. She found them in Derry's chamber. Morgan was standing over his brother, who was half reclining on a narrow bed.

"It must be done quickly, and she's already dealt with the cipher."

"No," Derry said.

"God's blood," Morgan said, "we've no time for quarreling. The ciphers must be translated, and your vision is still blurred from that potion. I can't do it, for I've the priest to hunt, unless you want him coming after you."

"She betrayed us to that priest, Morgan."

Morgan threw up his hands. "She says not, and besides, she need only write what you say. And look what your arguing has done to you. Lie back before you fall."

"Such tender care. I thought you wanted to kill me."

"Not until you're well enough to defend yourself."

Morgan stalked out of the chamber, leaving them alone. Thea glanced at Derry's expressionless features and scurried after him. The door shut in her face, and locked. She banged on it with both fists.

"Morgan St. John, you come back here at once! Morgan!"

"Cease that howling."

She rounded on Derry and stomped over to him. "This is your fault."

"How so? I'm not the one with a corrupt priest for a lover." He was lying on the bed with his arm over his eyes.

Rage burned a path through her skull. "Toad. You accuse me falsely when it is you who—who—" She couldn't think of words foul enough to use.

Derry lifted his arm. Surveying her with a blank gaze, he pointed to a table laden with writing materials.

"Then prove your honesty by writing what I say."

She lifted her chin and sniffed. "I need prove nothing."

Swinging his legs to the floor, Derry rose to a sitting position. Wary, Thea edged her way back to the locked door. He stood, feet planted apart, and hooked his thumbs in his belt. She had forgotten how he overshadowed her with his height. Though he stayed where he was, he managed to appear nearly as tall as the Black Tower.

"I can't see well enough to write, but I can see you. Thea *bella*," he said quietly. "I thought you'd learned what it is to be my enemy and defy me."

She couldn't think of anything to say that wouldn't provoke his anger, so she glared at him instead. He pointed at the table again. When she didn't move, he came toward her. She looked right and left. There was nowhere for her to run. By the time she'd decided on which way to go, he was on her.

He lunged for her as she sprinted to the left, caught her, and swung her against the door. Pressing his body against hers, he held her still. She clawed at his face, but he grabbed her hands. He was so close she could feel the heat of his body through their clothing. His lips touched her neck.

"You have a choice," he said against her throat. "Write, or submit to me."

Thea gasped, then stomped down hard with her foot. Her heel raked the inside of his leg and hit his boot. He yelped and jumped away from her. She darted from his grasp and stood, watching him hop and curse.

"I choose to write," she said.

Derry straightened. He touched his head, then closed his eyes for a moment. She almost went to him when she saw the blood drain from his face, but he looked at her with that empty gaze of his. He hadn't wanted her just then. He'd been using her, as always. She turned her back on him and stalked to the table.

Seating herself on a bench at the table, she took up a quill. Derry produced the cipher key and laid it in front of her.

"Write what I tell you."

He proceeded to recite the contents of the five button messages letter by letter. Using the cipher key, they translated and wrote the translations on a separate page. Thea finished the last message and read through the contents. All were couched in the same form.

*Triton pledges allegiance and fifteen hundred men to Icarus. Receives messages at the Bell and Dragon.*

"The Wyvern pledges the most men, two thousand," Thea said. "Look you. With the unicorn's five hundred, the griffin's nine hundred, and the ounce's one thousand, that's almost six thousand. God's mercy." She met Derry's gaze in horror. "Enough to start a war."

Derry rested his hip on the table near her and rubbed his temples. "Have I not been saying so to you for weeks?"

"And have I not attested that I've nothing to do with these cursed messages? Grandmother duped me."

Leaning on both arms, Derry looked down at her and smiled. "Sweet Thea *bella,* dupe or no, you're not to be trusted. Which means I must take the ciphers to London myself, and you will come with me. The Wyvern knows his messages have gone astray in your care. If you return to the city, he will seek you out. I'm taking you back to your father, and he will welcome me as your savior. Word will spread throughout London that you're home. I'll see to it. Bait, Thea *bella,* you're going to be my pretty, treacherous, seductive bait."

"I will not."

"I bethought me you might try to refuse." Derry leaned over to touch her cheek with his fingertips. "No doubt you took note of my father's greeting. He hates me, and for good reason. You see, Thea *bella,* when I was but a youth I ran my older brother through with a sword. Impaled him like a stoat. So you will hardly stand amazed if I promise to do the same to you if you fail to obey my least command. You will play the goat for me. I'll stake you out and, with good fortune, snare a dragon. Look not so furious, Mistress Hunt."

"Someday I hope to see you in torment."

Derry threw back his head and laughed, which made her long to punch him in a man's favorite parts.

"You like it not that I've discovered your base deceit," he said. He smiled sweetly at her, and the beauty of that smile fed her rage almost as much as the ballad he sang.

*They flee from me that sometime did me seek*
*With naked foot stalking in my chamber.*

*I have seen them gentle, tame, and meek*
*That now are wild and do not remember*
*That sometime they put themself in danger*
*To take bread at my hand . . .*

*Fathers, provoke not your children
to anger, lest they be discouraged.*

—Colossians 3:21

TWO DAYS PASSED AT Moorefield Garde in which Thea eschewed the company of Lord Derry. That is, when she was allowed to do so. At first his injuries forced him to rest while his brother searched for Jean-Paul, but the previous day he grew strong enough to harangue her about the priest. He berated her and then demanded to know the priest's designs.

She defied him, and their quarrel intensified until Viscount Moorefield himself appeared and ordered them to cease, saying he wouldn't have the peace of his manor disturbed. The appearance of his father wrought a sudden change in Derry. He closed up, clamlike, and transformed into a statue fashioned of ice.

At least he'd let her be after that, though he still refused to reveal Hobby's whereabouts. Today she'd been allowed the freedom of the castle as long as Inigo and Simon Spry accompanied her. She'd apologized for hitting them, but they seemed to consider her actions only to be expected. No doubt Derry had treated them far worse.

Thus they followed her patiently as she roamed about the castle. She visited the stables, the mews, and walked down to the outer ward to roam among the trees that surrounded the well there. By afternoon she had climbed back to the inner ward, where she found a walled garden next to the hall. The viscount had created a pruned and trimmed formal landscape. Box hedges bordered the garden while shrubs had been cut into spheres, rectangles, and cones.

The counterfeit and managed nature of the place made her long for home and her wanderings in the fields and woods. May was almost gone, and about now she would find pink clover in blossom, and perhaps blue field madder. The holly and maple trees would be in bloom. She was contemplating a cone-shaped bush with displeasure when she heard Inigo and Simon. They had been lounging beneath a tree, but the arched door in the wall swung open, and they scrambled to their feet.

Viscount Moorefield entered. As was his custom, he charged in, scowling, and jerked his head at the door. The two thieves fell over each other in their hurry to get out of the garden. He approached, his manner solemn yet courtly. He bowed and kissed her hand.

"Mistress Hunt, I'm glad to find you alone. May I speak with you?"

She nodded. This man who appeared to despise his oldest son confused her. Though they shared an antipathy for Derry, his continual state of rage made her uneasy. He conducted her to a bench and waited until she was seated before continuing.

"I confess I disbelieve this tale Morgan has told me. Did Derry deliver you from the hands of the outlaw Savage?"

She gaped at him.

"I thought not," the viscount said. He sat beside her. "He's cozened you into giving yourself to him, has he not, and now seeks to abandon you. You see, Mistress Hunt, I know my son."

She wet her lips. Better to allow Derry to be her rescuer rather than her seducer.

"You're mistaken, my lord. Your son delivered me from the highwayman Savage, as Morgan said."

"And then he seduced you."

She shook her head violently.

"Then how haps it that you can't remain in spitting range of each other without snarling and clawing like baited bears?"

"I—"

The viscount took her hand in his and regarded her with sadness. "I understand. You can't bear to speak of it. But I saw the hatred in your eyes yesterday. If you'd had a sword, you would have stuck it in his heart."

She swallowed and nodded, thinking of how besotted she'd been, and how Derry must have laughed at her.

"You're right to feel so," the viscount said. "He is my son, but I have come to admit his evil. No doubt you've learned that he killed his own brother."

"His brother?" She pulled her hand from the viscount's grasp and turned to face him on the bench.

He nodded. "Many years ago. Derry was always jealous of John, for he was the elder, and excelled at a man's pursuits, while Derry was poor-spirited and weak. To my shame, the boy preferred the pursuits of a clerk to those of a knight. I had to force him to become a man, and I will rue it until I die."

"But Derry fights like a Roman warrior."

"Not when he was young. John was the better knight,

and Derry knew it. One day they contested with swords. It was a practice match, but Derry took the opportunity of ridding himself of his rival. He killed his brother that day, and dealt me a mortal blow as well."

"Jesu Maria, now I remember hearing about an accident. Long ago it was."

She met the viscount's gaze, and found him studying her intensely.

"I thought I would run mad after he killed John, though everyone said it was an accident. Hark you, Mistress Hunt, there's mad blood running in Derry's veins."

She thought of what Derry had done to her. Was he so ruthless as to kill his own brother? She went cold at the thought of how much at his mercy she was.

"I can see you perceive the danger at last."

Viscount Moorefield glanced about the garden, then from a pouch at his belt withdrew a gold pomander suspended from a chain. Holding the filigree sphere, he opened it. Inside was another sphere of solid silver. He removed the silver ball and opened it to reveal a brown powder. Closing it, he replaced the silver sphere inside the pomander.

"Should you ever feel yourself in danger, this powder may aid you. It contains the essence of the fairy cap, or foxglove."

"But the fairy cap is deadly."

"Of course." Pressing the pomander into her hand, the viscount rose. "Once I had hopes of Morgan. I thought he loathed Derry as much as I, but now . . ." He shook his head in disappointment. "He falters, and I know not why."

She stood and looked at the pomander in her hand, then stared at the viscount. "In faith, I do believe you mean me to poison your son."

Lifting one brow, the viscount pursued his lips. "Marry, I but seek to arm you with a weapon for your protection, Mistress Hunt. I give you good morrow."

He left, but she shouted after him. "I'm not a murderer!"

Left alone she sank down on the bench again. Could she believe such a fantastical tale? Much as she despised her captor, she had to admit that he'd mistreated her in the name of loyalty to his queen. Had he been the greedy demon his father portrayed, would he not be crouched at the feet of the queen, flattering her, wooing her, rather than risking his life in her service? But then, what did she know of men and their designs? Hitherto, she'd been wrong in her judgments altogether.

She glanced down at the pomander in her hand, then fastened the chain to her waist. She opened the pomander and removed the silver sphere. Pouring the powder on the ground, she scuffed it into the dirt. Then she replaced the silver sphere and closed the pomander.

She was studying it when the snap of a twig made her jump. Turning, she found herself staring into deep blue eyes. She glanced back at the door through which the viscount had disappeared, and Derry smiled. He glanced from the pomander to the ground, where the powder had been dumped, then back to her.

"I was but fourteen, and yes, I did kill him. As I said, it's why you should take care to obey me."

She wanted to run, but he turned and walked to a gap in the box hedge that bordered the garden. He reached into the ivy covering the garden wall, turned a handle, and went through a concealed door.

The leafy door shut, and silence reigned. She glanced about the sun-bathed garden. Stillness enveloped the place, rendering it a bright painting bathed in gentle heat.

The quiet was so pervasive that in the end, she wondered if Derry had even been there at all.

*Several days later saw* her riding in a train of men-at-arms, servants, and baggage carts. She could have been any noblewoman on her way to court—a lucky one with a handsome, knightly escort. Derry rode beside her, but they had rarely spoken throughout the journey. On the first day she'd questioned him about his plans. He refused to answer, saying he did not confide in traitors. That remark sparked another quarrel. Distrustful of each other, weary of constant battles, they finally reached an unspoken agreement. The less they spoke, the less they would quarrel, and the easier they rested.

Thus she kept her eyes trained on the road ahead. He was silent as she.

Derry had threatened to stake her out as a lure to the Wyvern. Just how he would do this he wouldn't reveal. He wanted to use her, and she'd sworn she wouldn't become his tool again. He could hunt the Wyvern without her.

Every moment spent in his presence was filled with humiliation and a shameful longing. She had to escape him, but escaping Derry wasn't easily done. Mayhap when they reached Bridgestone Abbey she could simply send him away. Would he go? A foolish query. He'd been plotting and designing traps the whole journey. She could tell by the way he stared into the distance while others talked around him. She must watch for a chance to get rid of him as soon as they arrived.

Having come to this decision, she was surprised to see the towers of Bridgestone Abbey rising before her. Despite her unhappiness, Thea felt a flood of comfort wash over her.

A familiar place at last. If she was fortunate, Father would be there, having been called back to London by Grandmother's death. The sun was setting, and it set afire the windows of Bridgestone so that it appeared that they were riding into flames.

A porter opened the gates, and a cry went up among the gardeners and servants. By the time Derry helped her dismount, the household was streaming down the front steps. Her father burst from the midst of servants and pattered up to her. Always thin, he appeared to have lost much more weight than he could afford. He had more than his share of elbows, knees, and ankles, and what little hair he still had stuck out at all angles from his head.

"My little girl!"

Thea grinned and tried to stop her tears, but as he enfolded her in his bony arms, she laughed and sobbed at the same time. She listened to his babbling as he patted her head.

"That nice young man Cecil promised to find you, and he has. Are you well, my dear? Of course you are, or you wouldn't be standing here, would you? He said he'd send a great soldier to find you, and he did. What a horror! Your grandmother was killed, then you vanished, and no one seemed to know where you went. I don't like London. Too many people disappear or die."

After a few moments of hugging and head-patting, she was released. Grandmother's companion, Ellen Dowgate, greeted her solemnly. Ellen always reminded her of the late Queen Mary. Dour and disapproving, Ellen spent much of her time at mass or praying for those whom she considered sinful—which included almost everyone she knew.

"You must be the one who saved my little girl," her

father said. "My eternal gratitude, Lord—um, Lord, er, my boy."

Derry bowed to her father, smiling and gracious, while Thea longed to kick him off the steps. He came to stand beside her, and her father babbled praises and gratitude. She ground her teeth and glanced out at the mass of servants, grooms, and men-at-arms. It suddenly occurred to her that she could rid herself of this bastard at once.

"Father, Lord Derry must be on his w—mmmph."

A wide, lush mouth fastened on hers. Derry pulled her to his body, pressing her against him, and kissed her until she struggled for air. Freeing her, he spoke while she tried to catch her breath.

"A confession I must make, Lord Hunt. Since finding your lovely daughter, I've come to worship her, and find myself carried off by my devotion. Forgive me for my haste, but I would beg you to give your consent to our betrothal. My lord, I would marry your daughter."

As a cheer went up among the crowd on the front steps, Thea lost the breath she'd just regained. This was his plan. No wonder he refused to tell it to her! The facile duplicity with which he spouted his lies shouldn't have surprised her. Dear merciful God, he would pretend to love her so that he could be near and thus trap his precious traitor. A knot of outrage formed in her throat. Choking, she pounded her chest.

"Fa-father, n-n-n—"

He kissed her again, harder and longer this time, while her father laughed and led another cheer. Derry lifted his lips and whispered to her.

"Deny my tale, and I'll tell them I've debauched you already."

He kissed her again, and she bit his tongue. He cried out, jerked away, and hid his discomfort by hugging her until she thought she could suffocate. When he released her, she swayed. Picking her up, he headed for the house.

"I pray you," he said to Lord Hunt, "show me her chamber, for I fear Thea is quite weary, for all my care for her comfort."

Before she could recover, she was seated in her chamber alone with her father and Lord Derry.

"You must stay," Lord Hunt was saying. "We've the settlement to arrange, and we must begin to know each other. Indeed, my hospitality is but a small part of the great debt I owe you."

Derry inclined his head. "How can I refuse so hospitable an invitation, especially one that will keep me near the sunlight of my life, our dear Thea."

She scowled at him, then glanced down at the gold pomander swinging from her waist. Why hadn't she saved the powder Viscount Moorefield had given her? She could have used just a bit of it, not a mortal dose, just enough to make him sick, puking, spewing sick. If he had confided in her, told her his plans, she might have played her part willingly. Much as his presence pained her, she would have endured it to catch a traitor. But by all the saints, she wouldn't be handled, managed, and played with as though her own wishes mattered less than a dog's.

She rose from her chair and marched over to the two. Derry turned to her as she joined them, and she caught her breath at the way he smiled while gazing at her with the eyes of a killer. A dam formed in her throat, stopping her protests and denials. He bent over her hand. She felt his lips, then his tongue, and shivered. Then he was gone along with Father.

Thea strove for calm, for reason. What was she to do? If she revealed Derry's intrigues, she risked alerting the

Wyvern. Thus she couldn't rid herself of this mock betrothal without aiding a traitor.

She rubbed the back of her hand where he'd kissed it.
Beshrew him! He treated her with little more courtesy
than he'd show a common bawd and then expected her to
submit to his manipulations. And vexing as it was to
admit, she had little choice but to comply now that he'd
begun the game. Very well. She would endure awhile
longer for the sake of England. She wouldn't betray
the lies, but, by God's toes, she would do no more. Let the
master of dissimulations work his traps alone. She would
have nothing more to do with him.

Looking down at her hand, she noticed that it was red.
She'd rubbed it too hard trying to get rid of the feel of his
lips on her skin. Now it tingled. She rubbed it on the back
of her gown, but no matter how hard she rubbed, she
couldn't rid herself of the feel of his mouth, his breath
skimming along her skin, his tongue teasing her flesh.

*Within the walls of* London lay a great stone house surrounded by a high wall. It contained within it treasures
from Florence, Venice, Genoa, and Paris. Outside the
wall, guards paced, calling the hours of the night. One of
them strolled along the north wall and turned the corner.
As he vanished, something dark and lithe sped across the
cobbled street, scaled the wall, and leapt into the branches
of an ancient oak. Shadowy and silent, the cloaked man
shimmered down the tree trunk, across the grounds, and
to a door. He bent over the lock. It clicked, and the man
vanished inside.

The intruder glided quickly to the front of the house
and sailed upstairs to the third floor with the sureness of
familiarity. Slipping inside a pair of carved doors, he
slithered to an interior chamber. A page lay on a pallet

across the threshold. The figure paused, knocked the boy on the head with the hilt of a dagger, and stepped over the body.

Inside, a fire had died in the fireplace. The hangings on the bed were drawn, enclosing the owner of the house in warmth and privacy. The cloaked man drew them aside with one hand. Moving swiftly, he knelt on the edge of the bed and put his dagger to the throat of the man inside. There was a hiss of indrawn breath.

"Who are you?"

The dagger was withdrawn, the hangings shoved aside. The cloaked man lowered himself to sit on the edge of the bed.

"I have ridden without pause for days because of you, *mon ami. Bonsoir.*"

"Jean-Paul."

Jean-Paul's lip curled into a snarling smile. "Wyvern."

"You found them."

"I found them, and lost them."

"You lost them? How could you lose them? God's toes, they were only thieves."

"Wrong," Jean-Paul said. "They were much more than thieves and the abduction more than an abduction. They were noblemen; at least their leader was. This Savage is no savage at all, and no doubt serves the English queen. I had him until his minions attacked with hackbutts and routed my men. You're in trouble. *Le bon Dieu* only knows why I bothered to tell you, except that I must find him and kill him. He knows about me, and unless I misjudge him, he knows about you, or soon will."

The man in the bed sat up. "Who is he?"

"He is tall, with hair like wheat covered with dew and eyes like a New World sea. A man with the will and autocracy of a Roman god."

"Know you how many blond-haired, blue-eyed men there are in England?"

"Not like this one. He uses his sword with the skill of a fallen angel."

"I can think of at leave five men of such skill."

"Are they all quick-witted and capable of seducing Mistress Hunt?"

"Three men."

Jean-Paul leaned back on his arms and smiled at his host. "Which of them has a brother named Morgan?"

"Derry. Robin St. John, Lord Derry. Jesu preserve us." The man beside Jean-Paul made the sign against the evil eye. There was silence for long moments before he resumed. "Do you realize this man sups with the queen alone? Are you certain?"

"As it happens, I forced his name from him, and you have confirmed that he gave me his true one. *Sacré Dieu,* Lord Derry. How unfortunate for you."

The man launched himself at Jean-Paul. Grabbing the neck of his cloak and doublet, he forced the priest down on the bed on his back.

"And for you, my friend. If I'm to put my head on the block, I'll see to it that yours rolls to the ground before mine."

Jean-Paul smiled up at his captor, not bothering to try to free himself. "Be at ease. Why do you think I have come if not to rid the world of this golden-haired affliction? The Cardinal of Lorraine sent me to assist his niece in gaining the English throne. Lord Derry interferes with my task, and must be crushed."

The Wyvern lifted his weight slightly, but didn't release John-Paul. "And what of the woman?"

"You could have told me she was one of your intelligencers."

"She isn't."

"Then, *mon ami,* you have another enemy, and one who possesses the key to your cipher."

Again there was silence.

"It matters not. No one knows who I am. No names were used in the messages sent by her. The others can be warned, and then we will silence both of them. Where are they?"

"How could I know? I've been on my horse for days."

The Wyvern relaxed his grip on Jean-Paul. "I'll set inquiries afoot. You may rest while I search. When I find them, mayhap you'll turn your talents to conceiving a plan for killing them that won't create a furor."

# 15

*Great gifts are guiles and look for gifts again;*
*My trifles come as treasures from my mind.*

—ANONYMOUS

HE'D BEEN AT BRIDGESTONE Abbey for three days, stewing in his own pot of blended rage and lust. Derry stalked about his chamber. He prowled from one end to the other. Lord Hunt had given him Lady Hunt's chamber, and he lodged in drafty magnificence, surrounded by walls hung with Flemish tapestries and a plastered and gilded ceiling. Morgan lounged on the bed on his side with his gaze fixed on the carved tester. Inigo watched him as he paced about the room and looked ready to flee at the least sign of Derry's anger.

Derry stopped near the bed and glared at his brother. "Someone warned these men, the ounce and the triton and the others. We've watched the inns and taverns listed in the ciphers, and naught happened." Derry pointed at Morgan. "You're certain the Frenchman and his men fled north?"

"All the tracks I found headed north. I chased them to the border."

"Mayhap he circled around you and came south, to warn the traitors."

"It is possible," Morgan said, and turned to lay on his back and stare at the canopy supported by four heavy posts.

Derry stooped, knocked Morgan's crossed legs so that they fell apart, and sniped at his brother. "Lady Hunt was murdered in that bed."

Morgan glanced at the covers.

"They must have changed the sheets."

His lips curling into a smile, Derry resumed his stalking. "Lord Hunt removed all of his mother's possessions except the bed. I think he seeks to wipe out her influence by selling her petticoats and perfumes." He stopped by the chimney piece and touched the carved overmantel. It bore a scene of the Virgin and Christ Child. "Inigo, send for my players."

Inigo groaned. "Not them, my lord."

"And tell them they're to do the play of St. George and the dragon. But also tell them that they're to make certain changes in the dragon. They're to give it wings and two legs. It should be green with a red chest and belly, and red underwings."

"The Wyvern," Morgan said.

Derry turned his back to the chimney piece. "Tell them they're to perform the play in the yard of the White Hart Inn two nights hence."

Inigo left, and Morgan sat up on the bed.

"She still refuses to admit her guilt," Derry said.

"Marry, no doubt it's because there is none. Think. You'd had her locked up for many days. How would she know exactly where to meet the priest?"

"By prior arrangement."

"God's blood," Morgan said, "you've let the past color

your judgment. She's not your wife, Derry." He slipped off the bed. "Admit it. Your lust addled your wits, interfered with your reason, and you assumed treachery where there was none."

"And you see innocence where there is none. By the cross, Morgan, leave it."

"And let you use her to flush the Wyvern? I know what you're capable of, but I did think you'd learned a little charity for Mistress Hunt at least. When I saw her with the priest, she was trying to beat him off, not make love to him. And that's what pricks you, is it not? The thought that she might have welcomed him."

Derry cursed and headed for the door. "I don't make mistakes a second time. She's not to be trusted."

Leaving Morgan in the chamber, Derry crossed the house to the north wing. Ill fortune had pursued him since Thea had escaped. His luck had grown worse at Moorefield Garde. He had thought himself armored against any hurts she or his father might inflict. But he'd not counted on that scene in the garden. He'd followed Thea, suspicious of her, only to find himself a witness to a nightmare.

When his father had produced the poisoned pomander, he felt as if he'd left his body and was watching the scene from a great distance. Then his soul had grown numb, and he plopped back inside his body, void of feeling. Not even Thea's throwing the poison away had brought back his senses. Now there was a rock where his heart had been. For there had always been the hope before that Father would somehow see the truth.

He stopped at Thea's door. Thrusting it open, he entered her room without warning. She was still in her night rail. Since they'd arrived she had kept away from him by attending to neglected chores such as distilling rosewater and drying herbs. She looked up as he entered, then jumped from the chair, where she'd been huddled before a window. Hiding behind the chair, she ordered him to leave. He said nothing. Avoiding glancing at her body, he marched to a cupboard and pawed through gowns, sleeves, ruffs, and stomachers. Garments sailed out and landed on the floor around him. Thea stayed behind the chair.

"What mean you by this invasion, my lord? I shall call my father."

He found a gown suitable for town travel and threw it over his arm along with undergarments and a ruff. He approached Thea, tossed the garments at her, and laughed when a sleeve hit her in the face. She tore it from her head and threw it back at him.

"Dress," he said.

"What do you here? Why aren't you spying and creeping about the city, looking for traitors. Must I help you with that as well as the cipher? Get out."

He walked around the chair without responding, but she circled as he did. He stopped, cocked his head to the side, and surveyed her. In her anger she had forgotten her night rail. As she moved, it wrapped around her legs and drew tight so that he could see her legs and breasts through a film of white lawn.

"I like this new fashion of wearing gowns to bed," he murmured. "It tantalizes and provokes."

She looked down in the direction of his gaze, cried out, and scooped up the gown he'd thrown at her. Holding it in front of her, she snarled at him.

"Get out or I'll call my father."

"Your father is in a herbal fog. His new rosebushes arrived this morn, and he's choosing the planting spot for each. There are almost a hundred of them. Soon he's off to a fair to buy draft horses and pigs. He's forgotten I'm here at all."

"I'll remind him when I scream at him from my window."

He lunged at her. Reaching across the chair, he caught her arm and yanked her close. He crushed her to him, thankful that she was so stubborn and gave him the chance to touch her. For many nights now he'd longed to crawl all over her, rubbing his body against hers, and satisfying this appetite of which he longed to be rid. She scratched his neck. He wrapped his arms around her so that she couldn't lift her arms.

"'Never trust her at any time, when the calm sea shows her false alluring smile.' But then, I shouldn't compare you to a calm sea, a tempest, mayhap."

Breathing hard, she glared up at him. "I came to London. I've done my part."

Derry squeezed her, relishing the feel of her softness. "I'm the master player. Your part is what I wish it to be."

"When am I to be rid of you?"

"You know the answer. When I find the Wyvern."

"Then let us find him quickly, for that way I'll be rid of you the sooner."

He couldn't help chuckling any more than he could stop himself from brushing his lips down her neck. She twisted and writhed against his body.

"Release me." Her voice was ragged and breathless.

"When you promise to dress. You and I, Mistress Hunt, are going abroad in the city to shop."

Her mouth fell open. He couldn't help kissing her, but he drew back before she could bite him. He'd learned since his last attempt. After releasing her, he went out of the chamber but stuck his head back inside as she picked up a shoe and threw it at the door. It smacked against the frame, and he smiled.

"I'll send your maid. If you're not in the hall in an hour, I'll return and dress you myself. And, Thea *bella,* I can't promise that's all I'll do."

He waited in the hall, having asked Lord Hunt's permission to take Thea shopping, but he'd forgotten Ellen Dowgate. She appeared, capped and cloaked, with Thea close behind not half an hour after he'd left. He failed to notice her at first, for Thea had donned a gown of pale blue brocade that set off her night-black hair. He'd never seen such blackness. If the sun had turned black, it would have shone like her hair. He blinked, then chastised himself for losing track of his purpose. He looked down on Ellen Dowgate.

"Mistress Dowgate, we do not take a coach. I fear you will be discommoded. You remain at Bridgestone."

"I thank you for your courtesy, my lord, but Mistress Hunt does not go abroad without a companion. The grooms and gentleman usher await without."

He looked over Mistress Dowgate's head at Thea, but her eyes were cast down and she was stroking the folds of her gown. Her mouth curved in secret contentment, and he knew. She'd sent for Dowgate herself. He'd moved, and she had checked him. To whom would go the checkmate?

And so they rode into the city, he, the grooms and gentleman attendant, Ellen Dowgate, and Thea, lovely, black-haired, high-breasted Thea.

"Why don't you conduct your foul intrigues in your own house?" she asked, nearly spitting the words at him.

They were walking their horses out of the gates of Bridgestone Abbey. Outriders led the way, and Ellen Dowgate followed with the usher.

"Marry, lady, because you're at the cusp of this particular intrigue."

"And am I bait this afternoon?"

"Indeed. I'm going to parade you about the city so that every apprentice and duke knows you've been found."

"You'll be disappointed," she said. "This Wyvern cares not whether I'm in London or Hades, though I vow I've been in the latter since I met you."

He glanced at her, noting her flushed cheeks and snapping dark eyes. "It's only meet, since I have been there as well."

This time she met his gaze, but looked away quickly and reddened. They rode down the Strand to Fleet Street, and he could see the spires of London's churches, all except St. Paul's, which had been destroyed by lightning a few years before. He tried not to look at Thea again. Gazing upon her only made him want to bed her, despite his mistrust and anger. Thus he kept his gaze fastened on the road ahead.

Soon they had crossed the Fleet river, ridden through Ludgate and past St. Paul's. In the streets surrounding the church lay countless shops, those of waxchandlers, saddlers, drapers and mercers, cordwainers, coopers, and haberdashers. He led Thea to one of the more respectable streets. Its cobbles bore less litter, and the shops that lined it all had fresh plaster. Many boasted glass windows.

He dismounted and helped Thea. He grinned at the way she tried not to let her body touch his as he swung her down from her horse. While the grooms watched the horses, he paraded her down the street past four drapers' shops with their servants and Ellen Dowgate forming a train behind. Gallants and apprentices stepped out of their way, as did two water carriers bearing a wooden barrel on a pole. The hour was well past noon, and guild members and students alike hurried on their various errands.

They turned a corner. He saw a cart of wool, gripped Thea by the shoulders, and shoved her against a table in front of a ruffmaker's shop as its wheel splashed into a puddle. Muddy drops splattered around them, and they both ducked their heads. He stepped back, looked at her, and laughed. She scowled at him. He touched the tip of her nose and showed her the splotch of mud on his fingertip. Ellen Dowgate groaned behind them. She hadn't ducked in time, and now she wore a coat of slime. Her hair, already the same color as the mud, clung to her head, and her soggy ruff had wilted.

Hiding a smirk, Derry handed her several gold coins. "By my troth, Mistress Dowgate, you must forgive me for not giving warning. I insist that you go to that inn down the street and cleanse yourself. You"—he pointed to the gentleman usher—"go to that draper with Mistress Dowgate. She will need something to wear, if only a new cloak."

He'd been right. A glint appeared in Ellen's eyes as she rubbed the coins between her fingers. He watched her waver between duty and avarice. Avarice won, and Ellen Dowgate vanished with the remainder of their attendants.

Thea was looking at him suspiciously. He grabbed her hand, placed it on his arm, and resumed their walk. He glanced down at her, but his eye caught the shine of gold at her waist. He looked down at her skirt and saw the gold pomander, his father's deadly gift. Cursing, he launched into a swift walk. Thea protested, but he dragged her after him, turned down another street, and plunged into a shop past a startled apprentice on guard at the door.

Thea skittered in after him. Coming to an abrupt halt, he caught her as she bumped into him.

"Unthank!" he shouted.

Heads turned. The jeweler's shop held several satin- and brocade-clad customers. He glared at them all. A fat alderman and his wife left hurriedly while a middle-aged noblewoman and her gentleman companion turned and glared at him. Behind the wooden counter laden with treasures displayed for the noblewoman, an assistant gaped at Derry, excused himself, and disappeared into the workshop at the back of the building.

Thea had caught her breath. "You've the manners of a toad as well as the principles."

He met her gaze with as nasty a sneer as he could manage, but she only sneered back at him. So he bent, took hold of the gold chain that held the pomander and yanked it from her waist. She cried out, but he gathered it in his fist and shook it at her.

"You'll not wear this again."

"I will!" She grabbed for it, but he held it out of her reach. "I like it. It's beautiful, and——" She suddenly stopped trying to retrieve the pomander. Closing her mouth, she clasped her hands and lifted her chin. "Very well. I see you've taken to highwaymen's ways again."

She turned her back on him and would have left the shop if he hadn't snagged her arm and held her. They were scowling at each other when the shopkeeper returned with another man.

"My lord."

Derry left off the battle of mean looks. "Unthank. Here." He dropped the pomander in the jeweler's hand. "I like not this bauble and wish to purchase something else for my lady."

Unthank's brows climbed his forehead, but he refrained

from staring at Thea. He bowed, then conducted them upstairs to a room bright with sunlight from windows that looked out on the street. His assistant produced several wooden caskets and a flat, thick box. Derry led Thea to the only chair in the room and shoved her into it. She tried to rise, but he placed his hands on her shoulders and pushed her down again. He leaned over her and whispered.

"Peace, woman. I know you don't wish to accept a new one."

"Not from you."

He sighed, knelt at her feet, and continued in even lower tones than before. "I wish to make recompense—for Ravensmere, and—and the pit."

Thea turned her head to the side and appeared to be studying the window. He barely caught the slight nod of her head. He signaled to Unthank and his assistant, who had retreated to a far corner.

Unthank took the flat box from his assistant, held it before Thea, and opened it. Inside, on a lining of black velvet, lay seven pomanders of gold and silver. Thea had been glaring at Derry, but when Unthank opened the box, her gaze flew to it. He was surprised when her eyes widened to the size of plums. He heard her suck in her breath. He looked at the pomanders, but could see nothing that would elicit such wonder.

As he studied her, Thea slowly put out her hand and touched one of the pomanders, a gold one. It wasn't the most costly. It had no jewels at all while the others bore amethysts, diamonds, and pearls. Indeed, it was smaller than the rest, but for her it might well have been the only object in the box. Her fingers touched it lightly, then drew back as if it were hot.

Derry frowned and studied the pomander. Of gold

filigree, it was the size of a pigeon's egg. He leaned closer and saw that the gold work was in the pattern of ivy vines—tiny, veined, intricate. He should have guessed. Plants again. She loved plants far more than any object contrived by man.

He caught Unthank's eye and nodded. The jeweler produced a ball of ambergris perfume and slipped it inside the pomander. Next he conjured up dozens of chains. Derry selected one, and Unthank attached the pomander to it.

Derry picked up the resulting girdle and held it out to Thea. She stared at the pomander, then up at him and shook her head. Derry sighed, pulled her to her feet. Reaching around her, he fastened the chain to her waist.

Thea seemed to have lost her voice. She picked up the golden ball that hung from her waist and held it in both her palms. A smile filled with the sweetness of summer mornings spread over her face, and Derry felt the rock his heart had become begin to heat like an ingot in a furnace. Nonsense. One little smile couldn't burn away granite.

Then she looked up at him, bathing him with that summertime smile, and a painful knot formed at the base of his throat. The smile faltered. Her cheeks grew pink, and she looked away from him. She searched the room. He did as well, and found that Unthank and his man had left. He heard a little whisper.

"I have seldom received gifts. Father rarely remembers to . . . and Grandmother never . . . Why have you given me this?"

She was looking at him in wonder, but as he watched her, he saw the distrust fighting with the wonder. He was the one who had a right to distrust. He looked over her head at the bright windowpanes with their diamond shapes.

"Marry, Thea *bella*," he said quietly, "don't ask. When we speak, we quarrel. But accept the gift and ask no questions. I weary of battles."

His wits were frying in a saucepan. He quit the chamber before he spouted any more foolish prattle. She joined him below, and they were about to leave the shop when the noblewoman who had glared at them spoke.

"Thea? Mistress Thea Hunt!"

The woman stood, and they were forced to join her.

"You've returned," the woman said. "We thought you dead, child."

"My lady," Thea said. "No, I was abducted by—by a highwayman."

He finished for her. "And I plucked her from his clutches. The dowager Countess of Lynford, is it not?"

"Lord Derry," the woman said as she offered her cheek to be kissed. "To think that our courtly, dancing, amorous Derry vanquished a band of thieves and ruffians. I stand amazed."

He listened while the countess babbled questions at Thea. The more she was questioned, the more flustered Thea became. The woman looked Thea up and down as she would a lame horse. He could read her thoughts. An abducted woman was ruined, shamed woman. No doubt she thought Thea should have hidden herself away to conceal her dishonor. For the first time he felt a twinge of remorse. Thea would suffer from his treatment of her for the rest of her life.

"And for shame, Thea," the countess said. "You're prancing about the streets of London with a young man. Your grandmother would have fits."

"Indeed, my lady," he said. He would have liked to kick her. "Were it not that Mistress Hunt is soon to be my wife."

This remark produced an explosion of queries, but Derry managed to answer them without answering, a skill he'd learned from her majesty Queen Elizabeth. At last the countess summoned her escort, who had been talking with Unthank.

The man came forward, arms laden with packages. He was a stranger to Derry. The countess introduced him as Timothy Eyre, a friend of both the Earl of Lynford and dear Lady Hunt. A velvet cap covered his thin hair, and he appeared to be wearing most of the jewels in Unthank's shop on various parts of his clothing and body.

"Well met, Mistress Hunt," he said. "We all pray for your grandmother, and for you as well."

Timothy Eyre appeared to be in a hurry. He jostled past Derry with his load of packages without taking his leave. The countess said her good-byes with more decorum before she, too, quit the shop. He faced Thea.

"Two of your cohorts?"

"Two friends of my grandmother's."

"Then we progress."

She shook her head. "I see it not, my lord. My grandmother had many acquaintances. It was one of the reasons I was happier in the country. I like not crowds and meaningless carousing. Why do you think I refused the countess's invitation?"

"What invitation?"

"She asked us to a banquet three days hence. Said it would take my thoughts from the loss of my grandmother."

"We will attend."

"We will not! We can search for the Wyvern without going to cursed banquets."

He sighed and escorted her out of the shop. Standing outside, he held up a hand when she would have spoken.

"God's shroud, Thea, no arguments. I wish to go, and we will go. Marry, you would think by now you would have learned to obey me."

"Cease your prattling of obedience. I'll do what I must for England, even if I must suffer your persecutions."

Derry put a hand over his heart. "Saints! Has she decided to comply? I stand amazed. Thea Hunt has decided to become a loyal subject instead of conspire with traitors."

She turned her back on him. Before he could catch her she had marched down the street. The crowds of merchants, apprentices, shoppers, and laborers swallowed her. He shouldered his way after her, but she turned a corner, and he lost sight of her.

By the time he rounded the corner she was halfway down the street and approaching the courtyard of an inn. The sounds of banging and clashing metal came to him, and he called out to Thea. She didn't hear him. She marched on, eyes directed straight ahead. As he charged after her, he saw a crowd spill out of the courtyard and into the street, right into Thea's path. She stopped short as three rag-tag gallants tumbled over one another in a drunken melee with onlookers cheering and jeering at them. The crowd surged around Thea, and she vanished.

Derry shouted her name and broke into a run. As he bounced off a corn chandler and shoved a student aside, he caught sight of the inn sign. Swinging from a bar over the street, brightly painted wood gleamed in the sunlight. A red deer crowned with a rack of horns stared out at him, the symbol of the inn—the White Hart Inn.

# 16

*Take me to thee and thee to me.*
*"No, no, no, no, my dear, let be."*

—SIR PHILIP SYDNEY

SHE'D BEEN SO FURIOUS at Derry that she hadn't paid any heed to the noise coming from the inn. When the men rolled and tumbled into the street in front of her, she scuttled backward to avoid flying fists. As she stared at the snarled mass of legs and arms, people surged around her and shouted encouragement at the brawlers. A merchant knocked her aside in his haste to get a better view. She fell against a gallant in tattered velvet. He caught her, and she smelled cheap beer.

"Good morrow, mistress," the man said.

Thea coughed and turned her head away from the fumes rolling toward her. Shoving free, she tripped over the shoe of an apprentice while jeers and shouts rang in her ears. A hand shot out from the midst of closely packed bodies and grabbed her skirt. She was yanked off her feet.

Landing on hands and knees, she looked up to see Derry glaring at her. She gathered her feet under her as merchants and students surged around them. He was looking at her with that displeased-Roman-god look of his, hands planted on his hips. She began to rise, and as she did, she saw a knife behind Derry.

She never recalled much of the next few moments. She remembered a rusty knife, and brown teeth in a face that had never seen water or soap. The knife descended, aiming for Derry's back. She cried out and sprang. While still in the air she grabbed the arm below the knife. Derry turned. The knife sliced through his sleeve, and he cried out.

A fist knocked her head. She lost her grip on the arm and sat down hard on the cobblestones. There was a struggle above her head. She watched a sea of legs, heard a yelp. The legs receded, and Derry knelt in front of her. She was holding her head and trying to see something besides specks of dancing light. Her hands were pushed aside. He covered her eyes. Touching her cheek with his palm, he snarled at the onlookers nearby.

"Get you gone."

She squeezed her eyes shut, pulled his hands from her face, and opened her eyes again. His brilliant hair appeared, then worried blue eyes. The upper sleeve of his doublet had been sliced, and he was bleeding. She pressed her fingers to her temples, then tried to rise. He helped her stand and kept a hand under her arm.

"He hit me," she said. She felt it important for him to know.

Derry laughed. "He won't be hitting anyone else for months."

"On my head," she added to make herself clear.

She blinked at him several times. He studied her, then picked her up. She floated along the streets, content to observe the passing shops. It grew dark, and then she noticed the cause. They'd returned to the shop of the man called Unthank. She floated into a chair. Someone held a cup of wine to her lips. She sipped, then coughed and moaned. A cold wet cloth pressed against her forehead. Derry's voice wafted at her from above.

"Try to take deep breaths. God's toes, why did you spring at him? Why?"

She pressed her forehead against the hand that held the cloth and sighed at Derry's slowness. "Because he was going to kill you, of course."

There was silence. Thea decided she liked having her head bathed with a cool cloth. She sighed again. The cloth disappeared and she protested. Derry dropped to his knees before her.

"You would have been rid of me."

Suddenly rousing from her waking dream, Thea sat upright in the chair. "Unlike you, sirrah, I am not a murderer. If I were, I would have used your father's powder. Remember?"

He was staring at her still. She wished he wouldn't for his gaze bored into her like an iron spike into a tree, gouging out her secrets. Odd, since she hadn't concealed her hatred of him. She must have more courage, though she would rather run away than face that stare. She detested the way he could make her feel like a rabbit fleeing hounds. He had but to fix her with that devil's glance. And all the while she had to watch that body, that body that looked as if he swam miles each day just to make it lean and sculpted with muscles over the ribs—

She must have been hit terribly hard. She couldn't want this man. She couldn't. He was talking to her while she'd been lost in a lascivious dream.

She wet her lips. "What say you?"

He stood and folded his arms. "It's near a saint, you are, to save my life when you would rather end it."

"It was my Christian duty."

"Duty," he repeated.

She waited, but he appeared to be distracted by his own thoughts. He was staring at her again, and as the moments went by, his gaze changed. She wasn't sure how it changed, but gradually she realized that the threat in it had faded. Like embers smothered by a heavy mist, the anger dwindled. Then the embers glowed again, seeming to breathe, turn red and then gleam white.

"Thea *bella*."

The words were one long caress. She heard the deep tone—and fled. She rushed out of the shop and bumped into Ellen Dowgate.

"Mistress Hunt! Your gown." Ellen gawked at her rumpled and dirty gown, her mussed hair.

Derry appeared at the door, leaned on it, and grinned.

"I——I was jostled by a rowdy mob by the inn," Thea said. "Come, we must go home." She lifted her skirts and began to walk down the street in search of their servants and horses.

"Mistress Hunt."

Coming toward her from a haberdasher's shop, decked in brocade and a feathered cap, was Lord Gracechurch. Thea cursed her misfortune, then set her face in a pleased expression and accepted the man's greeting. She listened to his exclamations over her appearance while trying not to stare at his melon-like girth and flapping cheeks.

"Ruffians," Gracechurch was saying. "Cutpurses, louts, and ruffians in the streets day and night in spite of the watch. And you say they got away? Where are your servants, mistress?"

"I am her chief servant, my lord."

Gracechurch swung his belly around to face Derry, who had approached from the street. Derry sidestepped the paunch, which jiggled like custard.

"St. John," Gracechurch said.

Thea corrected him. "Derry."

More explanations, more exclamations on Gracechurch's part, more assessing looks from Derry. After courtly bows and protests of regret at not having the honor of his company, they were on their way once more. He didn't speak to her, but saw that she was mounted when they found their horses. Soon they were on the road home with Ellen trailing after them.

During the journey Thea had time to speculate upon her adventures. They'd been in the city little more than an hour before nearly coming to grief. Had the scuffle in front of the inn been a happenstance?

"Are all your friends papists?" Derry asked.

She gave him a disgusted look. "Gracechurch, the Lynfords, Eyre, they're my grandmother's friends, as you well know."

"And let us not forget the priest, who is much more than a priest and much more than a friend."

"God's patience!" Thea reined in her horse, reached across, and pulled on Derry's as well. Their whole party came to a halt. "I'll not endure your accusations, nor will I defend myself against them or beg forgiveness for transgressions I haven't committed. And another thing, have you noticed how dangerous it is for us to shop? Sometimes I marvel you've kept yourself alive so long."

Derry put his arm on his knee and leaned toward her. "You'll obey me nonetheless."

"I hate you."

"Do you?"

To her consternation, he laughed and patted the neck of his stallion. "Marry, I bid you hate me in such fashion as much as you will, for your hatred stirs me, Thea *bella,* so much that I begin to think you mistake yourself."

"You babble, sirrah."

"Mayhap you mistake the blaze of desire for this hatred of which you speak so often."

Her mouth worked. She opened it. She closed it. She stuttered.

"I'd—I'd as soon fall enamored of a—a plague-ridden, hairless rat."

Instead of becoming enraged, he sat there, at ease on that murderous stallion, and chuckled softly, as if he were in some woman's withdrawing chamber. "A cat in heat, squalling and scratching."

"Narcissus," she snapped. "In love with his own reflection."

He stopped chuckling then, to her satisfaction. He nudged his mount close to hers and whispered.

"Enough, you foul-tempered little shrew."

"You began it."

He groaned, then shook his head as if to clear it. "Peace, peace, woman. I know where such quarrels will lead us, if you do not. And I've no wish for such distraction when it could cost us our lives. Will you give me a truce?"

"A truce with a highwayman?" She sniffed. "To think you pretended not to know letters. You even told me the word 'Gracechurch' was too long. Does it please you to make me play the fool?"

He grinned at her. "Your face. When I said that, it was a sight, by the rood. No, now, don't loose that temper on my head again. I admit I might have played my part too well. Let us have the past behind us for now. Do we have a truce until our business is finished?"

"You mean until you're finished playing the spy in my father's house and finished trying to kill people and finished using me like a piss—"

"God's bones, woman! Do we have an agreement or not?"

"Yes, we have an agreement. If it means we find the traitors quick, and that you'll quit my presence forever once you've done intelligencing."

She waited for his answer. His gaze ran from her face, down her throat to her breasts, and then cascaded down her legs.

"Done," he said softly.

*That night she slept* heavily. Mayhap it was because of doing battle with Derry from morn until dark. Mayhap it was because seeing him at dinner, laughing and talking with her father, caused her to down more wine than was her custom. Her stomach contents turned to acid when she perceived that Derry was one of the few people who could draw her father out of his world of animals and herbs, draw him out and hold his attention for more than a quarter of an hour. Only she had ever been able to accomplish such a feat.

The ease with which Derry charmed Lord Hunt rankled. And the more rankled she felt, the more wine she drank. She'd weaved her way to bed as soon as she'd been able to excuse herself. In spite of her tipsy state, she'd lain sleepless. Try as she would, she failed to banish images of Derry. There was one particular image of his face, one in which he looked at once drowsy and yet fevered, his sunlight hair damp, his lips parted as though he'd just been kissed.

To ward off such visions, she'd thought about the web of treason surrounding her grandmother. Derry suspected everyone of plotting with this mysterious Wyvern. He suspected the dowager Countess of Lynford, Timothy

Eyre, the Earl of Lynford, Lord Gracechurch. He even suspected poor Ellen Dowgate.

She thought about Gracechurch. Could spies be pompous? A pig's belly and the manner of a fool would be the perfect guise for an intelligencer. The Earl of Lynford had the wits for intrigue, but a gentle and sorrowful nature that would make a poor spy. What of Timothy Eyre? Mayhap his Italian blood had given him a taste for spying. No, more like it would give him a brilliant mind. Timothy Eyre had no brilliance at all aside from his jewels. Of course, there was always the dowager Countess of Lynford. Thea had drifted into sleep, trying to imagine the busybody countess writing ciphers.

A buzzing in her head woke her—the effects of the wine. The bed hangings were drawn, and the chill air told her it was still night. She shoved the velvet folds aside and retrieved a cup of water. Draining it, she set it down and reached for the hangings to pull them back into place. A hand clasped her wrist. She squeaked, but another hand clamped over her mouth and a body loomed over her. She was shoved down on the bed and crushed beneath a long, hard body.

"Shhh. You'll wake everyone."

The hand on her mouth lifted, and she tried to scream. Derry clamped his hand back on her mouth. She felt his lips on her ear.

"Quiet," he breathed.

He lifted his hand, and she cursed him.

"Foul wretch. Get off me."

She tried to kick him, but the movement caused him to fall between her legs. He made a deep male-pleasure sound and thrust his hips into hers.

"Thea *bella*, we've other tasks this night, but if you keep offering yourself, I'll accept."

She filled her lungs so that she could scream, and he fastened his mouth on hers. The air rushed out between their lips, and she felt him smiling as he drove his tongue into her mouth. She began to kick again.

"Thea, listen. I mean no—uuugh!" His body jerked as her foot jabbed near his groin. "Damn you."

She barely heard him. Her body craved his, and she couldn't let him know. She wriggled, trying to burrow out from beneath him, but he only rubbed his body against hers.

"Don't," he said, but she knew he was lying. She could feel the heat of his response to her.

His voice sank until he was barely whispering. "God help me."

He trapped her arms against the bed, holding them with one hand while he caressed her with the other. There was a bulge in the leather that covered his hips. It nudged her between her thighs. She began to tingle.

All she had to do was forget. She could forget, for a few moments. She went still, then allowed him to shove her legs apart with his knees. She felt his fingers at her nipple, pinching and tugging. Then his lips replaced his fingers, which brushed their way down to the juncture of her thighs. A hot ache grew. Her flesh responded as he tongued his way down her body, kissed her. Then his mouth touched the place where his fingers had played, and she was jolted out of her sensual daze. She sank her hands in his hair and yanked. He almost cried out, then swore and tore her hands from his head.

He lunged at her, driving her body into the mattress, trapping her once more. She scratched his neck as she tried to free herself, biting and kicking. He subdued her by forcing her arms behind her back and lying on top of her. She couldn't move. Breathing hard, she lay beneath him and spat curses. She couldn't see him in the darkness, but she could feel his hands on her wrists, his legs pressing against hers, his hips butting against her own.

"It seems I must needs teach you the cost of teasing, Thea *bella*."

"No. I'll scream for my father."

The black shadow on top of her laughed softly. "And he'll have us married before dawn."

Her jaw clamped shut. She could suffer for a few minutes, or the rest of her life. She felt her night rail draw tight. He held her still with one hand while he tugged at the neck of the gown gently. Then he carefully ripped the lawn from her neck to her feet. One side of her body was bared. She shivered, then stifled a cry as she felt something brush her nipple. He had taken a feathery scrap of lawn between his fingers and was lightly brushing her breast with it.

"Teasing is an art, Thea *bella*. One I learned long ago."

She bit her lip, fearful of bringing a worse revenge on herself. The lawn skimmed in circles on her breast, then feathered down her ribs, touched between her legs, vanished. She let out her breath in relief, only to catch it again when his mouth fastened on her nipple. He sucked gently, then almost painfully, toying and playing with it with his tongue. His teeth grazed the hardening tip.

She was hot and cold at the same time. Finding her tongue, she began to protest only to have her words smothered by his mouth. His body shifted to the side, but his weight was still on her. She yelped into his mouth when she felt his fingers pinch her nipple and then move to the joining of her thighs. Light, teasing caresses, fingers playing, rubbing, plucking, then stopping to torment her nipples only to return again to their fondling until she nearly screamed with the ache between her legs. Desperation built until she longed for release. At last she felt his lips at her ear.

"You like my mouth, don't you, Thea the tease?"

He held her still, then touched her with his tongue. Thea heard her own rapid breathing. Heat suffused her body, burned away thoughts as he bathed her swollen flesh with his tongue, caressed it with his lips. When his mouth sucked at her, she did cry out, and found that her arms were free. She dug her fists into the covers, certain that she'd gone mad from the avalanche of swollen, aching torment. Her resolve breaking, she released the covers, slipped her arms under his, and pulled him up to ride between her legs.

Disregarding his quiet laughter, she yanked at the ties at his hips. Her hand touched rigid flesh. Derry caught her hands and shoved them above her head. He spread her legs with his, arched his body. She felt him nudge her, slide inside. Now she ached worse than ever, and he just lay there. She could feel him, ripe and swollen, but he didn't move. She tried to lift her hips, but he pushed her down and kept her there.

"The price of the tease," he murmured.

She lost track of the minutes. Just as she was about to scream again, he began to nibble at her breasts. Soon her nipples grew erect and the tingling between her legs increased. Still, he wouldn't move inside her. Then he lifted his body, slipped his hand between them to the place where they joined, and began to caress her. She lifted her hips, pressing against his hand, spreading her legs wider. When she arched her back, he withdrew his hand, trapped her arms again, and lowered his body on top of her.

This time he moved. Withdrawing slowly, he lifted his hips until he was barely inside her. He stopped again, so that she felt only the tip of him at her entrance, felt her own body quivering around it. He held himself still, his legs forcing hers apart and immobile. She waited while her body filled with the buzzing of mad wasps. His whisper came to her in the darkness.

"Are you a tease, Thea *bella*?"

She gritted her teeth as he nudged her.

"Say it."

"C-can't compare to you."

She heard him chuckle softly. His arms slid under her hips. He lifted them off the bed and drove inside her slowly, pausing, driving, pausing, driving. Their hips met, and he pulled himself back in a prolonged, lingering withdrawal. When he was almost out, he stopped again. Thea had to bite her lower lip to keep from protesting. His fingers touched her, danced over her flesh, parted her even wider. While he held her open, he began to insert himself again delicately, as if he had an eternity to enter her.

Without warning, as soon as he rested between her legs again, he pulled free. She cried out. Her arms came up. She clutched him, found his shoulders. Her nails dug into his flesh. His hands pressed her thighs apart, and she felt his sex brush her lightly, teasingly, so that she tried to lift her hips in response. He held her still with both hands and teased her with his body for a few moments.

He stopped again only to shove her roughly on her side. Lying behind her, he aligned his body with hers. Before she quite realized that she was free, he snaked an arm beneath her and wrapped it around her waist. Pushing his leg between hers, he slid his hand between them and cupped her. She flailed at him. Somehow she needed her hands on his body. She found his thigh and ran her hand up and down it. He paid no attention, but moved his hand from her waist to tweak her nipple while his other hand fondled her. She gasped and tore at the sheets, digging deep into the mattress.

This time he didn't stop. His hand kept her roused and writhing while he gradually moved so that he was pressing against her entrance. Suddenly his hands lifted her hips, and she felt him shove into her from behind. Cupping her flesh, he began to move at last. Driving up inside her, he worked back and forth, pumping slowly while his hands teased.

She felt him ramming his way home, pulling back, shoving inside. The tingling ache built. Her flesh ached with unsatisfied lust. She thrust her hips back against the flesh that prodded her, bucking wildly. His head sank to her shoulder. She felt his teeth grazing her skin as he cried out and thrust hard. Her flesh exploded while he held her against his own, and she felt him spear her over and over.

He shoved home one last time, holding her open as he sought his release. Then he allowed her to close her legs. Breathing in gulps, he settled on her, his leg draped over her, his arm circled beneath her breasts.

Thea lay beneath him, unable to move or prevent him from playing with her breasts as he recovered. Dazed, she could hardly summon the strength to move. She shivered at the thought of her own madness and at the way he had evoked it without effort. He had tricked her again. Dear God, he was a sorcerer. What else but evil enchantment could explain such power allied with such beauty?

She tried to move away from him. His arm tightened under her breasts and he thrust deeper inside her.

"Let me go," she said. "Haven't you used me enough?"

"Used?"

She felt his mouth on her neck.

"Used?" he said. "God's blood, is that the way you reason? Marry, I swear I've been used this night as well.

Who unlaced me and near scratched me with her nails, trying to put me inside her?"

She kicked backward and missed. Cursing, he slipped out of her, turned her to face him. Trapping her in his arms, he chuckled.

"Are we to fight again? Consider it well, Mistress Hunt, for you've just paid the price of our last quarrel."

Thea relinquished her useless struggle. She forced back the tears that gathered behind her eyes. "You did this apurpose, to torment me because I won't fawn at your feet, you vain satyr."

He didn't answer. She lay in his arms, hoping he wasn't going to begin his horrible, pleasureful teasing again. Finally he responded.

"In truth, Thea *bella,* I had no thought of taking you when I woke you."

His words alone wouldn't have convinced her. What made her believe him was the bewildered surprise in his voice.

"Then what do you want?" she asked.

"Mayhap I know not, Thea *bella.* Mayhap I never did."

*Where reason loathes, there fancy loves,*
*And overrules the captive will . . .*

—ROBERT SOUTHWELL

DERRY LIT A LAMP from the night candle in Thea's chamber and returned to the bed. He set the candle on a nearby table. Sinking down on the mattress, he regarded her while she wrapped a sheet about her body. Rousing himself from lustful memories, he set about restoring order to his own clothing. His hands trembled with the stirring of another bout of lust for her and tangled in the lacings of his codpiece.

"God's blood!" He yanked a finger free of a knot.

Thea brushed his hands aside, worked the knot, straightened the laces. He clenched his jaw and hissed at her.

"Let me be, woman. If you handle me much more, I'm going to lose all governance and we'll never get out of this bed."

She released him, and he made himself take several deep breaths before finishing the chore.

"Why did you do this to me?"

He glanced up from his work. She was gazing at him sorrowfully, her shining hair tousled over her shoulders, her lips swollen and red from kissing. God's blood! It was she who had done something to him. He bent to the floor to cover his frustration and confusion and fished about for his belt and dagger.

"Despite your opinion of me, I rarely invade women's chambers without invitation. If you had listened to me instead of trying to kick your foot through my gut, if you hadn't . . ." He tightened his belt around his waist while he searched for a word. "If you hadn't wriggled and, and—"

"You attacked me," she said with indignation.

"And moved!" He couldn't use any of the words he knew to describe what she'd done to him. She wouldn't understand them in any case. Driven past all courtly manners, he shoved her with each word that snapped through his lips. "You—wouldn't—listen."

She jumped each time he shoved her and finally fell on her bottom. Propping herself up on both hands, she stared at him through strands of gleaming black hair.

"Mean you that you came for another purpose?" Her voice sank to a whisper. "You didn't come to make sport of me, or to, to laugh at me for my—for the way I . . ."

Furrowing his brow, Derry tried to make sense of the timid half-sentences. Enlightenment burst upon him, and along with it shame. He rubbed his face and sighed, then took her hand.

"Thea *bella*, when I make love to you, that is what I am doing. Evil tricks have no place in what I feel for you. Marry, woman, when I touch you, I've no sense at all, or I would never have touched you from the first. Our dealings are so tangled."

She looked down at their joined hands. "I wish I could trust you."

"I wish I could trust you as well."

Freeing her hand, Thea brushed her hair back from her face. "What do you here?"

"I wanted you to come with me to meet someone."

"Now? Whom should I meet at such an hour?"

"Master Secretary Cecil. I thought if you spoke with him of your grandmother, he might gain some insight into this tangle of conspiracies. It's too late, thanks to your ungovernable passions."

"I am not the one with ungovernable passions. I am the one who likes not being pounced upon in her own bed."

"I did not pounce," Derry said as he slid off the bed and stood looking at her. "Tomorrow afternoon we go to a play of St. George and the dragon at the White Hart Inn."

She was no more eager to dwell upon the results of his pouncing on her than he was, so she nodded.

"I've been thinking about Timothy Eyre and some of the others," she said. "Timothy longs to be a great lord."

"Play bills have been sent to all your grandmother's friends."

"The Countess of Lynford has her own company of players. She won't come."

"Wear a mask as befits a lady," he said. "My betrothed mustn't be ogled by ruffians and bawds."

"The countess was grandmother's dear friend."

"You will watch the play from the gallery overlooking the inn yard."

"And she and Lord Gracechurch sent money to poor Catholic families in the North to provide for secret mass. Lord Anthony Clark helped."

"Morgan and Stubb will escort you."

"The Earl of Lynford watched his father die under the

headsman's sword on Tower Green. His father died at the order of the queen's father when he wouldn't recognize the king as head of the church instead of the pope. Grand-mother had many friends, but these are chief among them."

"Mistress Dowgate may come as well."

"Timothy Eyre is half Italian, and therefore Catholic."

He studied her bare shoulders. "And you, Thea *bella*, are half witch."

*Unlike the Bald Pelican,* a tavern frequented by the vulgar, cheap, and disreputable, the White Hart Inn had a reputation for courting the custom of gentlemen. Tim-bered, plastered, and glassed, it seldom endured indigni-ties such as the brawl of the previous day. That afternoon its patrons were to be entertained by a play concerning St. George and the dragon.

All day, pot boys and stable hands had been laboring to erect a stage consisting of planks set upon barrels at one end of the inn yard. A curtain hung at the back of this stage, painted and gilded to resemble a fantasy of moun-tains and clouds. Already the best seats in the galleries surrounding the yard had been reserved for gentlefolk and a few noble customers. The common crowd would stand in the yard. Already students and apprentices jostled each other for the best places, and quarrels broke out among these two traditional enemies.

Behind the curtain Derry watched as a group of blue-cloaked apprentices rushed a line of students in black. At his back and up one story in the first gallery the players wrestled with the papier-mâché dragon. Oofer Small stood with his legs thrust into hollow dragon feet while others tied a long dragon's tail to his waist.

Derry glanced up and over his shoulder and scowled. "I

told you red. The dragon's belly was to be red, not pink."

The player scratched his head. "Ran out o' red, my lord. Had to make do with thinning it."

"And the snout's askew," Derry said as he regarded the creature's head resting at Oofer's feet.

"He's snarling, my lord. See them teeth, them great yellow teeth? And look at them claws. Iron, that's what they are. Painted them silver so's the audience can see good." Oofer slipped his arms in the dragon arms and took a swipe at the air. A player dressed as the king ducked.

Derry threw up his hands as Oofer extolled the beauties of his dragon. A tall form loped by him in a dress. Derry groaned.

"Foxe."

The boy in the dress turned, gathered the bright yellow skirts in both fists, and stomped over to Derry.

"Foxe, you can't play the king's daughter. You're too tall. Saints, you must have grown a foot since last spring."

Foxe clapped a scarlet wig on his head, pursed his lips, and blew a kiss to Derry. The impression was spoiled by the deep voice issuing from painted lips.

"Got nobody else, my lord. Will's come down with an ague and can't speak lines for sneezing. Nice armor." Foxe marveled at Derry's chain mail.

"It's been in the family for a long time. Stubb polished it." Derry swept aside his white cloak with its red cross to reveal gleaming silver.

Foxe grinned and tugged on his lopsided wig. "You haven't joined us in months, my lord. We missed you."

"And I you. Marry, I'd have preferred my players to the hospitality of France, you may be sure. Now, get on with you."

Shaking his head, Derry watched Foxe slouch away. He hoped the lad could raise his voice an octave when he screamed for help. Oofer had donned the last of his dragon regalia and was shambling along the gallery. He would descend halfway downstairs and leap the rest of the way through the curtain and onto the stage. Oofer waved silver claws at him.

Derry waved back and moved to the spot where the backdrop met the side of the inn to wait for the play to begin. The yard and galleries were full now. He glanced at the stairs, the roof, the corners of the yard. Inigo and his men were dispersed around the inn so that they could watch for any of old Lady Hunt's friends. In the second gallery he found Thea. He could have recognized her despite the mask that covered the upper portion of her face, for her hair was a black jewel unlike the dull tresses of other women. She'd promised to survey the crowd for anyone who looked familiar. Ellen Dowgate and Stubb stood behind her.

Morgan also stood near Thea, but not so near that she appeared to be in his charge. Should anyone approach her, he would see them. Morgan had taunted him for setting him such a useless task. Should any traitors be discomforted by the play, he'd said, they would certainly not reveal it to the guileless Thea.

Thea had agreed with Morgan, and summoned another objection, a fanciful one.

"You're the one in danger," she had said before they left. "Who has a cut on his arm? Not I. I vow that priest has come after us and even now seeks your death. But have you given the possibility any thought at all? No, you spend your time dragging me to shops and silly plays."

He winced as he remembered how hard Morgan had laughed.

The play began. His players created a happy kingdom, kindly king, and his beautiful daughter. Then came the invasion of the terrible dragon. Oofer swooped down upon the stage with acrobatic vigor and attacked the players. The kingdom lay in waste. The dragon demanded tribute, and its people sacrificed their livestock to the dragon. Finally there were no more cattle or sheep, and the people drew lots to select a sacrifice. The king's daughter was selected.

Derry winced as Foxe's voice broke and his laments issued forth in a baritone. He recovered quickly, and the king stepped forth. Sinking to his knees, he prayed.

"Almighty God, I pray you send aid, for we are desolate. Send aid against this foul worm, this loathsome beast, this bloody wyvern!"

Derry drew his sword. It, too, had been polished for the occasion. Outside, the crowd hissed as the king's men bound the princess to a stake. Oofer had retreated behind the curtain and made a circuit after his last attack so that he once again perched on the stairs, ready to leap. The guards abandoned the princess, who began to weep.

"Boo-hoo-hoo. Hoo-hoo."

Derry rushed onstage so that he didn't have to listen to Foxe's hoots. They enacted the telling of the princess's plight. The dragon bellowed.

The audience gasped as Oofer the dragon pounced onstage in front of Derry. Ignoring the princess, he took three giant steps toward Derry, raised a claw, and sliced. The claws made a strange, evil sound. *Fffffzzzz. Fffzzz.* He ducked and cursed at the dragon under his breath.

"Damn you," he whispered, "attack the princess."

A giant row of silver claws batted at him. He dodged and parried with his sword, but the dragon swung his other paw. Derry hear a *ffffzzz*, then felt his head whip to the side. His body followed as he was thrown to the floor. Rolling, he came to his feet. A thin line of blood arced across his cheekbone. He touched it, stared, then looked at the dragon. He shook his head as the creature swung at him again.

He suddenly realized the blows always aimed for his head. He'd been careful to instruct Oofer to strike low. Derry leapt and dodged about the stage, parrying and striking at the iron claws. The audience howled with delight. Blood always excited them.

Derry sailed past the dragon and slammed the flat of his blade down on a green arm. Leaning close, he snarled at Oofer.

"What ails you, man? Strike low, or you'll behead me."

Spinning away, Derry swept his sword up over his head and down. The dragon lifted its claws—and grabbed Derry's sword. The great paw twitched, and the sword flew from Derry's hand. It fell to the floor and spun behind the green and pink tail.

Silver talons jabbed at him from two directions. Derry had no time to think and only moments to save his life. Dropping to his knees, he rolled and came upright again. The dragon followed much too quickly and slashed at him. There was a buzzing sound, and Derry felt the impact of the claws. They sank into the chain mail, snagged, then ripped. Two claws tore loose from the dragon paw. Derry hurled himself out of striking range. He landed on a rock near Foxe the princess. Panting and sweating, he grimaced as he pulled two curved iron claws from his chest. They had pierced him through the hollow rings of his chain mail.

"My lord!" It was Foxe using his falsetto. He could barely hear the boy above the roar of the audience. "My lord, that's not Oofer."

"I know that."

Derry thrust himself off his rock just in time to avoid

another swipe from bloodied claws. A second paw followed him, and he was pounded to the floor on his face. He rolled onto his back. A talon caught him, tore at his throat.

He fastened both hands on the paw, raised his legs, and jabbed the arm with his feet. The dragon roared, tearing its paw free. Derry coiled his body and spun with the force of the dragon's movement. He leapt over the tail and dived for his sword as the monster slithered around to deliver another slashing blow that nearly took his face off.

Spinning across the floor, Derry leapt to his feet again. The claws cut through the air. *Ffffzzzz.* Derry stooped quickly. He felt the rush of air as the claws tore at him. He lunged forward, sword extended, and stabbed into the pink underbelly.

He heard a grunt, then a yowl. The dragon's snout came down, knocking him in the head. Derry scrambled free of the faltering body. The tail snaked wildly as the creature writhed, the sword still sticking from its belly. The creature fell on its back. A crimson stain spread over the pink belly, radiating from the point where steel met cloth.

Cheers deafened him. Derry wiped sweat from his eyes. Shivering, he glanced at the audience, then up at the spot where Morgan had been. His brother had vanished. Derry glanced at the prone dragon, his body growing cold.

"Please, God, no." He closed his eyes briefly, then made himself open them and stare over the heads of the standing audience.

Thea was gaping at him, her lips parted and eyes wide. Flowers sailed at him. He whirled around and shouted at the players who had scrambled from behind the curtain to take bows.

"Stand in front of the dragon, you fools. You three, drag it behind the curtain."

He bowed quickly and left the stage. Behind the curtain Foxe was removing the dragon's head. Derry prayed silently as a man's shoulders appeared, then greasy brown hair. Derry bent over a pox-scarred face. His blood suddenly began to flow again, as if his heart had stopped beating while he waited to see the face of the dragon.

"Who's this, then?" Foxe asked.

"I know not."

"He tried to kill you."

"You're to hide him," Derry said as he searched the man's clothing. "I'll send Stubb to help you."

Finding nothing on the stranger, Derry rose and allowed the players to remove the body from the dragon costume. A trunk was quickly emptied of props and the body stuffed inside it. Derry left the stage. As he jumped from the planks, a hand shot out to steady him when he landed.

"Morgan." Derry almost smiled at his brother.

The younger man had his hand on his sword. "What happened?"

"You left her."

"Fear not, my love-smitten dragon-slayer. Stubb is with her."

Morgan pointed at the stairs in the corner opposite the stage. Thea was descending, followed by Stubb and Ellen Dowgate. Derry headed for them while trying to answer a deluge of questions from Morgan.

"I tell you, I know not who the bastard is, but I know who sent him."

"The Wyvern."

"You were always a clever—Morgan, look."

Thea was halfway downstairs. On the landing above, from a door to one of the rented chambers, burst a gaggle of apprentices. Blue cloaks flying, they rushed down the stairs, careening into the more decorous, bouncing off merchants and bankers. Derry and Morgan exchanged looks, and as one they bolted for the stairs.

Derry shouted at Thea, but the clamoring of apprentices drowned his warning. Her gaze was fixed on him, a distressed, fearful look that would have gratified him had he the time to think about it. He called out to her, but she only smiled and lifted her skirts higher. Her slipper lifted from the stair, and a blue cloak flipped in her face. As Derry sprang toward her, he watched a blue waterfall tumble on top of her. She was knocked aside and separated from Ellen Dowgate and Stubb.

As he jumped across the last few feet between them, he saw her fall sideways over the banister. He hurled himself beneath the railing and caught her as she hurtled toward the ground. The impact threw him backward into Morgan, who grasped them both as they tumbled in a heap.

He sat up and shifted Thea from his chest to his lap. Morgan pulled himself from the pile and sat on his haunches. Thea was snatched from him by Ellen, who fussed over her. Derry grabbed Morgan's cloak before he could chase after the apprentices. Under the cover of Ellen's chattering, he spoke to his brother.

"Don't bother. You won't catch them, and we've a matter of greater import to pursue."

"But they might have killed Thea!"

"Morgan, I was the real quarry this night. Listen to me. There's a body behind the curtain. In a trunk. With seven witless players sitting on it."

Morgan grasped the edge of Derry's cloak and tossed it aside to reveal bloodied links of mail. He lifted a brow and regarded Derry, unsmiling.

"I'll attend to it." He touched Derry's cheek with the tip of his finger and examined the blood that came away with it. "You, dear brother, must needs quit this inn along with your lady before one of you is killed."

"I know that."

"And mayhap on the way you'll think upon this—Thea was right. It was you who nearly lost his life. This Wyvern cares little for her and a great deal about you. If you continue to flaunt yourself about the city, you'll end up with a knife in your back or that sovereign-gold hair cleaved by an ax."

Derry stood and faced his brother. "Jesu, just get rid of the body, Morgan." They scowled at each other, but Derry remembered something. "I," he said with dignity, "am not love-smitten."

Morgan swung away from him, his scowl transforming into a grin.

"I'm not," Derry shouted after him.

"Not what?" Thea asked. Ellen had finished fussing over her and had gone ahead to the coach. "What a foolish trick."

Derry glanced at her innocently. "You falling off the stairs?"

"You know well what I mean. Risking dire hurt, and all for show. Well, sirrah, you've announced yourself to the Wyvern in a fantastical manner. No doubt he'll come for us quickly now. Only you're the bait as well, it seems."

"I didn't fall off the stairs."

She put her hands on her hips and looked him up and down. "And I'm not bleeding all over my antique armor."

Derry looked down at his chest. "Fah, mere scratches."

Stubb, who had been watching silently, gave a snort. "That weren't no player, that dragon."

"You be quiet," Derry said.

Thea gasped, then stepped closer to look at his wounds.

She grasped his chin and turned his face so that she could see the cut on his cheek clearly. She bit her lower lip and met his gaze. Color drained from her face. She released him and twisted her hands together.

"I was right," she said.

Derry took her arm and began escorting her to their coach. She stopped, bringing him up short.

"You knew," she said. "You knew all the time they would come for you."

"Come. Nightfall draws near."

"You were the bait as well as I."

"You're addled, Thea *bella*. It must be the fall."

"I'll go no farther until you answer."

He looked at the set of her chin and groaned. "I wasn't certain, but the more bait the better, I've always found."

"Lackwit."

"Call me no names. My plan worked, did it not. Only—"

"Only?"

He glanced up and saw Ellen coming toward them from the inn. "Only I didn't count on becoming enamored of the bait, Thea *bella*."

# 18

❧

*Be sober, be vigilant; because your adversary*
*the devil, as a roaring lion, walketh about,*
*seeking whom he may devour.*

—I Peter 5:8

T HEA ARRIVED HOME FROM the White Hart Inn
disheveled and fleeing to her chamber as if in fear of
demons. In truth, she raced upstairs and burst across
the threshold, distracted and unsettled because she'd
spent too much time in Derry's presence. On the trip, he'd
sat opposite her in their coach without saying a word. She
had flushed upon discovering that he was staring at her.
That unblinking gentian gaze rolled over her like the mist
that rose from a scalding bath on a winter morning.

Try as she would, she couldn't understand what she'd
done to merit such a scrutiny. True, she had objected upon
learning he'd been using himself as bait since their arrival
in London. The miscreant had lied to her again. He'd
protested that he'd lied for her own protection. She had
replied that the thought would be of small comfort if he
were dead.

After this retort he'd fallen silent and taken to examining her with that vexing, wordless, and intimidating stare

that never ceased. Which was why she now stood with her back to her chamber door, panting.

"Aaaow, my bones."

Thea whirled around, flung the door open, and stared. "Hobby?"

"Aaaow, mistress, my little mistress."

Hobby wrapped her in two plump arms and squeezed hard. Thea squeezed back.

"Hobbyhobbyhobbyhobby!"

Tugging the maid into her chamber, Thea clasped both her hands and shot questions at her.

"Where have you been? Are you well? God's mercy, I missed you. What did they do to you?"

Hobby tucked a stray lock back under her cap as they took seats on a bench beside the fireplace. "I been in a great castle. Locked up in a tower I was."

"Was it Moorefield Garde?" Thea asked. "I'll rip his golden hair from his head if he kept you from me at Moorefield Garde."

"Nah," Hobby said. "I been at some great border fortress. Its lord is a young beast name of Fitzstephen. I told him what would happen to him if he didn't let me go, but he just laughed, until his lady heard tell I was there. Oooo, you should have heard them fighting. The lady said she'd see me home herself if he didn't send me. That finished it, you see, because of her being with child. And here I am."

Turning to straddle the bench, Thea gaped at Hobby, who was calmly straightening her ruff. "Fitzstephen. The new Lord Fitzstephen?"

"So he sent me south, he did." Hobby touched Thea's sleeve. "And when I got here, the servants told me you were betrothed to the gallant lord who rescued you. Rescued! Lord Robin, bless my soul, not Robin Savage, oh, no, Lord Robin, Lord bloody Derry. The lying beast."

Thea patted Hobby's hand. "We've landed in a tempest, Hobby, and I fear I've made a grievous mistake in holding loyalty to Mary Stuart. She isn't what I thought she was."

Sighing, Thea told Hobby of her trials since they'd last seen each other. Peering at the maid, she could discern no injuries.

"That beast Stubbs, he didn't hurt you? That night in the forest, I heard you scream, and then they took you away. I was so frightened for you."

Hobby flushed with renewed ire. "The bloody jackanapes pulled my hair. I'd like to rip his out and use it for pillow stuffing."

"So it was another cursed trick," Thea said, her voice rising. "Sometimes I want to pull his lordship's hair out too. Especially when he won't tell me what he's about. Now he's trying to draw out this traitor, this Wyvern, but he won't confide in me. He said he was using me as bait, but I know that was only half a truth."

"How haps it that you're so fretted about his pretty skin? Let him get it sliced off his body."

Thea looked down at her hands, which were clasping the bench in front of her. "You don't understand. He guards me as if I were the Virgin Mother, risks his life to protect me, and yet he trusts me not. He tells me little. I think he's exposing himself to this traitor, hoping that the Wyvern will try to kill him."

"Good."

Pursing her lips, Thea glanced up at Hobby. "I don't think so."

"Not good?"

"No."

Hobby looked at her for a few moments, then moaned and clutched her head. "Saints and apostles protect us." Hobby's arms fell to her sides. Turning to face Thea, she patted her shoulder. "I heard talk of you two, but I didn't believe it."

"Hobby, I'm so muddled." Thea covered her face with her hands and whispered. "He—he orders me about as if I were a mucker of stables and then . . ."

"Ah-ha."

Thea uncovered her face. Hobby gave her a speculative look.

"I was afraid he would take you," Hobby said. "You being such a pretty maid and all."

Her face grew hot, and Thea ducked her head.

"Seems the talk was true, then. The servants say you're sick with love for him."

"I am not sick!" Thea lowered her voice. "He—he, oh, you don't understand. He's not a man who listens when he wants—and I don't seem to think at all when he—and he casts some sort of spell with his hands. I thought I hated him, but . . ."

The word ended on a groan, which stopped when she heard Hobby chuckling. She looked up and scowled.

"I forbid you to laugh."

Hobby covered her mouth. A snigger escaped, but she managed to assume a calm demeanor.

"Forgive me, mistress."

"Oh, Hobby, if only he weren't so, so—after all, he tricked me, and he tells me what to do all the time. He makes me so angry. And yet he protects me and, and I think he cares for me, Hobby, but he never speaks of it, and, and I told him to go away after he catches this traitor."

"Hmm. Never speaks of it?"

"Well, you see, we seem to spend a great deal of time in, um, discussion."

"Fight, do you?"

Thea sighed.

"Good."

"Oh, Hobby."

"It is," the maid replied. "Testing each other, that's what it is. You each got to know if the other will stay to the end, no matter the cost. Makes sense what with all that happened to him with his first wife."

"Wife?" Thea felt the earth slip out from under her.

"Don't get your farthingale in a tangle. She's dead. Betrayed him to old Bishop Bonner and got him tossed in the Tower when he was a youth. Accused him of plotting with Wyatt when he rebelled against the old queen, she did. If you listened to talk more instead of wandering in the country, you'd have heard the story."

Swallowing, Thea found her voice. "Did they hurt him?"

Hobby's usually loose mouth shut tight.

"Hobby, tell me."

"The rack."

Sweat broke out on her upper lip and brow. "And his wife was the one who betrayed him?"

"Lied, she did. But that was long ago, mistress, and now he's high in the favor of her majesty. They say she's so fond of him, she wanted to give him a palace, but he refused it."

At last an explanation. All these weeks she'd been subjected to Derry's unpredictable moods. He could lure her, sirenlike, only to become an adder, striking and spitting, venomous and frightening. Yet he came to her. Again and again he came to her despite his wariness.

She knew what it was to distrust someone. She understood all too well the hurt that lay beneath her own distant manner, her refusal to leave her country fastness. Yet for all his distrust, Derry had saved her life, risked his own life to protect her. What he would not admit, he revealed by his actions.

And this very night he would reveal himself again, for he would go to a banquet after having thrown down a gauntlet to the Wyvern, after surviving at least two attempts on his life. She couldn't prevent him. Mayhap she could protect him by watching over him. She could search for traitors as well as he.

Hopping up from the bench, she spoke to Hobby as she quitted her chamber. "Find a gown for me. I go to a banquet given by the Earl of Lynford this night. I must find Father and remind him. No doubt he's forgotten there is an Earl of Lynford."

She raced downstairs and out into the gardens at the back of the house. The sun was setting, but Father never gave up gardening until it was dark. She rounded a tall, cone-shaped bush and nearly ran into Derry. He caught her arm and pulled her around to face him.

"I was just coming to you," he said.

"I'm looking for Father."

"I sent him to his valet to change for the banquet."

"Then I will return to my chamber," she said. "I haven't begun to dress."

"There is no need."

"I can't attend in a soiled gown." She turned, but he fastened both hands on her shoulders.

"You're not going."

"Why not?"

"The danger is growing, Thea *bella*."

"It worried you not before."

"I always feared danger to you," he said, "but I needed

you to help lure the Wyvern. He's taken the bait now, and will transfer his attention to me, where it belongs."

"But you need my help. I know Grandmother's friends. I know more of them than you do."

"You forget who I am."

Thea shoved him away. "God's blood, I know who you are, and so does this traitor and his minions. I'm going."

She cried out as Derry suddenly swept her into his arms and brought her close so that their lips almost touched. His tongue touched her lower lip before he slowly lowered his mouth to hers. Bewildered, she held still while he sucked at her tongue. He lifted his mouth slightly and spoke against her lips.

"Thea *bella,* sweet, sweet *bella,* do you feel me?"

"Y-yes."

"God forgive me, but I want you. Here, on the ground."

He sucked at her lips again. "Don't fight me," he said between kisses that made her shiver. "Say you will obey me."

He lifted his mouth so that she could speak.

"No."

His talented lips paused, then pressed in a straight line.

Thea stuck her tongue between those lips and pulled him to her. She kissed him as deeply as he had kissed her, then released him. She was gratified to see that he was breathing as hard as she.

"You cozened me with your body once too often," she said. "You're a foul harlot to use my—my craving for you to bend me to your will. I'll not do it. Think you I'm some dull-witted bawd who loses her reason at your touch?"

He grinned at her, and her temper flared.

"You do!" she said.

"I never thought you were a bawd, or dull-witted."

She raised her chin. "I grow weary of your seductions

and tyrannies. That's what you do, you know, you seduce and tyrannize, seduce and tyrannize. I'm going."

He sighed and smiled at her. "I would have thought you'd learned to obey me by now."

She saw his eyes narrow, and she bolted. He caught up with her in three steps, lifted her in his arms, and continued walking with her toward Bridgestone. Ignoring her pounding fists and kicking legs, he marched past gawking servants and upstairs to her chamber. Hobby met them at the door.

Derry swung her onto the bed. Thea landed on her back, sat up, and began to climb off the mattress. Derry shoved her, and she landed on her back again. He pointed at her when she would have gotten up.

"You stay there."

"Go to—uhh!"

She lost her breath as Derry fell on top of her. He captured her wrists and held her still. Kissing her nose, he dragged one leg up the length of hers. She gasped and caught her lip between her teeth.

"You will remain in your chamber, Thea *bella*, or I'll use you so that you'll be too sore to do anything but lie abed." He emphasized his threat by thrusting his hips against hers.

"Here now, you stop that!" Hobby batted Derry on the shoulders with her fists.

Derry twisted around to glare at Hobby. The violence in that look caused Hobby to back away from him. He looked down at Thea, smiled, and kissed her on the nose again. Then he was gone.

Thea sat up while Hobby grumbled about licentious young noblemen. She climbed to the edge of the bed, where she sat, swinging her legs, deep in thought.

"Lascivious knave, foul, wanton lecher," Hobby ranted.

" 'Course I see what a trial it would be, having that man crawl all over you, specially with them long legs and that flat, flat belly and just the right kind of muscle on that pretty arse of his."

"Hobby." Thea's tone was loud in warning.

"Are you going to let him pin you to his sleeve like a love token?"

"Of course not." Thea jumped off the bed. "But I must wait until he and Father have left. If I try to disobey, he'll lock us both in this chamber."

"Then what are we going to do?"

"Why, I'm going to the banquet. Someone tried to kill him at the play, Hobby, and failed. The traitor will try again, and I fear it will be tonight."

"Then mayhap he's right, mistress. You shouldn't go."

Thea waved a hand at the maid. "I've been thinking, Hobby. For years I've been hiding from the world because I was afraid to be hurt. But then Derry came, and I couldn't run away from him. I couldn't hide because he wouldn't let me. And now, now I think I don't need to hide anymore. Besides, who else will protect him? Father? Morgan? Morgan wants to kill Derry himself."

"Oh?"

"I'll tell you about it later," Thea said. "Now, find me a gown."

*Thea followed Derry and* her father south across London to the Earl of Lynford's palace on the Thames. Lying between Bridewell Palace and Baynard's Castle, it nestled inside the old city wall. She instructed her coachman to keep a distance between them, and at the last moment, as the two dismounted and walked up the steps to the great house, the vehicle slowed to a stop before torch-bearing servants.

She maneuvered her farthingale through the door of the

coach, hopped down, and quickly mounted the stairs. As the men passed under the pointed arch of the entryway, she reached out and slipped her hand onto her father's arm.

"Thea, my dear." Lord Hunt peered down at her, vaguely puzzled. "I thought you were ill."

She glanced at Derry, who was eyeing her coldly, his hands trying to strangle his gloves.

"I recovered."

Lord Hunt resumed his progress with her on his arm. "That's nice. But, um, you know, my dear, I may be coming down with an ague myself. Might have to leave early. You brought Mistress Dowgate with you, did you not, and Lord—um, Lord—um . . ."

Father always disappeared from banquets and ceremonies at the first opportunity. Thea nodded without telling him she'd left Dowgate snoring in bed.

"Derry," Lord Hunt finished. He beamed in pride. "Knew I'd remember."

Derry leaned toward her and whispered. "Pray to all the pagan gods and demons. You'll need their aid when I find you alone."

Pulling closer to her father, Thea pressed her lips together and felt her heart thump as Derry inclined his head and accompanied them into the great hall, where they accepted the greetings of the earl and his mother. Lynford took her hand and expressed his sympathies upon the death of her grandmother.

"We were so distressed at your misfortune on your journey and rejoiced at your deliverance. Mayhap you'll tell me about this highwayman who abducted you."

Thea made courteous replies, all the while keeping track of Derry's whereabouts. He was angry with her, and she didn't want him coming upon her without warning.

The earl distracted her by placing her hand on his arm and asking for her company at his table during the banquet. She acquiesced because she knew of no way to refuse. Thus she was separated from Derry. At least he wouldn't be able to chastise her at the height of his anger.

For the first time, she gave the earl her full attention. It was odd how danger and Derry had changed the way she perceived people. No longer so afraid of men, she felt as if she were looking at Jonathan Taine for the first time. He was one of those men whose appearance fit his station in life. Tall enough to ride a knight's destrier with ease, well-proportioned of frame, he had an air of wistfulness and melancholy that intrigued and mystified.

He walked beside her, passing by candles in tall stands that cast golden beams on his hair and turned it a deep, rich chestnut. It curled in tight ringlets and sprang away from his face. In the past, the earl's dark looks had alarmed her. Now she remembered his easy courtesy, his lack of male hubris, his concern for her. Could it be that all along he might have guessed the reason for her fear of men?

She allowed the earl to conduct her through the throngs of guests toward the dais at the opposite end of the hall. She darted a look over her shoulder to see Derry in the clutches of the dowager countess. Catherine Taine had donned a red-gold wig. She glittered with gems. Every finger of the hand on Derry's arm boasted a ring. To Thea's mind, that hand gripped Derry far too tightly. Though mature, the countess was one of those ladies who trolled court waters for young gallants.

The earl seated Thea at his left between her father and himself while the countess seized Derry and put him at her side, far away from Thea. She contented herself with searching the hall for Lord Gracechurch. She found him at a table with Timothy Eyre. Both were cramming meat into their mouths.

The banquet proceeded as was customary, with a fanfare from the musicians above the screens, heralding the arrival of each course. Long tables stretched the length of the hall. Covered with the earl's finest linens, laden with silver plate, they nearly disappeared under the weight of swan, peacock, venison, and capon.

The earl lifted a Venetian glass goblet to his lips and drank while observing her. Her old discomfort in the company of men had assaulted her the moment she entered the hall. Nevertheless she was surprised to feel almost at ease under his temperate gaze. His glance wrought no devastation with her calm as did Derry's. She even relaxed enough to give him a small smile in return for a compliment.

"Mistress Hunt," the earl said, "I've a boon to ask you."

"What is it?"

"A masque will begin after the banquet." The earl touched the rim of his goblet with a finger. "And the countess begged me to participate in it." He grimaced and looked up from the goblet to meet her glance. "She says I'm far too reserved. I think she wants me to attract a new wife."

"Oh." Thea toyed with her eating knife. "My grandmother tried to make me do the same. Find a husband, that is."

"I know."

He smiled at her in sympathy, and she couldn't help smiling back.

"That is why I would beg you to be my partner," he continued. "When the masque begins, there will be a procession and mumming and poetry, and then, of course, we will take partners from among the guests. Would you be my partner?"

She hated dancing. Her gaze flitted over the earl's shoulder. The countess was holding a goblet to Derry's lips. At that moment a new thought came to her. Poison. An easy way to kill. Surely Derry understood the danger. She watched him drink from the countess's goblet. Indeed, he did. She'd been foolish. No doubt he'd survived countless intrigues and machinations through caution and his own particular wicked guile.

"Mistress Hunt, will you?" the earl was asking.

"Marry, my lord, I don't . . ."

"Your betrothed has already consented to partner Lady Beatrice, who is to play a sea nymph. It is called a Masque of the Sea, you know."

"He has?" She dragged her gaze from the sight of Derry offering a fruit pasty to the countess. "He has?" All fears for his life vanished.

"You may not know Lady Beatrice," the earl said. "She has been at the French court with the ambassador's household. They say she is most accomplished at all the new French pastimes. Lord Derry seemed to know her well."

She had never been jealous before. Having so little to do with men, she'd never had occasion. She didn't like it. Her head became an exploding hackbutt, and at the same time she wanted to debone Lady Beatrice like a fish. Most unpleasant. Thea turned to the earl, offered her hand, and consented to dance with him in the masque.

Around them the noise of the banquet had risen to fill the great hall. Laughter and applause rose and fell as tumblers and jesters cavorted. Gestures and balance became unsteady. The din echoed off the stone fan vaulting high above her head. Soon the tables were taken away and benches placed against the walls so that Nibbs the juggler could astonish the earl's guests by tossing and catching lit torches.

Fear returned to Thea. The hall was crowded, the guests more than half drunk on the earl's golden French wine. Someone could jostle Derry in the press of bodies, slip a stiletto between his ribs, and stroll on before she even knew it.

Thea sat on a stool while her father and the earl stood, flanking her. Derry lounged beside a bench holding the countess and another, younger, and far too pretty woman opposite them. Nibbs strolled by with his array of flying flames. After he passed, Thea looked back across the hall to the countess's bench. Derry was gone.

# 19

*No freeman shall be taken, or imprisoned . . .*
*except by the legal judgement of his peers*
*or by the law of the land.*

—MAGNA CARTA

GOD HAD AFFLICTED HIM with a disobedient woman. Derry skulked along a dark passage after Lord Gracechurch and promised himself he would punish Thea in ways most pleasureful to himself and most embarrassing to her. She had come to the banquet to vex him.

He slithered along a wall. The smell of soap told him he must be near the laundry. Gracechurch, Eyre, and Lord Anthony Clark had all attended the banquet. All except Gracechurch were still in the hall. He heard a grunt. Edging around a corner, he saw the bulbous form of Gracechurch. The man appeared to be assaulting a wall. Derry peered around the corner, puzzled as Gracechurch humped against stone. Then he heard an uncultured female voice, high and nasal.

"Ow yes, ow yes, ow yes, me lord."

Derry's gaze strayed to a scattering of coins on the floor, then to a pair of feet in leather slippers straining on tiptoe.

Withdrawing, Derry lifted his glance to the roof in disgust. He walked softly through a doorway and crossed the darkened laundry, nearly tripping over a large basin.

He opened a shutter. He was at the rear of the house, and it was late. Most of the activity among the servants was near the kitchens. He stared into the darkness and whistled. At a distance he heard an answer. After a short wait Inigo, Simon Spry, and Anthony Now-Now scuttled up to the window. Leaving Anthony on guard, the two thieves slipped inside.

"Try to get to his chamber first, and remember, I care not if he's a papist, I want evidence of the Wyvern, if there's any to be had," Derry said. "There's to be a masque, so you'll have time. Did anyone miss the stolen livery?"

"No, my lord," Inigo said. "I paid well for it."

"Very well. Get you gone, and no stealing. I'll have to answer to Christian if you're hanged."

He sent Inigo and Simon Spry up the back stairs toward the private apartments of the earl and countess. Gliding down the passage, he entered the hall in the midst of the Masque of the Sea.

Myriad green-clad dancers floated down the center of the hall. Their bodies painted sea green, their hair silver and gold, they bore torches and banners aloft and marched to the haunting call of lute and harp. The hall had been darkened for the occasion so that the firelight gave the scene a liquid quality. Derry skirted the crowds of guests, satisfied himself that Thea was still sitting beside her father, and rejoined the importunate countess as a float bearing Neptune entered.

He paid little attention to Neptune other than to note that like the other mermen he wore little clothing. What there was consisted of a mask, silver seaweed, and gilded leather sandals. His curling locks bore a crown of palest sea green studded with mock diamonds. Derry searched the hall for Timothy Eyre, whom he'd last seen guzzling wine. All at once his gaze veered to Neptune again, for he had stopped and dismounted from his floating throne to stand before Thea.

Lady Beatrice blocked his view. Bobbing in front of him in green robes of near transparency, she tugged at his hand. He allowed her to pull him to the center of the floor, for it brought him nearer to Thea. To his consternation, she rose and placed her hand in Neptune's. Derry craned his neck to see over Beatrice's head as the music began. She led him to stand behind Neptune while the god guided Thea through a stately march. Derry scowled at the man, only to end up gawking as Neptune removed his mask, and he recognized the Earl of Lynford.

She was dancing. She hated dancing. He remembered her telling him so. Inconstant little witch. Mayhap now that he'd awakened her, she lusted after other men. His wife had. God's blood, he would see to it that she danced no longer. No, he couldn't do that. He would have to wait to hurl chastisements at her.

He managed to do three things at once—dance a gaillard with Beatrice, watch for Lord Gracechurch to reappear, and keep his eye on Thea. Perhaps this multitude of tasks accounted for his lack of attention to Beatrice. She pinched his thigh as they came together, arms linked. He almost cried out at the pain, and scowled at her.

She glided away from him and curtsied, then came back. When their hands joined, she dipped her body toward his, and he felt her hand where no lady's should be. His eyes flew wide open. Gasping, he shoved her from him under the guise of lifting her in the air. The dance speeded up, and he managed to avoid her groping by spinning her so fast, she grew dizzy.

As the dance ended, he swept the participants with a glance and spied Thea receiving a kiss on the hand from the earl. He dragged Beatrice behind him and swooped down on Thea. In a few moments he'd maneuvered so that they exchanged partners for a slow pavane.

Squeezing her hand, he hissed at her. "So, you detest dancing. Marry, I see how you detest dancing. You detest it so much that you move as if your feet were enchanted."

"I never said I knew not how to dance, only that I didn't like it."

"But you did it." Derry knelt while Thea marched gracefully around him. "You lied. I'll never believe you again—"

"God's patience!" Thea lowered her voice as other dancers looked their way. "Am I not allowed to change, to grow, to leave behind me unpleasant memories of old hurts?"

"Oh."

"Well?"

"You could have decided to improve yourself with me instead of that green lecher. Or have you decided that a papist earl is more to your liking?"

"You lascivious insect."

Derry cut off her tirade by squeezing her waist. As they danced, he'd been looking about the hall, watching for Gracechurch. As he squeezed Thea, he saw a round figure in damask amble out from behind a screen. She scratched the back of his hand, and he stopped squeezing.

"Shhh!" He bent over and whispered to her as they passed in procession down the length of the hall. "Behind us. Gracechurch."

They reached the end of the hall and turned to march back the way they'd come.

"Look," Thea said, barely moving her lips. "He speaks with Timothy Eyre. They're arguing."

"Do they quarrel often?" he asked.

She stretched her neck as Derry paced around her. "I've never seen it. Derry, I think Eyre gave him something. Or perhaps it was the other way round."

Derry had his back to the men.

"Are you certain? It's dark and crowded. What was it?"

"I know not. It was too small, and Gracechurch hid it with his belly."

"Damnation. Where is your father?"

Thea gave him a wry glance. "Gone. He said his ague had arrived."

"God's blood, woman, I can't follow those two and protect you at the same time."

"I'll come with you."

He suddenly bent to hiss in her ear. "Try and you'll pay, my willful. Have a care, for your offense is already like to cause you grief."

When she didn't answer, he glanced down at her to see her swallow hard. Good. Let her suffer unease over what he was going to do to her. Mayhap then she would obey him.

For the remainder of their time at the banquet he and Thea watched Eyre and Gracechurch. The two seemed enamored of each other's company. Once, the Earl of Lynford engaged them in conversation, but he moved on quickly. Derry glanced at Thea.

"Gracechurch annoys Lynford," she said. "Gracechurch has a fantasy that he's clever, which is indeed a fantasy."

"Or mayhap a pretended foolishness."

Thea lifted her brows in surprise. "Think you so? Surely no one could play the lackwit so convincingly?" She paused, glanced at him, and pursed her lips. "No one but you, mayhap."

"Are you ever going to forget Rob Savage?"

"No."

He had to be content with glaring at her. Finally the hour arrived when they could take leave without causing comment. He hurried through their leavetaking, deposited her in the coach, and climbed in after her. She gave him a startled look that told him she'd expected him to ride his horse back.

He lowered himself beside her, swirled his cloak back over his shoulders, and smiled at her. When they'd left the earl's palace behind, he spoke to her quietly.

"I had other business than looking after you this night."

"No doubt you had your ruffians crawling all over poor Lynford's house."

He paused, for that was what he'd done. "I ordered you to remain at home, and you disobeyed me." His fingers curled around her arm and squeezed. "Mayhap you've forgotten what happens when you disobey me."

"Recently? Of late you make love to me as if doing so would save your life."

He stopped again, for she'd answered in a calm tone that held no trace of fear. He would have to play the part of ruthless intelligencer all that much better.

He couldn't make her see how dangerous it was to run about the city without him. He would have to settle for blind compliance. He lunged at her, covered her with his body, and drove her down on the seat. He raked his fingers through her hair and pulled her close so that her breasts pressed against him.

"Your pudding-headed father has let you have your way too long. You may choose your punishment. I could stop the coach and find a switch to take to your pretty legs. The coachman and footmen would be most entertained."

He felt her suck in her breath. Moonlight passed over her face, and he saw her blinking at him.

"Or," he continued, "you may scrub the floors of my apartments on your hands and knees, ten times. Or, and this is my preference, you may come to my chamber for the next five nights and show me how repentant you are by obeying me completely, no matter what I command you to do."

She squirmed against him and mused softly, "Five nights?"

Never had a woman so baffled him. Aggrieved, he raised his voice. "God's blood, you're supposed to cringe, not sound as if five nights weren't enough!"

Even as she chuckled he heard the report of a hackbutt. The coach swerved. The wheel hit the ditch at the side of the road and sank. Horses screamed. The vehicle swerved, and he heard wood crack and splinter as he scooped Thea in one arm and braced himself with the other.

He used all his strength, but they were thrown like dice in a box when the coach toppled on its side. He landed on top of Thea and banged his head on the door. He rolled off her while listening to the sounds of fighting outside.

"Thea?"

"I'm unhurt. What happened?"

"Stay here." He drew his sword and dagger. Kneeling beside her, he touched her cheek with the hand that held the dagger. "Thea *bella,* my love, this time you must obey me. If not for your sake, for mine. Remain within. If you distract me, it could mean my death."

"Why do I never have my crossbow at hand when these things happen?" She put her hand on his. "I promise."

He looked outside from the door that had landed uppermost. All he could see were dark blurs and the dull gleam of swords. Throwing the door open, he vaulted out and onto the ground. A man rose up from behind the wheel of the coach, a cudgel in his hand. The cudgel swung at Derry's head as he landed. He ducked and lunged at the same time. The man grunted, then clutched his belly.

Derry didn't wait to see the man fall. He leapt over the body of the coachman and thrust at one of the two ruffians, trying to gut a footman. He pricked the man in the leg, and he dropped to the ground, screaming. The second man turned, but not in time to stop Derry's sword from slicing a gash in his throat. The footman cried out.

Derry whirled and parried a thrust from another man. A lucky move, for he'd seen his opponent's sword only at the last moment, when a cloud blew free of the moon. He took the force of the blow with his sword arm, sank to his knees, and drove his dagger into the man's gut as he rushed forward under the impetus of his own attack.

Blood gushed over his hand and sleeve. Derry pulled his weapon free and jumped to his feet. He swung around in a circle, but found no on.

"They ran, my lord."

"How many?"

"Two."

He assured himself that all the attackers were dead or fleeing while the footman attended to the bodies of the coachman and his fellows. He came upon the man he'd pricked in the leg.

"Help! I'm bleeding to death."

Derry stood over the man and glanced at his wound. Bloody, but no major vessel had been cut. Ignoring the man's wails, he bound him to the coach wheel with his own belt. His lips curled. He hadn't planned on capturing one of the Wyvern's men so soon. He must be closer to the bastard than he thought. Having secured his victim, he banged on the coach door with the hilt of his dagger.

"Thea, you may come out." There was no answer. He waited a moment. "Thea?"

He heard his prisoner snigger. The sound caused him to lose all the heat from his body. Jumping onto the coach, he wrenched the door open and peered inside at the emptiness. He bent over and retrieved Thea's cloak. His fingers sank into wet velvet. He dropped the cloak and held his hand up. Blood.

He hurled himself from the coach and onto the prisoner with such speed the man squawked in surprise. Fastening his hands around a dirty neck, Derry squeezed, pressing his thumbs into the man's throat. He made choking sounds and writhed, but Derry had pinned him to the wheel with his weight. When the ruffian's face had swelled and darkened like a ripe turnip, he eased the pressure of his hands. The man wheezed.

Derry spoke quietly. "Where have they taken her?" He didn't wait for an answer. Drawing his dagger, he stuck it in the man's wounded leg. After he finished screaming, Derry spoke as if he were not at all interested in the answer. "Where?"

The man babbled and begged, whimpered and whined. Hearing the note of terror in his victim's voice, Derry repeated his question.

"I will ask you once more before I cut your nose from your face." He placed the dagger inside the man's nostril.

"God's t-truth, I swear by my life, master, my lord. I know not. They told me nothing about taking the woman."

Derry listened to the man's ravings. He'd been as frightened as his victim, and in much more pain. He'd told the truth, and no one had believed him. Gazing on the wreckage before him, he withdrew his dagger. As he stepped away from the coach wheel, Inigo, Simon, and Anthony Now-Now came galloping down the road. He stood still while the three gathered around him and jabbered questions at him. The footman joined in, but their noise faded as he summoned his reason.

Anguish battered at him, but he fought it back, knowing that to lose control could mean Thea's death. Galloping off in search of her in darkness would gain him nothing. He needed light by which to track. They were over halfway to Bridgestone Abbey, outside the city walls on the road north of Westminster. The road was deserted. The attackers had chosen a stretch of it that passed through a meadow. Far off he could see the vague lines of houses to the south, those that clustered near Ludgate. Yes, he must wait for light, but he needn't remain idle.

He silenced his men with a downward slice of his arm and stalked back to his prisoner. They followed him and gathered behind him to stare at the groaning ruffian. Derry drew his dagger again, which made the man cringe. Derry almost smiled.

"Simon, build a fire." He took a step nearer his victim. "My good fellow. You and I will have converse for a space. I will ask questions, and you will answer. Quickly and truthfully. For if you do not, you will wish yourself in Spain and the prisoner of the Inquisition."

He never imagined he'd be glad of his experience in the Tower. The man's little courage held out less than a quarter hour.

"It was some lord, but I know him not," the man whined. "All smothered in a cloak and hood, he was. A big man. But I never saw his face."

Derry removed his dagger from its resting place at the prisoner's groin. "Mean you that he was tall, or wide?"

"Wide."

Sheathing his dagger, Derry turned to Inigo. "Go to Bridgestone for fresh horses and bring Stubb. We ride at first light, so you must hurry."

"But what will I tell Lord Hunt?"

"He'll be abed. We've no time for explaining, and you'll not have to if you hurry."

He passed the time by questioning his prisoner further. Unfortunately, the man knew little beyond the fact that he'd been hired for the night by a fellow rogue the previous morning.

"What was his name?" Derry asked.

"Smythe."

"Inky Smythe?"

The man nodded. Derry fell silent. Inky Smythe. A petty rogue who dealt more in forged papers than bloody robberies. Inky hadn't been among the attackers. He would have been useless. And this attack, it was a break in the shield of secrecy surrounding the Wyvern. Most likely the man behind this attempt on his life was Gracechurch. Mayhap Inky Smythe could confirm that Gracechurch was the Wyvern.

Inigo returned with Stubb and the horses. Derry prowled the scene of the attack restlessly, waiting for the first gray light in the sky. He picked up a log from the fire and held the burning end near the ground. He began to circle the coach, his gaze pinned to the ground. He paced around the vehicle in a widening circle. His eyes strained to discern the marks of a small pair of slippers. He knelt twenty paces from the coach, in the meadow. The grass had been crushed beneath boots. He touched his fingers to dried blood.

A shout from Inigo made him lift his head. A mounted man galloped toward him. Too late he realized how far from his men he'd come. They were racing to join him, but the rider would reach him first. He dropped his makeshift torch.

Derry drew his sword and turned so that his body was placed sideways to the rider. He lifted his weapon, but the newcomer slowed, swerved before him, and threw something. A woman's chain girdle and pomander landed at his feet. The rider continued his race, this time galloping off in the direction from which he'd come.

Derry knelt and picked up the chain. It was wrapped around a rolled piece of paper, and at its end was the ivy-leaf pomander. Thea's pomander. Closing a fist around the golden trinket, Derry clenched his jaw, then opened the paper and read.

*An hour past midnight. St. Botolph's. I will exchange her for you. I need not tell you to come alone.*

The note was unsigned, but below the message a wyvern had been drawn, crouching, its wings spread.

Stubb and the others gathered around him, but he crumpled the note. Striding quickly away from them, he returned to the dying fire and shoved the paper into the flames. By the time the others caught up with him, it was gone.

# 20

*Thou art a slave to fate, chance, kings
and desperate men.*

—JOHN DONNE

THEA TRIED TO TEAR the gag from her mouth and the
blindfold from her eyes, but her captor knocked her
bound hands from her face. It was a gentle blow. He
hadn't hurt her at all, not even when she'd grabbed a
discarded dagger and stabbed his hand as he dragged her
from the coach.

There were three of them—masked, silent, purposeful.
When Derry had burst from the coach and killed several
men without effort, her tall captor had separated from the
rest and come for her. Now they were riding at a gallop,
back into the city. She could tell because they'd left the
dirt road behind and clattered down a cobbled street.

She couldn't tell what direction they took, for they'd
turned down several crooked streets. They stopped suddenly, and she was taken down by the same strong, gentle
hands that had captured her. The man lifted her without
effort and carried her inside a building. She could tell she
was inside a structure by the sound of his boots against

wooden floorboards. A door creaked on its hinges. She sailed downward, then across a room.

The man holding her set her down, and she planted her feet apart to keep from losing her balance. She felt the brush of air that meant he'd moved. Footsteps retreated. Then a door slammed and she heard a bar drop into place across it.

Thea lifted her hands to her face slowly. No one stopped her, so she pulled the cloth from her mouth and eyes. Blinking, she waited for her eyes to adjust to the darkness. She turned in a circle, dread and old fears growing as she realized she was alone. She was in a dark pit again.

She covered her dry mouth with one hand and fought back tears of fright. Then she forgot her tears, for she perceived a dim sliver of light high in the air across the room. Rubbing her sore mouth, she crept closer to it. Her foot hit something solid, and she cursed and hopped on one foot.

Thea waved her hands in front of her. One of them hit a banister. She clutched it and mounted the stairs. As she ascended, the light grew. She wasn't in a black pit after all, only a cellar. Though she knew it was futile, she tried the door when she reached the landing. Of course it was blocked.

She sighed and sat down on the first step. She had feared for Derry when she should have been afraid for herself. Lizards wriggled in her stomach as she contemplated her own danger. God's mercy, she'd been abducted again, but this time she was certain her captor was no loyal subject protecting his queen. Rubbing her face with both hands, she tried to think clearly in spite of her dread.

Why would the Wyvern take her? She knew little, and it was Derry who was the threat. Derry! She was to be bait again, bait to lure Derry to his death. The word clanged in

her head, a giant clapper in the bell of her mind. *Death.*
Derry's death. Derry couldn't die. Threading her fingers,
she pressed them to her forehead so hard that they went
numb, and still the fear slithered up and down her body.
Derry couldn't die. What would she do if he died? Her
hands dropped to her lap as she discerned the answer. If he
died, she would want to follow him. By the Holy Father,
he had become necessary to her continuance.

As she pondered, she heard the clump of boots outside.
The sound sent her scampering down the stairs. She'd
been sitting on her bottom instead of trying to find a
weapon with which to protect herself. She raced across the
cellar, her eyes now accustomed to the dimness, and
searched among the boxes, barrels, and jars. She encountered a shelf against the far wall as the door opened. Her
hand hit an earthenware jar, then closed around it.

A wide form blocked most of the light from the passage
beyond the door. Thea thrust the jar behind her back and
waited as the man in the doorway came down the stairs,
followed by another. Both were cloaked and hooded, but
she recognized the spherical shape that bounced toward
her.

"Gracechurch."

The large figure paused at the foot of the stairs.

"You might as well reveal yourself, sirrah," Thea continued, "for I can see that belly from here. You look as if
you'd swallowed the moon."

A startled sound of annoyance almost made her smile.
Gracechurch threw off the cloak and hurled it at the man
behind him. He stalked over to her, his layers of chins and
his stomach leading the way. He stopped and looked down
his bulbous nose at her.

"Ill-mannered little annoyance."

"You release me at once, Gracechurch."

A pudgy hand reached out and slapped her. She cried out more from surprise than the pain, then threw the jar at his head. Unfortunately Lord Gracechurch was more agile than his bulk made him appear. He ducked, and the jar crashed to the floor. The other man didn't move.

"Enough of this." Gracechurch shoved her, and she stumbled against the shelves behind her. "I've questions to put to you, and little patience. If you wish to be left in peace, answer them."

To her amazement, Gracechurch plucked a folded piece of paper from his sleeve, opened it, and held it up so that it caught the meager light.

"Oh, yes," he said. He stuck the paper back in his sleeve and folded his hands over his belly. Speaking as though reciting to an audience, he went on. "Does Lord Derry know the true name of the Wyvern?"

She stared at him, her brow furrowed. When she failed to answer, Gracechurch continued.

"Does he know my allies?"

She glanced over his shoulder at the shrouded figure.

"Has he translated all the messages I sent by you?"

Thea wrinkled her forehead until her brows arched toward her hairline, but she said nothing. Gracechurch glanced over his shoulder, then turned and shouted at her.

"Answer me!"

He startled her, but she wasn't frightened. Gracechurch only annoyed her. She kicked his shin. He bellowed and scooted out of her reach. The man at his back reached for him. Thea saw a bejeweled hand fasten on Gracechurch's arm. A diamond glinted at her, and she discerned a ruby and an amethyst. It was then that she remembered the countess and her hands decked with rings.

"My lady?" she queried.

The hooded figure withdrew its hand. Gracechurch

cursed and waddled in the direction of the stairs. The cloaked person followed. Before Thea could call out to them, they'd gone.

"Curse it."

Thea banged her fist on the top of a barrel. She glared at the door, but her gaze caught the glint of gold. She raced to the landing. Near the threshold lay a brooch, a large one suitable for pinning cloaks. Thea picked it up and held it near the light coming from beneath the door. It was shaped like a dragon, enameled in green, with a red belly and arched wings. A wyvern.

Thea rubbed her fingertips over the cool enamel and resumed her seat on the top stair. The Wyvern. The clever, devious Wyvern. Why had such an adroit intelligencer suddenly become clumsy and dropped so revealing a token at her feet? Thea tapped her finger on the dragon. She was being manipulated, by the rood, manipulated and used. And if Gracechurch were the Wyvern, why had he exposed himself to her?

Shivering, Thea clasped her arms about her body as the answer came to her. He'd shown himself because such an action suited his purpose—and because she wasn't going to be allowed to live to reveal his name.

*The main kitchen at* Bridgestone Abbey slept in darkness except for the light of one candle resting on a cutting table. Derry sat on the table, one leg bent under him and the other braced on the floor. He held a butchering knife which he jabbed into the tabletop repeatedly, without looking at it.

Along the wall to his left stretched three cavernous fireplaces, each framed by brick arches. The fires had burned low. Before them slept kitchen boys and cooks' assistants too exhausted from the day's labors to care if he'd decided to loot Lord Hunt's pantry.

"Well met, brother."

Derry paused in his dissection of the table, then resumed his jabbing. "You were keeping watch of the inns. What do you away from the Angel and the Golden Bull?"

"I've caught two rats, noble vermin whose minions hadn't the sense to keep their mouths closed when they were sent for messages. Sir Gideon Walbrook and Lord Anthony Clark, who now lodge in the Tower. I've come by way of Traitor's Gate to find your men sulking in their shed by the stable."

"Get you some rest," Derry said. "I've matters to attend to that will keep me from my bed."

Morgan walked around a brazier set on tall legs and straddled a bench on the opposite side of Derry's table. "Inigo told me you've misplaced your betrothed."

"Did he?" Derry asked lightly. "I'll have to prick his tongue with my dagger to teach him reticence."

"Poor Inigo. I've already frightened him until his bones shook to get the story out of him. He didn't want to tell me. Said you'd drown him in a horse trough."

Derry sighed and slid off the table. He found the cloak he'd slung on a stool, but when he straightened he found Morgan blocking his way. Throwing the cloak over one shoulder, he rested his hands on his hips and lifted a brow.

Morgan shrugged. "We all know they've taken her. The others don't know why. I, however, was trained by Christian de Rivers, as you were. I know they took her to get you."

"Rejoice, then. I'll most likely be dead by sunrise."

Derry stepped to the side, but Morgan moved with him

and put a hand on his arm. Derry glanced at the hand, and Morgan dropped it to his side.

"You'll most certainly be dead by sunrise if you comply with the order to go alone."

"You would have me bring my men? We speak of the Wyvern, who has killed quite frequently of late. I'm not enamored of retrieving her with her throat cut."

"So you will allow him to cut yours after he's burned and broken you for your knowledge."

"As I said, rejoice." Derry tried to step around Morgan again, and again his way was blocked. "Sweet brother of black eyes and blacker temperament, I've no time for dancing. Get out of my way, or I'll truss you up and hang you from one of the spits."

Derry dodged left and sprang to the right, leaving Morgan spinning. He raced to the stairs that would let him out into the kitchen yard. As he moved, he felt a hand fasten onto his arm, and he swung in a half circle to face his brother's dagger. Morgan tossed a lock of midnight-dark hair from his forehead and inclined his head.

"You need me," he said.

"I think not," Derry replied. "Now run along, for I've no patience with your quarreling at the moment."

Morgan sprang away from him and raced halfway up the stairs to stand like a slim portcullis impeding Derry's exit. Derry ran up the steps, swearing, only to come up against Morgan's dagger. The tip of the weapon touched the laces of the leather jerkin he wore.

"By God's arse, I thought you prayed for my death. Stand aside and I'll try to oblige you."

Morgan's gaunt features took on the expressionless quality of a saint in a stained glass window. "But Derry, I don't want you killed unless I perform the task myself."

Desperation clawed at his forbearance. Derry knocked

the dagger aside, stuck his face close to Morgan's, and hissed.

"I did stab him, you know. Apurpose, for the title, and the lands, and the riches. I knew I'd won when I felt his blood spilling over my bare hands."

Morgan closed his eyes briefly and grimaced, then opened them to gaze blankly at Derry. Before he could react, Derry slapped him. Morgan's head snapped back. Derry caught him and tossed him over the banister. He charged out of the kitchen without waiting to see his brother hit the floor.

Racing to the stables, he found Stubb holding Jove saddled and dancing in the night's coolness. He mounted while his servant held the stallion still.

"I like it not, your going off alone. Got no right to hie yourself off like this. Where's your brother?"

"Asleep."

Derry slapped the reins against Jove's withers, and the animal sprang into motion. He galloped away from the house, leaving Stubb behind.

The journey to the ruins of St. Botolph's took less than an hour. He walked his horse to within a half league of the church, tethered him, and crept from hillock to bush the rest of the way.

St. Botolph's lay in fields that had once been church grounds and a cemetery beside a portion of Bishopsgate Street that ran outside the city walls. To the north and south, houses and craftsmen's halls lined the road, but Londoners avoided St. Botolph's. It was said to be haunted by the ghosts of a Norman lord and the Saxon prince he murdered. If this rumor weren't adequate, the hooting of unseen owls in the cemetery was enough to discourage would-be builders.

Derry snaked his body through the tall grass in a field

that bordered the cemetery. Lifting his head, he raked the headstones, trees, and fallen blocks of stone for signs of Thea's captors. He'd come well over an hour early, yet he could see at least half a dozen men in various places of concealment. He was watching a man scurry to a hiding place behind a tree, when a vise closed around his ankle.

He jackknifed his body, but a great weight landed on him. He was flattened on his back, and a gloved hand clamped over his mouth.

"Shhh," came a whisper. "Do you want to warn them?"

The hand lifted, and Derry whispered back fiercely at his brother. "Get off me, God curse you. If you ruin— *mmphf.*" He whipped his head from side to side, but Morgan's hand stayed put.

"Be still."

If he fought Morgan, he would lose Thea. He let his body grow limp and glared up at his brother. What he saw caused a moment of consternation, for Morgan's smooth and almost boylike features had contorted with remorse.

"Derry, forgive me, I beg of you."

"You're mad."

"No," Morgan said, shaking his head, "not now, though I have been since the—the accident. No, listen before you reply." Morgan's head sank to Derry's chest, then he lifted it again. "Why did you not deny Father's accusations? Why did you let me believe you killed him apurpose?"

"Morgan, this is not the time."

"Why?"

"Because I would have too closely mimicked Pontius Pilate—'I am innocent of the blood of this just person.'"

He looked away from Morgan's shock and stared at a dark screen of grass. To his relief, Morgan released him from his unsettling stare and rolled off him. He turned over to face him, and they ended up nose to nose.

Morgan grimaced. "Do you know how I woke to the truth? You confessed. At last you said what I'd been trying to make you say all these years. I'd longed to hear you babbling your guilt, and when you complied . . . How was I to know I couldn't believe you? A pox on it, Derry, why didn't you tell me the truth?"

"You didn't want to hear it, and in any case, silence preserves innocence, or in this instance, your life and mine. If I had protested against your accusations, you would have fought me all the more. Now, by your leave, I am in haste to deliver my Thea *bella* from these sodding whoresons."

"I shall assist you."

Morgan drew a knife.

"Wait," Derry said. "You mustn't touch any of them until I show myself. Otherwise someone may notice they're missing. I've searched completely around the church. There are seven men."

Together they planned their stratagem, then returned to the place where he'd tethered Jove. Derry led the horse openly down the road while Morgan crept upon the outermost guards. He passed the first, who signaled to the second. Congratulating himself on his caution, Derry didn't look back. He thought he heard the barest trace of a thud, then another as Morgan felled the two guards after each had given his signal.

He dropped Jove's reins before he turned off the road. The animal halted and began to graze. He walked into the field in front of the rounded stone arch that once formed the entry to the church. He stopped, letting his arms hang loosely at his sides, and waited.

He heard the scrape of flint. A torch flared, casting long

shadows inside the hollow of the church. The torch floated
to the threshold. Attached to it was Thea's arm. She held
it aloft in bound hands and gazed at him. She was gagged.
After glancing over her shoulder, she stumbled out of the
ruins. Behind her, sword tip nudging his captive, came
Lord Gracechurch. Three men walked behind Gracechurch. The group halted twenty paces from Derry.

Gracechurch called out to him. "Your sword, my lord."

"It's Gracechurch," Derry said on a laugh. "Well met,
sirrah, and a game well played." Derry drew his blade and
tossed it aside.

"Now come here."

He shook his head. "Release Mistress Hunt."

Gracechurch lowered his sword and shoved Thea toward Derry. She took three steps.

Then Gracechurch shouted, "Take him!"

The three men behind Gracechurch rushed past Thea.
Derry dived for his sword as an arrow whizzed by and
impaled the first man. He heard Gracechurch screaming
for his hidden guards, his voice rising in panic as no one
came to his aid. Derry rolled to his feet, sword in hand, as
the two guards reached him. He parried a thrust from one,
leaned sideways so that his torso was parallel with the
ground, and kicked the man in the gut.

The second man was on him as he straightened. Derry
brought his blade up to counter his overhand slice, but the
man was heavy, and his arm bent. He went with the force
of the blow, letting himself fall to the ground. He rolled
and crashed into the man's legs. His opponent dived and
hit his shoulder against a building stone encased in lichen.
Derry was about to leap to his feet, when the tip of a sword
touched his throat.

"No more of that," said the second guard. His gaze
flickered as he looked over Derry's shoulder.

Derry heard a buzz. Another blade flashed, and the guard's sword left him. Metal clashed against metal. Derry thrust himself aside as Morgan rained blows on the guard. The man recovered from his surprise, however, and countered with an offensive that drove Morgan backward.

As Derry turned to search for Thea, Morgan cried out. His heel caught a broken gravestone, and he fell. The guard ran at him, sword raised. Derry palmed his dagger as the man raised his sword over Morgan's unprotected chest. The guard stabbed down at Morgan, who parried, but the sword slid down his blade. Derry saw the tip pierce Morgan's shoulder. Derry's thumb pressed into the flat of the blade. His arm cocked and he threw hard.

As the guard pulled his sword free to deliver another thrust, the dagger hit between his shoulders and sank in to the hilt. The man's body jerked. The sword wavered over Morgan's limp body, then the guard dropped to the ground. Derry immediately turned and searched for Thea.

She was standing between him and the church, torch in both hands. She swung the flame at Gracechurch. The man hopped and dodged the brand while trying to avoid the last guard, who was rolling on the ground, clutching his burning face. She jabbed at Gracechurch's stomach, but he countered by bringing his sword down on the torch. It flew from her hands. Derry raced for her.

"Thea, run!"

She turned at the sound of his voice. He cursed himself as Gracechurch aimed his sword at the middle of her back.

# 21

*Full many a bloody deed was done.*

—HENRY HOWARD, EARL OF SURREY

THEA WHIRLED TO FACE Derry. At once she realized her mistake, even without the horrified look on Derry's face. She dropped to the ground with a jolt, and Gracechurch's sword jabbed into the earth before her face. At the same time, Derry's boot landed by her cheek. She heard a grunt, and what felt like a pair of oxen landed on her. The world vanished, as did the breath in her body. She flailed her arms, and the oxen rolled off her.

Wheezing, she lay quietly until she was scooped up into Derry's arms. Warm lips devoured her cheeks and ears, and she smiled even as she panted. Then she looked down at Gracechurch. He lay belly uppermost with Derry's sword still protruding from his gut.

"You shouldn't have killed him!"

"Shouldn't have killed him?" Derry dropped her legs and stood her on her feet so that he could glare at her face-to-face. "Shouldn't have killed him? He was going to skewer you!"

"But something's wrong. Derry, he's not the Wyvern. I'm certain of it. Hark you, I've seen someone, not closely, but someone. Someone who wears many rings and jewels, like your dear Countess of Lynford."

"I know Gracechurch isn't the Wyvern," Derry said. He began dragging her to where Morgan lay against a gravestone. "I wanted to keep him alive, but the fool attacked you. God's blood, think you I'd believed Gracechurch the master of a ring of traitors? Gracechurch, in faith."

They knelt beside Morgan, who in the moonlight appeared as pale as the gravestone that supported him. Thea drew his hand from the wound, and Derry tore jerkin and shirt to expose the injury. Thea produced yards of petticoat. Derry lowered Morgan to the ground.

"Attend to him while I make certain we're safe and find Jove."

She pressed upon the wound with a thick wad of cloth until the bleeding ebbed. By the time she'd constructed a bandage, Derry returned with Jove and Morgan's horse. With her help he put Morgan on Jove and mounted behind him while she took the other horse. Riding slowly, they made their way west to Bridgestone Abbey.

It was still dark when they rode up to the front steps. Morgan had fainted, but his bleeding had slowed. She helped Derry lift him from the stallion. To her surprise, Derry hefted his brother into his arms almost as easily as he lifted her. She went ahead to bang on the doors and raise the household.

When she reached the threshold, her hand met an open door. No doubt the alarm had been raised at her absence, for a diffuse light came from the entry that ran between the doors and the screens to the hall. She shoved the doors open, entered quickly, and returned with a lit candle from a wall sconce as Derry came inside. Leading the way, she passed through the arch in the screen, then slowed as misgiving overtook her. The house was silent. When her father was alarmed he was never silent.

"Derry, go back."

"What's wrong?"

"Go back at once," she said as she hurried back the way they'd come.

A voice boomed at them from the stairs at the other end of the hall and echoed off the hammerbeams high above.

"I would have preferred that you dealt with Grace-church."

They turned to see two men descend the stairs. Timothy Eyre led the way, bearing a candelabrum, and behind him came the Earl of Lynford. Thea swallowed hard as she noticed the bandage on Lynford's hand.

"You," she said, "you were the one."

Lynford favored her with a sweet smile as he came toward them, then transferred his gaze to Derry. The loathing she saw in his face made her draw closer to Derry. Unlike herself, Derry appeared not at all startled by Lynford's appearance.

"I had a list," Derry said as he lowered his brother to the floor. "A short one with three names on it. Yours, my lord, was the last of the three. But I confess I would have thought having failed again to kill me this night, you'd have had the sense to flee England."

"What have you done with my father?" Thea asked.

The earl hardly bothered to glance at her. "I clapped him in the stables with the rest of the household." He stared at Derry. "There's going to be a hellish fire. A most lamentable accident. Soon. But fear not, my lord. You and your lady won't perish. Not yet. You see, there's a certain Frenchman who longs to have converse with both of you. I promised I'd bring you north with me."

"We have Walbrook and Clark," Derry said.

"But not the others, who have been warned." Lynford glanced down at Morgan. "I confess I shall enjoy your anguish when you see the boy engulfed in flames, for you've near ruined me by forcing me into the open with your antics. But I take heart, for I've lands in Scotland, and can act from there."

"You had Gracechurch play the Wyvern," Thea said, her voice sharp with indignation. "You threw Timothy Eyre, and even your own mother in our path—"

"So that we'd not suspect you," Derry finished. "Sending an assassin to play the dragon to my St. George, that was indeed clever."

Lynford inclined his head in acceptance of the praise.

"I thank you. It's lamentable that I've no time to hear more compliments or witness my revenge." He glanced at his men. "Gentlemen."

Lynford fastened his hand on Thea's arm.

"Wait!" She twisted in his grasp. "At least tell me why you've betrayed her majesty and England."

A spasm distorted the earl's upper lip into a sneer. "Her majesty. The spawn of that monster, good King Henry. He killed my father, may God curse his name to eternity. I watched the headsman chop through his neck, you know. I can still hear the ax. It made this peculiar thud, and then there was a cracking sound as it cut the neck bones. I hear that cracking, and Mother screaming. I'll never forget."

Lynford was staring at Thea without seeming to recognize her. "When I was younger, Mother would remind me of how it was, if I began to forget."

The earl shook his head. Thea could see his gaze clear and fasten upon her. He dragged her to him and called to four men who emerged from the shadows near the stairs.

One bore a crossbow aimed at Derry. The rest surrounded Derry and disarmed him. The crossbowman stopped beside Thea, his weapon still aimed at Derry's heart.

Thea kept her gaze fixed on Derry. One of the men began to drag Morgan away, and she knew Derry would fight for his brother. Though her legs felt as weak as rotten timber, she readied herself to come to his aid. The man dragging Morgan was drawing his burden through the arch in the screen. One of the guards was binding Derry's hands. Body trembling, Thea tried not to hold her breath while she waited.

She was forcing herself to breathe, when she heard a crash. Thunder sounded behind the screen, and the guard holding Morgan cried out and dived out of sight. At the same time, Derry jammed his elbow into the belly of one of his guards. As he moved, Thea recovered her wits and kicked the crossbow. The weapon darted toward the ceiling and fired.

Lynford grabbed her, swearing, as Thea poked him on the nose. He bent low and threw her over his shoulder. She kicked at him uselessly as he carried her toward the other end of the hall.

Just then her father clattered into the hall astride a massive draft horse, brandishing a garden hoe.

"Trample my roses, will you! Steal my animals!" Lord Hunt roared.

Inigo Culpepper followed him on another thundering animal and drove a herd of squealing and furious pigs in front of him. Several of Lynford's men followed, stumbling over pigs and falling under the great hooves of the draft horses.

Before Lynford bore her out of the hall, she saw Derry run his sword through the last of his captors and dodge a candelabrum thrown by Timothy Eyre. She screamed his name and he looked up at her, horror plain in his eyes. The earl bounded through the house so quickly, her head knocked against his belt. She saw the floors of various chambers and passages, then the flagstones of the terrace that led to the gardens at the rear of the house.

On the terrace the earl paused, turned to face the house, then in the direction of the stables. She could hear the melee inside and a similar one in progress in the stables.

As her head bumped the earl's belt again, Thea's fear turned to rage. She wasn't going to be abducted a third time. Her hand slipped around Lynford's waist, groped for and found a knife. She drew it and stabbed at the earl's back.

Though the blade hit steel armor, Lynford cried out and threw her from his shoulder. She landed on her back. Her arms hit the flagstones, and the knife was jolted out of her hand. It skidded across the flagstones. She scrambled into a sitting position, pushing back her tousled hair. The earl was walking away from her toward the knife.

She jumped to her feet and tried to run, but Lynford picked up the knife and caught her quickly. He drew her close so that her back was to his chest.

"By the true church, it seems I must settle for killing the lady instead of the brother. No matter, Lord Derry will suffer as much, mayhap more."

She felt a gloved hand clamp down on her jaw. It dragged her head to the side, exposing her throat. She gasped when she felt the edge of the knife press against her skin.

"I shall leave you here bleeding, your throat gaping open, for him to find."

Thea shrieked as the blade sliced. But then Lynford's body jerked, and the hand holding the knife went stiff. There was a moment when they stood still, he poised to cut her throat, she straining to pull his hands from her. Then the earl's arms dropped. She turned to ward him off, but his legs buckled even as he stared at her, mouth working. He sank to the flagstones.

Thea skipped backward out of his way. From his back protruded the quarrel of a crossbow. Stunned, Thea looked at it blankly. She raised her head. Across the terrace, on the steps, knelt Derry, crossbow still aimed. He, too, had been staring at Lynford. She jumped as the crossbow fell from his hands. He looked up at her, his gaze filled with alarm.

"Thea?" His voice was hoarse. "Thea?"

She ran. Skirts flying, she raced across the terrace and threw herself into his arms as he stood. He kept muttering her name as he lifted her and squeezed hard. She wrapped her arms around his neck and hugged, pressing her face into his neck.

"Jesu Maria," he said. "But a second later and—"

She cut him off with a kiss, then lifted her mouth. "My father!"

Derry gave a short laugh. "Your father is busy trampling traitors. He's quite well and happy. Lynford's men are fleeing."

Thea kicked her feet. "Put me down."

Derry set her on her feet, but her knees bent. He slipped an arm about her waist, and they began to walk toward the house. Inside, the hall was filled with the squealing of pigs and clattering of hooves. The bodies of dead men lay scattered across the floor, and Inigo and her father were directing their disposition.

"Ah!" Lord Hunt said as they joined him. "Found her, did you, Lord—uh—my boy? Excellent. Really, Thea, you shouldn't run off when we're killing people. Bad manners."

"Father, I've never seen you fight," Thea said.

Lord Hunt snorted. "They were going to steal my horses, and they trampled my roses. Killing's the least they deserved."

Thea glanced at Derry, who shook his head in sympathy. Luckily they spotted Morgan lying on a table by the screen with Hobby and Simon Spry in attendance. Excusing themselves, they went to him.

"Aaow, my lady, what a hurly-burly, what a horrible mess. And look at this poor boy. Needs a physician, he does."

"I know, Hobby. Now, stand aside so that Lord Derry can lift him."

Derry picked up his brother. Thea took her skirts in one hand and a candle offered by Simon in the other.

"This is where we began," she said.

Derry glanced up from studying his brother and smiled at her. In a short time they had Morgan in bed and his wound cleansed and bound. Thea sent for a physician and ordered a watch by his bedside.

Hobby tended him first, and as the woman took her place in an armchair, Thea noticed the sun shining through a window. She leaned on a bedpost. Her eyelids felt heavy and dry, and her body felt as if it had been trampled by one of her father's draft horses. Derry left Morgan's side and came to her.

"You're weary."

"Near dead," she replied without moving.

Her eyes closed and her head began to drop. Startled, she caught herself. Her head jerked back and she stumbled against Derry. He chuckled and lifted her. She almost fell asleep by the time he lowered her into her own bed.

His hands moved over her body, undressing her. She protested, but he ignored her and threw the covers over her, drawing them up over her bare breasts to her chin. He bent and kissed her. She latched onto his hand when he tried to leave her, and he sat on the edge of the bed.

"Sleep, Thea *bella*. You must rest, or you'll become ill."

"Tell me," she said. It was an effort to keep her eyes open. She grasped his jerkin and pulled him nearer. "Tell me. Did you come for the Wyvern, or for me?"

"Both," he said. He touched her cheek with the backs of his fingers. "But hark you, Thea *bella*. I will always come for you, no matter the cost."

For a bright instant her weariness vanished. She sank her hands in his sunlight hair and drew him down to her. She opened her mouth to him, and he kissed her, drawing her tongue deep into his own mouth.

His lips lifted slightly and whispered, "Sleep, Thea *bella*. And ask no more foolish questions. I will come for you, 'as long as rivers shall run down to the sea, or shadows touch the mountain slopes, or stars graze in the vault of heaven.'"

He left her then, and as the door closed and she began to sink into sleep, she suddenly came fully awake. Her eyes flew open. He'd said he would always come for her, but she's made him promise to leave. He would leave. She said the words aloud, and they caused a winter gale in her stomach. She wouldn't lose him to death, but she would lose him all the same. She couldn't bear losing him when she lo—Thea sat up. The covers dropped away from her body unnoticed. She loved him!

Astonished, startled, amazed—none of the words that came to her seemed adequate to expressed the turmoil that possessed her. She lay back and tried to calm herself. The weariness of her body warred with the agitation of her mind until, at last, weariness triumphed. She fell asleep with Derry's words chasing each other in her imagination. *I will come for you "as long as rivers shall run down to the sea, or shadows touch the mountain slopes, or stars graze in the vault of heaven."*

*She woke late in* the afternoon of the next day to find that the signs of the previous night's battle had been cleared away under the direction of her father. She bathed and dressed while waiting for Hobby to bring her a meal. Dabbing lotion on the cut at her throat, Thea mused over the betrayal of the Earl of Lynford. The man hadn't served the Scots queen's cause for his own gain. He had wealth enough. Why had he risked everything? For what he called the true faith, for power? Mayhap he'd but desired vengeance upon the daughter of the king who killed his father.

Hobby came in with a tray of food. Thea drew a stool up to a table beside the fireplace and began to devour roast partridge and hot bread. Her stomach was so empty, she could feel it twisting into dry, empty knots. Chewing thoughtfully on a hunk of bread, she watched Hobby move about the room, picking up clothing and shoving bath cloths out the door.

"Hobby." She swallowed a piece of bread and took a sip of ale. "Hobby, where is Lord Derry?"

Hobby kicked the last cloth outside and shut the door. She moaned and pressed her hand to the small of her back.

"Galloped off, he has. That man vanishes like a merchant at tax time. Aaow, my bones. He rushed about all day, ordering folks about, having them villains rounded up and taken off someplace, then all at once he disappeared."

"And my father?"

"Still in the stables, conversing with the horses. He was all amazed at the earl, him turning vicious and all. Curious, he was, but Lord Derry made up some story about you spurning the earl for him and the earl going mad."

"A pox on him! Why must he cast the blame on me?"

Thea dropped her bread and rested her chin on her hand. She hadn't had time to tell Derry more about the countess, and now he'd gone off without telling her when he'd return. No matter. She would tell him when he came back. After all, the countess wouldn't be allowed to leave England now that her son had been revealed as a traitor.

But had Derry really triumphed? He'd destroyed a hive of traitorous wasps, but the Scots queen remained a threat. Thea felt a twinge of regret. Mary Stuart had once been kind and possessed of fine sensibility to the suffering of others. How could she hatch such foul designs that could result only in the death of innocent subjects? The more she thought, the more Thea realized that England and Queen Elizabeth would never be safe with the Queen of Scots lurking on their doorstep.

She stuffed a candied fig in her mouth as she contemplated the possibility that Elizabeth might not survive the secret battle with Mary Stuart. A quiver traveled through her body at the idea. A plague take Mary Stuart. She had no right to interfere with the peace of England.

Thea dipped her fingers in a bowl of water and wiped them on her napkin. Hobby had dragged out one of her gowns and was sitting on a cushion, mending it. Outside in the court below her room, she could hear a servant raking the gravel that covered the ground. A moment of peace. A rarity since she'd encountered Derry. Derry— she'd been avoiding thinking about Derry's leaving, about her revelation of last night.

Soon she would have many peaceful moments, for Derry would leave and she would go home to rural tranquility. There the days would lengthen into warmth and placidity.

She had never noticed the monotony. But that was before Derry. Now when she thought of going home, the prospect no longer offered comfort, but desolation, for at home there would be no Derry. No lordly whirlwind to try her patience with his imperious demands and ruthless temper, no unpredictable enticer bent on luring her to his bed.

She sneaked a glance at Hobby. What she needed was some of Hobby's forwardness. Her brash maid would give no thought to telling a man that she wanted him to stay. Mayhap she'd have some advice.

"Um, Hobby?" Thea rose when the maid looked up from her sewing. She left the table and picked up the sewing basket lying at Hobby's feet, and studied its contents. "Um, Lord Derry said he would go away once he'd caught the traitors, but . . ."

Hobby let her sewing fall to her lap and shook her finger at Thea. "Now, you listen to me, mistress. That man loves you. Young lords don't tear about the countryside, risking their lives for ladies they don't like. It's time you stopped hiding. You take that young man for yourself before some rich court lady does."

"But how?" Thea asked, almost wailing. "I never had a suitor, not a real one."

"Forget courtly manners." Hobby tossed her sewing aside and went to Thea. She dug her elbow into Thea's arm. "There's not a man living who wouldn't give his fortune for a pretty girl to pursue him. You just tell him. No drivel, no lolling about or dithering. After all, he can barely keep out of your gown. Think you he's hot to run off where he can't touch you?"

Thea bit her lip and impatiently brushed away a tear: "Hobby, are you certain? What if he doesn't want me?"

"Not want you! Did I not see him near make love to you on that very bed. And last night, when he wasn't looking at that brother of his, he was casting looks at you like he was a fly and you were a fresh carcass."

Thea wrinkled her nose. "Afore God, Hobby, leave off your comparisons."

Hobby poked her with an elbow again and lowered her voice. "Know what?"

Thea shook her head.

"He come in here while you was asleep. A few hours ago. I found him hanging over the bed, staring, just staring. He touched his fingertips to his lips and then pressed them to your cheek. 'Course, he wouldn't have done that if he'd seen me."

She widened her eyes, and Hobby grinned at her. Derry? Derry hovering over her like an enamored gallant? Slowly her lips spread in a smile. He loved her. He'd saved her life, vowed to do so always, and he sighed over her as she slept. He loved her!

She was grinning at Hobby, when the noise of several horses sounded outside. Racing to the window, she beheld Derry dismounting along with Stubb and Inigo. Whirling, she faced Hobby.

"He's returned. God's mercy, he's returned." She put her hands to her cheeks. They were hot. "I must have courage."

Hobby snorted. "You'll need all of it married to that one."

"Peace, woman. Go to him. Ask him to meet me—oh, where?"

"I know," Hobby said. "That little stream her ladyship had built beside the garden."

"The aqueduct?"

"Aquaduck?"

"Duct, Hobby. Yes, ask him to meet me by the aqueduck—duct. Hurry."

They left. Hobby went in search of Derry while Thea raced out of the house and into the garden. She must ask him at once, for if she delayed, thoughts of France would rob her of courage. And Hobby was right, she would need all her courage if she were to ask Derry for his hand in marriage.

# 22

*Love is a fervent fire*
*Kindled by hot desire . . .*

—Sir Thomas Wyatt

Thea hurried to the aqueduct so that she would have a few moments before Derry arrived. The stone channel ran along the edge of the garden toward Grandmother's rectangular pool and fountain. Since the water was clear, she could see the pebbles and rocks at the bottom. Ferns and saplings hugged the rectangular stones that had been set on end to contain the stream.

Thea hopped from stone to stone along the path to the aqueduct. A breeze stirred as she reached the channel, and it rippled the surface of the water. Stooping, she dipped her hand in it and pressed her damp palm to her face. She didn't want Derry to find her with burning cheeks.

"Courage," she said to herself. "He mislikes cowering."

She pulled her shoulders back. As she cleared her throat, she heard a door slam. Derry came racing toward her from the house. The sun was dropping below the towers of Bridgestone and cast a deep gold aura behind him that turned his hair to flame. Thea ran her tongue around her

dry mouth and squeezed her hands together to conceal
their trembling. Derry dashed along the stone path and
came to a precipitate halt, only to scoop her into his arms
and kiss her hard.

Thea's apprehension vanished as he drove his tongue
into her mouth. She almost forgot her task, but as his hand
roamed over her back, she came to herself. Capturing his
hands, she held them in hers. He grinned at her. Darting
at her like a snake, he planted kisses on her forehead,
cheeks, and chin.

"Derry, I would speak with you."

"Yes?" He freed his hands and put them on her waist.

"Derry! Please, I would talk with you."

"I just handed Timothy Eyre to Master Secretary Cecil.
Our jeweled peacock was screeching names of traitors so
loudly, I needed someone with a host of clerks at his beck."

"And what of the dowager countess?"

"There's no proof against her, Thea *bella*. You saw a
jewel-laden hand, but it could have been Eyre's. Cecil will
question him about Lady Lynford. God's blood, I'm relieved to be rid of this infestation. I nearly went mad with
terror when you vanished. And like a dolt I had ordered
you to remain in the coach."

Thea put her hand over Derry's mouth. "Afore God,
will you stop chattering and listen to me? I must speak
before I lose my courage."

Staring at her, Derry kissed the hand over his mouth,
then sank to the ground. He pulled her down, and she
knelt in front of him. She sank back on her heels. Her
intention had been to look at him, but she found it
impossible to move her lips while gazing into those gentian eyes. She looked at her clasped hands instead.

"You said you would come for me as long as rivers run
down to the sea." She glanced at him quickly. His brows

had drawn together, but a trace of his smile still lingered. "And you have cared for me as no other has, not even my father, especially my father."

"And endangered you as well."

She leaned closer to him and touched his sleeve. "But hark you, though we've quarreled more than we've agreed, since you came, I've learned to—to go among people again. And to be brave."

"You have always been brave. When I cast you—best not call forth such unhappy memories." Derry kissed her hand. "You are the bravest of women."

"I hope so, for I've a thing to ask you." She took in a deep breath, and as she let it out the words came also. "You said you would leave when the traitors were caught, but I no longer wish you gone. You are—I find that your presence is necessary to my happiness." Peering at his startled features, she touched his hand. "I would ask you to—"

"Stop."

She sank back to gaze at him, dread growing as she beheld the way he glanced away from her.

"You know little of me."

"I know you're a highwayman and intelligencer and abductor of women. I know you can kill as easily and as skillfully as you kiss. God's patience, I even know about your mean-spirited father and his ridiculous accusations."

"And do you know about my wife?"

"Dead."

"Yes, she died before me, but not for want of trying to send me first. Much as I desire you, Thea *bella*, I'll not trust myself to marriage again and risk death."

She hesitated for a moment, trying to guess what he was feeling, but he'd closed himself up like a corked bottle.

"Leave it," he said softly.

"I can't."

"Please."

She shook her head. "I love you."

Derry shot to his feet, and she scrambled up as well. He took a few steps back down the path to the house.

"Did you hear me?" she asked.

Derry paused without turning around. "I begged you to leave the matter be, but you force me to be plain with you. I want no more wives, no more danger sleeping in my bed. Again I ask you to stop."

She went to him and grasped his wrist so that he looked at her.

"Don't you want me?"

"Always," he said. "Now cease, for by my troth, this talk of marriage summons demons within me best left undisturbed."

He tried to free his wrist, but Thea only tightened her hold.

"But those are old demons with gray beards. I would never betray you."

Derry had grown pale, and his body tensed when she refused to release him.

"I beg of you, speak no more of it." His voice rose.

"You're afraid."

"God's blood!" Derry turned on her. He yanked his wrist free and put both hands behind his back. "You've seen the scars on my body. I defy you to say you could acquire the like and not be wary of the cause. I bear them because of a woman. No woman will ever hold me in her power again."

Thea didn't know why she threw herself into his arms. Mayhap she only wanted to stop him from talking. She fastened her arms around his neck and pulled his head down. Capturing his lips, she kissed him fiercely, thrusting her tongue into his mouth.

His arms began to shove her, then lifted her to meet his answering kiss. Thea devoured his lips. As she drove her tongue into his mouth again, he gasped. She was torn from him and set on her feet. Swaying, she reached for him, but he held her off with an outthrust arm.

"No," he said. "I can be your lover, but no more."

"You can't be my lover, but you can be much more. Please, Derry."

"Jesu Maria!" He lunged at her. Grasping her by the shoulders, he snarled at her. "I offer you pleasure and the gift of fidelity, and you want my soul. You can't have it, do you hear? It's dead. It died in the Tower when I was seventeen."

Thea cried out as his fingers pressed into her flesh. He cursed and thrust her from him. He ran from her then, as if she were some witchly hag trying to dine on his flesh. He was gone from her sight before it occurred to her to run after him.

There was an imprint of his boot in the soil beside the path. She gazed at it, unable to perceive any of her own emotions. They seemed to have flown from her body as Derry had fled from her. She wandered back to the aqueduct and stood staring at the water.

She had offered her love, and he had turned his face from her as if he'd been presented a rancid dish at table. She'd spoken of love, and he'd answered with talk of lust and pleasure. She had been wrong—again.

He didn't want her, except to make use of her. Thea sank to her knees and squeezed her eyes shut as pain stabbed through her chest. God, she might as well have been a beggar holding out her bowl to him, a peddler offering cheap baubles. Was that how he valued her, as a cheap bauble not worth the price asked for it? Doubling over, she hugged herself. At last the tears came, and with them the knowledge that she was unwanted. Sobs tore from deep inside her body as she realized how greatly she'd feared this very thing.

Was it wrong to want someone to stand at her side before God and man, to long for him to offer her more than affection and pleasure when convenient for him? Thea dropped on her stomach and thrust her fist into her mouth to stifle the noise of her crying. She should never have come to London, never trusted Grandmother, never trusted him. Better a lifetime of loneliness than this pain.

*Derry quit Bridgestone Abbey* almost as soon as he'd left her. She had watched him ride away on Jove from her window, knowing she would never see him again. In the depths of summer, winter settled into her bones and suffused her being. Three days went by without her observing their passage. Somehow they vanished while she sat at her window, shrouded in her grief.

Upon the morning of the fourth day she answered a knock at her chamber door. Stubb stood without, offering a sealed note. He'd remained behind with Inigo to care for Morgan, who could not be moved at once. She broke the seal on the paper and read: *Will you see me? Morgan.* She hesitated, then nodded her assent. If she didn't go to him, Morgan was stubborn enough to come to her chamber.

Morgan was dressed and lying atop the covers of his bed. His arm was bound to his chest. She noted that the wound fever had left him, and that he'd gained some color. He had been dozing when she entered, escorted by Stubb. He roused, but she forbade him to rise and ensconced herself in a chair beside the bed.

"Are you better, my lord?"

Morgan gave her a sidelong glance. "Yes, I thank you, mistress." He propped himself up on an elbow, gazing at her solemnly all the while as if measuring her worth. "The Queen of Scots is well enamored of Lord Darnley now. We've had word that she will wed him in a few weeks."

Thea smoothed a wrinkle from a sheet, then met his gaze without smiling. "A deserved fate. I hope Darnley is even more of a fool and an arse than your brother."

"My brother has indeed played the fool with you, I fear," Morgan said gravely.

Refusing to change her indifferent expression, she said, "I was most concerned for your health."

"His behavior to you is right marvelous, you know. He seldom plays the horse's arse with women, for he never relinquishes command of himself."

"Your fever is gone."

"You mustn't let him run away."

"I will ask Cook to prepare fruit pasties for you. They build strength."

Morgan sat up, swung his legs over the side of the bed, and peered at her. "He loves you."

"Good morrow to you, my lord."

His hand shot out to restrain her. "Have you never been frightened?"

She cast him an incredulous glance.

"Then," Morgan said, "you should understand. He was little more than a boy when that bitch fed him to Bloody Bonner. Thea, he used to follow her about Moorefield Garde along with her pet spaniel. You must understand that his fears have nothing to do with you. They're from the past, and they intrude upon the present."

"He doesn't want me."

"Of course he wants you. Why else would he have fled like a rat chased by a terrier?"

"Then why did he abandon me?"

"Because you asked of him something he fears more than the pox. Marry, lady, I think he's bargained with Satan for the gift of artifice, and mayhap therein lies the secret. Since he was released from the Tower, he has practiced his wiles upon many women, played with them, spun a web of lies and charm in which to tangle them, but never trusted them with his love. But you are different. You he loves, though he refuses to admit it. He can't rid himself of this love, but he can't marry you. Therefore he flees."

Thea gripped the arms of her chair. "Why do you tell me these things? He's gone."

Morgan took her hand and kissed it. "I owe my brother an unpayable debt. This is my way of settling part of it. Thea, you're the only woman who has ever withstood Derry, his evil games, his dragonlike temper, his chameleon nature. You're the only woman for whom he's ever shed all these disguises and defenses."

"The only one," she repeated. Understanding began to light her gloomy world.

"Don't let him go," Morgan said, squeezing her hand. "He came to me before he left, and I heard him mutter something."

"What was it?"

"'Shall she never out of my mind/Nor shall I never out of this pain?'"

She left Morgan and retired to her chamber to contemplate his revelations. She thought for two days. Longing for Derry battled with pain and the fear of being hurt again. To her dismay, Hobby had discovered the details of her conversation with Morgan. She suspected that Stubb had eavesdropped. Now Hobby urged her to precipitate action.

She stood over Thea, plump arms folded, and chided her. "It's time you stopped being like your father."

"I'm not like him!"

"Mayhap you've a better memory, but both of you run away, mistress. He ran away from his mother and from the world; you run away from that tasty young man and from the world. Admit it. You're going back to the country."

Thea traced a join in the floorboards with the toe of her slipper. "Not right away."

"See?"

"I can't face him." Thea fled to the window and curled up in its seat. She whispered, "Hobby, I think I would die if he cast me aside again."

Hobby marched over to stand before her and shake a finger at her. "You listen to me, mistress. A man like that, who will give his life for you, who admires you and looks part stallion and part angel, a man like that is worth any risk." Hobby paused and glanced at her sideways. "Or are you such a shivering little trout that you'd rather let some court bawd have him than fight for him yourself?"

Thea uncurled her body. "What court bawd?"

"It's bruited about the city that the queen would have Lord Derry married. She likes it not that he's heir to Moorefield and has no babes of his own. I heard she's to look to the matter herself."

"He won't marry a silly maid."

"If the queen commands, he'll have no choice."

"Afore God!"

Hobby grinned at her. Thea ignored her. She tapped her slipper on the floor as she considered the prospect. Another woman might capture Derry simply because she was too cowardly to fight for him. Another woman might share his bed, receive the gift of his smiles.

"Not if I have to tie him down while the minister performs the ceremony."

"What?" Hobby asked.

Thea turned to the window. In the court below, Morgan was making ready to leave. He was mending rapidly, and he'd told her he would join Derry at his house in Charterhouse Lane. Thea twisted the latch and shoved open the window. As she stuck her head out, Morgan put his left boot in the stirrup and swung his long leg over the back of his stallion. That smooth, graceful movement sent her spinning back in time. She saw Derry perform that same action with the same ease and grace. She saw him riding toward her, body bent over Jove's neck. He reached out, scooped her up as if as if she were a sack of leaves. . . .

Blinking, Thea recovered her wits. "God's mercy." She leaned out of the window. "Morgan! Morgan, hold a moment."

She leapt out of the window seat. Scurrying out of the house with Hobby close behind, she ran up to Morgan and beckoned to him. He dismounted, smiling at her haste, and bent to listen to her low converse. After moment he straightened, and his smile had spread into a grin.

"It will serve," he said. "By God's nightshirt, it will serve right well."

They grinned at each other while Hobby stood near, bursting with curiosity. Just then Lord Hunt wandered around the corner of the house carrying a rosebush. The knees of his hose were brown and soggy from kneeling in the dirt. His progress was marked by a trail of clods and sprays of soil from the roots of the bush.

"Ah, Thea, my dear. There you are. This is the last of the bushes, and I thought you might like to plant it yourself. Those ruffians destroyed many of them, but I've sent for more." Lord Hunt paused to study Morgan. "My boy, I'm sure you had golden hair." He turned to Thea. "My dear, Lord—um, Lord—um, he's turned his hair black. Don't approve, my boy. Not at all. A French trick. Englishmen don't do it."

Muttering to himself, Lord Hunt continued on around the house toward the garden, leaving Thea to stare after him in exasperation while Morgan tried to conceal his mirth.

"Shall we ask your father to help us?"

"A pox on you, Morgan St. John, you're not a chivalrous man."

# 23

*But true love is a durable fire*
*In the mind ever burning;*
*Never sick, never old, never dead,*
*From itself never turning.*

—SIR WALTER RALEIGH

FRIGHTENING TIMOTHY EYRE HADN'T distracted Derry from his pain. Since he'd refused Thea, he'd spent his days prowling his house in Charterhouse Lane and his nights threatening Timothy with his most artful forms of persecution. He had but to describe them to make Eyre chatter like a jackdaw. Cecil's clerks had been taxed to keep up with him. Yet the pain remained.

It had settled throughout his body, a diffuse, pervasive ache, constant and wearing to the spirit. The world had lost its bright colors, the morning its hope. To have the woman he wanted he must do the thing that would destroy him.

Even his treasure room held no joy. As usual, since he lost Thea, he couldn't sleep. He'd come to the chamber to find solace, for it was there that he felt the most at peace. No longer.

He'd promised himself the pleasure of showing it to Thea, for she would love it as he did. He had risen at the hour after midnight and dressed. He'd gone there and lit dozens of candles so that he could see the paintings, the vases, the books and statues.

The chamber was long, almost as long as the gallery beside it. The walls bore paintings by Botticelli, Uccello, Rapheal, and Tintoretto. They were cast in shadow now, as was his latest purchase, a bronze by Benvenuto Cellini. His father had tried to crush his love of art. To survive, he'd hidden the love until he grew strong enough to nourish it himself. Often he wished he'd been born soon enough to have known Michelangelo Buonarroti. The treasure room had been his soul's nourishment—until Thea. She was the greatest treasure of all.

Derry wandered to a table and rested his hand on a small silver-gilt box he'd purchased from the Farnese family. Molded in the shape of a Greek building, it bore mythical scenes in carved rock crystal on its sides. Within lay a manuscript by da Vinci. He had longed to show it to Thea, for he knew he would have seen the same look of awe that had been on his own countenance upon beholding the drawings. As he gazed at the box, the first hint of light touched its shining surface. He glanced at the window, and heard horses entering the courtyard at a gallop.

When he looked out, he saw Morgan dismounting. To his surprise, his brother ran up the steps two at a time. Curse the fool, he would rip his wound open. Derry stalked across the room, but the door flew open and Morgan charged in, slamming it behind him.

Panting, he grabbed Derry. "She's gone."

"Thea? She's gone north?"

Morgan nodded and gulped in air.

"Why such haste to tell me?" Derry removed himself from Morgan's grasp. "It is her custom to hide in the country."

"No." Morgan advanced on him. "She's furious at being scorned. Derry, she's gone north to Scotland. She intends to speak to the Queen of Scots."

"You're right mad."

"I've had it from her maid."

Rage erupted, burning through his mind, his reason. He'd been duped. He'd been fooled by her shy airs, her passion, her pretended honesty.

"By God's entrails, this time I'll deal with her as I would the meanest trull. Inigo!"

Bellowing for the thief, he stormed out of the treasure room. Morgan followed, and he locked the door before stomping downstairs to gather his men. He was so furious he could hardly wait for Jove to be saddled, but in less than an hour he and his party were ready. Morgan joined him.

"You're not well enough to come," Derry said as he gathered his horse's reins.

"She left two days ago. You'll need me to help find her."

"Anthony."

Derry watched Anthony Now-Now clamp a massive hand on Morgan's arm. Morgan was dragged gently from his horse.

"Derry, you sodding arse, tell him to let me loose."

"I can't, sweet brother. He's your new nurse. God rest you, Morgan."

With a wave of his hand he set off. He set a swift pace but not a killing one. After all, Thea would travel woman-style, with many stops and an easy pace. She would have baggage carts, slow, clumsy vehicles that stuck in mud and tipped over in ruts, and most roads in England con-sisted of mud and ruts.

Fortune was with him, and three days' riding saw him far north of London and about to pounce upon Dorothea Philadelphia Hunt. He'd had all that time to contemplate her punishment. He was going to abduct her again. The fright would serve as her first taste of retribution. Afterward he would give her to Cecil, for he no longer trusted himself with her.

He and his men camped when Thea did. She was traveling as quickly as she could, but that morning she'd left the road to cut across country. Thus she'd forgone the dubious comfort of the few inns scattered along the road. As darkness fell, he reflected upon how incongruous it was that they once more drew close to Ravensmere. The castle lay less than an hour by foot to the west. No doubt Thea was unaware of its nearness.

Derry sat before the fire with Inigo and Stubb and tossed the dregs of his ale at the flames. Earlier he'd crept close to Thea's camp and watched her. Seeing her again had aroused both his lust and his rage. She seemed so tranquil, not at all as if she were defying him and betraying her queen. He smiled, causing Inigo to stir uneasily.

"Please, my lord," Inigo said, "don't do that."

"What?"

"Smile at me. Gives me chills, it does. I feel like Death himself is leering at me."

"I must remember to smile when we catch Mistress Hunt." Derry rose and took up his cloak. "You will remain here until I return with her."

"But someone should go with—ow!"

Derry glanced down to see Inigo rubbing his arm while Stubb calmly sipped his ale. "I need no assistance in plucking her from that nest of fat geese. I'll return anon."

By moonlight the journey to Thea's camp took little time at all. The only difficulty was that the camp wasn't where he'd left it. It had been perched on the edge of a stream at a bend that curved around an archaic oak. Now all that was left of Thea and her escort was a black pile of burnt and wet wood, the remains of a doused fire. Derry knelt and touched the wood. Still warm. He raised his head and strained to see through the darkness to the darker shadows of the trees.

He turned and swept his gaze in a circle. Nothing. He was about to find dry wood to make a torch, when he caught a glimpse of yellow through the trees. A dot of light receded in the distance, bobbing occasionally. A torch held by someone foolish enough to travel at night and clumsy with haste. Thea.

Springing up, Derry dashed after the light. At the last moment he dodged an overhanging limb. He'd been so intent upon pursuit, he'd forgotten to keep his gaze on the space directly in front of him. Pausing, he cursed his own negligence, then resumed the pursuit, this time glancing from the light to his surroundings and back again.

Moving swiftly, he soon caught up with the dancing light. It wove way in a direction that he soon recognized. Ahead, past the frothy, hissing stream lay Ravensmere. Derry raced across the stone bridge, plunged into the wood once more, and approached the disintegrated curtain wall. As he emerged from the wood, the floating light vanished through a gap in the wall. He climbed a spray of fallen blocks of stone and peeped over the top of the wall.

The inner ward was dark. He slipped inside and slinked over and around debris until he saw a dim light through the arrow slits in one of the towers, the tower in which he'd kept Thea. As he approached, the light moved up the stairs. He darted inside. Holding his scabbard so that it wouldn't clank against the tower wall, he crept after the light. He stopped a few steps below the landing that led to Thea's old chamber.

For the first time since he'd begun to chase the light, he

paused. There was an unnatural quiet. No raven stirred. No owl hooted. He listened, but could hear not the slightest creak of old wood. If this was Thea he'd followed, where were her men-at-arms, her servants? What would make her plunge into a dark wood alone? Derry pulled his dagger and slowly, silently, unsheathed his sword.

Flattening himself against the wall, he eased up the steps to the open doorway of Thea's chamber. The light had come to rest inside, but he first glanced up the staircase and the blackness leading to the next floor. Then he carefully stuck his head around the door frame.

The torch had been stuck in a wall sconce near the threshold. It burned low and now cast but a dull, diffuse pool of light upon the doorway. Derry had to direct his gaze away from the light to be able to distinguish shapes in the room beyond. As his eyes adjusted, he perceived movement.

"Come in, Derry."

"Thea Hunt, what means all this creeping about at night?"

"Come in, and I will tell you."

Sheathing his weapons, he stalked into the chamber. A rustle at his back caused him to whirl and draw his sword. The door slammed in his face. He heard a bar drop into place, whipped around with his back to the portal, and peered into the darkness.

"Thea, you evil little blight, what are you about?"

There was no answer. He grabbed the torch as its flames dwindled and thrust it in Thea's direction. The flames died as he moved the torch, but before it sputtered out, the dim light flickered over an expanse of flesh—bare, smooth flesh. He heard himself make a guttural sound.

An unclothed arm appeared, and the window was shoved open, letting in moonlight. Thea stepped into the beams, and Derry dropped the torch. A silver aura caressed her body. She was smiling at him, a wraithlike apparition he could barely refrain from touching. He knew she'd tricked him, but he was unwilling to do anything to destroy the air of combined sorcery and seduction. Whatever her plot, he could thwart it at any time. But not now.

She was still smiling at him. "I missed you."

He only nodded, but she seemed to understand that he'd longed for her as well. Without warning she floated up to him, and his arms were full of soft, gently squirming Thea. Her breasts flattened against his chest as she fastened her arms around his neck. He dove at her mouth, but she put her fingers over his lips.

"You're furious."

He captured her hand, then smoothed his palms over her bare shoulders. "Please, no talking. Not now." He traced the outline of her body with his fingertips while he kissed her neck.

"He said you would be."

Derry's fingers paused. Several moments passed before his head jerked up and he met her gaze. Moonlight gleamed off the tip of her nose and her teeth. She was smiling at him again. He grasped her wrists and pulled her arms from his neck.

"You and—and my brother?"

She nodded, and this time her smile burgeoned into a grin.

He snarled and whipped away from her. "Two traitors!"

A muffled voice came from behind the door. "I told you. He's so afrighted of marriage, he'd rather think we're criminals."

Derry sprang at the door, pounded on it, and shouted. "Morgan! Morgan, you deceitful little whelp, open this door. By my troth, I'll beat you senseless this time."

His answer was a shower of laughter that receded as Morgan descended from the tower. Derry flew to the window and stuck out his head. Morgan danced out of the tower.

"Come back here, Morgan St. John."

"Fare you well, sweet brother. I'll return. Soon."

Derry filled his lungs and bellowed. "Mor—gan!"

"He won't listen."

Turning, he found Thea looking at him. She had donned a cloak against the chill of the night. His boot touched something on the floor. He bent and touched a loaded crossbow.

"It belongs to Morgan," Thea said. "He said he wasn't trotting about a forest alone at night without arms."

He scowled at her. "What do you want?"

She cocked her head to the side. Her upper lip was caught between her teeth.

"I want you."

Derry stared at her, his consternation growing. "Mean you that this chase across country was some foul plot to trap me into marriage. God's blood, I'll not be forced."

At that moment Thea shoved the cloak back over her shoulders. He forgot what he was saying as she went to the bed, curled up on it, and drew the cloak over her legs.

He said again, "I'll not be—"

"Yes?"

Derry had been aware of a growing fullness, a swelling ache. He swallowed.

"I'll not . . ."

The cloak dropped low on her shoulder, and before he realized it, he had begun to approach the bed. He sat on the edge, never taking his gaze from the rounded curve. He reached out and touched her throat. There was nothing softer, not a dove's breast, nor the breath of a babe. What was he going to do?

"Derry."

"Hmm." His fingertips smoothed down her neck to rest above the swell of her breast.

"Awake, Derry."

He shifted his attention to her words.

"Hark you," she said, her tone grave. "Father Jean-Paul could have been behind that door as easily as Morgan."

He began to speak, but she rushed on.

"I could have led you into a trap far more treacherous than this." She got to her knees and brought her face close, pinning him with her gaze. "I could have betrayed you to your death with this machination, and mark you, we're not even betrothed, much less married."

"Women are deceitful and marriage dangerous."

"Prejudice, born of one horrible experience and one only."

"I," Derry said with rancor, "am not small-minded."

"Just cowardly."

He couldn't allow her to see how foolish he was beginning to feel. He had good reasons for his dislike, good reasons.

"Derry," she said softly, "you taught me not to run away. You taught me that a life without risk is a life without reward."

Somehow he ended up with his face close to hers. He felt as if two dragons were doing battle inside his head. Marriage. A wife. Death. Her lips touched his, and he sprang off the bed. Going to the window, he thrust his head out and gulped in cool air. When he faced Thea again, she was sitting on the side of the bed, the cloak drawn around her.

"No," he said.

She lowered her head and remained silent for a long time. Then her head came up and she sighed.

"Than I shall have to find another."

"Another what?"

"Why, another man."

His jaw fell open. Thea? Thea and another man? Thea disliked going among strangers, much less hunting for a man.

She sighed again. "I shall ask Father. No, that would be useless. I'll consult Ellen Dowgate. Grandmother and she were trying to get me married before all this plotting interfered. No doubt Ellen made a list of all the handsome young men who need good marriages." Thea tapped her finger on her chin. "There must be many pleasing young men in need of a wealthy mate. He can't be dark though. I dislike dark-haired men."

"Enough!"

"Now that I think of it, I remember Grandmother mentioning Sir Peter Bethell."

He couldn't have heard aright. "Peter Bethell has but sixteen years."

"All the better. He needs my wealth, and since I'm older, I can guide him. It will be much like keeping him for a pet, a beautiful young colt."

He felt as if he were strangling on his own rage. He flew to the bed and stood over her. Grasping her arms, he dragged her up to face him and shook her.

"I forbid it!" He stopped shaking her so that he could glare into her eyes. "No one but I will ever be your mate."

She asked him quietly, "And how will you prevent it?"

He knew her. He could see the apprehension in her eyes. His anger drained from him, and he released her.

"By God, Mistress Hunt, you could give lessons in deceit to Satan."

She winced, but he refused to let himself be maneuvered further. When he only stood staring at her, she turned away and slumped down on the bed.

"The door isn't barred. That, too, was a ruse."

He hesitated, then opened the door. It swung toward him easily. Glancing back, he found her looking at him, eyes wide and pleading. All he had to do was take at step toward her.

"Good e'en to you, Mistress Hunt."

He left then, and charged down the stairs, heedless of the dark. He burst out of the tower and stopped. The darkness had lightened, a harbinger of the coming day. He walked a few steps, then stopped again. He heard a sob, faint and desolate. He began to walk again, but his steps slowed. Thea had lied, led him on a wild chase, trapped him and cast snares to trick him. Thea, who was afraid to dance, who had been hurt near to death by trusting a man.

*"Jesu Maria."*

Derry turned and faced the tower. Without thinking he began to walk toward it. His steps quickened. As he approached, he heard a crack.

Something hit the wall of the tower level with his shoulder and clattered to the ground. He dropped to the ground as shards of stone flew at him. He heard a buzz. Then an arrow shot into the ground by his face.

He rolled quickly, until he reached the tower entrance. He flipped his body over and dove for the threshold. As he moved, an arrow impaled his sleeve to the wooden frame. He sat up and tore at the material.

"You killed my son."

He went still. The dowager Countess of Lynford stood in the courtyard, a bow and arrow in her hands. She raised the bow. The arrow pointed at his heart, and he dared not move.

# 24

*They are not wise, then, who stand forth to
buffet against Love; for Love rules the gods
as he will, and me.*

—SOPHOCLES

THEA HAD BEEN CRYING, when she heard the strange
cracking sound outside the window. Derry hadn't
valued her enough to fight his own demons. Her
heart felt as if it had been encased in forge-hot iron. The
burning pain manifested her despair and desolation. Once
again she had been scorned as a partner, only this time not
for a dance, but for life. Unable to contain her grief, she
buried her face in the folds of her cloak.

Then she heard the crack. Wiping her eyes, she went to
the window and looked down at the courtyard. She saw
Derry at once. He was rolling on the ground toward the
tower. Thea could barely make out the figure of the
stranger holding the bow. The stranger shot another arrow. Thea leaned out and looked down at the entrance to
the tower. Derry was struggling to free himself, for the
arrow had pinned his sleeve to the door frame.

Giving a little cry, Thea ducked back into the chamber.
She thrust her hands about on the floor, retrieved Mor-

gan's crossbow, and angled it so that it would fit through the window. She braced her elbows against the stone ledge. There was no time to check if the bolt was lodged securely in the groove. Bracing the stock as best she could with one hand, she curled her finger around the trigger.

The stranger had come closer to Derry after missing him.

"You killed my son."

Thea's attention was so fixed upon aiming at the killer, she could barely heard this remark. She could see better now, could make out the outlines of a cloak, a skirt. She aimed for the woman's chest and held her breath. The countess raised the bow, and Thea fired. She heard a snap. The crossbow jerked. Lowering it, she stared down at the scene in the courtyard.

The countess lay on her back. The short crossbow quarrel protruded from her breast, and the bow lay beside her. Thea let out her breath as Derry walked to the body. He glanced from it to her.

"I was coming back to you, you know."

Thea wondered if he felt as cold as she. "I couldn't let her kill you."

"I love you, Thea *bella.*"

"She's dead."

She couldn't stop staring at the body. She'd never killed anyone before, but then she remembered what the woman would have done to Derry. A ravening fury inflamed her shivering body. Her hand clenched on the stock of the crossbow.

"I would do it again, were she to threaten you."

Derry threw his cloak over the countess, and at last Thea was able to look away from the body. Derry was looking up at her, hands on his hips.

"You're a terrifying foe, Dorothea Philadelphia Hunt."

Thea glanced at the crossbow. "I've never aimed at a person before, only at targets. She was there, you know, when I was abducted and put in that cellar. I suppose she dropped that dragon brooch on purpose to make me think Gracechurch was the Wyvern. She must have thought I was to be released unharmed."

"Um, Thea, your logic is sensible, but mayhap you should withdraw from the window. Dawn approaches, and much as I love your body, I don't wish it displayed in so lofty a manner."

She looked down and saw that in her haste she had thrown the cloak back and over her shoulders. Braced in the window as she was, her upper body was exposed. Sudden mortification jolted through her. She dropped the crossbow, and it tipped out the window, banged against the tower wall, and hit the ground. Turtlelike, Thea bolted back inside and dove for the gown she'd placed on a stool near the bed. She pulled it on and, leaving it untied, hastily drew on the cloak again.

Donning her slippers, she ran out of the tower in such haste, she failed to notice that Derry stood with his back to her, his sword drawn. She slowed, then halted as she perceived a rider coming toward them between the broken pillars of the old gate house. A glance behind her found the crossbow, but she remembered Morgan had the pouch of spare bolts. And it wasn't time for Morgan to return.

She joined Derry, and he guided her to stand behind him. She stood on tiptoe and peeked over his shoulder as the rider walked his horse to within speaking distance. The rider shoved the hood of his cloak back.

"The priest," she said.

Derry inclined his head, never letting his gaze waver from Jean-Paul.

Jean-Paul bowed in the saddle. "*Anglais, ma petite*, this foiling of my plans must cease."

"You," Thea said, "you sent her to kill us."

"A chance opportunity," Jean-Paul replied. "After you and the *Anglais* ruined years of work on the part of my master, I decided London no longer held interest for me. Therefore I was returning to Scotland. The countess begged me to take her as well, and since I hate leaving talkative women where they may do damage, I agreed."

"And you camped at Ravensmere," Derry said.

"*Oui, Anglais.* But the woman grew tiresome with her whining about her dead son. I was about to rid myself of the nuisance, when Mistress Hunt and her party arrived, forcing me into hiding. When you were lured here soon after, I couldn't resist crafting a design by which I would avenge myself upon you and rid myself of the woman."

"You were a fool to take the chance," Derry said.

Jean-Paul shrugged. "The timing of the matter was intricate, but I succeeded in rousing the countess to a fever of malice and set her upon you."

"And I killed her," Thea said from behind Derry's back.

Jean-Paul leered at her. "*Oui, ma petite,* and the sight of a naked Amazon defending her mate was worth losing my pawn."

Thea blushed and ducked behind Derry to peer around his shoulder.

Derry flicked the tip of his sword in Jean-Paul's direction. "Get on with it, priest. You haven't come to prattle about my lady's beauty."

"*C'est vrai, mon ami.* Shall I hear your confession before I kill you?"

Derry shoved Thea away from him, lifted his sword, and said, "Confess to yourself, priest, though it will do you no good in hell."

Jean-Paul's hand went to his sword, but as he began to draw, a hunting horn sounded in the woods nearby.

"It's Morgan," Thea said. "Hie you hence, priest, for that is the signal of his approach, and he brings my men and his and Derry's as well."

Jean-Paul released his sword, staring at her all the while. Derry moved between Thea and the priest and raised his sword level with Jean-Paul's eyes.

"Not in all your imaginings, for I will cut your cock in twain before you reach her."

The hunting horn sounded again. Jean-Paul glanced from Thea to Derry.

"I believe you mean it, *Anglais.* Very well. Perchance we will meet in the future. Until then I will bethink me of other methods of vengeance. Look for me, *Anglais.* Look for me."

Hauling his mount in a swift turn, Jean-Paul galloped out of the courtyard, leaving Thea to rush into Derry's arms. He smiled at her ruefully.

"I've no horse with which to pursue him."

"Good." She gazed up at him, uncertain.

"Thea, will you now grant me the favor of putting on your clothes properly before more men come?"

She looked down at the gaping neck of her gown. "God's mercy." She whirled and ran back to the tower.

In her chamber she was fumbling with laces, when a hand touched her cheek. She gasped and twisted around to face Derry. He was smiling at her, but somehow this smile was different. It held no mockery, no distrust, no concealment. He opened himself to her with that smile, of his own choice it seemed. And in that smile she perceived the gift of his trust, and his love.

"Thea *bella*," he said, pulling her hands from the laces, "I have been a fool."

"As have I."

"But you must believe me. I would have come for you had there been no murderess chasing me."

"'As long as rivers shall run down to the sea, or shadows touch the mountain slopes'?"

He chuckled and took her hands in his. "'Or stars graze in the vault of heaven.'" He kissed her fingertips and pulled her close. "It seems I must hazard the dangers of remaining with you, for the risk is scant when compared with the mortal peril of not having you at all."

She remained still, hardly daring to speak for fear her wits had frayed and she was imagining him. Then he kissed her, his warmth surrounding her, invading her mouth, and she knew her reason tarried with her still. But as his hands slipped inside her gown, she realized it wouldn't tarry long.

A piercing whistle made her start and caused Derry to curse. He set her from him and went to the window. Morgan, Stubb, and Inigo were standing by the countess's body and looking up at the tower.

"By all the saints, brother, I leave you to reconcile with a maid, and you kill a countess."

"Thea did that, you scourge upon mankind. The woman tried to kill me."

Thea dragged Derry from the window and took his place, popping out at the men on the ground like a disturbed owl.

"Morgan St. John, you said all the traitors were in gaol."

"We hadn't arrested the countess yet," Morgan said. "Timothy Eyre hadn't yet confessed that she knew of her son's plotting."

She leaned farther out the window and scowled at Morgan. "But you said Cecil was having her watched. You said—"

"Derry," Morgan shouted. "Derry, curb your tigress. By my troth, she's about to leap at me from her perch."

An arm curled around her waist. Derry lifted her out of the window and into his arms. He kissed her to stop her protests. They were still kissing when Morgan burst into the chamber.

"She was traveling with someone else," he said.

Derry lifted his lips from Thea's. They all spoke at the same time.

"The priest."

"Father Jean-Paul."

"The bastard was in London all along," Morgan said.

"And now he's here," Derry replied. "He left not a quarter of an hour ago."

Thea frowned at Morgan. "You said he had gone back to Scotland."

Morgan cast a pleading glance at Derry, who set Thea on her feet.

"Have forbearance, my love. The priest is the most cunning of adversaries, and Morgan is but a boy."

Outraged, Morgan said, "A pox on you."

"I remember you in smocks," Derry said.

"Why are you standing there?" Thea asked Morgan. "You should be chasing Jean-Paul."

"I am waiting, Mistress Know-All, for my men and horses."

"Peace," Derry said. "Get you hence, Morgan. I must take Thea back to London. You'll send word of how you do?"

Morgan grinned at him. "You're not coming?"

"I'll trust Thea's safety to no one else. You lost the whoreson. He's yours. We're returning to London."

"But mark you," Thea said to Morgan. "He's threatened Derry. When you find him, see that he's no longer able to carry out his threats."

"Christ, Derry, she's become a devil."

Derry laughed and hugged Thea to him. "An enchanting devil."

Morgan took his leave, and soon Ravensmere was deserted once more. Derry had sent his men to prepare for their journey, and Thea had resumed her struggle with the laces. As she pulled them tight, they slipped from her grasp. Derry dropped them and slipped his arms about her from behind. His lips touched the curve of her neck and kissed their way to her shoulders.

"Will you ask me for my hand again, Thea *bella?* No, this time I will ask." He knelt, kissed her hands, and looked up at her. "Will you do me the honor of marrying me, Mistress Hunt?"

Thea dropped to her knees in front of him. "I will."

She leaned forward and kissed him. He surrounded her with his arms but lifted his head to stare into her eyes.

"I must warn you that my father won't welcome you. His hatred of me will encompass my wife."

"I know," she said softly. "He won't change. Not after all these years."

Derry gave her a sad smile. "He can't. If he were to admit that I'm guiltless, he would have to admit that he deserves the blame for what happened. It was he who goaded me into challenging my brother, and he who allowed us to fight so violently."

"You're at peace."

"Now that Morgan no longer wants to kill me."

Laying her head on Derry's shoulder, Thea sighed. "I should follow your example. Sometimes I pray so hard for Father to notice me instead of his rosebushes."

"Think of me instead, Thea *bella.* I notice nothing else

but you. Jesu Maria, feeling you this close is like to turn me into a ravaging Saracen."

She giggled, then lifted her head and moved away from him to see his face. As she moved, he pulled her loosened gown from her shoulders. It dropped to the floor. As she'd worn nothing under it, she was in his arms nude. Her stomach grazed against his belt, and she jumped. Pulling on it, she set about ridding him of his clothing. When he was bare, he encircled her with his arms again.

He touched his lips to her forehead, then her temples and cheeks and before they fastened over her mouth. As she nestled into his arms, she heard him whisper.

> *Without love I had thought to live*
> *All this my life henceforth in peace,*
> *But passion has drawn back again*
> *My heart when it had found release;*
> *A greater madness I pursue*
> *Than foolish child who makes his cry*
> *To have the fair and lovely star*
> *Shining above him bright on high.*

She tilted her head back to gaze at him. "You thought to live your whole life without love?"

"When you asked for my hand, you forced me to admit my folly, if only to myself," Derry said. "You see, Thea *bella,* I feared a far greater hurt than any I'd been dealt before, for by my troth, I loved you a thousand, no, a thousand thousand times more than I ever loved my first wife."

"I, too, am afraid, but not so much that I would surrender my claim to you."

"And I thank God and his angels that you didn't, for indeed, I shall love you as long as the stars graze the vault of heaven."

SUZANNE ROBINSON

loves to hear from readers. You can write to her at
the following address:

P.O. Box 700321
San Antonio, TX 78270-0321

## About The Author

SUZANNE ROBINSON has a doctoral degree in anthropology with a specialty in ancient Middle Eastern archaeology. After spending years doing fieldwork in both the U.S. and the Middle East, Suzanne has now turned her attention to the creation of the fascinating fictional characters in her unforgettable historical romances.

Suzanne lives in San Antonio with her husband and her two English springer spaniels. She divides her time between writing and teaching.

# Don't miss these fabulous Bantam women's fiction titles on sale in July

## CRY WOLF

☐ 56160-X $5.50/6.50 in Canada
### by Tami Hoag
Author of STILL WATERS

*A juicy novel of romantic suspense set in the steamy Louisiana Bayou by the author Publishers Weekly called "a master of the genre."*

## FANTA C

☐ 28999-3 $5.99/6.99 in Canada
### by Sandra Brown
Author of TEMPERATURES RISING

*A single mother struggles to balance the needs of work, home, and the passionate desires of her own heart.*

## TWICE IN A LIFETIME

☐ 56298-3 $4.99/5.99 in Canada
### by Christy Cohen
Author of PRIVATE SCANDALS

*A gripping story of two women who find their friendship threatened when they each fall in love with the other's husband.*

## THE TESTIMONY

☐ 29948-4 $4.50/5.50 in Canada
### by Sharon and Tom Curtis
Authors of SUNSHINE AND SHADOW

*"[THE TESTIMONY] is one of the finest books I've ever read."* —Romantic Times.